MW00713963

THE
PHASES
OF
HARRY
MOON

THOMAS SULLIVAN

THE PHASES OF HARRY MOON

E. P. DUTTON NEW YORK

Copyright © 1988 by Thomas Sullivan
All rights reserved. Printed in the U.S.A.

Publisher's Note: *This novel is a work of fiction. Names, charac-*
ters, places, and incidents either are the product of the author's
imagination or are used fictitiously, and any resemblance to actual
persons, living or dead, events, or locales is entirely coincidental.

No part of this publication may be reproduced or transmitted in
any form or by any means, electronic or mechanical, including
photocopy, recording, or any information storage and retrieval sys-
tem now known or to be invented, without permission in writing
from the publisher, except by a reviewer who wishes to quote brief
passages in connection with a review written for inclusion in a
magazine, newspaper, or broadcast.

Published in the United States by E. P. Dutton,
a division of NAL Penguin Inc.,
2 Park Avenue, New York, N.Y. 10016.

Published simultaneously in Canada
by Fitzhenry and Whiteside, Limited, Toronto.

Library of Congress Cataloging-in-Publication Data
Sullivan, Thomas.
The phases of Harry Moon.
I. Title.
PS3569.U3579P47   1988   813'.54   88-3842
ISBN: 0-525-24656-8

Designed by David Lui

1   3   5   7   9   10   8   6   4   2

First Edition

For Ray,
whose quiet voice still resounds,
and for my parents,
whose love still spans the distance.

ACKNOWLEDGMENTS

An adaptation of the third chapter, titled "Investitures," won a cash prize in a literary contest and was subsequently purchased and published by *The Detroit News* in its *Michigan Magazine,* April 20, 1986. License has been taken with the advent of the fad known as "droodles," which arose primarily through the publications and TV shows of Roger Price perhaps some three or four years later than the 1962 date I have used.

The author wishes to give special thanks to JoAnne Lamun for her critical review of the book in manuscript, as well as all the members of the Society of the Black Bull for their unstinting enthusiasm.

Contents

PEDIGREES

The brothers Moon were kicked out of England in 1767. Up until then they lived in their father's Cotswold cottage near Gloucestershire. Gloucestershire was quiet, the Cotswold Hills were quiet, all of southwest England was quiet, but the brothers Moon were noisy. They were, in fact, "a despicable din and blemish on the breastplate of society," according to the bishop. Possibly if their errors and omissions had been committed quietly they would have been just like everyone else.

Jonathan was the oldest and loudest of the four. At the age of eight he stole a decanter of port from an inn and got falling-down drunk. The innkeeper's wife found him out cold in her cellar and rolled him home in a wheelbarrow. Jonathan's mother doused him with chamomile tea. Jonathan's father threw him in the sheep-dip trough. He remained more or less drunk for the rest of his life and got to know sheep-dip troughs as well as any man might. It became true that he never felt quite sodden enough until he was immersed at the end of a binge, thus saturating himself inside and out.

By the time he was twelve he was extremely quarrelsome and apt to kick anyone who touched him when he was drunk. In that condition he nearly disemboweled the blacksmith with the point of his boot one night and earned a cuff on the ear that rang in his head forever. When he himself clouted his mother at the age of fourteen, he sorely repented, even to the point of attending church, where the minister soon insisted he be baptized. To appease his mother, he consented; but the sacrament left him feeling halved rather than whole—it was the immersion without the binge—and he went out afterward to complete the ceremony in his own fashion. Baptism, he decided, was a conclusion without a beginning.

Despite being perpetually drunk, he grew strong and robust. The quarrels became fights, the fights brawls. The world was Jonathan Moon's pigpen, and he wallowed in it, rarely letting the muck dry before rolling deeper.

After Jonathan came Samuel. He had none of his older brother's appetite for the world. He was sad-eyed and spoke in a slur with his teeth locked together, the words somehow leaking out the side of his mouth. But the main thing about Samuel was his clubfoot. It dragged along with him and when he stood still seemed to take root, as if he were tied to some inanimate post driven into the ground. He often stood still. It looked better that way than the limp, he thought. If a crowd overtook him he would freeze, like a hunting dog coming to point, and, when they jostled past, continue on. As a boy he would arrive at the schoolhouse long before anyone else and stay after school until he was alone. "The first to arrive, the last to go, and ne'er present in between," said his first schoolmaster. He had a fondness for braining toads with his cane, Samuel did, which made him odious as well as pathetic in his schoolmates' eyes. They avoided the things he touched.

When he reached puberty he began to peep in at windows. But the first time he came upon a naked woman, she looked up, saw his distorted face through the bull's-eye in the glass, and screamed. It was the baker's wife, Goody Joiner, and she was eight months pregnant. When she gave birth prematurely to a Mongoloid infant, uneasy mutterings were heard to the effect that Samuel Moon might be responsible for the misfortune. Pregnant women were subject to that kind of thing—frighten one with a toad and her baby was likely to develop warts. And here was grotesque Samuel Moon, and there was Goody Joiner's Mongoloid. It was cause and effect. Maybe it was even *deliberate* cause and effect. Satan was alive and well in the Cotswolds.

The matter hung in the air like dead smoke, intensifying but going nowhere. No one accused Samuel directly, but people now turned away from the very sound of him, dragging along behind a hedge or around a wall. The whole thing might have stayed like that if Samuel had not made another enemy. Again, it was peeping through a window that was his undoing. This time he came face to face with the local magistrate flouncing his fat body up and down on the naked frailness of a scullery maid. Samuel knew his fate was sealed. It was just a matter of time.

It was then that old Erasmus Moon began telling his sons they should go abroad. He knew nothing of the magistrate's sexual affairs, but it was clear to him that Samuel had the Devil's mark on him and that the collective memory of the Cotswold district would dredge up evidence from his son's childhood bit by bit until there was enough to start a fire under him. And it was only a matter of time before Jonathan would kill someone in a drunken rage or get a wench in trouble. Erasmus included his youngest sons, Benjamin and Alexander, in the planned exile. Benjamin was a sneak thief, and Alexander was simple-minded.

Alexander had angered the bishop, and in Cotswold he might as well have angered God. This occurred during an investiture. With the bishop presiding, Alexander's dimly lit mind flickered and went out. As he slept, his breathing deepened into snores until Erasmus was obliged to throw an elbow into him. Alexander awoke with a fart. The bishop cringed and swept the congregation with baleful eyes. He was a strict and unforgiving man, and when he later discovered Alexander urinating on his gatepost, he saw clearly that the lad would be happier among his own kind in London's Bedlam insane asylum.

"You have disgraced the name of Moon," Erasmus told his sons. "For the good of the whole, and your own personal welfare, you must now leave England. I do not care where you go, so long as you do not travel to the New World. Go to France, go to Vienna, go to the West Indies, but do not go to the Colonies. When you have become respected and honorable men you may return home."

They went to the Colonies, of course. And they never returned to England.

Jonathan died some six years later in Boston Harbor while
attending the famous Tea Party. Undressed as an Indian, he
crept aboard one of the three East India Company ships at anchor there and joined in heaving tea chests overboard. He was
still an alcoholic, however, and something in the way this drink-
able commodity splashed into the harbor must have triggered
pleasant associations, because he suddenly leaped in among the
bobbing chests. Grabbing one of these, he began kicking toward
shore. But he was a poor swimmer, and the split chest was sinking. Jonathan went down gulping cold, salty tea. It was his old
nostrum—drink and immersion.

Many years passed before another one of them died; this
time it was Samuel. Ugly, clubfooted Samuel had rarely found
himself welcome in the same place twice. He lived out his life in
a series of one-act plays in which he entered a tavern once but
was barred the next night or was hired one day and fired the
next. Naturally this meant that Samuel Moon was much traveled and widely experienced. Toward the end it seemed to him
that he had done nearly everything once. He died of syphilis
contracted in a union with a deaconess who screamed "Rape!"
when they were about to be discovered. Samuel fled but the
syphilis lingered on. Like everything else in his life, he had
made love only once.

Next was Benjamin, the petty thief. Besides his compulsion
to abscond with a watermelon here and there, Benjamin was
proud and stubborn as a rusty nail. His chief error in life came
when he stole a chicken in the village of New Penance and fled
to the church belfry within sight of the minister. The good reverend was sure he had his man when tufts of chicken fluff
began floating down like condemning angels. This particular
minister was strong on irony and a shade vindictive (the same
who had surprised Samuel having intercourse with the deaconess). Fingering the bell rope, he gave it an experimental tug.
Thung! it went; he thought he heard a gasp and more chicken
fluff rained down. He yanked harder, and the bell pealed out
unfettered this time. It seemed to satisfy the minister, who then
began to flow with the rope, up and down, as if he had primed
a pump, tasted the discharge, and found it worthy of a long
draught. Sound bubbled forth, overflowing in torrents, washing
the air, the rope, the bell tower itself in vibrations. It spread to

the town, drawing the curious a few at a time until a fair crowd had gathered. Someone began to help the reverend with the bell rope, and though he said nothing it became clear by the reverend's intensity, his gaze, and the chicken fluff on the bell-tower floor that a human drama was unfolding in the belfry itself.

Even before it was fully understood, the thing was compelling. People came hour by hour to stand in the trembling lunacy beneath the bells. They took turns at the rope, spelling the minister, vaguely aware that they were punishing someone, that they were taking their individual throws in a stoning. Martyred on high, Benjamin clung to his pride and his chicken. He had throttled the latter to keep it from squawking, but his pride was silent and bled like a fresh wound that did not coagulate for a day and a night. The eerie thing ended when the chicken fell to the ground. The bell ringers stopped then, and as the sound coiled away like smoke from ashes, Benjamin Moon crept slowly down, stunned and stone deaf. He stumbled to an outhouse and later died of a nervous disorder. For years afterward it was often said of anyone who died in that county that they "threw down the chicken."

Alexander outlived them all. On his one hundred and third birthday he suddenly remembered his father's injunction to return one day to England. "I'm coming, Father," he tremoloed, then farted with the effort of gaining his feet and died. His father had been dead three quarters of a century by this time, however, and it hardly mattered to anyone what old Alexander said anyway because he had been insane for eighty-one years. Shortly after arriving in the colonies he had begun to suffer fits of melancholy. Leeches were prescribed to alter his humors. Alexander had always been terrified by anything that crawled, coiled, or slithered, and when the nasty creatures were scooped fresh out of the Roanoke Island mud and affixed to his nose he fell to the floor, thrashing and rolling. He had decided to become a leech. There is safety, after all, in numbers. Quietly insane, he thus lived out his life and died, if not the oldest of his adopted species, at least the oldest of the brothers Moon.

These then were the earliest American ancestors of Harold Matthew Moon.

NEW
MOON

{ 1 }

When Harry Moon was born in 1950 the doctor gave him a five on the one-to-ten scale with which they secretly rate newborns. Anything below seven was not particularly good. Six equaled minimum hamburger standards in Bangladesh (East Pakistan at that time), and five could be used to describe carrots. Harry's rating was primarily because he didn't cry and stayed blue for too long, and because Dr. Ufunker had been called out of bed in a snowstorm and nicked the garage with the right front fender of his blue Kaiser Deluxe. The blue Kaiser Deluxe got a ten before the nick, but little Harry "blue" Moon got a five. People underestimated Harry even then.

Actually he had been a phenomenal sperm. The chances of his making it to the egg at all were slim to none. His mother, Alice Viola, and his father, Edward Winslow, were using three forms of birth control at the time. This was because they had already found out how unusually fertile they were. The names of the ways they had found this out were Nicki, Stu, and Stanley.

The first time Alice Viola had gotten pregnant they were using only one method: rhythm. Alice was nothing if not regular—regular and self-assured. She had grown up a Stenner in Chewbagin, Vermont. Stenners ran the post office, the hardware, the gas station–grocery, the restaurant, and the historical society. Vermont itself was regular and self-assured. The seasons relieved each other like clockwork sentries; the tennis players left and the skiers arrived; the stones in the creeks lay gluey and green beneath spring runoff, or white and dry in August, or like lumpy oatmeal in March, but always like so many anchors tethering the mountains round which the creek beds and roads ran. The mountains were granite and resisted settlement; thus, those clots of people who chipped a town out here and there must necessarily be regular and self-assured. So the first time Alice Moon got pregnant while relying on the rhythm method was not because she was not regular. It was because she lied.

God had told her to do this, she felt. For a long time she had wanted a child, and God knew it, and every time she turned around she seemed to find an omen to tell her so. One night she asked him if she should have a baby. (She had already asked Winslow, and he had said no.) The next day she opened her Bible and immediately read "Go forth and multiply." So she gave God three months to make her pregnant, since he had done this kind of thing before, but the Almighty declined. She began to see she would have to use Winslow for God's will.

It would not be a regular lie, she decided; she wouldn't have to say a thing. Winslow never asked her when she had ovulated. She just took a hot bath with dish detergent in it, wrapped her hair in a towel, and dabbed some fruity essence on her breasts that was so old it had begun to ferment. Winslow did the rest. She was the calendar keeper, regular and self-assured. If she took a hot bath in dish detergent and her breasts smelled faintly organic, it must be the right time. Winslow fondled and thrust into her with all the faith of a wire walker falling into a safety net.

Afterward Alice felt a trifle guilty. But the natural odds of becoming pregnant from one such union were still against conception. Winslow was reluctantly happy when she announced her pregnancy, and nine months later they named the immaculate deception Nicholas.

The second pregnancy was unplanned and came about because Winslow's trust in the rhythm method was shot. He had never had good timing, he knew. The day before lead-based paint was found on Mexican pottery, he had bought eight place settings for Alice. His lone venture into the stock market heralded the collapse of a major zipper manufacturer. One day he had noticed his fly down and thought what an indispensable item a zipper was. Hence, he surveyed the industry and bought stock in what he considered to be the only worthwhile zipper on the market. Zippers subsequently plunged, and Winslow imagined everyone going around with open flies.

He had always marveled at people who flowed with events, sensed disaster, or listened to some secret rhythm of good fortune. Winslow swam upstream and heard nothing. For a while he had thought Alice's regularity would offset his naturally bad timing, but now he believed his only salvation was a good zipper that stayed shut twenty-four hours a day. Since he had already closed down the only worthwhile manufacturer, he would have to find a substitute birth control. So he went to the drugstore and asked to see the pharmacist. The girl at the counter fled as if he had propositioned her, but the pharmacist appeared immediately, looking dispassionate and parental. Behind him the counter girl now snickered to the cashier. Winslow felt as though his fly were open again. He had only asked to see the pharmacist, and already everyone in the store knew what he was there for. So instead of inquiring about condoms, he asked loudly what to do about hemorrhoids. The druggist recommended ointment. Winslow bought a tube and went to another drugstore. This time he lurked among the diapers until a stock boy happened by. With a wink and a quarter tip he asked to see the man in charge, and the stock boy, somewhat warily, delivered the message. In due course the pharmacist found him, and there, among the powders and pacifiers, they discussed birth control. Winslow inadvertently took the hemorrhoidal ointment out of his pocket and thereupon felt obliged to pay for it again rather than appear habituated to pharmacies. He left with the overpriced ointment and a pack of condoms.

When he explained the pharmacist's recommendation to Alice she recoiled in horror. The condoms were made from animal membranes, and she had no intention of coming in contact with "the intestines of lambs." She promptly wrote a letter to the Society for the Prevention of Cruelty to Animals, while Winslow returned to yet another drugstore for genuine rubber rubbers.

He followed the directions on the package precisely, pinching the receptacle end as he unrolled it and withdrawing immediately after his climax. There was no point in using the rhythm method anymore, he thought. Picking the right moment would be a shell game played on a calendar, for him. Is the egg on this day, or that? He would always guess wrong. So he trusted latex, and in due time Alice conceived again.

They named the baby Stuart. Alice was overjoyed. The whole point of marriage was to have a family, and her favorite book was *Cheaper by the Dozen*. If only, she thought, they would have a girl as well, someone to sew dresses for, whose hair needed braiding, and to whom she might pass on her bounty of feminine lore. She had no idea, of course, that little Stu would someday desire all three.

Winslow took the second baby in stride. Timing. He had done something wrong. He had put the latex fraud on too late, or withdrawn after it had loosened up, or maybe he had just wandered into the wrong drugstore at the wrong time, the stock boy having just stuck a pin through the particular box he would buy. There was nothing more to do about it, except that they began using a cream, so that now they had two methods. He wanted to get a vasectomy, but Alice convinced him it was tantamount to suicide.

"God made you a man and you have no right to undo that," she said.

"I'm not going to cut it off, just the tubes," he argued. "The tubes are going to be cut. I'll function just like before."

"And where do you think your sperm is going to go? What happens to all those seeds?" He couldn't answer. "I'll tell you where," she fluoresced. "Into your kidneys, that's where. And your liver. And your heart. You'll be so chock full of seeds after a while that you'll get arthritis and die."

"No one's ever died that way," he mumbled.

"How do you know? It's pretty new, isn't it?"

He didn't know, didn't want to know. But years later he would read a newspaper article that said higher cholesterol levels had been reported in men with vasectomies. This was attributed to the leakage of sperm into their bloodstreams. Alice was right, he would think. All those seeds go to the heart.

She would not have her tubes tied either. God didn't want knots in her belly, she said. So they resumed intercourse with condom and cream, and that was the way Stanley was conceived.

There would be no early retirement, no cabin up north. Winslow loved his three sons, but another child would impoverish the family, he felt. So in addition to the condom and the cream, he told Alice he wanted to go back to the rhythm method.

Thus, Harry Moon had to have been a phenomenal sperm.

Never mind Dr. Ufunker's five on the newborn scale. An egg is just an egg, but a phenomenal sperm has *timing*.

The egg, of course, contained the genes for regularity and self-assurance. Alice imagined them labeled and swimming around like pollywogs. This baby felt lighter than the others somehow, and she had a sense of equilibrium with it that she interpreted as compatibility with her body and therefore with her Stenner heritage.

That was important.

She had been an elementary-school teacher before she got married. Her expectations had been that there would be an unending stream of neophytes passing through her life and that her love and good judgment would expand with them like an exhilarating ether. But then she met Winslow and was overwhelmed by his sadness. It never occurred to her that such fatalistic genes might be dominant.

He was so much a victim. She could always conjure back those first feelings she had for him by a table of wool hats at Kresge's. It was an unadvertised special, the voice over the P.A. exhorting haste and a clerk waving a red pennant above the display. The winter crowd was compacting like a giant sponge, the smell of wet wool wafting out of its pores. When she came even with Winslow, his hands looked so dry and ghostly that she glanced at his face. It was mortar dust that made him look chalky—he was a bricklayer—but she thought he was somehow impregnated with the stuff of the hereafter. And that was sad. They wedged in together. He was erect, a shuffler, no press at all, and she outreached him for the final hat. Their glances met, and she saw that his eyes were moist and sad.

"Here," she said bluntly, "take the hat. I pushed you out of the way."

He shrugged. "That's life."

"No, it isn't. Take the hat."

"First come, first served."

"But you were first, you just didn't grab fast enough."

"Survival of the fittest."

"Stop saying things like that. You have no right to feel that way."

They ended up sharing the hat, because they got married. He was a natural-born victim, and she was a natural-born do-gooder. She knew now that the Moon pedigree had no champions, and her first three sons were already inclining toward their paternal heritage. That was why the sense of compatibility with her Stenner bloodline was important. Harry was going to represent hope.

} 2 }

When Harry was four, his father galloped under a low arch in the dining room. This in itself would not have been remarkable except that Harry was on his shoulders at the time.

Dr. Ufunker, who had sold the blue Kaiser Deluxe and now drove a red Mercedes, ordered a half dozen X rays. His overuse of this diagnostic tool was legendary. He had once requested a battery of exposures on a cadaver, mistaking it for a comatose patient. A colleague put a sign on his door advertising "still life portfolios." If Humpty Dumpty had arrived with a damaged yolk, Ufunker would have fried him with radiation.

"Six?" Winslow asked incredulously.

The doctor gave him a dry look that invited challenge. Too many? Too few? Would you like some eight-by-ten glossies framed in cardboard? Some extra prints maybe?

"I just wondered, that's all." Winslow banished himself to the waiting room.

Since he had only given Harry a five at birth, the doctor was not surprised that he had collided with a wall. Fives floundered, fell, and fractured themselves, and Ufunker assumed the boy had somehow caused the accident himself. He told Alice that Harry needed glasses.

Winslow got the news in the waiting room, where he sat stupefied with guilt before a radio. An opera star was singing about migraines.

"When your head is simply spli-iting..."

"Harry needs glasses," Alice said.

"Don't just sit there di-itling..."

"The doctor saw something in the X rays and says he needs glasses. I'm afraid it's some kind of brain damage."

"Alka-Seltzer, Alka-Seltzer, Alka-Seltzer...."

The afternoon was spent with a succession of optometrists, each of whom denied both the brain damage and the need for glasses. Alice remained undaunted. Optometry would discover the predicted defect at some later date, she said, her faith in Ufunker unshaken. "In the meantime we're going to eat carrots. Lots and lots."

But carrots were nothing much to wake up to. They tasted lousy with milk and sugar and could not be toasted or scrambled. Armed with only regularity and self-assurance, Alice set out to discover a universe between hard-cold and limp-soggy.

Her recipe for carrot creole won a prize at the PTA bake-off, eventually finding its way into a book put out by a local talk-show host. She appeared on the show twice. A famous comedian was on the first time, and Alice said almost nothing. But the second time, she loosened up and they had to cue her to shut up. She was making carrot soup on that occasion, and the talk-show host burned his lips so badly on a sample taste that he could hardly close the program. He was supposed to say "May the Lord bless you and keep you!" but it came forth "A-ay the Lord 'less you and kee-kee you." As soon as the red light on the camera went out he lunged for the water cooler. They had to cancel the next two segments, which were shot back-to-back.

But he was not one to bear a grudge, and when his book came out he sent Alice five dollars for her carrot creole recipe.

Harry became something of a cause célèbre in the world of carrots and could even chew them to the tune of "Yankee Doodle" by gauging the timbre of macerated chunks with his tongue. The end came at a wedding reception for an older cousin—his mother's niece. Spurred on by admiring bridesmaids, he tossed off a pitcher of Shirley Temples made with carrot juice and promptly threw up on the bride. Thus his ardor for all things carroty cooled, eventually becoming a mockery. In college he was to use vegetables for doorstops.

Meanwhile, the crunch of carrots drove Winslow to distraction. It was the sound of frontal lobes shattering on a dining room arch, and though he strove to hide this, everyone understood his guilt. You could wave a carrot at Winslow and he would shrink back like a vampire from the sign of the cross; if a plate of them pointed at him he would turn it sideways or change seats.

Even before fatherhood, Winslow was vulnerable to minor acts of fate. He braked on green lights because they would turn amber before he got there; he bought a newspaper to read before going to the bank because the line would be up and communications down; he bought duplicates of everything —pickles, jam, toothpaste, bandages—and hid them in bureau drawers, because whatever he needed or wanted they would have just run out of. Toilet paper upstairs in his bureau would do him no good when he got to the end of the roll downstairs in the bathroom. So there were always four or five packages crammed into the vanity. These extreme preparations were, of course, their own penalty, but somehow they set him at ease with his off-stride universe. He was taking away fate's opportunity to stick it to him. The problem with children was that his vulnerability had multiplied, and no amount of toilet paper stuffed in the vanity would ever again be enough.

So he embarked on a campaign of heroic countermeasures. He placed training wheels fore and aft on Nicki's bike, for instance. This meant that Nicki could remain upright in earthquakes and high winds, and that he would never turn into the street at the wrong moment. In fact, he would never turn anywhere at all. There was something reassuring, Winslow felt, in watching his eldest son ease majestically down the sidewalk, dismount, drag his bike around, and come creeping back. Little

Stu's clumsiness was another source of vulnerability. What if he slipped on the basement stairs while carrying scissors? What if the moment after he popped a sucker in his tiny mouth he did a full gainer layout over his shoelaces? Methodically, Winslow ground off the points on their scissors, put up handrails, laid abrasive treads on the stairs, and placed a foam rubber pad at the bottom. He trimmed Stu's shoelaces. He even trimmed his sucker handles and popsicle sticks on occasion. For all this he received protests and scorn. He invalidated himself, becoming a caricature of authority, an oppressive force to be ignored. But when he discovered asthmatic Stanley nearly suffocating in his sleep because he had taken his space helmet to bed with him—a helmet Winslow had recently drilled two air holes in—he knew it was necessary. And when he kissed Harry's warm, silken hair at night and saw him snuggle and smile in his sleep, he knew it was worth it.

The ill-timing that had conceived four sons for him seemed, then, a blessing after all. He could no longer imagine that their existence had ever been in question. Wondering about cause and effect was the closest Winslow ever got to philosophy, but he vaguely mistrusted conclusions. Edward Winslow Moon never made up his mind about anything.

Two weeks after the accident, Harry began to read. His flawless recitation of six pages from *Winnie-the-Pooh* elated Alice and terrified Winslow. This was a consequence of the collision with the dining room arch, Winslow knew, and he suffered nightmares in which Harry sat across the breakfast table reading almanacs, his tongue smoking, red veins swelling out of his eyes. One morning the nightmares started to come true.

"*Tengo hambre*," Harry said at the breakfast table. (I am hungry.)

Neither Winslow nor Alice spoke Spanish.

"*Tengo hambre y sed*," Harry elaborated. (I am hungry and thirsty.)

Winslow pushed back from the table as if he wanted to look at Alice but couldn't tear himself away.

"Why, Harry," she said, "is that Spanish?"

"*Quiero comida*." (I want food.)

Winslow groaned.

"That's wonderful, Harry," Alice said. "Where did you learn that?"

"*Mierda de toro*." (Bullshit.) He smiled.

"Our boy speaks Spanish, Winslow." Alice stepped behind her husband's chair and pinched his neck. "Don't you think that's wonderful, dear? How lucky we are!"

Alice decided he learned it from the radio, but Winslow was dead certain it was a cosmic fluke related to the accident. Actually, Harry had heard the phrases at a playmate's house, where a senile grandfather was kept out of sight in an upstairs room. The gentleman's name was Castillo, but the family surname was Donaldson. While Harry played with Billy Donaldson in his bedroom, the old man pleaded for things through the floor register that connected the rooms. Harry did not understand that he was a virtual prisoner. He thought the voice through the register was a game.

"Tengo hambre."

"Tengo hambre," Harry would repeat.

"Quiero comida." Plaintively.

"Quiero comida."

"Mierda de toro." Exasperated.

"Mierda de toro."

After a week of hearing Harry celebrated as a language prodigy, his brothers decided that three was company and four was grounds for homicide. From the time little Harry had endearingly described his favorite food as "roast beast," they had foreseen death and dismemberment for the runt of the litter. What was so cute about a speech impediment? Even then they had understood that he was somehow compensation for them, that their redemption was his intended destiny. It was decided to act collectively; thus they led him several blocks from home and abandoned him in an empty lot. It was the old close-your-eyes-and-count-to-twenty trick. When Harry opened them again, they were gone.

His father came looking around sundown and found him outside a bakery half a mile away. By that time Harry had picked up a stray, which was coincidental because Winslow was being trailed by an incredibly lean whippet.

It was not unusual for Winslow to find canine company. One of the great symbols in his life was the dog. Dogs dogged him. He did not know why. It was not as if he encouraged them. He did not trust any creature with hair growing on its nose instead of in it. In fact, he had spent many years repelling them with sticks, shouts, and kicks. Among those people he silently hated were the love-me-love-my-dogshit people. Typically, they loosed their animals against overly polite neighbors and gazed at squirrel nests when faithful Pounds-o'-Poop unloaded, or—if the neighbors were outraged beyond embarrassment—freed their fecal warriors after sunset and in the early dawn. Against these Winslow had launched many campaigns. He had sprinkled lawns with hot pepper, laced meatballs with Ex-Lax, set traps, and even embarked on a "spray-a-stray" program with red enamel. Still they followed him on the streets as if recognizing in his gaunt, mortar-washed appearance some fraternal companion.

"Where'd you get the dog?" he asked his son as they walked home.

"He followed me," Harry said.

"You sure you didn't encourage him?"

"Nope." He cocked his head, trying to read his father's expression. "Hey, Dad, can I keep him?"

"No, son." The dogs had fallen in behind them. "But there'll be others."

Stu, especially, hated Harry. If Harry stuck six new three-cent stamps to a doorknob it was cute. Let Harry drop his turtle in the toilet, and when Daddy flushed it away the consolation poured in, not to mention a replacement hamster. Even when the hamster got *its* swimming lesson nobody cared. Mother lifted the lid and there it was, frantically clawing its way around the waterline. After she got her breath back, she said that was cute too. Once, Stu was cute. Now he was naughty and had a kidney infection all the time. You didn't win praise for urine specimens. They wrapped the jars in wax paper and put them in sacks in the refrigerator. It was even worse when they had to take a stool sample to check for worms. Stu's stool. They put that one in a carton like the cartons for chop suey. Stu would never in his life be able to eat food that came in cartons. Ice cream came in cartons.

All Harry's fault.

Stu provoked Harry with prods and pushes and broke his toys. He even wet Harry's bed for him when Harry woke up dry and went into the bathroom. By the time Stu was nine, he was seeing a psychiatrist.

Harry got along best with Stanley, who was as pliant as a rubber plant. Nothing disturbed Stanley; Stanley disturbed no one. Out of sheer dispassion he achieved a kind of secret witness status among his brothers. There was Harry's specimen-taking, for instance. The time Harry did that, Stanley and Stu watched.

It began with a half-full bottle of ginger ale. Harry brought it up to capacity, and Stanley marveled at his aim. When Winslow took it out of the refrigerator later that evening, Stanley was the only one on hand. Winslow flipped the cap off with his thumb and took a long draft. Stanley was impressed but said nothing.

"God, that's awful," Winslow complained. "I've tasted better piss!"

Stanley smiled faintly.

Winslow belched.

Harry was upset when he looked in the refrigerator and couldn't find his specimen. Then it occurred to him that they had taken it to Dr. Ufunker. Somehow he thought this would make him and Stu closer—urine brothers.

Harry could be tenacious, especially about relationships. He was tenacious about Stu exactly 490 times. That was because he learned in Sunday school that you were supposed to forgive your enemy "seventy times seven." He got his mother to work out the math and began counting. Poor Stu didn't know he had a quota, and so he kept transgressing with equanimity. When Harry came home from school pinching a large sheet of limp poster paper between his fingers, saying it was sunset on a lake with lots of ducks and their mother ooh-ed and aah-ed and told him she knew it was a lake because the blue water was still wet, Stu waylaid Harry up in his room and tore off a corner.

"Don't like it," he said.

"Thirty-nine," said Harry.

Stu laughed and tore the poster down the middle.

"Forty."

All in all, it took five weeks. Some of the therapy—the cutting of ten bicycle spokes with a hacksaw, the flattening of Harry's Sunday school pin with a hammer—actually made Stu feel crummy. But he carnaged on, and when he reached 490, Harry beat the living daylights out of him. After that, Stu just got quietly sicker.

Tenacity. Harry reeked with it.

And he never gave up on the dream that began in July of 1955 when Disneyland opened. "I'm going to be Walt Disney someday," he told his mother. "I'm going to have my own land."

Alice told Winslow that he should take Harry to Disneyland. Their son had the capacity for visions, she said. Wasn't that what Einstein had? Someday Harry would look into the universe and it would all come clear to him, she told him. Winslow wondered if Einstein's father had ever galloped him under a low arch.

∤ 3 ∤

Harry fell in love for the first time when he was twelve. This was in 1962; he had just started junior high. The name of the femme fatale was Heather Latko. It was a sacred relationship. He didn't tell Heather for fourteen years.

This was not a case of love at first sight. The first time he saw her was at a Brownie investiture at the age of seven. He went with his mother, who, because of her ties with school, had consented to be a troop leader. He remembered the occasion vividly because he walked and sat and, in a sense, talked with the fathers who were there to see their little girls invested into Troop 63. It made him feel very grown up to be privy to those murmured remarks made mostly over his head. The fathers were being irreverent because the thing had started out badly and was getting worse. They waited nearly an hour in a parking lot until everyone showed, then marched in two groups through a nearby woods to the pondside setting where the ceremony was to take place. The first group, composed of veteran Brownies, led the way, lacing the trail with strips of toilet paper which members of the second group, those to be invested, were supposed to follow. Alice Moon kept yelling, "Tie one on! Tie one on!" about the strips, and the fathers joked about tying one on until the girls ran out of toilet paper halfway and had to use hot dog buns, which a cold dog, cold and hungry, running loose in the woods promptly devoured. So the second group got lost. Eventually Harry was sent back to find them, and that was when he discovered Heather Latko. She was wandering a little ahead of the others, looking for toilet paper.

"You a Brownie?" he demanded.

She regarded him coldly, her dark eyes—regal even then—narrowing. "I'm going to be infested," she said scornfully.

"Well, you're lost, don'tcha know," he announced archly.

"I am not lost," she replied.

"You're all lost and I'm gonna show you the way." He waited a moment but she showed no gratitude. "It's that way," he said, pointing.

"I *know*," said Heather frostily.

Just then the flustered mother in charge saw him and called, "Did they send you back, Harry?"

"I'm supposed to lead you!" he shouted.

"Good!" The mother nodded excessively. "Lead on!"

"I don't need you to lead *me* out," said the little girl with the dark eyes who was on her way to be infested. And her apricot mouth and pearl-like teeth and dusky cheeks stirred something in Harry's breast he couldn't identify.

The cold stray dog found Harry then, sniffed his pant cuffs, and fell in step.

When they finally got to the pond, the first group was coming apart. They were tired and bored, and some of the girls had to go to the bathroom. The two flag bearers ("flag draggers," one of the fathers called them) were beating each other with their staffs. Walter Cronkite could have explained the universe, evolution, and the Korean War in the time it had taken Troop 63 to walk that trail, yet the light poles in the parking lot were clearly visible above the trees. The trail had merely wound around two sides of it. They had come nowhere to do nothing.

At last the first group shaped up, hollering in unison, "Who comes to this Brownie ring?"

"We do!" chorused the second.

"What do you want?" from the first.

"We want to be Brownies!" the second.

"Come ahead, then!"

Harry took his place among the fathers, whose self-control

was fast deteriorating. They were gripped in the kind of forbidden humor that magnifies the funniness of asinine remarks.

"Don't wake the sleeping bags," said one, who smoked what Harry thought looked like a piece of dog poop.

"I'm from *National Geographic*," snickered another, tears starting to his eyes. He brandished a camera. "I'm here"—snicker—"to film"—snicker, snicker—"these hidden rites neverbeforeseenby—" He raced the last words together but still couldn't finish.

The man with the poop observed that Alice Moon should put her Jesus shoes on and walk across the pond.

The girls all had pieces of Naugahyde called "sit-upons," which they had crafted the week before. Alice was trying to get them to form a horseshoe of the sit-upons so that the ceremony could begin. "Sit down in the horseshoe," Alice said, only she let the last syllable tail off and through the din it reached the fathers as "Sit down in the horsesh—" Naturally, they thought that was hysterical and that it adequately explained the need for sit-upons.

Then it began to rain.

Nothing was going to go right. The girl in charge of introducing the initiates picked her nose and no one would hold her hand. Eventually, as they were about to leave, a veteran Brownie informed the men that they had been sitting in poison ivy. Alice shrugged benignly, and Troop 63 marched off singing, "We're jolly, jolly juniors."

Harry caught a last glimpse of Heather, regarding him like some kind of useless object, unplugged, broken, disassembled. She made him feel that he was somehow already a part of her past, without present or future. The entire farce dissolved in a day-long rain, remaining submerged until years later when Harry would return to this very same spot to see the investiture of his own daughter. The weather would be better then, and the savant who could explain the universe and evolution before they traveled from parking lot to pond would be Carl Sagan instead of Walter Cronkite, and the song...the song would have lost its innocence. No longer "Jolly, jolly juniors!" the refrain would be "Sexy, sexy seniors!"

When Harry saw Heather again five years later, he knew immediately who she was. She stood out of the whole imbroglio of that day like a photo with dim edges, her image soft but articulate against a kind of halo. In actuality, that dimness was the formlessness of her childhood, from which she had emerged a budding, brittle adolescent. Harry saw the budding but did not understand the brittleness. That which looked perfect must *be* perfect, he felt instinctively.

This, then, was far more than sexual passion. Not that he was any kind of an expert. As far as he knew, sex was a rumor. He masturbated, which seemed to confirm something, but his knowledge of the female form was limited to Vargas calendar girls, *Gray's Anatomy,* and what he could see of Carrie Reske.

Carrie Reske was one of those gals who used to be "one of the fellas." In the good old days Carrie had bravado, a foul mouth, and an arm like Virgil Trucks. Now Carrie just had "tits." At least that was all the boys could see, and they could see a lot on Carrie Reske. Rumor had it she was still one of the fellas, a real bosom buddy to everyone with fingers, but the rumors were wrong. Carrie put out about as often as a slot machine, and the payoffs were small. She knew, for instance, why Harry Moon kept challenging her to compare heights.

"Hey, I'm almost up to your shoulder now," Harry would say cleverly.

"Wanna bet?" She would feign stupidity.

Harry would start to sweat, lechery making an intense waffle of his face. Licking his lips, he would assume a ramrod posture—the vertical equivalent of an erection.

"See?" he would pant.

Carrie Reske would then unlimber, thrusting herself up—and out, her turgid breasts nearly touching his face.

He could stand only a few moments of this sublime nubile heat before wilting. When it was over, he would try to say something but his speech would dissolve into carnal rumbles. He sounded rather like a car engine trying to talk. Yes, Carrie Reske knew precisely who was pulling her handle and how much the payoff should be.

From this little charade Harry extracted the idea that he was a slick operator. And from his dreams he developed suave still shots of himself making time with Heather Latko. He was, at that time, rather short, with large eyes and a thin face. The size of his hands and feet promised more growth, but for the time being he resembled a rabbit (small wonder, with all the carrots he had eaten). His marks were average, he spoke in a Lilliputian voice, and his parents were becoming an embarrassment to him. Like his father, he was stalked by bad timing. Tin grins were not in when he got his braces. Hair was. He had this thin, untrainable stuff, and he wore a hat whenever he could. Hats were out. When he finally learned to use a hula hoop, no one would be caught dead with one.

On the theory that history repeats, he borrowed the artifacts of Nicki's past to fill the cultural void in his present. There were two 45 RPMs, a pink shirt, 3-D glasses, and a small book of "droodles" by Roger Price, liberally appended to by Nicki. Thus he exploded into the sixties like a tardy sonic boom.

Harry painstakingly memorized the records, but his thin voice sounded like escaping steam. He was a pigeon cooing to crows, a rooster crowing at dusk—the wrong species, the wrong time. Likewise the pink shirt was the wrong plumage. He wore the 3-D glasses to school, but the contrasting red and green cellophane lenses made it impossible for him to distinguish traffic lights, and at the very first corner he caused a cruising taxi to swerve into some garbage cans. The sound of crumpling metal and the sight of mangled bones flying through the air panicked him, and he ran away. The bones were from a dozen dinners served by the fried chicken restaurant that owned the garbage cans, but Harry feared that some, at least, were human. He hoped they were only the bones of stray cats feeding in the can, but perhaps the cab had killed a midget who was reaching up to pry off the lid.

A stray dog fell in behind him, and he took this as a good omen. Nevertheless he dropped the 3-D glasses in a sewer and prayed. At that moment the dog following him saw a squirrel and gave chase. Squirrels were about the size of cats, and Harry took this as another good sign. Maybe it was even squirrels in the garbage can.

That night he searched the paper for conclusive evidence and, finding none, stole back to the scene. The bones were gone but there were some bits of yellow plastic and broken glass from the taxi's lights. Harry looked into the first of the garbage cans, and what should flow out but a randy-looking cat. It was the final omen. The anguished beast must be holding a vigil for its mate. For a time thereafter, the howl of a cat could, for some unrecallable reason, shred his composure.

All the artifacts Harry had borrowed from Nicki's dead culture had been tried now except for the droodles, so he took that to school. Droodles were simple line drawings of magnified details the viewer was supposed to figure out. For example, there was the single dot on a white sheet of paper. That was a cinder in the eye of a ghost. He showed it to Nino Torkie first, and Nino couldn't get enough of it.

"Boy, that's rich, Moon!" He guffawed. "How'd you think of that one?" The whole process of thought was a flat-out mystery to Nino. He had an interesting head from a ballistics point of view and had once spent an hour trying to open a hockey puck.

"Simple," Harry said, and Nino thought he'd been answered.

"I got to try that out. A cinder in a ghost's eye! Where do you put the cinder, hey, Moonie? Up high? Hey?"

"High is okay," Harry said.

"A cinder in a ghost's eye," Nino repeated and went off howling.

By noon there were dots all over the school. This made Harry feel like Walt Disney in embryo. It was time to proliferate something new: a rectangle with two small circles on it and a curlicue coming up from its top edge. When he got the rectangle down, someone might blurt, "It's a coffin!" Methodically he would add the circles, and everyone would know it was not a coffin. When he added the curlicue there would be an eager silence.

"A pig in a drawer," Harry Moon would say then, basking in the uproar.

The uproar convinced him he was ready for Heather Latko. She was there in the cafeteria at noon, super-groomed and formidable, flanked at a long table by two girls known for their exploits in chess and forensics. God, she was beautiful! He must be crazy going over to the most perfect human being on earth with a trayful of macaroni and cheese to show her his droodles, he thought. He would have a better chance with the Wizard of Oz, asking for brains, courage, and Kansas.

The two on either side of her were eating soup, their heads alternately bobbing, so that they looked like offset cams on the same shaft. In between, the goddess of symmetry nibbled a grape as if it had good parts and bad.

Harry sat down with a clatter and stabbed his macaroni as though he were harpooning Moby Dick. The two cams stopped bobbing.

"Macaroni's tough today," one said.

"Like chopped clothesline," agreed the second.

They were a team, Tweedledee and Tweedledum. In between, Heather Latko nibbled an endless grape.

Harry chewed the punctured macaroni to bits while fumbling through a fistful of pencils. With a flourish, he whipped one free and drove it into a paper napkin, snapping off the lead. The dot was mostly lost in the lower layers of paper and almost invisible.

"Whazzat?" he demanded, spinning the napkin across the table.

The two-headed machine for eating soup nearly threw an axle exchanging glances. H. Latko consumed another grape.

"It'saghostwithacinderinitseye," Harry rattled. "Cinder," he repeated, his right hand flopping over like a bellied-up fish.

Tweedledee looked distressed, Tweedledum looked dumb. They glanced at each other.

Heather nibbled.

Harry wished he were dead.

Humming dementedly, he wrenched a sheet of paper from his notebook and began the more elaborate pig in a drawer. But the rectangle came out like a trapezoid, and the broken lead crumbled on the curlicue, making the pig's tail look grubby. Then, when he tried to spin the droodle across the table with a cavalier flick of the wrist, it landed edge-on in Tweedledum's soup.

Nobody moved to fish it out.

"Pig in a drawer!" he gunned across the void a little too intensely.

There was another ghastly silence. Tweedledum fished the pig in a drawer out of her soup. Heather stopped nibbling the infinite grape. Harry felt wretched.

Suddenly he realized how immature he was, how absolutely infantile this must seem to someone like Heather Latko. He had been successful with his classmates because they were mere children. But Heather Latko was not a child. Anyone could look into her cool, dark eyes and see that you couldn't dazzle her with droodles.

Gesturing away the picture he volunteered archly, "I voted for Kennedy."

For years after, he wondered if she understood that he meant the straw vote in social studies class or if she, in fact, thought he was being impossibly adult. I voted.... The soul withers.

What she actually said was, "Oh. You're the one who was going to lead us out of the woods in Brownies that day. Now I understand."

¾ 4 ¾

Winslow worried about Harry's sexuality. He should have worried about Stu's because Stu had begun to collect women's underwear, but he knew nothing of that and regarded Stu's interest in lingerie ads and fashion magazines as a healthy sign of manhood. Nicki was a carnal beast, and even Stanley had a pornographic study of Buck Rogers hidden in his closet. This was healthy, Winslow thought. But Harry was not healthy. Harry never mentioned girls, never lingered over a picture of a bikini or a nyloned leg. How could he take his son to Disneyland when what he really needed was a locker room attitude toward sex? So he encouraged him to go out for sports instead.

The first sport Harry tried was cross-country. He liked the solitude and freedom of running; you left the gym when you were done stretching and ran through the neighborhoods. There were six routes, and they led past such places as a bakery, a park with a pond, a burlesque house with appealing notices out front. Harry liked to circle the pond. It was the first hint he had of his lifelong affinity for water. His ancestor back in Gloucestershire had been Jonathan Moon, the oldest of the four expatriate Moon brothers, the one who loved drink and immersion and later drowned at the Boston Tea Party. There were four brothers then and four brothers now; something cyclic was happening, but history was repeating its atavisms as if through a kind of reduction valve. The current brothers bore similarities to all of the earlier four, even though their bloodline passed through only one. The similarities extended to the events of their lives, though Harry knew none of this. Odious, clubfooted Samuel, who peeped through windows, was a little like sexually maladjusted Stu, for example. And Nicki, who was fast bullying his way to the head of a junior mafia, was something like chicken thief Benjamin. Dreamy Stanley bore a kinship to bereft Alexander, who died at the age of 103. That left Jonathan for Harry to emulate. Thus he circled the pond again and again in his runs, fascinated by its winks of light and the languid waving of submerged weeds. It was as if someone were beckoning him.

Harry liked the cross-country coach. His name was Mr. Schroeder, and he talked a lot about how running felt. You got the impression that he was talking about flying, really, because he made it seem like a weightless, soaring form of concentration, and he had, in fact, once been a pilot. His license was revoked because he forgot to put the wheels down on a Beechcraft going into La Porte, Indiana. The story got around that his touch was so good that the plane glided smoothly to a halt and his two passengers never knew about the wheels. Actually, he tore the bottom off the craft in a blaze of sparks, furrowed the runway, and spun the Beechcraft around, giving one of the passengers whiplash. His insurance wouldn't pay to resurface the runway, and the passenger with the whiplash—his mother-in-law—sued. He ended up divorced and never applied to have his license reinstated. Now when he talked about pace and rhythm he seemed filled with nostalgia for flight, and his runners left these lectures overflowing with a kind of religious ecstasy.

Though Harry's stride was short, he probably would have stuck with cross-country if it hadn't been for the injury. This was something called plantar fascitis. He was coming down a steep hill one day, and instead of leaning back and shortening up, he stretched out his stride to the point of almost falling. It was near-flight, he felt: Schroeder's soaring. But it stressed a tendon in his left foot. When the injury didn't heal, Alice took him to Dr. Ufunker.

"He can hardly walk, doctor," she said. "And he's on the cross-country team. Is there anything you can do?"

Dr. Ufunker had done enough when he gave Harry a mere five at birth. He remembered the boy's head injury; where were the glasses he had prescribed? He had been driving a red Mercedes then, and now, six cars later, here was Harry Moon with no glasses. Harry had made a dozen visits in the interim, but this was the first time Dr. Ufunker remembered the glasses.

"Orthotics," he said, without taking off the boy's shoe.

His standard cure for anything below the waist was orthotics. If you had tire tracks across your thighs, Dr. Ufunker would tell you to put orthotics in your shoes. Later, Harry would be afraid to stick out his tongue for fear Ufunker would put an orthotic on it. Got a cold? Take two orthotics and call me in the morning.

A nurse made a plaster cast of Harry's feet while the doctor left for the day in his yellow Alfa-Romeo. The orthotics were made from the cast and cost seventy-five dollars. Harry was supposed to be able to run in them, but they made his hip hurt when he came down on his heel. He was afraid to tell his mother for fear she would take him back to Ufunker. So he said good-bye to the bakery, the park, and the pond, the burlesque, the dogs that followed him, and the coach, and he quit.

Alice was satisfied. Ufunker's orthotics had allowed her son to finish a phase of his life. Harry had tried cross-country and it was not for him. He had seen it through. He was more regular and self-assured for the experience, just like all those good old Stenners from Vermont. Dr. Ufunker, she felt, should have his head on Mount Rushmore.

Winslow agreed. Ufunker's head was made of the same material, as far as he was concerned. He was outraged over the seventy-five dollars for the orthotics, followed by Harry's quitting the team. But if he mentioned money to Alice, she would say she should go back to teaching to help pay for things. Even now, after all the years of not working, Alice could go out and in one day get a job that brought home more money than he did. So he let it pass. Football season started later than cross-country, and there was still time for Harry to try out for that.

The football coach had a voice that would saw young boys in half. He was the bluster and bluff type and he had come out of the Marines, so hardly anyone cared to discuss their personal problems with him. There *were* no personal problems. There were only *team* problems. If you had personal problems you were weak, spineless, and despicable, Coach Coomes assured them. Harry donated his earthly flesh to the team and subordinated his soul. Coach Coomes said he had possibilities.

There were moments in the primitive frenzy of a halftime talk when Coach Coomes could have said, Nino Torkie, your mother is your enemy; tackle her the next time you see her, and Nino would have done it. Of course, Nino was not bright. He had once tried to inflate a sweat sock, and another time a football with his mouth. But the primitive energy of the assembled group, uniformed and distinguished solely by numerals, and Coach Coomes's voice sawing through them, produced a kamikaze-like dedication.

Still, deep down, the players hated him. Yet they also feared being hated by him, because he represented maleness. It was exactly what Winslow wanted for Harry. Maleness.

Harry did not like football. He missed the individuality of running and the poetic reveries of Coach Schroeder, so much like the winged kingdoms of Disneyland. But he wanted to impress Heather Latko, of course, and that was why he stuck it out for as long as he did. He even hung around after practice sometimes, taking extra laps when his foot wasn't bothering him. On those occasions he might share the main shower room with Coach Coomes.

He liked showers. They provided a refuge of sound and touch and temperature most closely associated with the womb. The timpani of the spray was also pleasant, and the acoustics of the tiled room purified voices. He liked to hear Coach Coomes singing on those nights when they shared a late departure. Then the saw-toothed voice would soften and soar like one of Mr. Schroeder's reveries. "Ooo-de-ooo-de-yo-dah!" Coomes would sing. Harry never spoke. Coomes, conscious of his performance, never spoke either. "Ooo-de-ooo-de-yo-dah!..."

Harry's last game was Homecoming. That was when they met their arch rival in a cliff-hanger. The outcome was very much in doubt at halftime. Coach Coomes drilled holes through their very souls as well as sawing them in half with his voice in the locker room. The spirit of the kill was intense. Coach Coomes even prayed aloud, as if he were Jesus talking to the Father. After he said "Amen" the team raced onto the field like an epidemic and managed to eke out a four-point lead by the last minute of play. Then they fumbled on their own twelve-yard line. The inert mass was twenty-two players high, but everyone had seen Harry Moon and Nino Torkie come down on the ball. In the dark, stinking crush at the bottom, neither of these two could be sure who the owner of the other hand was.

"Nino?" Harry wheezed. "That you?"

Nino grunted. Whistles were blowing like a firemen's field day.

"Tap my hand if it's you," Harry squeezed out.

Tap my hand if it's you! An immortal stupidity. Even Nino knew it was stupid. Suddenly everyone tapped everybody, Harry released the ball, and the subsequent infighting was like a freed log jam. The ball turned over.

Ordinarily twelve yards is across the galaxy for junior high football players. Embalmed as they are in pads and equipment, they are prone to stumble into each other in huge, doughy collisions. A player hanging his head after a play may merely be gathering the strength to raise his neck. But a great moan of disappointment from the crowd fell heavily on the home team now. In the very next play they crumbled like stale bread, and the enemy fullback lumbered into the end zone.

Harry found isolation beneath the bleachers. The sound of boards snapping and rumbling above him as the crowd left was penance. People were walking over him. When the field was long empty, he trudged into the locker room and heard Coach Coomes singing in the showers. "Ooo-de-ooo-de-yo-dah." The tone was flat and mournful.

No one else was around, and Harry walked slowly to the mouth of the shower room. A cloud of steam separated them, each seeing the other like a ghost.

Harry looked at Coach Coomes's nakedness, his slack neck, his pouchy eyes, his sagging belly weedy with wet hair, and wondered why he had ever been afraid of this man. Football was just a game and Coomes a spectator, after all. He was powerless except for the strength of some brainwashed boys. Harry had made him strong. Harry had made him fail. He had never realized how vulnerable Coomes was.

"Do you think I should quit?" he murmured.

"Ooo-de-ooo-de-yo-dah," sang Coach Coomes, as if entranced in self-therapy.

"It was my fault," Harry said loudly. "The team will be better off without me."

"Ooo-de-ooo-de—"

Coach had written him off. He turned back to his locker and slowly peeled off his uniform, dressed without a shower, and left. All the way through the empty gym he heard the showers and Coach Coomes singing "Ooo-de-ooo-de-yo-dah," and he thought that the marvelous sound of water was now purer than the soaring voice.

MOON
RIVERS

╏ 5 ╏

That summer Alice took her boys home to Vermont. There were exciting reasons for this. Nicki had become a thief, Stu a pervert, Stanley an addict, and Harry a manic depressive.

Nicki's larceny began for Alice the day she opened a drawer that smelled sweetly of butter rum and chlorophyll. Under Nicki's shorts were twenty-seven packs of Life Savers and breath mints. There were also shoelaces, dental floss, bouillon cubes, nail clippers, and six bottles of wart remover. The urge to own things was eccentric, and she said nothing until the day Nicki brought her a huge sport coat to be altered. Then she burst into tears.

"You think I stole that, huh?" he blurted. "Is that what you think? Huh?"

"I think you stole it." She shuddered.

"Momma, Momma, I didn't. I swear—"

She held up a palm in dismay. "No more lies, Nicki. Please."

And he cried too.

When Winslow found out about this, he battered Nicki around the house with a slipper. Alice was terrified and called the police. When they arrived they took his slipper away—as if only that half of the pair were dangerous—and spoke privately and patiently to him about the benefits of analysis. Winslow promised to get help, and they departed with his slipper. He had no idea why they kept it but imagined all sorts of bureaucratic consequences. In his file would be three photos: heel, sole, uppers. Interpol and the FBI would have his footprint in their archives. Whatever was afoot, so to speak, would implicate him, and he would sit home forever, nervously waiting for the other shoe to drop. So to speak.

Alice considered talking to Dr. Ufunker. Omnipotent Ufunker would know what to do. But what if he turned Nicki in? A doctor wasn't under an oath of secrecy like a priest. That was why she decided to take Nicki to Vermont. After all, what was there to steal in Chewbagin?

As for Stu, there was no question that he had begun to do a grotesque and disturbing thing. One day, while making his bed, she pulled six bras and three pairs of panties from under the mattress. None of them were new, nor were they the same sizes. He was only fourteen and very clumsy, and she did not consider it likely that he could have such power over older women. Judging by the sizes, they had to be older women. Oh, Stu, oh, Stu! her heart cried out. She took the garments away but the next week found a ragged girdle in his lunch box, as if his monstrous sexual appetite had devoured an innocent matron as part of a mundane repast. After that it was nylons in his shoes, and then a garter belt tucked in the left leg of his corduroys hanging from a hook.

All the garments were clean. She guessed, therefore, that he hadn't taken them off their owners, as she first had feared, but rather off clotheslines or out of laundromats. He seemed to prefer blue.

He had seen a child psychiatrist for six months when he was nine because he murdered a cat. The cat was hanging from the cross brace of the backyard swing when Winslow took out the garbage one evening. Stu confessed with a shrug. The psychiatrist told them he had a lot of pent-up hostility and to try to "channel it away." Alice gazed heartsick at Stu's collection and wondered if this was a channel. If so, she would gladly buy him a cat today, tomorrow, and yesterday. Cats returned to the elements but girdles stretched on forever. The cats in Vermont were hard to catch, the laundromats few, she recalled, and added Stu to the homecoming.

Part of Stu's problem was that Stanley had eaten his tranquilizers every day for the past six months. This was also part of Stanley's problem. He was a devotee of aspirins and Coke, Midol, and all things reputed to dull or enliven the senses. He had tried wood alcohol, vanilla extract, rum cake, and every brown bottle in the house. The manner of ingestion hardly mattered. Stanley believed there were many pathways to the brain. He had seven bodily orifices and used them all. This gave him an edge in the field of exotic sensations. Hardly anyone on his block had experienced a peppermint enema or the sensual tingle of orange crush in one ear. It bothered him that his navel led nowhere.

He was absolutely guiltless about such things. At the age of six he had asked permission to smoke. Once, on Palm Sunday, he ate half of the frond given him at the altar. Still more sensational, the sight of countless fur coats in a department store produced the desire in him to flow naked through the racks. Divesting himself, he had scampered ecstatically among the beavers and hares until brought down by a security guard and a fake fox boa.

He explained these episodes in terms of apocalyptic visions, and Alice always listened, impressed but doubtful. It was really hard to indict Stanley for such foolishness. Whatever he did, he did sincerely. And when the school sent him home for trying to cut a Hostess Twinkie in half on the school table saw, she simply asked if he couldn't find a knife. Stanley's sins were always murky. Vermont, she thought.

In her despair, Vermont shone like a white castle on a darkling plain. All roads, twisted, tangled, or perverse, led to Vermont. That was *her* apocalyptic vision, and she was riding into it with her own four horsemen at full gallop.

The potential for disaster, then, accompanied her to Chewbagin. It was like carrying diphtheria, rubella, chicken pox, and whooping cough into a nursery school and hoping no one would breathe, sneeze, or touch anything. The one antibody she had was Harry, the Moons' great hope. True, he had been depressed lately, but that was because he had hurled a god-awful strike in Pony League baseball just as the umpire bent over to dust the plate. The ensuing rectal agony so upset the ump that he threw Harry out of the game. Alice thought he had made rather much of the incident for a grown man.

Everyone blames the ump.

Actually, Harry was not depressed because he had thrown the perfect strike and gotten only bowels from the umpire, he was depressed because he was going to Vermont.

The final and most vexing reason for Alice's return to her roots was to air out her marriage. The exhilarating ether she had once breathed was now carbon monoxide. She had ceased to feel sorry for Winslow; he was happy being a victim. Crisis and failure confirmed his existence and fit smugly into his expectations. He clutched at them like vines, swinging through the jungle of life. There would always be enough failure and disappointment to support Winslow, but that wasn't her element. She couldn't float in it. She needed to function, to move forward, to share in the social and civic goodness of life. Winslow was dead in the water, and the current was pulling her onward.

Just before she left, they had a brief flare-up. Exasperated that she had become a social insect communicating to the world by phone, Winslow went out one morning and called in. It took a while to get through, but she finally answered in a bright voice he hadn't heard in years.

"Where's my razor?" he demanded bluntly.

"You don't have a razor," she said, dropping an octave. "You use mine. Since I'm taking it with me to Vermont, I'll get you your own."

As a gesture of conciliation, she bought him an electric one with combs that you had to blow through to clear when you finished and gave it to him the morning of their departure. But Winslow was in the habit of eating his breakfast while he shaved, and standing there in his one slipper, he casually blew a mouthful of Cream of Wheat through the razor head. That was the way she wanted to remember him, she thought, and left without saying good-bye.

They went to Chewbagin by train, and Alice couldn't wait for the state line. The Vermont human being in her memory was God's archetype for the species. But at Brattleboro three hippies got on.

The hippies were followed at the next stop by three young

blacks, and then three Peace Corps volunteers. In each case the trios were constituted two thirds male or female, and Alice discerned something universally troilistic about Vermont youth that she had never discerned before. She was relieved when a pair of wholesome teenage boys boarded in suits and ties. They were followed by a mother and daughter. But at the next stop the mother and daughter got off, and the teenage boys began holding hands. Terminal saturation came with the inclusion of three young pacifists, a trio of albino-looking Nazis who would have been overdressed in anyone's Reich, and a lone haggard-eyed soldier in a green beret.

Alice was plainly worried. Festive young people had always migrated to the resort areas in summer, but this assortment looked too purposeful to be either festive or young. Why were they all wearing buttons? Was there some sort of identity crisis she hadn't heard about?

The Peace Corps trio wore GIVE A DAMN and APATHY but were neutralized by the hippies, whose logos included TURN ON, TUNE IN, DROP OUT, HANDS OFF TIM LEARY, and GET STONED. One of the hippies wore only a bikini and a belly button painted to read MY BUTTON LOVES YOUR BUTTON. Stanley was fascinated by this gaudy orifice. Stu coveted her tiny bra. Alice tried not to notice, but the shameless child swayed up and down the aisle passing out flowers. When she got to the pacifists, one of them offered to pay for a daisy by reading his poem. He wore two buttons, MORATORIUM and WE SHALL OVERKILL. The flower child promptly crossed her legs and sat down on the floor of the train.

"I just wrote this in the train station," he said, pulling out a typed scroll. "It's called 'Some Thoughts in a Train Station.' It's got two stanzas." His face grew intense.

"This little flower, so tender and pale,
　Can withstand the rain and the snow and the gale
　To come out of the earth in the spring without fail.
　But when the bomb drops this baby will sail!

"God gave us life this side of the veil,
　Some with wings, some with fur, some with snout, some
　　with tail.
　Rock-a-bye baby so tiny and frail,
　But when the bomb drops this baby will wail."

The girl nodded profoundly. "Heavy," she said.

Alice wondered where the young man had seen a flower in a train station.

After that, another one of the pacifists stood up and delivered a speech. "Good afternoon, fellow travelers," he began. "We journey this shimmering set of rails to a certain destination together, but I tell you today that the road we are traveling to the future is less certain. The specter of nuclear annihilation hovers over us all. There is no reason for this. Why can't we live in peace? Our needs are the same. We must put our weapons aside and join hands at the equator. Only then will we understand tolerance and brotherhood. Where are our principles? Where is our love? Where is our compassion? Come and hold hands with us today, or we will be forced to blow your fucking heads off." With that, the three pacifists pulled out pistols and waved them around.

Alice's jaw dropped. Harry went white. Stu whimpered. Nicki studied the pistols reverently. The Peace Corps volunteers applauded.

"This train car is hereby commandeered by the Committee to Hold Hands at the Equator," said the young man. "We will hold it until our demands are met."

The Peace Corps people clapped some more. "We would like to join you, brothers and sisters," one of them said.

"So be it," said the spokesman for the pacifists.

The flower child stuck a daisy in each of the guns.

"What's goin' down with the bread?" one of the blacks demanded, bobbing out of his seat like spring steel. He sported the obligatory pair of buttons, WE SHALL OVERCOME and BURN BABY BURN. "I mean like all that money that don't go for bombs got to go for reparations to the Africans." As he spoke, he riveted the air with a diving finger, and his companions raised clenched fists.

"Agreed," said the spokesman for the pacifists. "All funds deleted from Defense shall go for Social Justice."

Cries of "right on!" swelled the coalition to twelve.

Alice felt as though she were falling slowly downstairs. The other members of the car had defected, or were arguing back, or—in the case of the two teenage boys in suits and ties—were practicing holding hands presumably for reasons equatorial. Should she swear allegiance to the imbeciles of the world? For all their pronouncements she still did not know exactly what their demands were. Surely they did not believe they could form a ring at the equator?

The soldier put it succinctly. "The least you could have done is picked a meridian that stayed over land most the way, you stupid pricks."

The Nazi laughed.

"Who you callin' a prick, honky?" blurted one of the blacks.

The soldier took off his beret, revealing the tight curls of a Negro.

"Sumbitch . . . we got a Oreo here," said the black.

The Nazis then sneered at the pseudo-Aryan soldier, who redonned his beret in rabbinical fashion, smiled, and gently informed them that Hitler was one quarter Jewish.

"Stop it, stop it!" cried the pacifist spokesman, wringing his hands. The pistol he held thereupon discharged, ricocheting off the cloche brim of one of the helmets and spidering the window behind the Nazi's neck. If the Führer himself had spoken the next words, he could not have commanded more attention from the Nazis. "You people make me sick!" screamed the pacifist. And just at that moment they entered a tunnel.

An eerie silence ensued, with just the imperfections in the tracks and Stu's whimpering heard. When the light flooded back, the Nazis were gone, the soldier was gone, the teenagers in suits and ties were gone, and Alice and her boys sat facing the twelve-person Committee to Hold Hands at the Equator.

"Well?" demanded the spokesman.

"I don't like bombs," Alice said.

The pacifist nodded grimly. "This is a hell of a siege," he said and put his pistol away.

"Talk, talk, white folk ain't nothin' but talk," muttered the first black, and the trios seemed to drift apart without actually moving.

"Wouldn't have worked anyway," said one of the Peace Corps volunteers. "I spent two years on the equator in Sumatra, and you can't stop slapping mosquitoes long enough to hold hands."

The teenage boys had not left the train after all but had worked their way down to the floor between seats. They got off at the next station and went directly to the bathroom. There was only one facility, and Alice had to stand outside waiting with Stu because all the excitement had upset his bowels again. When the two teenagers finally came out, she noticed they had switched ties. Since she did not think they had gone in there for the sole purpose of switching ties, she was somewhat reluctant to let Stu enter next, but there was no longer any real choice. When her turn came she was further dismayed to find the human condition graphically displayed in all its alarming detail on an interior wall. The great variety of passions was at least as encompassing as anything Michelangelo had done, and Alice realized that no single artist—or pair of artists, for that matter —could have quickly rendered it. Vermont had slipped. Vermont was teetering as though its great granite mountains were as honeycombed with faults as the rest of the world. Vermont, Vermont. . . . Alice Stenner Moon had arrived too late to save or be saved by it.

{ 6 }

Winslow had understood that they were parting when he blew Cream of Wheat through his razor. Alice was going home to Vermont and taking the children. She was turning her back on him because his problem was one too many now that the boys were so screwed up. A mother had to look after her children first. The razor was a consolation prize.

He wasn't hurt or angry. Actually he wanted to be alone. He went to the bathroom with the door open, belched, farted, scratched anywhere he itched, and undressed as he walked from room to room. Like Goldilocks, he slept in whatever bed he wanted and drank out of everyone's favorite glass. When the phone rang he didn't answer it, and the mail piled up on the porch. It was the season for construction, but he contracted no new jobs. He could only have been happier if he had opened the paper and discovered his own obituary, services private.

Going Goldilocks one better, he began to wear Nicki's T-shirts when his own were all used up. If he was sparing, he might only have to launder once all summer. But Nicki had small feet, so when Winslow ran out of socks he went to Stu's room. That was how he found the silk panties and the padded bra. They were in with the socks. Trophies of the hunt, he reflected with a touch of pride, but the more he looked at them the more he saw that these were not the wrinkled remnants of passion.

He was devastated.

First Harry's sexuality, now Stu's.

How long had this been going on? Cell by cell his sons had accumulated into small human beings until in a blinding sleight of hand they had grown up. Had he missed the signs? He had tried to play with them, to be interested in their games, but all he had ever been able to do was hug and kiss. He had never even taken Harry to Disneyland. Overcome with remorse, Winslow wept.

Stu's socks were too small also, and rather than washing clothes he went out to buy new ones. Invigorated by fresh air and his first exercise in days, he felt like a lily-white cadaver emerging unshaven into a hereafter of sunshine and tans. He was self-conscious about his naked ankles, and he had been eating garlic for days. He kept excusing himself to the store clerks and customers upon whom he breathed. The dogs that followed him were farther back than usual. He returned with new socks and the conviction that life had to go on.

Alice and he had simply rusted apart. They were like a gate hasp and staple whose lock disintegrates. The parts are still there but the gate swings open, and now Winslow swung with it. He was dismayed at how easy it was. All those years together. It would have taken next to nothing to avoid: a word here, a touch there. If they had just continued to talk to each other, if they had worked at mutual respect, if they had not become the tedious fulfillment of each other's lessened expectations....

But the marriage was dead; mortar-washed, ephemeral Winslow Moon was laying it to rest.

He hated bars because of the smoke. He hated crowds too. He hated dance halls. He hated libraries. He hated concerts. That left movies and restaurants. He liked movies if they weren't crowded or pretentious. There in the cool darkness he might find an uncomplicated, undemanding, unpossessive, reasonably sane, hygienic human being who was also a good bang. The trouble was that anyone who met these qualifications would be too good for him, he thought. Anyone who was half these things would be happily married.

Already defeated, he went to the Comet Theater, but then he remembered he had taken Alice there on her birthday, and he left for the Washington Cinema down the street. As soon as he sat down, Tommy Rettig came on the screen and discovered Lassie lying in a ditch. Something about Tommy's shocked mouth and stricken eyes reminded him of Harry, and he recalled that he had refused to let Harry keep the dog that was following him the day they walked home from the bakery. He got through four more minutes, then left. But his sons were on his mind now, and he found himself sadly engrossed in a Walt Disney rerun at the next theater. So far he had purchased three tickets to six movies, and all he had to show for it was four minutes of Lassie lying in a ditch and the guilt-provoking flight of Peter Pan.

Next, he chose a foreign film with subtitles. Europeans were blasé about the sort of thing he was going to do, he thought, and women who came to see these kinds of films would not be offended by directness. Better still, the film was French and starred Brigitte Bardot. He took a back-row seat until his eyes grew accustomed to the gloom. The place was two thirds empty, but in the third or fourth row he saw a lone female outlined in the glow of the screen. He waited a few minutes to make sure no one was going to return from the lobby with popcorn to join her, then rose and stalked down the aisle. Each step seemed to catapult him faster into a moral descent from which there was no return. He felt inevitable and foreboding. Let her turn out to be a male hippie with long hair, he prayed; let her be a transvestite with a dress and hairy legs. She was quite feminine, in fact, with a petite nose and rouge that was evident even in the dim theater. He sat down, and she glanced noncommittally his way. He waited a few minutes, then said, "I'm married and I have four sons but I'm lonely."

She kept on gazing at the screen, but her eyes glassed over. He thought it might be because she felt sorry for him. Brigitte Bardot was taking off her clothes for a man at a desk, and he didn't see anything sad about that.

"Don't say anything," he said, and she kept on saying nothing. "I'm going to put my hand on your knee now. But if you don't want me to, just say no."

It occurred to him in a kind of fog that he had just told her to say nothing before that, but she looked at him noncommittally again and he thought it was all right.

Gracefully, he dropped his hand on her knee.

"*Non, Monsieur!*" she cried, popping straight up.

Brigitte Bardot's naked fanny was directly overhead; if it wasn't for that distraction the whole theater might have descended on him. He beat a hasty retreat to the rest room, where he grasped the edges of a sink and stared at himself in the mirror. "Stupid, stupid," he said to his image. "She spoke French!"

He stopped lamenting as he became aware of euphoric moans behind him. There was no need to turn around. In the mirror he could see the green door of the toilet stall and, below that, leather shoes—four of them. The exact nature of the act he was witnessing was unclear, but the shoes all pointed in the same direction, one pair behind the other, and the green door began to thump fervently against the lock.

"Fire," he husked urgently, "fire!" and went home to bed.

The next night he tried the strictly adult Roxy on the theory that if there was another soul as lonely and desperate as he on the planet Earth they would eventually go to just such a place. There were only six people in the theater, and the dim interior smelled like alcohol and cigarettes, but luckily one was a woman—a palpably comely woman with the correct number of limbs, only two of which were on the floor—and she was sitting alone in the front row.

Like the other one, her eyes got suddenly glassy when he slid in. This time the scene that loomed enormously overhead was a Roman orgy and definitely not melancholy. No one sitting this close could possibly make anything out of it, and he sensed that she was only waiting.

"I'm married and I have four sons but I'm lonely," he said. "May I put my hand on your knee?"

She sighed and looked at him then, an unbearably sad look that matched his own, and pulled his fingers into her lap.

"My name is Crystal," she said.

* * *

· **49** ·

She was undemanding, unpossessive, reasonably sane, hygienic, and a good bang, but she chain-smoked and was not uncomplicated as he had hoped. On the other hand, she had been hoping for a black 220-pound football star with a Ph.D. in psychoanalysis. She settled for Winslow because she said only someone with as much tragedy as he had written on his face could possibly believe all the cruel ironies life had played on her.

She was married but hadn't seen her husband since he was kidnapped on the Iberian peninsula by a kiddie porn syndicate. He had told her he was a journalist investigating white slavery in the Mideast, but the Spanish police claimed he was dealing in it in Europe. She had spent all her money trying to find him, but when the pornographers sent her a left shoe with a foot still in it, the Spanish police took the foot and closed the case. How could she be sure the foot was really her husband's? she said; they had only been married a few months, and she never got below his waist. And even if it was his foot, he might still be alive. What did he need a left foot for anyway? The Barcelona authorities canceled her visa when she continued to holler, and she was forced to fly home.

Back in the States she applied for her husband's life insurance, but there was a clause in the policy that said, in so many words, produce the body. She wrote the Spanish authorities asking for her husband's foot, and they sent her a plastic jar of formaldehyde with a human nose in it. She realized that someone had screwed up a translation, but she submitted the nose to the insurance company and got back a check for $875.16, representing partial payment, prorated according to how much of the body she had produced. She appealed the award but the court ruled the payment generous and said that if more parts of the body were forthcoming she could continue to collect. She decided she would take it to a higher court if the kiddie porn syndicate continued to send her husband back in bits and pieces, but she wondered how much of him it would take to prove he was totally dead. And then a letter arrived from a woman in Madrid whose brother had lost his nose and wanted it returned for sentimental reasons. The letter was written in broken English and carried an element of pathos and accusation:

You got Fernando's nose by mistake. Is a good nose he lose in fight. The policia keep it for evadence but they send to you and Fernando wants back. You got no right to Fernando's nose.

Crystal realized her mistake. She felt guilty for swindling the insurance company, guilty for tying up the courts, guilty for keeping Fernando's nose. But what could she do?

Then the insurance company found out her husband had been involved in international prostitution at the time of his disappearance and demanded its $875.16 back. They said Zolton —that was her husband's name—was a pornographic movie star and that he had fled the country to avoid prosecution for sodomy and other involuntary acts. Incensed at these new accusations, she launched her own investigation, and that was how she discovered Zolton on the silver screen. She had never seen him commit any involuntary acts, but there could be no doubt he performed in legal adult films. She had seen all his roles, she thought, and that was what she was doing in the Roxy the night she met Winslow. The reason she sat in the first row was so she could study Zolton's foot. The severed foot in Spain had a hammertoe, she said.

Winslow listened to all this sympathetically. "Forget your husband's foot," he advised.

"I can't," she said plaintively. "Not until I know for sure."

"Do you still have the insurance money?"

"Yes."

"Then you should go to an adult bookstore and look for your husband's films. I've got a sixteen-millimeter projector with stop action. We can study them frame by frame for a hammertoe."

He went with her, and they came back loaded down with reels. Not only did they find the suspect hammertoe but all the involuntary acts as well. It was a great ending, and a great beginning too. Crystal felt relieved to know the truth. She got a job in a fur salon, paid back the insurance company, and she and Winslow had sex regularly at her apartment. When another letter came from Madrid—"What good is Fernando's nose to you? Why you no send back?"—she badgered the insurance company for its return and shipped it to the owner. Minus a nose, she breathed a lot easier.

"Oh, Winslow," Crystal cried, "do I have some flawed gene that invites bureaucracies to pick on me? Let's forget the past. Let's forget everything but us and the present."

She hadn't mentioned the future, he noticed.

{ 7 }

It was raining when Alice and her four sons finally got to Chewbagin. The wind whipped gray veils across the town as they bumped along under yellow slickers with their luggage to the biggest house on the street. There was no need to ring the bell because the dogs announced their arrival. Then the door opened and a clump of strangers paraded onto the veranda, surrounding and dismantling them like a ravaged float after Homecoming.

The house smelled of mint, mold, and tobacco. Stu immediately got sick and asked for the bathroom, where he not only relieved himself but fondled the nylons strung over the tub. Stanley wandered off like a scenting hound to lick mothballs and sample solvents in the cellar. Nicki went back out in the rain to size up his new territory. But Harry was carried through lengthy introductions at his mother's behest. Stenner eyes searched him. They ransacked his face like an old suit of clothes, pulling out his most innocent and false expressions. He was the tribal emblem, the totem; whatever judgments were made should be based on this son, his mother seemed to be saying, and whatever the sins of the other Moons, let Harry's account square the record.

He was faintly shocked that the house and his relatives looked so squalid. The floors dipped, the ceilings swelled, and gummy cracks linked the two over flaking plaster walls. The cracks seemed to extend to the human faces—weathered, settled faces, heavy with some strange force.

What he was seeing, but did not understand, was that parallel lines met in Chewbagin. The town, conceived on a precipice, owed its accommodation to a variety of warps. All laws obeyed gravity. Time and tempo, matter and mood, these paid duty to the mountain. Momentum in Chewbagin was angular.

There were seven adults not counting Edgar, the hired help. This included his grandparents, two sets of uncles and aunts, and one great-uncle. There were also five cousins. The cousins were unremarkable except for Donald, who had a speech impediment and thus commanded ungodly sympathetic silences whenever he labored through a statement.

"Tha-that's Rodney," twisted free of his lips as he pointed to one of the cocker spaniels, which had already begun to follow Harry. "Do-do-don't l-let him wr-wrap his p-paws around your l-leg like th-that 'ca-'cause he's trying to *mate!*" He squeezed this last word out with glee while everyone grinned ponderously. This was followed by his own hideous laugh as the disgraced Rodney was shooed.

"Anyone feel like eatin'?" Grandma Stenner bawled.

The table stretched from kitchen to parlor like a highway dotted with organic flotsam. There were seventeen place settings for Alice and her family, her two brothers' families, Grandma Elvira, Grampa Caldwell, and his brother Jules. Jules wore a vestment and a Roman collar, but just as he led them in bowing their heads, Donald fired up for Harry's benefit: "Y-you do-don't have to w-worry about Quee-Queenie, sh-she don't m-m-mate no more." All eyes remained down. "A-and even if sh-she did, sh-she don't d-do it that w-way."

"Donald, dear," said his mother with saccharine charm, "we're going to thank God now."

Jules cleared everything from his throat, closed his large, luminous eyes, and began the saving grace.

"Glorious Father, Creator of all things, Architect of the universe, Author of our being, divine Comforter, Alpha and Omega, hear our prayer. We are humbly grateful to you for our daily bread, and doubly grateful this day when you have brought us all together here in this room—all except Winslow—to celebrate our love and share your bounty. And what a bounty it is! Apples from your tree of wisdom—permissible now since the Fall—bread from your wheat fields, wine from your vineyards"—Jules's large, luminous eyes flashed open as if awakening to glory—"mashed potatoes and squash and cranberry sauce! Oh, dear Lord, we thank you for your pickles!" His eyes swept the table like flashlights seeking items of indebtedness. His hands made lifting motions. He beatified the china, the silverware, the napkins. Everyone was staring wide-eyed at his ecstasy when he suddenly noticed the chicken, the giblets, and the meat loaf. "And now as we gaze at the ruins of these animals both large and small," he rumbled, "we are filled with remorse. 'Is any sick among you? let him call for the elders of the church; and let them pray over him, anointing him with oil in the name of the Lord.'" Here he began basting the chicken with the giblet gravy. "'And the prayer of faith shall save the sick, and the Lord shall raise him up; and if he have committed sins, they shall be forgiven him.'" Having finished giving extreme unction to the hamburger, he gestured catholically, sat back down, and ate several portions.

With a long look Elvira telegraphed that this was a standard deviation, but Alice was devastated. The siege of the train, the pathetic passions on the bathroom wall, little Donald's infirmity, and Jules's senile raptures were too much for one day. Had Vermont been declared insane by an Act of Congress? She remembered Winslow standing in his lone slipper blowing Cream of Wheat through his new razor and thought he looked rather suave in retrospect.

Nothing Jules said made any sense, but there was something in the self-assured, sadly philosophical way he said it that convinced Harry he was listening to great truths. Jules's thin dry lips and waxy crags were like one of Vermont's mountains, and when you followed them all the way up, there were those wide, empty eyes. Harry learned to love eternity and infinity, looking in those eyes, and to find peace in the crash of waves, or in the perpetuity of the wind, or in silence.

"There is a gold mine in every town on earth," Jules told him one day. "It lies in plain view and is known by all. Yet no one extracts its wealth."

"Where?" asked Harry.

"Follow me."

He took him to the edge of town, where Harry's eyes went quite naturally up the green flank of the mountain to the sun-shot mist at the top.

"I don't see it," he said.

"Look lower."

Down the road there was a sign, advertising antiques and maple syrup, and a lone house that seemed to have slid away from the town.

Jules gestured expansively. "The churchyard." His hands dropped on the iron pickets in front of them. "We bury the dead with their jewelry, their fillings, their watches. I have known some to carry their wallets to the grave. How inappropriate! Their maker delivered them in flesh and bones and they return in silk and worsted, clutching their Diner's Cards and driver's licenses. Dead leaves wear the brightest colors. We should strip the dead of their possessions, their vanities, their materialistic sentimentalities. Let the poor harvest them. It is not too late. The gold mines of the earth lie waiting. What a simple solution for human misery."

He seemed to be addressing the rows of cream-colored tablets that rose like amphitheater seats on the hillside. Harry followed him inside while he chastised the dead for their conceits. Over the scrolled name *Hugh Stenner* he stopped and told a dirty joke.

"I've told him that before, but he never remembers," he said. "Most of them don't remember very well. That's because death consists of old memory. Old memory and old association. They get confused by that. I've given some of them last rites three or four times."

He went into the adjacent church and played the national anthem on the organ. He played it twice.

"They like music," he said. "Music is the aphrodisiac of the heart, the ordering of the mind, the hemming and unraveling of the soul."

Harry didn't know whether they heard his music or not, but when he looked in Jules's eyes he felt as he had on Coach Schroeder's cross-country team, circling the pond in the park and gazing into its waving depths at something beckoning and indiscernible.

Jules's senile reveries always ended painfully. He would suddenly remember the earth as it was and smack his palm against his balding brow. The sound of flesh against flesh was like a wet towel on a tile floor, and Harry hated it. It had once stood for football, locker rooms, and Coach Coomes. Now it was the sound of Jules falling to earth.

Despite the Roman collar and his preoccupation with last rites, Jules attended a Presbyterian church. One Sunday that summer he stepped into the pulpit ahead of the minister, who stood shocked and uncertain in the apse. The congregation held its breath. "There are three things a man must deal with in this life: sex, the army, and money," he said. But then his nostrils began to palpitate like a rabbit's. A hermetic silence sealed him off, and he rolled his enormous eyes slowly over the worshipers. Harry watched him slap his brow, heard the sound. It was like wooden pallets dropping this time. The congregation started forward in sympathy, but Jules kept doing it, wooden pallets, over and over.

They led him gently away. He was grinning sheepishly then, hunched and humiliated, and Harry felt the inexorable pull of Chewbagin's gravity reassert itself.

It was Stanley who finally cured Donald of his speech impediment. He did it by getting him to relax, which he did by getting him stoned.

"Rodney tried to screw Queenie," Donald enunciated clearly to the assembled adults one afternoon.

They had just sat down to lunch, and Donald's father, Lester, inhaled an olive and began to strangle. Everyone was drawn to this new emergency, but Donald just giggled. Grampa Caldwell and Edgar took turns clubbing Lester to the floor while his wife, Veronica, poured water in the vicinity of his mouth. When the olive finally passed, Lester gestured feebly toward his son but was unable to express his outrage. Veronica moved quickly to save the situation.

"Yes, Lester, yes," she said with revelation, "his stuttering is gone."

Donald giggled. "Good ol' Stanley," he said.

Alice froze.

"Stanley?" Veronica repeated.

"You should've seen Rodney tryin' to screw Queenie. He just couldn't find her—"

"Donald!" Lester barked.

Donald giggled and circled the table, appropriating an olive, a pickle, a handful of nuts.

Alice quietly withdrew.

She found Stanley in the garage immersed in his new enterprise. Cigarette papers fluttered like moths in the draw of the door as she opened it and stood glaring through a sickly sweet blast of smoke. Three children she neither looked at nor cared to see scurried past with the last of the vapors.

"Hi, Mom."

Stanley waved languidly from behind a wooden keg heaped with something shredded and pubic-looking. This she took to be the offending substance.

"Where did you get this?" she demanded, snatching up a handful and shaking it in his face.

"It's a sin to waste food," he said, regarding the gentle rain of leaves to the floor.

"Food! You call this food?"

"Everything is food," he murmured.

This was pretty much true as far as Stanley was concerned. Few people put into their mouths the things he had and lived to tell about it. If you are what you eat, Stanley was universal.

For the second time in her life, Alice drew on some secret fund of biochemical insights she didn't know she had. The first time had been when she warned Winslow about vasectomies cluttering up his organs with "seeds," and now the nature of evolution came clear to her in a flash. "God gave you a body for digesting chemicals, my son," she said, "and it took millions of years to refine it to the particular ones called food. A baby learns this evolution in a few short years, depending on its sense of taste and a loving mother. If neither the baby nor the mother poisons it, that child will become a person of good judgment— of good taste—and avoid chemicals that are incompatible with what evolution equipped it to digest. Evidently I have failed you, because you don't know any better than to shove weeds in your mouth and light them on fire, or inhale adhesives, or swallow dangerous tonics. It's a wonder to me that with all the solvents in your body, nothing has cleansed your mind."

"Oh, wow," said Stanley.

"What do you mean, 'Oh, wow'? You sound just like that little tart who was passing out flowers on the train."

Stanley surveyed the weeds on the floor. "You ought to try some of this yourself. I mean, like, look what it did for Donald. He was all uptight too, and now he's beautiful."

"That's the worst of it: my son the doctor. Stanley, where did you get this?"

"From the earth . . . the natural earth."

"You grew this?"

"Nicki grew it."

Nicki had a nice little cash crop growing on the side of the mountain. He had taken it over from Constable Bullard's son after a fistfight. Alice tried to burn it, and that was how she set fire to the mountain.

The wind was gusting to twenty miles an hour when she started sprinkling gasoline, but she wouldn't have cared if a tornado were raging. As soon as the marijuana began to burn, the wind shifted and she saw that she was on her way to joining Nero of Rome and Mrs. O'Leary of Chicago. She took off her sweater and began to beat the flames, but it caught on fire. Then she took off her blouse and flailed with that until it ignited. There was nothing left but her skirt. Her skirt and Chewbagin.

Back on the veranda of the Stenner homestead, Nicki and Stanley watched the black smoke curling over the trees and had no idea that it contained the combustion by-products of their mother's sweater and blouse. Constable Bullard was the first to arrive on the scene, and he was astonished to find Alice Moon hopping up and down three scorched acres of mountain in her bra and panties. With some difficulty he captured her in a blanket and delivered her to Doc Kraft for treatment of second-degree burns.

She would have snaked out of town on her belly if she could have collected her sons en route, and there was no consolation in the fact that the town knew nothing of Nicki's cash crop and regarded her as heroic. They eventually presented her with a citation, which had to be mailed, because by that time she had left Chewbagin forever.

She said only one word on the day after the fire, but she said it four times. "Pack," she said.

When Donald learned that Stanley was leaving, it made him so angry that his speech impediment returned, and by morning when the Moons departed he could only utter "G-gghgggh . . . g-gg," so that Alice wasn't sure whether it was "Go," "Good," or "Good-bye."

The trip home by train was uneventful this time, but she was surprised and disappointed to find Winslow thriving and apparently happier than he had been in years. The laundry was done, the pantry well stocked, and the house had the stately ease of a freshly oiled hinge about it.

It was the final imperfect result of her imperfect decision to go to Vermont. She had been surrounded by caricatures and had gone to Vermont seeking substance for them. Now to come home and find Winslow whole again seemed to make her the caricature. She had the feeling then that she had been watched all summer—watched and tested and satirized—and that somewhere some lofty power was laughing and saying, in a voice that might have been Donald's, "A-bedee, a-bedee—that's all, folks!"

⧘ **8** ⧘

Harry was still a virgin when he finally discovered swimming in high school, but the juices were fairly gushing by then and he fell in the pool out of a dawning awareness that all ecstasy is related to liquids. It did not surprise him to learn that the human body is 84 percent water or that his very earliest ancestor was a single cell in a primeval pond. His Gloucestershire ancestor, Jonathan Moon, had drowned in the depths of Boston Harbor, and out of his seed Harry had arisen like an echo of creation.

This instinct, then, is what drew him to the subterranean depths of the school where they kept the pool and everything was tiled. The day of tryouts he stood naked on the deck with sixty other boys, most of whom had better builds and a respectable amount of pubic hair. Steam came off the surface of the water each time some exhibitionist opened the balcony doors, the chlorine ate his nostrils, and the debilitating shrills of adolescents bounced off the walls like spear thrusts. Coach Hockney blew a whistle and commanded them to the diving end of the pool. The coach had been one of the Allies who liberated Buchenwald in 1945, and the sinewy, nude boys cowering to hide their nakedness at the edge of his pool always reminded him of forlorn Jews at the brink of a pit, prompting something unconsciously authoritarian and German in his voice.

"You will each dive in and swim one length!" he shouted. "You will swim your best stroke! You will swim one at a time on command! Line up!"

The first dozen or so were returning lettermen, but the rest were country-club issue, and none of these knew how to dive. They soared and flopped and hit the water as if capsized from a canoe or bailing out of an airplane, and each time one of them stung a flank an appreciative "aaaahh" went up from the rest. Now aquatic, they thrashed and flailed like newborn ducks. A few simply sank and were gaffed by the shepherd's crook in Hockney's hands.

Despite his instincts, Harry was inexperienced, and the procession of gasping souls climbing and sliding down whitecaps intimidated him. Where was the serenity, the peace, the harmony he associated with water? To top it off, the boy in front of him was his friend Nino Torkie, and Nino swam fly for an AAU team. Nothing looked more dynamic than those swooping double-arm pulls launched off undulating kicks. Hurling himself into the maelstrom left by Nino's dolphin, Harry broke loose with a weak but functional crawl. He took six strokes without a breath before colliding head-on with Nino, who had taken the turn. The coach dropped his shepherd's crook and jumped in. The varsity jumped in. The spew and foam of thirty bodies effectively hid the victims. Rescue was certain, but it would take a while.

Nino, having been hit solidly in the head, was unscathed, but Harry was out cold. He lay on the bottom of the pool closer to Jonathan and his essential element than he had ever been before. It was his baptism. Jonathan's immersion had been in the sheep-dip troughs of Gloucestershire; Harry's took place on the bottom of a high school pool.

His mother called Ufunker when she learned of the accident, and the doctor drove his yellow Porsche straight to Emergency, where he ran off enough X rays to fill the high school yearbook with Harry's brains. Nino's mother, a first-generation Italian of good heart and many anxieties, begged to take Nino to the hospital with Alice. When they got to Emergency, Ufunker resisted her.

"Madam, I do not tolerate other physicians treating my patients when I am available, and I certainly practice what I preach. May I ask your physician's name?"

"Giuseppe," she murmured disconsolately.

"That is his last name?"

"Giuseppe Bertelli."

"You know him well enough to call him by his first name, I'm sure he would be disappointed to learn that you went to someone else."

"I don' think so," Mrs. Torkie said slowly in a thick accent.

"Perhaps you should call him."

"I don' know his number."

Ufunker sighed. Speech was a direct measure of intelligence, he felt, and all knowledge was first expressed in English, then gradually paraphrased into lesser languages beginning with Latin. This woman was obviously helpless because she was a foreigner.

"Where is your physician's office?" he asked.

"Mola," she answered lugubriously.

"Mola Street?"

"Mola, Italia."

"Italy?" he translated against the grain of knowledge. "He lives in Italy?"

"Sure," she said.

Nino grinned healthily and Ufunker cleared his throat. "What's wrong with him?"

Mrs. Torkie looked confused. "That's what I'm askin' you," she said with a forceful thrust of three fingers.

"Harry had a headache," piped Alice, trying to be helpful.

"I'll have to take X rays."

"Nino ain't got no headache," said Mrs. Torkie. "Nino ain't got nothin'."

This was true. X rays of Nino's skull would be like snapshots of Mammoth Cave at midnight with no flash.

"You'll have to sign a release," Ufunker said.

"I don' write so good."

"Is the boy's father here?"

"Nino ain't got no father. Nino ain't got nothin'."

Ufunker went over to the boy and spread his eyelids one at a time with his thumb. Then he looked at *Harry's* X rays. Then he rapped a knuckle on Nino's skull.

Nino grinned.

"Madam," said Ufunker, "your boy will be fine. He ain't got nothin'."

Coach Hockney made Harry a distance freestyler and Nino a sprinter. In Harry's case he recognized regularity, pluck, and a sheer love for the water that could sustain him through monotonous workouts. Nino, by contrast, had reflexes, strength, and coordination but lacked concentration. Anyone who lost count on a one-length swim had a limited future beyond a hundred yards, Hockney realized. On the other hand, Nino could develop fixations that surpassed mere concentration. At the first home meet a small boy in the bleachers yelled "Bang!" as the swimmers came down for the start of the fifty free, and Nino took off, sprinting over the recall rope and through a half dozen teammates who leaped in to stop him. After the meet Hockney took Nino into the coach's office and closed the door. Subsequently four shots rang out. Parents and swimmers alike were aghast. Then coach's voice was heard: "Bang! bang! bang! bang! Can you tell the difference now, you nincompoop?"

No one asked questions.

The thing Harry liked most about training was the opportunity to think. A pool was a womb that deadened sounds, dimmed sights, and insulated the sense of touch. In such a medium, thought was inevitable. At first you thought about pace and your catch, your breathing pattern, kicking in and out of the turns, the subtleties of fluid mechanics, of eddy resistance and laminar flow, of pressing through; then you thought about goals; and finally you reached free association, which had a dreamy quality that, like the water, seemed to defy physics. Formless thought and movement. Harry got off on both.

The thing he thought about most was Heather Latko. She had metamorphosed into a still more elegant queen than before. There was her symmetry, the pale-to-starkness skin, her broad thin shoulders, her expressive wrists and fingers, her puffy immutable lips, her dusky cheeks, her dark bobbed hair as rich and jagged as quills, a precise nose, carved nostrils, damp and dark brows and lashes, translucent shell-like teeth, and something divinely labial about her earlobes that he saw but hadn't yet identified. With all this superfacial (and superficial) perfection, pitched battles were fought over her in locker rooms. She was worth two touchdowns, a dozen rebounds, or a new record in the pole vault, depending on whose bleachers her profoundly round little bottom graced. That she was actually intelligent seemed ostentatious and unnecessary to the vulgar masses who paraded after her into the library, chomping gum and seeking only carnal knowledge.

Harry carried sandpaper in his pocket and regularly surveyed each of the school's sixty-two toilets for defamation of her character. He called her parents in the middle of the night, purporting to be one or another of her beaus. And when he got hold of her personal phone number, he did his futile best to tie up her line so that no one else got through. He never actually talked—she would have hung up in nanoseconds—but she evidently got a lot of heavy breathers, tongue-tied idiots, and teasers because she would stay on for precious minutes if he played a Beatles record, rang bells, or tooted a kazoo. The list of names she went through trying to guess his identity was appallingly long. "Is this Billy, Brad, Eddie"—*toot, toot*—"Boyd, Harvey, Felix—*" toot, toot.* When she guessed Rumpelstiltskin and his name still hadn't come up, it was something of a blow. He developed cold sores from talking through the kazoo and contrived to stay home until the disfigurement healed. During this time he made up an anonymous note file of the names she had guessed and wrote stinging slanders to their mothers.

Dear _____,
Since I am the mother of six boys myself I know just how your heart must ache to hear bad things about _____. But "Spare the rod and spoil the child" they say so I'm going to tell you just what your _____ did so you can save him before it's too late. You know the bathroom in the boys' locker room, well, _____ wrote obscene things about Heather Latko on the wall. He also made some dirty pictures which it would be too embarrassing for me to repeat here, so take my word for it they were dirty. If I were you I would keep _____ away from Heather since I also have four daughters and know just what kind of trouble they can get in. I'm sure you know what I mean.
                                        Sincerely,
                                        A minister's wife

Then one day Carrie Reske showed up in the pool balcony (the boys wore suits when the season started). She had gone back into her past looking for security, and there he was. Sexless Harry Moon: old buddy. The reason for this was because her precocious breasts had continued to grow, past voluptuousness, past all useful proportions. To her horror, they had turned toward the center of the earth. She felt bovine and gravity-conscious. It brought about a reformation in her moral character, and she took to wearing frilly blouses and bulky sweaters, clutching her books maternally, and never stretching. This only maddened the boys, who thought there couldn't be enough of a good thing, but it drove Carrie Reske into chastity. Hence, Harry Moon.

Harry's self-esteem chugged on unawares. The first hint he had of where their relationship was going was at Brandywine Mall at Christmas. In each other's company they enjoyed a strange inversion: he seemed to acquire the sexual status she shed. "Sister Carrie," he called her. So they went to Brandywine, where he eventually got in line to buy two hot pretzels and she sat on the edge of a fountain. When he looked back he saw that a wandering Santa Claus had stopped to talk to her. He wished he could speed up the pretzel line, but the man in front of him was wearing galoshes, coveralls, a blue mackintosh, a red transparent slicker, and yellow mittens and couldn't find his wallet. He kept adding to his order.

"Better make that two more softies, one with mustard, one without. Also one plain, one garlic, and one onion."

Harry looked back. Santa was still there. Carrie was laughing now.

"Gimme two more softies with raisins," said the man in the galoshes, as if to delay payment.

Once, Harry and his mother had waited forty-five minutes to see Santa, and just before their turn Santa threw up and had to be led away. It was because of all the sick children who sat on Santa's lap, his mother had told him. Santa was germy.

"I can't find my wallet," said the man in front.

The clerk shrugged.

"Look, my wife's around somewhere, her name is Faye, and

if you'd just call her on your public address system, she could pay for all this."

"We ain't got no P.A.," said the clerk.

Harry looked back. This Santa looked healthy. The way he was ho-hoing around, he must be feeling pretty good.

"What d'you mean you ain't got no P.A.? All malls got P.A.s!" asserted the man in galoshes.

Santa was waiting for him, Harry knew. Alone and healthy, waiting for *him*.

"The P.A. is at the information desk," said the clerk. "It's up past Sears."

"Sears! That's way the hell down by the other end. This is ridiculous. Faye! Faye!" The man began to shout.

Jolly old St. Nick was stroking Carrie's hair now. "Ho-ho-ho!"

"Your order," the clerk droned.

Harry spun around. "Two," he said.

"Two what?"

"Pretzels."

"Soft, crisp, plain, salted, cheese, garlic, onion, egg, or raisin?"

"Hey, son, I don't suppose—" began the man in galoshes.

"All I got is two dollars," Harry rasped. "Soft," he said to the clerk, glancing back. Santa was squeezing Carrie's shoulders. She had taken off her coat before sitting down, and her breasts were shadowed provocatively by the mall lighting.

"Mustard?" asked the clerk.

"Faye!" bellowed the galoshes.

"Yeah," grated Harry.

The clerk lathered two pretzels with yellow soup, and Harry bolted off minus a dollar. Santa was still squeezing and stroking. Carrie's smile looked numb and uncertain. "I'll bet you've got lots of boyfriends," the old reprobate was saying.

Harry grinned hideously. "Excuse me, Santa, but what the hell are you doing?"

"Ho-ho-ho, so you do have a boyfriend!" He was still fondling. "Well, now, don't be jealous of Father Christmas—"

It was very plain to Harry what the old fool was doing. First he ho-ho-hoed her, then he asked about her love life, then he started pawing her. "Hands off, fatso!" he shouted.

Santa leered but continued to pat Carrie, as if to settle a large dog by proxy.

Harry had a pretzel in each hand, and he lashed out without thinking. The yellow stain transferred to Santa's white beard as he fell backward into the fountain. The rest was a dim nightmare from which they ran through the mall, past pretzels and horrified toddlers, up and down ramps and stairs and circuitous mazes, the substance of symbols, of children lost and damned forever and lonely figures drifting through space wailing "Faye! Faye!" Indelible was the image of Santa sitting in the fountain, his yellow beard clinging to his face. And was that *weed* floating up from his pockets? Surely the brother of Stanley knew weed when he saw it.

As for Carrie, she felt like a pair of tits again, but somehow it seemed all right. "Oh, Harry," she said, "you saved me from Santa's claws."

If this was not true heroism, there were moments in Harry's adolescence which came nearer and which presaged that side of his character his mother knew was struggling to emerge. It was the Stenner heritage at last, she thought. The warps of Winslow's legacy might yet dovetail to the nobility of her own.

There was, for example, the business of the lion. This happened in Harry's second year of high school. He was doing a post-season run on some back roads when he came upon a film crew making a commercial by a pond. The commercial was for a Plymouth Barracuda, and the idea was that when an announcer with a fishing pole opened the hatch and said, "You never know what you might catch with a Barracuda," a trained lion sprang out of the bushes and into the trunk. The announcer thereupon slammed the hatch without taking his eye from the camera. On the first three takes the announcer flinched each time the lion sprang, and on the fourth the big cat merely ambled out and placed his paws on the rear bumper. But the fifth was a wrap—as far as it went. "You never know what you might catch with a Barracuda," said the announcer, and the lion soared gracefully into the trunk. *Slam!* went the hatch. And that was when the Barracuda began to dance, because the lion's tail was caught under the lid.

"Cut!" yelled the director.

"Oh, lordy," said the announcer.

The Barracuda roared like a Sherman tank, while upholstery foam rained off the windows as thick as snow in a bottle.

"Somebody do something!" the director ranted, but all

around him was the look of Lilliputians who had gone fishing with a Barracuda and now were afraid of the bounding mane.

"Give me the trunk key," said the trainer who had brought the cat. He took the key from the announcer while everyone scrambled away. Then he locked the trunk. "I'm not crazy," he said. "Get the police out here."

Harry was shocked. Here was a dumb animal victimized, and there were the agents of his misfortune procrastinating the obvious solution. Darting forward, he snatched the key from the trainer and ran to the car. By the time he got the hatch up, the entire shooting crew had made thirty yards through the bush. And by the time the first of them were cautiously returning, he and the lion were sitting docilely together in the trunk of the wrecked Barracuda.

"Androcles," said the director.

They got another car and Harry did the commercial because the lion wouldn't work with anyone else.

Alice was immensely proud. There were elements of true greatness in her youngest son. She could not imagine the final distillation being anything but vintage Stenner, pure and unadulterated.

} 9 }

Winslow felt the gears shift, felt his life slip into reverse. Since this was the direction he had always wanted to go in, he found moral disintegration fulfilling. Infidelity, it seemed, was a wonderful way to fail.

His damnation had the tragic quality of a curse about it. He loved to slink around to the back door of Crystal's apartment, to meet her in dismal places sparsely populated with sodden and coughing humanity. Such wretchedness sustained him far more than their sexual relationship. It made him feel he was at last at the bottom of the ladder, with nowhere to go but up. He even looked the part. Over the months he lost weight, spoke in a voice increasingly hoarse with fatalism, and suffered night sweats. Alice thought he was sick, and finally, at her insistence, he went to see Dr. Ufunker.

The waiting room was occupied by two men and a woman on crutches. One of the men must have been incredibly old, judging by his corrugated skin. The other was quite bald and had a gold tooth like Daddy Warbucks. Winslow took a seat in the only remaining corner, and they all stared at each other. There were no magazines, no lamps, no carpet, and no bulb in the ceiling fixture. Winslow wondered if Ufunker specialized in patients with light-sensitive eyes. The receptionist sat with her back to them in a glass cage that looked like it might be bullet-proof.

"Damn!" erupted the bald-headed man who looked like Daddy Warbucks.

"I'm just here for a checkup," said the ancient one with the corrugated skin. "But I'm in great shape. Used to box. Fought out of New Amsterdam, you know."

"Where's New Amsterdam?" Winslow asked politely.

"New Amsterdam, New Amsterdam, right there on the coast with the lady in the harbor, you know."

"You mean New York," Winslow corrected.

"Yeah, right there below Plymouth Rock."

Daddy Warbucks's gold tooth glistened in the gloom. "They changed the name to New York because Ethel Merman couldn't sing 'New Amsterdam, New Amsterdam, it's a wonderful town,'" he said. "Son of a bitch!"

"What're you here for?" the ancient one asked him.

"Head lice."

The lady looked at his bald head and planted her crutches as if to bolt for the door.

"Wanta see me do a push-up?" The old man dropped to the floor and crept into the center of the room. There he braced his wrists and for a while they heard him expelling his breath in little grunts, but nothing else happened, and for all his stillness he might have expired. The lady on crutches got up then and painfully made her way out, planting one of her tips alarmingly high between the old man's legs as she passed over his prostrate form.

Daddy Warbucks and Winslow now gazed at each other in the twilight of the waiting room, and something as relaxed as truth traveled between them. "I'm not really here for head lice," admitted the one.

"I didn't think so," Winslow said and coughed.

"Shit! Damn! Son of a bitch!"

"You said that already."

"I know. I've got Gilles de la Tourette's disease. That's where you can't stop swearing. Asshole!"

Winslow nodded sadly.

"Dr. Ufunker X-rayed my brain, but he couldn't find anything. So he told me to move to France. That way if I swore in English I wouldn't offend anyone. But it didn't work."

"Why not?"

Daddy Warbucks swore in French.

"Oh," said Winslow.

"Next I moved to Spain. But that didn't work either." He swore in Spanish. *Mierda de toro,* he said, and Winslow remembered that was what Harry had said after he had galloped him into the dining room arch. "Then I moved to Rome," Daddy Warbucks continued. "That lasted three months. One day I went to St. Peter's Square and started swearing during a blessing by the Pope. I heard later that he forgave me, but the crowd wanted me castrated. Then it was Germany, Poland, Finland, Japan. Always with the same result."

"You learned to swear in Finnish and Japanese?"

"I can speak sixteen languages and forty-three dialects now. I've been offered a job translating at the United Nations, but how long can I last if—shit, damn, son of a bitch!"

"I see what you mean."

"So I've come back to Dr. Ufunker."

Winslow looked down at the ancient pugilist stretched out flat on his face. "Do you want some help?" he asked.

"I'm in great shape," came back from the floor like a record playing too slowly. "Used to box. Fought out of New Amsterdam, you know."

"Bastard!" said Daddy Warbucks.

When Winslow's turn came he underwent the obligatory carnage of X rays and took a seat in Ufunker's inner sanctum to await judgment. Most doctors had diplomas and certificates on their walls, but Ufunker's were covered with colored glossies of all the cars he had owned. Two X rays were also framed but unlabeled, and Winslow imagined they might be baby pictures of Ufunker's children.

"Well, now, Mr. Moon, just a few more questions and then I can give you a complete state of your health," the doctor said jovially as he entered with a sheaf of exposures. "How is your appetite? your bowels? your sleep? Do you have any pain when you urinate? Are you ever constipated? Are you dizzy when you stand up?"

Winslow said "no" reflexively.

"Mm-hmm, mm-hmm, mm-hmm," mused Ufunker, seemingly preoccupied with a glass bottle on his desk, containing a nondescript lump of flesh.

Winslow wondered if it could somehow be Fernando's nose, arrived in some unfathomable way to indict him for having engaged in an affair with Crystal. Ufunker was about to tell him he was suffering from infidelity. The cure would be confession and abstinence, and of course he would have to wear Fernando's nose around his neck.

"Any headaches, trouble breathing, stomach pains? Frequent heartburn? Are you always thirsty? Do you catch cold easily? Do you itch? Is there blood in your sputum?"

"No, no, no," said Winslow and, when Ufunker looked directly at him, added "no."

"Well, Mr. Moon," the doctor said then, "everything seems to be good except your chest. I'm afraid you have some lung cancer."

Some.

Like a rash. Like acne.

It was more than some. More than a fistful. It was a lungful. Winslow's clock was ticking down.

The next thing he remembered he was sitting in an adult movie theater, the same one where he had met Crystal. He was in the first row and couldn't see anything. It was as though he had found his way back to a fork in the road where he had gotten lost. For the first time in his life, the thought of sympathy was abhorrent to him. After years of rehearsing, he played tragedy badly.

There was no way he could go back—the slow erosion of his marriage was irreversible—yet he felt he must do something for his family. But what? He was not even sure he understood the process that had taken place, only that two people had disappointed each other in too many ways. Thank God there was still time to take Harry to Disneyland.

He walked home from Ufunker's, and the world seemed to spite him. Women strode briskly past, freed to such legginess by microskirts and miniskirts. Edwardian men in Peter Max ties whose designs seemed distorted by the forces of speed and gravity chased them. The population of the city was engaged in a frenetic chase for sex and success and survival while Winslow plodded along dying, unable to overcome inertia, unable to overcome cancer. The very fact that it was lung cancer made it clear to him that this was no idle stroke of misfortune. How could he have lung cancer? He had always believed in God, he realized now, and this was divine retribution. Crystal, with her cigarettes, was the angel of death. Most lovers gave their consorts VD, but his had given him lung cancer. It must have been a special kind, quick-acting, maybe feeding on the chemistry of guilt. He was on an accelerated dying program, faster even than the deteriorations of all those smokers he had avoided in the past.

As he crossed a boulevard he saw a church. It was a church he had seen many times before, but now it had a special meaning, and he went in to make peace with the forces of retribution. He had always believed in God, he reaffirmed, but he had never believed in churches. They were like museums of human fallacy. On the one hand there was the dogma, beautiful and compelling, and on the other there were the living displays of contradictory frailty: here in the first pew we present the sanctimonious, the crisply fashioned Pharisees, singing loudest, humbly heaping the collection plate with fat envelopes and personalized checks; and in the middle the insecure, the gossips, and backbiters, deeming themselves worthy by comparison with those they malign; and finally, tucked into the back, we have the fearful, the guilt-ridden, afraid to live, afraid to die, accumulating penance by the very act of worship. Such cynicism left no place for Winslow to sit down, and that was why he hadn't been to church since Harry's baptism.

"May I help you?" came a voice from the pulpit. Winslow discerned a man crouching there. "I'm working on the speaker wires. Last Sunday's service sounded like it came from Hawaii over a crystal set. Know anything about sound systems?"

Winslow climbed the altar steps and knelt beside him. "I'm a bricklayer," he said. "The doctor says I have lung cancer..."

The kindly face turned full upon him. "...and you had to tell someone," he finished for him.

Winslow shrugged. "I suppose so."

"Is it terminal?"

"Yes."

"You've come here for reassurance then, isn't that it?" When he spoke, his lower jaw stayed more or less stationary and the top of his head went up and down. It made him seem very enthusiastic. Winslow wished he had such joy.

"I don't belong to a church," he said.

"Well, it's never too late, you know. Last week one of our members celebrated his one hundredth birthday, and he didn't join until he was seventy-three. He said he was hoping for an eleventh-hour salvation, and if he'd known he was going to miss it by twenty-seven years, he would have sinned a whole lot longer."

Winslow didn't see the purpose of this story. He already knew he wasn't going to reach a hundred. "I'd like to believe Jesus is the son of God," he said. "But I've got four sons, and all of them were accidents. I know how those things can happen."

"Oh, it's the virgin thing, then. You think Mary told a whopper."

Winslow had never heard it put just that way before, but he nodded his head.

"Hmm. Lucky it turned out to be a boy, eh?"

"A boy?"

"I mean, after Mary told that whopper about conceiving the son of God and everything, it would have been the end of her if it had turned out to be a girl. Or twins," he added enthusiastically. "Or if she miscarried. Or if anything was wrong with the baby. Very un-God-like. She took quite a chance, didn't she?"

Winslow felt strengthened. "I never thought of it that way," he said.

"Lucky it fit the scriptures too," said the self-assured voice. "I mean, someone had to claim the Messiah."

"Yes, yes," said Winslow.

"And Jesus himself must have thought he was the son of God. Otherwise he was committing the greatest possible blasphemy of all time. Unless he was an atheist. But then what was his angle? He certainly didn't get much of a reward here on earth."

The man's openness was contagious. Winslow felt a great avenue of hope opening up for him. "Thank you, pastor," he said hoarsely. "You've restored my faith. I want to join your church. When I die, I want the funeral service to be held here. And I want you to know that you've got a loose connection in your sound system. Tighten that wire there."

"Ah. A loose connection. Thank *you*. But...I don't think you should join this church. If you truly believe, then don't press your luck. Stay away, that's my advice."

"Stay away?"

"Let the moment of your conversion be the last word on the subject for you. You haven't got long to live; it should hold you to the end. I know your type, wavering, wavering, always wavering. You're like candle flames. One good blow to your faith and you go out. Stay away from church. Otherwise you'll be like that hundred-year-old man, a good convert who got bored waiting around to die. Believe me, your soul is in danger here."

Winslow's eyes brimmed over as he looked in the kindly face. Then he turned and left.

When he was gone, the man tightened the connection and mounted the pulpit. "Dearly beloved," he said into the microphone, "we are all ministers of the faith. Lawyers, salesmen, store clerks. Housewives, teachers, firemen. And even church gardeners like me."

Winslow told Alice he passed the physical.

"Passed?" she repeated. "You mean you got a 'C'? Of course you passed. But what's wrong with you? Did he take X rays? Did he say why you've lost so much weight?"

"He said I should eat more." Winslow grinned too suddenly.

She sensed his evasion then. Her eyes sparked once with fear and banked into a steadily burning sympathy. "What is it?"

He knew he had to meet her gaze or forget it. Once, he would have founded his love on that kind of sympathy; now it compounded the dying. "Your cooking," he said, and his eyes took on the exquisite green of a deep, unbroken wave.

So her cooking improved and grew prolific. It was the same fanaticism that had produced carrot creole for Harry's condemned vision. Multiple-course meals haunted Winslow. And though he lay awake nights detecting the insidious metabolic theft that fed his cancer cell by cell, he ate and ate and ate....

{10{

"Listen, listen," said Harry Moon. "You hear that?"

"Hear what?" asked Carrie Reske, standing in the exceptional silence of a Sunday morning waiting for the traffic light to change.

"The splashing. They're working out at Vespers and New Trier and Santa Clara."

"Santa Clara is three thousand miles away. It's four A.M. there."

"Schollander and Spitz are loosening up," he declared with a sense of urgency.

"Schollander and who?"

"Spitz, Spitz, Spitz!"

She spit three times and grinned.

"I've got to pick it up," he said. "I appreciate your company, but I have to run my own pace now."

"You're trying to tell me something."

"I can hear Spitz's heart," he said. "One-eighty. He's starting his repeats."

"Do me a favor, tune in New York and tell me what Bob Dylan's doing?" She stopped running. At seven A.M. Dylan was probably brushing his teeth *before* going to bed. "Hey, Moon!" she hollered. "Never speak to me again, okay?"

He was out of human earshot, but if he heard Spitz splashing in California, she was sure he heard her. She was tempted to sprint past him. He was a lousy runner. She could take him, except that her breasts were so large and pendulous that a full-out gallop meant two black eyes.

It was their junior year, and they were no more intimate than they had ever been. Less, in fact. They had been more intimate at the age of six when they pulled down their suits in her backyard pool. She should have known then that his sexuality was ineffably bound to water.

A quarter mile ahead, he cut through a band of trees onto the country club's third fairway. The course was empty, but on fairway number six a faucial voice rose and swelled like the languid outrage of a sea lion. "Hey-y!"

Harry looked down the lime-misted arbor leading to the green and recognized in the paid-for privileges of an old duffer a sense of Eden violated. He felt at once sympathy and rejection of the idea that the grass, the mist, and the trees could be owned. Who told such men as these that they could stake off a part of the earth and possess it? Did the grass acknowledge contracts? Did the dew have landing rights? Was the aroma of the evergreens part of the deal? Some day the men would die and be possessed much more certainly by the earth in turn.

"Hey! Hey!" shouted the duffer.

Harry grinned gregariously and waved. "The squirrels own this place, you crumby old piece of shit," he said under his breath.

On the seventeenth, a stressed tendon pulled him up lame; then a caddy cart whined over the brow of the hill and was on him.

"Hey!" shouted a uniformed guard. It must have been a shibboleth of authority. "Hey! Don't try to get away!"

Since he was sitting on the grass holding his foot, the circling caddy cart had a Keystone exuberance about it.

"You think you can trespass anytime you feel like it?" shouted the guard. "This is private property and the members are pretty damn angry—pretty *damn* angry. I'm gonna make an example out of you, fella."

Harry pointed to his lips and touched his ear. He scribed a circle with his pinkie, raised three fingers, cupped his hands.

"Don't think you can pull anything on me," said the guard.

Harry used both hands, tapping, twirling, scribing, cupping, clenching, and hooking.

"Oh," said the guard.

He was not much older than Harry, and he licked his lips in indecision. Harry retied his shoe, rose, started off.

"That's right, get the hell out of here—" The guard remembered he was talking to himself.

Then Carrie's voice floated over the course: "Haa-ry!" It lofted over twice, like a nine-iron, then whipped cleanly like a driver. Harry kept walking but heard the guard explaining.

Carrie's laugh was curt. "Deaf and dumb? Dumb, maybe. But he can hear Mark Spitz splashing all the way out in California."

"Hey!"

Harry limped faster, but the caddy cart whined after him and cut him off.

"Deaf and dumb, huh?" The guard looked passionate in the sunrise. "You little bastard."

Carrie arrived in a papulous rush. "Easy, Chet," she said to the guard. "He punched out Santa Claus once."

"You get out of here, Carrie. I'm gonna make an example of this twerp."

He looked at her, she looked at him, Harry looked at them both.

"Oh, Chet," she cooed, "you always made such a fuss about everything. Like that time on Thanksgiving when we were down in the basement. Remember that time down in the basement, Chet? I took a pair of pliers and pinched your—"

"Okay!" blurted Chet, "one more chance."

When they crossed the trestle that bordered the eighteenth, she explained to Harry. "That's my cousin Chet. He's the one whose father reached for a foul ball and fell out of the second deck. Very athletic family. Think you can keep up with me now, sport?"

Whatever it was she had pinched with the pliers, Harry bet she had pinched it hard. She seemed dedicated to unmasking the male gender in general and him in particular, this despite the dependency she painstakingly nurtured between them. Like Cinderella, she had taken a cast-off in her environment and was transforming him into high fashion for herself. She could be dogmatic, psychic, even tolerant at this. An example of all three was how she sat in the pool balcony night after night, divining his dreams of Heather Latko and offering him patient, forgiving looks. The dreams now had a possessive quality, and he surrendered himself to the pace and rhythm of the accompanying swims like an addict experiencing a rush. There was a real danger, he sometimes felt, that the dream and the swim might never end, that the ecstasy of introspection might carry him back to that beckoning figure in the pond of his cross-country running days. He would look to her in the balcony then like a little boy, frightened by the surrealism of a mirrored merry-go-round, glancing suddenly and anxiously toward his mother. It never occurred to him that she was bonding him until the evidence accumulated suddenly for him in the person of his father just before Christmas.

The snow was coming down in enormous sticky flakes and the wind kicked up chunks of it like piecrust on the day he saw Winslow with the other woman. He remembered the snow because it made the world seem clownish and misproportioned. She was blond, petite, well-dressed, and she wore the tragic expression that fading beauty wears. That was all he could see through the window of the restaurant as he trudged home from workout, except that she smoked a cigarette. He thought she was sympathetic looking. His father must have valued the sympathy a lot, because he hated cigarettes. They were a couple of consolation prizes making up for each other's losses. And that's how it was between him and Carrie. But at that moment, standing beneath the crushing weight of enormous snowflakes and listening to the roar of silence, Harry thought only of his mother.

Crystal's cigarette became the symbol for his father's betrayal, slowly consuming itself and leaving only ashes. It was this that may have triggered Harry's actions in a supermarket later that same year. He was standing in line at the checkout with a bottle of soda in his hand when the lady behind him lit up. She was blond and petite, as Crystal was, and she wore a wedding ring on the hand with the cigarette. Harry had never thought twice about the state law prohibiting smoking in food stores, but now he turned and said, "Would you mind putting that out?"

She gave him back a sneer glazed with horror. "I'm not hurting you, child."

"We don't have to argue about it. All you have to do is obey the law."

"What's it to you?"

Harry leaned past the next person in line and asked the cashier to tell the lady to put her cigarette out.

"We don't enforce that kind of thing," the cashier said. "It's just like a request, you know?"

"It's the state law," Harry said.

The cashier shrugged.

Harry took off his shoes and socks. By this time nothing was being rung through, and some twenty people were watching him.

"Hey, no bare feet!" the cashier said.

Harry began unbuttoning his shirt.

"Hey, you've got to wear a top in here!"

The manager arrived and asked him what he was doing.

"You don't enforce your posted no-smoking sign, so I guess your other signs don't mean anything either," Harry said.

"If you don't put your shoes and shirt back on, sonny, you're going to have to leave the store," said the manager.

"What about her?"

The lady with the cigarette took a long, slow drag.

"Stock boy!" the manager called and scooped up Harry's shoes.

Jeers began to float out of the crowd, and a stout woman kicked off her sandals. "Why don't you tell her to put her cigarette out?" someone demanded.

The manager tried to appear resolute, but he gave Harry another warning, and now an old man was pulling his shirttails loose.

"What makes her so special?" asked the stout lady.

Shoes were dropping all over the place as the manager turned to the petite blonde. "Would you please put that out?"

She was trembling, but she took another long draw on the cigarette and began to unbutton her blouse. Catcalls and whistles rained down. "If you don't stop, I'm going to call the police!" the manager threatened. She had her blouse open then, and as she pulled the lapels back with her hands the manager plucked the cigarette from her lips and threw it into the bean sprout bin.

A great cheer went up and the petite blonde slapped the manager and stormed out of the market. The cheering turned to respectful applause then as Harry began to dress. He got another hand after he paid for his soda and was leaving. But it was not something he wanted to savor. Whether for nonsmokers' rights or out of anger at his father's adulteress, it had been an act of self-righteousness—that old Vermont self-righteousness his mother would have proudly identified. If she had known.

But he never told her.

} 11 {

Winslow knew he had reached the bedrock of his remaining days when Alice bought tickets to a world heavyweight championship fight. It was like a going-away present—farewell to the dying man. She had such a distaste for violence that this radiant betrayal of her pacifism seemed no less than the capitulation of a virgin to a soldier bound for a far-off land of war and darkness. He had never told her he was dying; she had never acknowledged it. Yet she got three tickets to the fight and pointedly invited Dr. Ufunker, as if his presence in this final gesture was required and appropriate.

The doctor reciprocated by inviting them to his home for dinner before the fight, where he prefaced the salad by playing the national anthem on the violin. He was not an especially good player but he was very fervent about patriotism, and when Alice said she had always thought "America the Beautiful" ought to be the anthem, Ufunker found a book of hymns and sawed through that one as well. An NFL play-off game was being televised, and the set remained on while they ate chicken tetrazzini and stuffed mushrooms.

"Most fans identify with the players," Ufunker confided, "but I empathize with the refs. They are the ones charged with preserving the laws of the game and with making order out of chaos. That they do this expeditiously and without drawing attention to themselves is a marvel of execution, don't you think?"

"A marvel," Winslow agreed. Actually he had been engrossed in the commercial of an opera star singing about antacid. He seemed to remember the opera star from somewhere. Perhaps the chicken tetrazzini was going to come up on him and that was why the antacid commercial seemed familiar.

After dinner they squeezed into Ufunker's new T-Bird and drove all the way to Boston. The arena was jammed. Winslow's cough grew worse in the acrid pool of smoke, and he couldn't imagine how Alice could enjoy the evening. She seemed enormously delighted. He wondered if the smell of sweat and the coarse language hadn't touched some latent, lusty chord that he had never been able to arouse. They had seats on the aisle right by the champ's corner, but he was too sick to appreciate any of this. Alice's gift of the tickets, the chicken tetrazzini, the long drive to Boston, the smoke-filled arena, and now the excitement his wife and his doctor seemed to be sharing struck him collectively as an act of infidelity and a mocking of his death.

"The referee is from Buffalo," said Ufunker.

"What pretty robes!" exclaimed Alice when the fighters reached the ring.

"I've got an aunt in Buffalo," Ufunker informed them.

"What pretty bodies!" Alice went on.

"I've noticed that a lot of refs come from Buffalo," the doctor continued. "There's a certain innocuousness about someone from—"

Just then a scratchy recording of the national anthem began, and Ufunker leaped to his feet. So far as Winslow could tell, he was the only one singing. Then the bell rang, like a lone buoy announcing disaster.

The noise and the sweat and the nakedness of the principals united the delirium into something raw and starving. An appetite was about to be served, and to Winslow, already close to death, the impending brutality seemed unbearable. Were these his mourners? Was this the undisguised ferment of his own funeral?

The fight lasted less than three rounds. In the first, the

champ went down twice. In the second, he walked into a stiff left and plummeted to the canvas like a stone, but it was ruled a slip. The delirium turned nasty. A swarm of voices, like killer bees, assaulted the ring, and when the challenger was cut and lost on a TKO in the third, the roar became hysterical. Hardly had the bell finished tolling for the announcement, and a tiny man confirmed the outrage in a voice that seemed thrown from a departing train, than chairs started to fly and skirmishes erupted. The challenger ran from official to official shaking his head and pleading. The champ was hit on the shoulder by a hurled shoe as he clambered from the ring surrounded by police.

That was when Alice rose to her feet.

Winslow was astonished to see her step into the aisle and begin swinging her purse at would-be assailants who were after the champ. His wife, Alice Moon, was defending the heavyweight champion of the world! She swung right and left with abandonment until by the sheer intensity of her will, it seemed, the crowd gave way. He understood something about her courage then, her strength of purpose, her perseverance. She had stuck with him through the divergence of their lives, through infidelity, through cancer, through the ultimate abandonment of death. She had a sense of duty and resolve that was, perhaps, worth more than romantic love. You can't depend on love, Winslow thought, but you can depend on a sense of duty if you're lucky enough to be its object.

Driving home from Boston, listening to Ufunker describe the most damaging punches of the fight, Winslow remembered the opera star then. The one he had seen on television that night singing about antacid was the same one who had sung about migraines in Ufunker's office the day he galloped Harry into the arch.

When he got home he went to Harry's room. He and Alice had achieved peace, he thought, and it seemed imperative that he extend this healing process to his sons at once. He was going to make a firm commitment to take Harry at last to Disneyland, but he was asleep and Winslow feared waking him lest he find out the interruption somehow jeopardized Harry's athletic career. Since both Nicki and Stu had moved out of the house, that left Stanley for reunification.

He claimed Stanley as a tax deduction, but he wasn't sure

that Stanley fell under his roof. Actually Stanley fell under a lot of roofs—wherever he happened to get drunk or stoned for the night. In the process of dying, Winslow had rationalized that there wasn't enough time to rehabilitate him but that he and Stanley understood each other. Now, standing outside his son's room, he felt as though he were facing the door of a foreign consulate. Beyond was a land of inexplicable indulgence, a Sodom and Gomorrah of eating. The creatures of this place imbibed chemicals that in Winslow's society belonged to the industrialists, the carpenters, and the dry cleaners. He did not know their language and had no travel permit. His sole hope of communion lay in the faint, symbol-laden issue of light from under the door. He knocked.

He knocked three times.

Whether or not this was the correct signal, or his son had merely separated the reality of the knock from whatever state he was in, a forlorn acknowledgment like the call of a Canadian goose came to him.

"It's me," Winslow said. "Can I talk to you?"

A sound of indifference, again forlorn, arose in the room. It sounded as though Stanley had been to the dentist.

Winslow tried the door. "It's locked," he said. The door was always locked. No one had been in Stanley's inner sanctum for months. "I'd really like to talk to you," said Winslow.

Presently a bolt clicked, a chain fell, a hook unsnapped. As the door opened, the air inside wobbled like a wall of Jell-O and held. Winslow felt as though he were walking through cotton candy. The arena in Boston was pure ether by comparison. He looked around, nodding appreciatively at the psychedelic walls, the posters, the incense burners and water pipes, then sat down on some sort of Apache throne that seemed to be molting.

"Nice," he said.

"You really think so?"

"A little dusty."

"Dust is natural."

"It always makes me sneeze," Winslow ventured.

"That's because you keep trying to get rid of it." Stanley smiled benignly. "If you leave it alone, it clumps together in chains and doesn't float around. Dust is natural."

Why are we talking about dust? Winslow wondered. "I

worry about you, son," he said. "I worry about whether you eat enough. You never come to the table anymore."

"Nicki got me that little refrigerator there," Stanley replied. "When I'm hungry I open it and eat whatever doesn't have fuzz on it. Sometimes I eat the fuzz too."

"Molds are bad for you, son. Why do you eat molds when we've got mock duck downstairs?"

"Mock duck is fake. Molds are natural. They make penicillin from molds. Yogurt is mold."

"I miss you at the dinner table, son," Winslow pleaded. "It seems like we never run across each other anymore."

"I'm a hippie, Dad. I don't go in much for schedules. Schedules are unnatural."

Winslow reached out and plucked a button off the wall. TAKE A HIPPIE TO LUNCH, it read. "Why don't I do this," he said. "Next time you're hungry, why don't we go out somewhere together?"

Stanley shrugged.

"How about going to church with me, then?" Winslow asked with sudden inspiration.

"Oh, wow."

"It would mean a lot to me, son." Stanley looked too sapped to refuse an earnest request, he thought.

"You want me to hit on religion, is that it?"

"I just want you to sit in church with me once. You don't have to pray or sing or anything. Just be there, just...make a memory with me. Okay?"

Stanley grinned slowly. "Okay," he said, holding out a twist of grass. "But first you try my religion."

They went the next Sunday, which happened to be Holy Communion. Stanley wore sunglasses and sat instinctively in the third pew, left side. It was the family pew of the Moon family back in Gloucestershire. He was quite ignorant of this, of course, and also of the fact that he most closely resembled bereft Alexander of the original brothers four. Two hundred years earlier, Alexander had farted in front of the bishop. Now Stanley Moon felt vaguely imperiled by a force equally as compelling as gas.

While Stanley's uneasiness grew, Winslow searched for salvation and meaning in the service. He would have preferred to sit in the balcony for perspective's sake, because all he could see was the choir, and the only thing he knew about the congregation was that they couldn't read in unison. Behind him, strident voices crosscut mumblers, dramatic soliloquies counterpointed the Gregorian faithful. The choir did a little better, and there was one soloist who filled him with joy and optimism. She had a censorial aspect behind wire-rim glasses, but her voice was pure syrup. He decided he wanted her to sing at his funeral. He wrote her a note on the back of a pledge card and placed it on the collection plate in an act of blind faith. This was the same church he had visited after learning of his cancer, and he wondered where the minister he had talked to was.

When the Communion wafer and the grape juice came around, Stanley's sense of peril eased. Here was a rite that dealt in substances; he could identify with that. Deciding to eat the wafer like a graham cracker, he dipped it in the juice and was astonished to see it dissolve. It was his moment of conversion. If the mere symbol was this potent, what must be the actual power of Christ's blood? Euphoric—and uninformed as to the purpose of the holes in the hymnal rack—he left the Communion glass on the wooden pew when the congregation rose to pray. The moment of historical truth was now upon him. Two hundred years earlier his vastly removed uncle, bereft Alexander, had sensationalized the church; could Alexander's vastly removed nephew do less? With a grinding crunch and a piercing cry, Stanley sat down on his Communion glass.

His conversion was possibly the shortest on record, and it was ironic that he should find salvation too hazardous when every day he took substances into his body that played Russian roulette with his genes. The sad history of Alexander approximating itself in the twentieth century may, in fact, have been a kind of genetic punishment for Stanley's excesses. His father never knew. What Winslow did know was that it took thirty-four stitches to close the wound, and that his son swore before an entire congregation and its spiritual leader never to "haul his bloody ass" to church again. Later Stanley was to comment philosophically that it hadn't been all bad, that the single Communion had "kept him on his feet for a long time afterward," but by then it was too late to tell his father. Winslow died in a state of grace, more or less reconciled to those around him. He was refused by three funeral homes, all of which had sent him free calendars for years only to be booked solid when he died. But when the funeral did take place, the soloist who had filled him with joy and optimism sang "Ave Maria" over him, the church groundskeeper read a prayer, and a cortege of somber dogs that had trailed him for weeks got up and followed Harry from the gates of the cemetery.

{12}

Harry's senior year began with a splash and ended with a bang. The splash was the start of the swimming season; the bang was Carrie Reske.

Actually the swimming season never really ended. Since Harry had now joined Nino Torkie's AAU team, he worked out all year long. This was a tremendous advantage in a sport that was fundamentally ridiculous—to hurl bodies into an alien medium, prescribe limitations on their movements, time them from point A to point B. At the end of a single long-course summer swum in a 50-meter pool Harry was among the top three distance freestylers in the state.

"You are a *machine*, Moonie!" deemed Nino, himself given to inhuman performances.

Nino was so prone to violence that he was in danger of drowning while brushing his teeth. Nino ate banana peels. Nino tried to unzip baseballs. Nino sprinted into the gutter at the end of the pool and fractured his wrist. Had man assembled his elements instead of nature, he would have burned gasoline and dug excavations.

The AAU team traveled a lot, and this developed character. Love, honor, and acne were all magnified in the privations of crowded motel rooms or tents. Three days and two nights of sleeping in a nest of elbows, of interminable waits in restaurants, of long car rides with drivers who smoked or whistled or listened to news, left one longing to go off alone and emit gas. Harry saw his first fresh fatality on the highway to Boston and his first live copulation in the parking lot of a municipal swimming pool; he was robbed for the first time in a motel room, by a wealthy but troubled teammate; he experienced his first thrill of victory in the fog-bound prelims of a parkside pool and suffered his first major agony of defeat that evening in the finals. There was nausea and diarrhea and heartache, but the bottom line was character. When Harry stood on a starting block in the chill of a morning and saw the sky and his own silhouette in the smoking surface of the pool, he knew he was caught between two planes of existence. And as his character developed, he recognized which one he was. He was the beckoning figure in the pond, he was water, and he would unfurl himself off the block to embrace his roots.

The big meet that year was the state championship. They had to travel two hours to the pool, which was so old it was ringed with gargoyles. An immense sign on the wall read BATHER LIMIT 131. Harry wondered if the 131 were tall or short, fat or skinny. Had the public safety officials who made the sign taken this into consideration? Would it make a difference if the Boston Celtics decided to swim here? Could a jockey club fit in 145? The figure 131 was very precise and disturbing, as if 132 might cause a mass beaching.

Nino actually took a count. He stood on the starting block jabbing his forefinger at heads. But this caused him to miss most of the warm-up. In an effort to stimulate circulation he went into the locker room and covered his whole body with Ben-Gay. This set his genitalia ablaze, and when he tried to pick his nose with one of the fingers that had applied the cream, it slid halfway into his brain, igniting mucous membranes along the way. Breathing was hell; the nostril felt like a smoking gunport. He tried cramming wet toilet paper up the orifice and ended by stoppering it with an ear plug. But he still wasn't loose, and when he barely qualified for the 200 IM, Coach Hockney was disgusted.

"You are really stupid, Nino, you know that? Stupid, stupid, stupid. Eight thousand yards a day, six days a week, and you come up here and don't even loosen up. Stupid."

Nino felt stupid. He asked Harry, and Harry even said he was stupid. He went out to Howard Johnson's and drank a glass of raw eggs. When he argued with the waitress over what the charge should be, she said that drinking raw eggs was stupid. Then he went back to the motel where they were staying and shaved his legs. This was supposed to cut water resistance. But one of the backstrokers said it was stupid. So he shaved his arms, his head and his eyebrows. Next he shaved his pubic hair and trimmed his lashes. He looked like an obscene baby; that made him feel even more stupid. Without lashes his eyes continually watered, so he began using eye drops. Coach had said he wouldn't be able to see the fastest qualifier in the middle of the pool due to the fact that he had only qualified for lane eight after tightening up, so Nino kept putting in eye drops.

An hour before the finals the team went back to Howard Johnson's. They got the same waitress who had called Nino's raw egg drinking stupid. She looked at his shaved head, smooth brows, and stubby lashes and gave him ten feet.

"I told you not to drink raw eggs," she said. "Now your hair has all fallen out. If you think you're going to sue Howard Johnson's, forget it."

"It didn't fall out, I shaved it." She was just a blur to his watery eyes, and when he tried to glare the tears overflowed. Also, he breathed excessively through the unplugged nostril. It looked to her like he was crying and had asthma. She sucked her cheek, softening.

"Oh, yeah," she said, "I can see all the little cuts. What'd you use, a machete? Lucky for you, you didn't bleed to death."

"I used a mill file."

"Oh. Well, you should've used a depilatory, you know. Files clog up. What'll you have? We're all out of raw eggs."

"Is the maple syrup free?"

"French toast, waffles, and pancakes are only on the breakfast menu."

"Is the syrup free?"

She looked at him critically, but his eyes were overflowing and in the heat of the restaurant one of the shaving nicks had reopened. A large drop of blood rolled down his skull, circled his ear, and ran laterally along his neck. He looked like a Christian martyr. "Over there," she said about the syrup. "On the sideboard."

Everybody else ordered orange juice.

When the juice came, a dozen hands reached for a dozen packets of sugar. As if by ritual, these were torn open and poured in the juice. A dozen spoons stirred.

"Hey, Nino, watcha gonna put the syrup on?" Harry wanted to know.

"No pancakes," Hockney warned from the end of the table.

The lid on Nino's syrup grated. It looked like a can of motor oil going down—one long gluey quaff.

When the waitress returned, she looked at the empty jar and she looked at Nino. "Honey," she said—a synonym for syrup—"if you were anyone else, I'd say you stole that. If you were anyone else, I'd say everybody at this table helped you get rid of it. But you're different, and I don't want to know what you did with that maple syrup. I'm not even going to tell the manager. It's yours. Free. Take the pitcher too, if you want. And here's a bonus." She handed him a tube of depilatory. "You need that more than I do. I'm just asking one thing. If you ever come in here again, don't sit at any of my tables. Okay? You're sweet," she added softly.

Sweet. By the time he got to the pool, any doctor except Ufunker would have diagnosed him as comatose; Ufunker would have taken X rays and recommended orthotics for his shoes. Nino had always distinguished himself with unusual entries into the water—once, when Hockney had hollered for him to swim backstroke, he rolled over in midair and landed on his back—but now, barely conscious, he canted off the edge, landing on his face. The shock brought him around sufficiently to warm up. There may have been more than 131 in the pool. He couldn't tell; everything was a blur. The eye drops had dilated his pupils and the chlorine ate pits into them.

"Okay, Nino," Coach said at the end of warm-up. "I guess you know how important this two hundred IM is. I don't want to make you nervous, but if you win we've got it made and I keep my job; if you lose, we hitchhike home and nobody talks to us for a year. I'll have to sell my kid's cat." Nino tried to focus his feral red eyes, and Coach thought he had fired him up. "I was just kidding about the cat," he said.

When the IM came up, Nino found lane eight. Weak, nauseated, and blind, he stumbled into the block. His head was bleeding. The swimmer next to him kept hyperventilating.

"Take your marks!" ordered the starter.

Nino bent over and fell in the pool. As he crawled out, lane seven said, "You look like a ferret." He didn't know what a ferret was, but it sounded homosexual.

"Take your marks!" said the starter.

He bent over and fell in the pool again. "Your mother sucks," he said as he crawled by lane seven.

There was increased tension now. Anyone who committed the third false start would be disqualified. The starter moved to within a yard and when the gun went off a spark hit Nino's shaved head, furthering his sense of crisis. At the end of the fifty he had an unbelievable lead, but he came off the wall all over the ropes on the backstroke leg. At the turn he clunked his head but still held the lead going into the breaststroke. By now he was legally blind. His eyes felt pinned in their sockets and looked like artichokes in buttermilk as he gaped at the timers. His underwater pull took him under the marker, where he promptly kicked lane seven in the head. From there he went on to lanes six, five, and four, kicking each in the head before he strangled on a marker and got turned around. He worked his way back, kicking four and five again, missing six, and getting seven in the face. Lane three won the race.

It took forty minutes to figure out the finish, treat the injuries, and mollify the outraged coaches. Five teams filed protests. The prospects for a team championship were considerably altered with four swimmers suffering degrees of whiplash. No one knew how it would turn out.

"Nino is stupid," Coach kept saying and wrote it on his clipboard as if to give it permanence.

But for Hockney and his cat, his swimmers, and especially Harry, victory grinned. Not only did they win the championship, Harry Moon capped it with an upset win in the 500 free. They threw the coach in the pool and dove in with their sweats on. Then Harry saw Nino go into the locker room, and after a few minutes of splashing around he went to find him.

Nino was alone in the showers. It made Harry think of himself with Coach Coomes after he had lost the football game.

"You okay, Nino?" he asked.

"Yeah," Nino said, but his head was in the cascade from the shower and Harry thought he might be crying.

"You sure?"

"Sure."

Harry got in a shower across from him.

"What's a ferret?" Nino asked.

"A weasel-like animal that eats rats," said Harry.

Nino turned the shower off. He never turned showers off. "I'm gonna walk back to the motel," he said.

"Want some company?"

"Naw."

While he was walking back he began to hear a ringing in his ears. This did not surprise him, since the starter's pistol had nearly blown his head off. Swimming meets were scream city, anyway, and the noise had all seemed against him, so now his ears rang. It sounded just like a phone ringing. He passed a few more shops, and it kept getting louder. It was a phone. He stepped into the booth on the corner and picked up the receiver.

"This is station WBOO in Chester calling you with another 'Biology Bounty' question! Answer this one correctly and you win five free karate lessons from Mr. Moto! And now for the question: Name a weasel-like animal that eats rats!"

"Lane seven," said Nino.

"Wrong," said WBOO. "Sorry."

Nino hung up and saw that he was outside Howard Johnson's. He could see his favorite waitress through the window. He waited until she had her back to him, then slipped in and left three dollars on one of her tables. The tube of depilatory was the kindest thing that had happened to him all day.

So Harry was the hero. His single unexpected victory outweighed the predicted ones of his teammates. The students pampered him, the teachers respected him, even Heather Latko must know he existed, he thought, and on the strength of that he decided to ask her to the senior prom. Success had gone to his head.

He brushed his teeth, put on an extra sweater to keep from shivering, wrote the date and time on the wall, and called. It was March 19th, 8:33 P.M.—but the line was busy. He went through the same preparation on March 20th, with the same result. On the 21st he tried sixteen times, and on the 22nd thirty-one. He wondered if it was the same conversation. With all the historical moments written on the wall by the phone it looked like a number painting. Then on the 29th, at exactly 6:05, Heather's phone began to ring. It rang for three hours and forty-two minutes. After his kidneys reached toxic levels, he had to run to the bathroom or die of uremic poisoning.

When he returned to where the phone lay, it was making an oscillating noise like an anguished cat. There was something stridently mocking in that sound, and he sulked for three days. On the next attempt his sense of history failed him, and he neither recorded the moment, nor brushed his teeth, nor donned an extra sweater to keep from shivering. This time the phone rang and was answered immediately.

"Hello-o-o."

He cleared his throat.

"Hello-o-o," she said again.

"Hi," he squeaked. It was the voice he had abandoned in adolescence.

"Hello?" she asked sharply.

The change in tone terrified him. He reached for his trusty kazoo: *Toot, toot.*

"Oh. You again."

Toot.

"Do you take requests?"

Toot.

"Good. Drop dead."

She hung up, and his sense of history promptly returned. It was April Fool's Day, 1968.

He wound up taking Carrie to the prom. This was the first overtly romantic date they had ever had, and she was extremely nervous. She wore no makeup but consumed large numbers of Chap Sticks the week before to condition her lips.

"You're with *me* tonight, sport," she said when he picked her up in his mother's car. "Try not to make me look like a consolation prize. Do not let your eyes roam Heather and thither like you usually do."

"Yeah? Is that right? Is that what you think?"

She smiled smugly. "Did Daddy read you the rules—no touching below the throat, drive with the emergency brake on, nothing stronger than Grape Nehi?"

"He showed me a bunch of clippings of car accidents."

"Ah. His portfolio. No threats?"

"He kept punching me in the shoulder."

"Yes, Daddy used to box. He was the first and last fighter ever to enter the ring with glasses on."

"That's amazing."

"Not really. He got his eyes lacerated."

Harry never knew when she was kidding.

The country club where the dance was held was the same one he had been thrown off of while jogging, only now its permanence seemed incontestable. Smelling the newly mown grass, he peered from the parking lot into the gloom of the fairways and seemed to hear the outraged duffer of that day crying, "Hey! Hey!" They passed through the doors into a state of acquired grace, as though traveling from the amnesty of childhood into an adult world of pretentiousness and responsibility. Sandwiched between crystal and stone and parquetry were the friends and enemies of their youth, ceremented for a final reckoning before diverging into separate judgments. Life was over; life was beginning. It seemed to Harry that whatever relationships he wanted must be cemented here and now or they would slip from his grasp forever.

But all he wanted was Heather Latko.

The object of this desire was wearing something passionately pink and as arresting as her arrogance. Her escort was a gifted athlete on his way to a Rhodes scholarship, and the light around them seemed to fall off in expanding circles so that they made radiant passes around the floor in a kind of gossamer glow. He and Carrie, on the other hand, glazed a path across the room like a relentless Zamboni. When they had done this three times they took a break.

"Guess I'll check out the punch bowl," he said.

An amorphous lump of his own kind clung to the serving table. There he learned that the in crowd was heading for Lake Seymour after the prom. Lake Seymour was pronounced with a carnal leer. Sexual excesses were automatic on its beaches, and colonies of latex bobbed in its shallows. He was still a virgin, and, since he had no intention of deflowering Carrie, Lake Seymour sounded threatening. But it was where Heather and her Adonis would be. Like the severed claw of a vanquished crab, Harry kept trying to get hold of something.

"Say, why don't we go to ol' Lake Seymour and skip stones?" he said.

Carrie's eyes trained on him like gun barrels, but her voice was loaded with innocence. "Oh, Harry," she said, "all the bad kids go to Lake Seymour. Are you sure we want to go *there?* I mean, it's got such a bad reputation and everything. Oh, Harry, are we bad kids?"

She was already groping for the Chap Stick.

He led her out, left her to open the car door herself, and peeled off in the best tradition of Grand Prix.

"Don't you think we ought to go home and change first?" she said.

"You've got eight minutes," he told her at the door to her house.

He went back to the car, took a pair of paint-spattered jeans out of the trunk, and began to change in the driveway. Then the porch light came on.

"Harry?" It was Mr. Reske.

He tried to hop behind the dark side of the car, but old man Reske sauntered out.

"Ah, there you are. Why are you in your shorts? Say, what have you been up to?"

"Nobody wears a tux after the dance, Mr. Reske," Harry said. He tried to pull the cummerbund down without unhooking it and it stuck on his hips.

Mr. Reske peered at the tux lying twisted in the trunk. "That looks pretty silly."

"Yes, sir." Harry pulled harder and his shorts came off with the cummerbund.

"You're supposed to take the sash off first. How the hell did you get the tux trousers down, anyway?"

He got so close that Harry felt apprehensive about his sexuality. Then he realized that he just wanted to smell his breath. "I don't remember," he said.

"Got another picture here." Mr. Reske grunted. "See this?"

It was a glossy of a twisted wreck. The driver hung limply out the window, blood coagulating darkly below his extended arm.

"Nice," Harry said.

"Drunk," said Mr. Reske. "Lots of kids out there drinking tonight."

"Not us, Mr. Reske." He had managed to get his pants back on.

"That's my little girl you've got there."

"I'll be careful." Harry met his gaze, but he was looking for lacerations that might have been caused by boxing with glasses on.

"'Early to bed, early to rise, makes a man healthy, wealthy, and wise,'" said Mr. Reske.

Early to bed, early to rise, makes a man healthy, wealthy,

and tired as shit, thought Harry, and just then Carrie returned. They settled in the front seat and Harry roared out of the pits.

"Lake Seymour." She sighed. "To skip rocks. We'll be the only ones."

"What?"

"Skipping rocks. We'll be the only ones. Everyone else will be spawning."

Harry pictured Heather Latko spawning.

"How'd you like it if I raped *you*?" he asked peevishly, and a profound silence kept him from looking across the seat.

When they got to Lake Seymour there were cars and bodies all over the beach. It looked like a rookery.

"Where the hell are you going?" Carrie demanded when he began to troop among them as methodically as a behavioral psychologist.

He saw Heather and Adonis then, cuddling in the hollow of a weathered log that had been dragged along the sand. They still had their clothes on, and he took this as a kind of reprieve. Waving Carrie to a spot forty yards away, he slogged on.

"Terrific run," she groused, huffing and puffing after him.

The sand was fine-grained and yielding, and he plopped down with a sense of finality. Like soft wax, the beach took impressions and made them permanent. All around him the sexual ferment of his generation was resolving itself two by two in the sensuous sand and a warm, velvet night. "I forgot something," he said and struggled up, retracing his steps to the weathered log. When he saw that his rival's right hand was in Heather's blouse, his blood froze. The moonlight made white things look swollen, and he watched heartsick as a massive left hand slid down and disappeared into the darkness of her jeans.

"What did you forget?" Carrie asked him when he got back. She imagined some appliance of love to have been the object.

He grunted. "Nothin'."

"Sure is a lot of he-ing and she-ing going on."

"I forgot something else."

"What?" She sounded incredulous.

"My wallet. I must've dropped it."

Ah. His wallet. Can't spawn without a wallet, she thought.

He went back to the log. "Police!" he called softly. To his right, a startled couple fled like flushed partridge. When nothing else happened, he edged forward, and there, stark and flowing as dunes, was the naked act he feared.

He heard the waves then. They came in little surges, purer than the rhythm of his imperfect queen and her defiler. He was the water's lover. Hydroponic Harry Moon, having arisen from Jonathan's seed which drowned in Boston Harbor, could always find release and consolation in his own element. He trudged to the shore, kicked off his shoes, and crouched in the shallows.

Carrie came and squatted beside him.

Somewhere in the night an owl called, a truck climbed a grade, running lights crossed on the far side of the lake. When a few cars began to leave, he stood.

"You've got sand on your fly," she said. She had sand on her blouse, too. Gently she stroked his fly and he brushed her blouse, and that was how he discovered she wasn't wearing any bra. All at once they were stroking and brushing all over the place. She pulled him down into the water and the dampness penetrated their clothes. He ran a fingernail down the crotch of her canvas shorts and sculpted her breasts. She kneaded his torso and slid her palms together between his legs.

It was the water that turned him on. The wet clothes peeled off, exposing a damp sexual essence, like pulpy fruit, dewy, dissolving. He fell into her with a splash. For long exquisite moments the liquid surged from some disguised beginning, then eddied, melting the last rigidity of his flesh in coursing currents. His body congealed again on top of hers. He was faintly shocked to find himself naked and stuck inside her. She had always been a blouse and skirt, or a sweater and jeans, or at least a bathing suit. Those parts of her which were important—her face, her hands—stuck out of her clothes. But now she seemed overwhelmingly composed of sexual parts, wide-flung thighs and gaping hips and stark, jutting breasts. What had he done? What irrevocably adult thing had taken place? "Oh, my God," he said.

She moaned and held him. "Stay," she said.

The water stirred their bodies, and they started up like soft machines driven by a single well-lubed piston. This time the climax built slowly and was extremely intense. The water seemed to lift them in a crest and dash them on the beach, thin and spent and utterly melted in an ecstasy of elements.

Harry felt as though his body had opened to some supersaturated atmosphere where oxygen flowed in through every pore. It was exactly the feeling he got from a good workout. Even the afterglow was the same. There was an all-pervasive sense of relaxation, an opening of doors that allowed his strength to flow back. But following his sexual awakening this return seemed particularly complex and meaningful. He felt himself collecting in the sand in puddles and clues dredged up from an ancestral ocean.

Carrie felt something else. She had always known exactly what was happening inside her. Something pivotal was taking place and spreading to her brain like an enchantment. "Harry," she whispered with magic in her voice, "I'm pregnant."

{13}

The one person who might have celebrated Harry's impregnating a girl was dead. Another case of bad timing for Winslow. Harry had let him slip into the hereafter without proof of his prowess; but then, his father had never taken him to Disneyland. The story of his father's virility had come to him in bits and pieces, and now he wondered if he too was cursed with some relentless potency, a super sperm that penetrated all flesh as easily as DMSO. Was that why Carrie had blurted that she was pregnant only moments after his climax? How could she know? Where was the missed period? Where was morning sickness?

He went to the library to bone up on obstetrics and was surprised to find books on female anatomy and sexuality right out in the open. These were the same pictures that covered the wall of the library's men's room, only with clinical captions instead of various human pleas, and he read furtively in the narrow aisles. But the oldest librarian in the world somehow stole up to his shoulder and leered until he slammed the book shut.

"May I help you?" she asked snidely.

"I was just admiring your orgasm," he whispered rapidly. Orgasm? Did he say orgasm? He had meant to say organization. "I mean your organ," he said. "Your orgasmization. Orga... org," he finished pitifully.

She took the book, fingered the spine, and smiled pertly. *"Your Vaginal Health,"* she read.

"I thought it was about ferns."

"No. It's about women. See? Does that look like a fern to you?"

He tried to clear his throat but only croaked.

She took off her glasses, and her eyes were full of knowledge. "This is the labia majora, and this is the labia minora. Ever see one of these before? Better than a fern, eh?"

"Well, I'm looking for ferns," he said. "Which way to the ferns?" Waving rigidly, he backed out of the stacks.

The world was full of carnivorous women, he thought.

On the way home he read a bank advertisement that told him more about his sexual episode with Carrie than anything he had read in the library. No penalty for early withdrawal, it said. Put something away for the future and watch your deposit grow.

She had guaranteed him maximum interest, and he had made the deposit, but there was no certainty about the account. When three weeks passed and nothing seemed to happen, he took her back to Lake Seymour and they lay on the beach in the dead of night while he rationalized.

"You probably thought you were pregnant because you wanted to be. That's natural. All girls want to be mothers. But believe me, you're not. It wasn't at all likely anyway, and now three weeks have gone by, so I know for sure you're not."

"I missed my period," she said.

Harry realized two things then. The first was that a giant shadow had fallen oppressively over his life. The second was that he was looking deeply into her toes and talking to her feet.

There was nothing left to do but go to Ufunker.

She couldn't see her own doctor for fear it would get back to her parents, so he took her to Ufunker just before the Fourth of July weekend. She went in alone, and he stayed behind in the barren waiting room.

"Been coming here long?" one of the other two men who were waiting addressed him presently.

"All my life," he said.

The stranger grinned toothlessly. "That long? I been coming here twenty-two years, and I didn't start till I retired." He could have been sixty or ninety.

"What did you do before you retired?" asked Harry.

"I followed the lure of the canvas."

"Ah, an artist."

"No. A boxer. Fought out of New Amsterdam. Wanta see me do a push-up?"

"Strawberry royale!" exclaimed the remaining man. Harry noticed he was bald and had a gold tooth like Daddy Warbucks.

"Don't mind him," said the old boxer. "He's here for head lice."

"Mocha chip!" said Daddy Warbucks. "I've got Gilles de la Tourette's disease. That's a disease where you can't stop swearing. Vanilla!"

They were the same two Winslow had met the day he found out he had cancer, and now, like harbingers of ill tidings, they had come together at a critical conjunction in Harry's life. The only one missing was the old woman on crutches.

"To you it probably sounds like I'm saying ice cream flavors, but to me these are swear words," said Daddy Warbucks. "I used to say really bad stuff, like...banana almond fudge! Then Dr. Ufunker told me to move to a foreign country where they wouldn't understand English. I lived all over the world and learned to swear in sixteen languages and forty-three dialects. Then the UN offered me a job as a translator. Pistachio! So I went to a hypnotist and he turned my swear words into ice cream flavors. Everything went great until this morning when I addressed the ambassador from Venezuela on behalf of his neighbor to the south as a Brazilian banana nut. Then I had the representative from South Africa calling the President of Nigeria a chocolate chimp. After that, the Soviet Union promised a rocky road in any future arms talks and Uncle Sam offered to make heavenly hash out of all the double dips in the Moslem world. By this time an international crisis was brewing, so I slipped out and came here. They're probably still trying to figure out who said what, and come tomorrow the world may lie waste in the aftermath of nuclear war. Molten marblecake!"

"Happy Fourth of July," murmured the old boxer, who was down on the floor again trying to do a push-up.

Harry drew his feet onto the chair rung. Who were these people, and what was he doing here? Was this life after high school? Was he being punished for infidelity to Heather Latko?

Just then the outer door opened, and the woman on crutches stumped in. "Holy shit," she said. "Nothing ever heals." And she stumped out again.

"When are you going to tell Father?" Carrie asked him after they left the office.

"Tell him? You mean you really are pregnant?" His voice rose two notes at a time.

"Oh, I'm pregnant all right."

"Ufunker said that?"

"More or less."

"More or less pregnant?"

"He recommended orthotics. And he said you were a five at birth. I have no idea what your being a five means, but he obviously thinks I'm going to have a load on my feet. He took a urine sample and rambled on about rabbits, and when we call back in a couple days he'll tell me I'm pregnant."

Her assurance seemed to sever his heart from its arteries. The sense of fatalism he had once shared with his father was his alone now. There would always be boxers from New Amsterdam and people who swore in ice cream flavors cluttering his life, and where there were choices, he would always choose wrong. Against the lucklessness of his timing, blessed lives would unfold on the other side of the universe.

"Okay," he said. "You're pregnant."

An accomplished fact; they marched along stricken with awareness. What must come next could crush either one of them, but the choice was his. He dreaded breaking the silence; she ached with it. The well-dressed oaks of summer seemed to usher them toward the river and seclusion as they passed near a downtown park. In a matter of hours the park would resound and flash with pyrotechnic effects but now it held its green breath. They walked and walked and walked, trying to establish meaning through the sound and cadence of their steps, until their feet fell silent over the grass.

"My brother Nicki can arrange an abortion," he said at last. The crucial noun fell leadenly into an environment of verbs and adjectives, a piece of dead mineral flattening pliant stems and garish flowers. The park wind blew all around it, and Harry sought to soften its outline. "That's one choice," he said.

"Is that what you want?"

"It would be best for the baby."

"You don't have to marry me anyway, you know."

"I don't?"

"Poor dumb jock, what would I want to marry you for? It would spoil a beautiful friendship."

She sauntered off, and he stood there as if she had left him chained to a fence. He had never realized how easygoing she could be in a crisis. Good old Carrie. It was a rotten deal but she wasn't going to make it sticky for him. She must be peanut brittle inside. God, all they'd been through. She must have sat through five hundred workouts. And even when he took her to the prom just to be close to Heather, she took that too. It reminded him of his mother sitting home while his father drank coffee with some petite blonde in a restaurant.

She was almost to the bridge. Against the expanse of the river she looked lonely and impermanent. The bridge! he thought. She got to the crest and placed one hand on the rail. Then she leaned over. He came at a dead run.

"Don't do it!" he shouted.

She turned and waited. "Do what? Jump? You think I'd jump for you? What a dumb jock—what a dumb jock snob. Next you'll imagine I was going to do it just to get rescued by you just because you're such a great swimmer and everything."

He saw it all clearly now. She was going to do just that. Luckily, he hadn't turned away after they said good-bye. Fate was giving him another chance. Water had brought them together, water had triggered their sexual encounter, water was coursing beneath them, offering them a choice.

"If you jump, I jump," he said.

"Big deal. You couldn't drown in the Atlantic." Then she said carefully, "We could commit hara-kiri."

The loaded pun seized him like a hand in the dark. "Why don't we?" he asked huskily. "Harry-Carrie. Us. Forever."

"You mean get married?"

"Yes."

"Because you don't love me, that's why," she said. "It wouldn't work out. You can't build a marriage on guilt and obligation."

"Who says I don't love you? I've always loved you. Didn't I punch out Santa Claus for you?"

"What about Heather?"

He gestured carelessly.

She sighed. "No, I don't think so. You'd end up hating me and the baby. You just don't love me."

"I'll prove it," he stammered.

"How?"

He turned around, as if to find the evidence, but ended up taking out his wallet. "My driver's license," he blurted. "I'll tear it in half."

She burst out laughing. "Oh, Harry, Harry, you're such a child!" Then she thought: she was a child, and she was bearing a child. Plucking the license from his fingers, she held it gingerly over the water and released it. "Regrets?"

He watched intently as it fluttered into the river. "Naw," he said. "It was only good for four more years anyway."

You needed a license or a permit or a certificate to do almost anything, Harry soon discovered. You couldn't be legally alive or dead unless some piece of paper said you were. The document supplied by the hospital he was born in was only gratuitous, he was told, and he had to apply for a valid birth certificate. This together with certification from Ufunker that he did not have venereal disease and was in fact a male, accompanied by a consent form for minors, eventually permitted him to apply for a license to get married. Since the Secretary of State's office was in the same building, he applied for a duplicate driver's license there as well but was told that he needed proof of insurance and a valid vehicle registration, which he had left in the car. When he went out to get this, it was 12:01 and a meter maid was ticketing his car because it was a permit-only parking space from noon till 12:30. He argued with the meter maid and ended up moving the car to a 30-minute parking zone, after which he returned to the Secretary of State's office with the proof of insurance and vehicle registration. The person who had been processing his application was going out to lunch by then, and he had to move to a long line behind another clerk. By the time he had applied for the duplicate driver's license, a half hour had passed and he rushed out to find the meter maid writing him a second ticket.

"It's not expired yet!" he shouted, coming across the street.

"It will be by the time I finish this," she said. "I can tell by the little clicks they make. Some hum, some whir, but this one clicks. Down on East Butternut all the meters are spring-loaded and—"

"But I'm here!"

"You need another penny."

"I'm all out of change."

"Oh. That's too bad. Sometimes you can find one lying in the gutter."

Harry glanced frantically at the pavement.

"Over there!" she said excitedly. "Quick, oh, quick. It's clicking! Isn't that a penny?"

He ran to where she was pointing.

"It's a bottle cap!" he cried.

"Too bad," she said with genuine concern.

"Why can't I just move the car?" he demanded.

"Good idea," she said.

Harry yanked open the door and popped into the driver's seat.

"Time's up!" boomed the meter maid.

He came out of the car spitting venom. It was the same fearless passion that had faced down a raging lion and stood on principle in a supermarket. Here was the mindless agent of everything that licensed, validated, and certified. He had boiled over at the first ticket, but now he steamed quietly down the street to a bank. He did not have proper proof of his family's commerce with the bank, but he argued that his mother had a "certificate" account and at last the teller transacted two rolls of pennies in exchange for a paper dollar. Returning to his car, Harry put three pennies in the meter and hurried past the maid, where for the next two hours he deposited pennies in every slot that hummed, whirred, or clicked before she got there. Four times he had to race her back to his own expiring meter.

"A penny for your thoughts," he said when he got to the last one of the second roll.

Not even the fact that the Secretary of State's office had misunderstood his request and eventually sent him duplicate plates rather than a duplicate license dampened the victory.

{14}

When Stu heard that his younger brother had gotten a girl pregnant, he was filled with jealousy and hate. Harry could piss in a bottle of ginger ale and it was cute. Harry ravished girls. Stu kept a bowel chart and dated women's underwear; Nicki was in and out of jail; Stanley was a junkie. It seemed to Stu that the collective virtue and virility of the Moon family was being drained off by its youngest son, leaving the rest of them sapped and twisted with moral malnutrition.

He showed up one evening in Stanley's room with a Bible in his hand and read him the story of Joseph's brothers casting him into a pit. When he was done, Stanley slowly raised his face and asked him what he wanted. Leafing back in search of a stronger immoral imperative, Stu then read him the Cain and Abel story. After that Stanley nodded languidly and said, "Fundamental, man."

"Don't you get it?" Stu cried in dismay. "We've got to do something about Harry."

The light glittered off Stanley's unmoving glasses. "Are you Jesus, man?"

Stu hung his head. "I am a pathetic pervert," he said. "You are a junkie. Nicki is a con. But Harry—hah—Harry is a state champion swimmer. Harry is a *B* student. Harry knocks up women. Don't you see, he's stealing our energy. There's some kind of pipeline in this family, and the faucet is in Harry's genes."

Stanley nodded.

"So now you see what we've got to do?"

"Fundamental, man."

"Good. The question is how. I've been racking my brains over this for a week, and I need help with the answer. Maybe I need courage, too. You always understood everything, Stanley, so I've come to you first. Can you give me what I need? Can you give me courage and answers?"

"Fundamental, man." Stanley reached under his bed and pulled out an army grenade belt decorated with peace symbols. "Here. Take this." He extracted a plastic bag. "It's an aphrodisiac. You need a good lay."

Stu took the bag, went back to his room, and stared at himself in the mirror. "Fundamental, man," he said.

The next morning he took the plastic bag down to the corner. Before him stretched the houses of the women of his neighborhood, the ones with families, the childless, the singles, the widowed and divorced. He had worn the intimate apparel of most of them at one time or another—these were the women whose bras and panties he had taken, whose scents were in his nostrils, yet whom he had never spoken to—but today he was wearing K-Mart jockeys with a rooster on the crotch and a red torso shirt. One by one the husbands came out and drove off to work. Here and there children followed, on bikes, on skateboards, or on foot. They carried their bats and rackets and disseminated to the fields of their youth, leaving an assortment of vulnerable mothers behind. Stu kept track.

At nine ten he opened the plastic bag and stuck his tongue in the leaves. They tasted like oregano and spinach, but he knew no one understood more about substances than Stanley and immediately felt a glow in his belly. It was the same kind of crawling heat that preceded a bowel attack, but this time it was headed toward his loins. He imagined Harry feeling suddenly diluted as his sexual potency waned.

The first door he tried belonged to Mrs. Fletcher. She was a chunk of femininity who could hit a golf ball 200 yards and whose husband was superintendent of schools. Her four children were away at church camp for a week.

"Hi," he said. "I'm here to make an introductory offer. How would you like my cherry?"

"I b-beg your pardon," she said, clutching her robe at the throat.

"You know, my cherry. Me."

Her brow knit, her lips opened dryly. "What's wrong with you?" she said. "You shouldn't be doing this. You shouldn't be coming around here saying that to me." She kept listing what he shouldn't be doing, but she stayed in the doorway and her voice got weaker and weaker.

"I can't wait long," he interrupted and the protests died. "May I come in now?"

She let him in, and they made love there in the vestibule on a blue shag rug. The whole thing took four minutes. "I hope you're not pregnant," he said ingenuously and checked the view through the mail slot in the door before leaving.

The next house belonged to Mrs. Mallory. She burst out laughing, thought it over, and hooked him by the neck. She had been doing her morning exercises to Jack LaLanne and insisted they copulate to the music and movements that remained. "Thrust one, thrust two, thrust three," said Jack LaLanne, and they complied to the end of the program. "You're very athletic," she told him as he was leaving. "There's another show at twelve thirty, if you want to come back."

"I don't know if I can keep it up," he said. "Maybe tomorrow."

He thought he would try one more house and call it a day. Pale and prim Mrs. Prittikin was aching with secret lust. He had once worn her bra, a tightly woven B cup with no lace, plain white. He had sensed repression when he put it on. Here was frustration; here was boredom and fantasy and longing. Fidelity was shackling her like her bra. He flicked his tongue into the plastic bag and knocked on the door.

It was barely nine thirty and she was already dressed in nylons, skirt, and a high-necked blouse. Her eyes met his in a straightforward manner, and she said nothing, as if she had already granted him an audience just by opening the door.

"Hi," he said. "I'm here to make you an introductory offer. How would you like my cherry?"

She understood, and was sure she understood, instantly. The concussion seemed to spread from her eyes to her lips to her neck, all of which quivered and tensed. "How dare you proposition me," she said shakily. "What do you think I am?"

"Sexy."

Her breathing got out of control, and her lips stayed parted. "You little arrogant bastard," she said.

He stepped in alongside her.

"I could have you arrested for this," she said and closed the door.

His own hands were trembling as he ran them down her front. She shut her eyes and stood fast. He unbuttoned and unzipped her. Silk rustled, elastic snapped. She gasped as his fingers created moist suction.

"You bastard..." she whispered.

She pushed him into the bathroom and opened the faucets to the tub. Then she undressed him, poured detergent into the bath, and lowered herself into the steamy water. She had her eyes tightly closed as she began an act of self-gratification.

This familiarity fascinated Stu, who, despite the pace of his sexual initiation, thought he would presently erupt like a volcano. When she began to groan and gasp loudly, he clambered in between her knees and there received an education that reviewed all the stages of infancy, adolescence, and adulthood. Unable to reach a third climax, he stayed erect through each position.

"You bastard," she said again as he rested his head against her breast. But there was no strength in her voice. "We can do this Tuesdays and Fridays."

"I work at the supermarket Fridays."

"Thursday then. But not until noon. Tony doesn't leave for work until ten thirty."

He wanted to ask if she had done this before, but he knew she hadn't. She had just fantasized it so thoroughly and often that there were no decisions left to make.

"I can't come Thursdays either," he said.

Pain began to creep into her eyes.

"Or Tuesdays," he said.

The pain turned to hate.

He was riveted on her eyes, but it seemed to him they were his eyes and he was feeling self-pity. Until this morning *he* had been the pathetic sexual entity. Until Stanley had given him the aphrodisiac he had been worse off than she. Then he had tapped the sexual energy hoarded by his brother and now the wretchedness was leaving him, draining into Mrs. Prittikin. How would she get rid of it? How would she recoup her self-esteem? By more affairs? By diminishing her husband so that she wouldn't be unworthy of him?

Stu picked up her underpants on his way through the living room. Old habits die hard.

{15}

Mr. Reske was insecure to begin with, and when his daughter announced her pregnancy all his Freudian bonds tensed. This showed particularly well in his nostrils, which distended as if they had been widened with a can opener. He remembered the driveway on the night of the prom and Harry standing there, the tux lying twisted in the trunk, and he imagined he had missed the very act of insemination by only minutes. I must kill the boy, he said to himself. When Harry came through the back door later that afternoon, he stalked him up and down staircases. His wife and daughter rolled in front of him like a shock wave, allowing Harry time to hole up in a cedar closet. "Come out of there, you little asshole creep!" he cried. "Come out or I'll kick the door down!" He delivered three kicks to make his point.

"What are you going to do to me?" It sounded like Harry was at least a mile away.

"I'm going to kill you, you little shit." The closet was silent, and Mr. Reske resumed kicking. "Come out or I'll burn you out. Where's my lighter?"

"You used to be a boxer, Mr. Reske, your hands are lethal weapons."

"Come out of there, you dirty little bastard. . . . Bastard!" He despaired and sank to the floor against the door. "I'm going to be the grandfather of a bastard."

Harry heard him weeping and tried to push the door open, but he couldn't move Mr. Reske's bulk. He had read Balzac's *La Grande Bretêche* in senior English, and it occurred to him that he might be sealed up forever in a closet like the discovered lover of that tale. "Mr. Reske," he called, "if you promise not to hit me, I'll come out."

"Grampa's bastard," the dejected flesh sobbed.

"I'm going to marry your daughter," said Harry.

"Gramma's bastard."

"We'll get married right away. Didn't you think I'd do that, Mr. Reske? You bring a preacher to the closet door, and we'll get married right now."

"Gramma and Grampa's bastard."

"You'd better bring witnesses too. Someone official, like the chief of police. He can bring along homicide and one or two precincts. Mr. Reske? Please let me out."

Mr. Reske stood up. "I'll think about it," he said.

Harry heard the key turn, heard the women protest, heard them walk away. Six hours later, Carrie returned and let him out.

"The wedding is all set," she said. "Two weeks. Your side gets to choose the church."

Harry went back in the closet and cried.

She wanted a big one. A full house and a reception. Her father agreed. He wanted to murder all the doubters, and a big wedding seemed to be the best way to confront everyone.

Harry had no input whatsoever. All he had was a sense of falling through space. In the coolness of space, the heated movements of others seemed like a gross overreaction. The whole concept of fatherhood was analogous to some disease process, he felt, and he was becoming an invalid. There were moments when he simply stopped functioning.

"May I help you?" asked the manager of Grand Union one day, discovering him on his knees near the vegetables.

"I can't walk," he said.

"Then perhaps you would like one of our motorized wheelchairs."

The manager sent a stock boy for the chair, and Harry

spent forty minutes whining up and down the aisles of canned goods and boxes.

When he finally got home and gave his mother the flashlight batteries she had sent him for, she put one in each hand and delivered a speech as though she were drawing current. "I've come to a decision," she said. "Your father's insurance money is a tidy sum, and I thought at first I'd invest it in African dance lessons and open a studio in Miami. I got the idea in church when I noticed how much better everyone sings when they have to keep getting up and down. It's like calisthenics. The ministers keep them hopping up and down on purpose. Breathing is the key to life," she disclosed, and then her voice dropped. "But when you committed your act of passion, I realized how utterly I've failed you.

"I want you to go to college, Harry, and I want you to become a teacher. Teachers are innocuous. If you'll become innocuous, I'll put you through school."

"I can't let you do that," he said.

"You mean you won't become innocuous?"

"It doesn't really matter what I become. It's the money."

"It's my money. I could give it to Nicki and he'd gamble it away; Stu would buy out Frederick's of Hollywood; Stanley would spend it on drugs. But if I use it to make you a teacher, I'll be satisfied the rest of my days. So don't tell me no. 'No' is an arrow in my heart. I'm buying forgiveness for leading you into your act of passion. It's a wedding present. You're going to college, and that's that."

He accepted it without further protest. His mother had assumed his guilt, and it seemed to him that he had just stopped falling through space.

The wedding was marred by a freak midsummer hailstorm and the fact that Stanley refused to enter the church because it was the same one where he had sat on the Communion glass. He had missed his father's funeral and now his brother's wedding, but even the hailstorm couldn't drive him inside. When the wedding party emerged they found him waiting on the steps in his tux with frost on his shoulders like a chilled bottle of Black & White. But he looked no worse than the best man, Nino Torkie, who had rented his tux with the assurance that one size fit all.

Stu popped up among the bridesmaids and caught the

garter. He had returned to his old fetish after contracting genital herpes from one of the women who had accepted his introductory offer. That his ancestor, Samuel Moon, had gotten syphilis two hundred years earlier from a single experience with a deaconess was unknown to him, and he blamed Harry for his condition. Harry had somehow blocked him from regaining his sexual energy, and he had done it in such a way as to turn him off women forever. Of course, Stu had never had any sexual energy to begin with (Stanley's aphrodisiac had only stimulated him psychologically), but he scored it as a loss and blamed Harry. Standing now among the bridesmaids he felt like a white blood cell surrounded by infection; all around him were aggressive, inflamed clitorises.

Nicki was awaiting trial for grand theft auto and was the only one not at the reception. The Stenners of Chewbagin had arrived on three separate trains, the last of which, to Harry's delight, bore Jules, wearing his Roman collar and granting last rites to the caboose. When Jules recognized Stanley at the reception as the young man who had stayed outside on the steps of the church he asked him if he believed in God.

"Man, I believe in nature," Stanley answered.

"Piffle," said Jules.

"Nature is fundamental."

"Piffle."

"I tried church. It was a pain in the ass."

"Church? Church is the God-politics of man. I asked you if you believed in God. Church is a hiatus."

Stanley peered hard at him through his wire-rim glasses. He did not know what "hiatus" meant, but it sounded like a group sex act committed on drugs.

"Fundamental, man," he said.

"Piffle," said Jules and gave him last rites.

Alice stood stoically at the very center of the room. In her purse was the lone slipper the police had taken from Winslow the day he had used it on Nicki to punish him for stealing. It had been returned three months after Winslow's death, and she brought it to the wedding as a way of including him. It was a rather small room for a reception, but it seemed to her to go on forever. There were French windows and balconies on either side, and these resembled small gloomy stages on which various paradigms of her life were being played out. The actors and actresses had aged and become bigger than life; their smiles were exaggerated, their gestures flamboyant; and she wondered if this false joy, this charade of color and companionship, wasn't all for her benefit. She felt like the epicenter of events whose effects were beyond her, and thus she was responsible if not accountable. Winslow's death, Harry's passion, the hail on the church steps instead of rice—these facts accumulated like wrinkles and rust, like corrosive pieces of a jigsaw puzzle whose final distortion she dreaded. Was this a mocking or merely a test of her good intentions? Around and around her the insanity flowed, and the only other person in the room who seemed to understand this was incendiary Mr. Reske, equally frustrated, who hovered at the flash point of human flesh.

By this time Stanley had eaten half the inorganic trimmings on the cake and was feeling better than anyone else. The mother of the bride was named Jean, and as he deviated around the floor he periodically turned and shouted, "Hi, Jean!" For a while this brought smiles, but gradually it wore, until Mrs. Reske began to hunch with a distinctly ursine character each time she heard the voice. Mr. Reske, ever alert to dishonor, closed in.

"What do you mean by this, young man? Why are you shouting at my wife?"

"I was just practicing good hygiene," chirped Stanley. "Hi, Jean!"

"Who the hell do you think you are?"

"Man, my ancestors came over on the *Niña,* the *Pinta,* and the *Piña Colada.*" Finding a finger alongside his face that was not his own, Stanley hooked his nose over it.

The father of the bride's index finger was stuck up the groom's brother's nose, and it seemed to Mr. Reske that he had left his body and was observing this outstanding phenomenon. What kind of person hooked his nose over your finger? Did it matter what such people thought? Suddenly the young man's own middle finger rose into view and a voice laden with inflection said nasally, "Get pronged, man." Withdrawing his finger, Mr. Reske collared Stanley and aimed him toward the nearest balcony.

But Alice saw them coming and immediately divined the meaning of the false gregariousness all around her. It was because everyone hated her sons. She had once defended the heavyweight champion of the world; now her own flesh and blood cried out. Unsnapping her purse, she grasped Winslow's slipper and began rapping Mr. Reske on the head with it.

"Run for it!" she cried. Mr. Reske released Stanley and stared dumbfounded. "Run for it!" she shouted, slapping him across the skull this way and that. It occurred to her now that her finest moments had been violent ones—beating out the fire in Chewbagin, defending the champ—she was at the top of her form with aggression.

As she rapped away, the slipper began to lose flecks of leather and quickly dwindled into a twist of cardboard insole tufted with wool. The fact that Mr. Reske never moved, that Alice had a slipper in her purse to begin with, and that the instrument of assault was disintegrating in a rain of fluff left a comic uncertainty in the minds of the guests.

"Good God, Alice, you're beating the stuffing out of him!" her brother Harvey guffawed from one of the balconies, and everyone laughed tentatively.

"If we all picked each other's noses, we'd be too busy to fight," observed Stanley.

Alice discarded the useless insole, and a nervous calm was restored. "G-god b-bless us, ev-every one!" said cousin Donald. Then Harry and Carrie slipped away, and Jules magnanimously conferred last rites en masse and on the bride and groom in absentia.

"I can't wait!" Carrie said as soon as they got in the car.

"What do you mean you can't wait, we're in the middle of downtown."

"I want to do it now. I can't wait any longer."

"All right," he said. "But not here. We'll do it in the park."

It was the same park he had proposed to her in—if he had proposed at all.

"Hurry," she said. "Hurry, Harry."

They found a spot under a loquacious willow and hastily divested themselves of their burdens. Then they began opening the wedding presents.

"Electric can opener," she said.

"Sheets," he announced momentarily.

"Steam iron. Oooh, this is fun."

"Bedpan."

"Bedpan? That's a long-handled popcorn popper, dummy."

"Hah! Look what Stanley gave us."

"It's probably dope," she said, hefting the glassine bag.

"Probably an aphrodisiac."

"Useless."

"Look what Stu gave us."

"A six-pack of ginger ale and garter belts? Goody. Why are there corks in the bottles?"

It was still dusk, but a flashlight beam spilled over them, and the silence of an Orwellian society descended. The beam picked out details like an accusing finger. When it came to rest on the glassine bag, Harry said, "Hi, we just got married."

The policeman raised the bag and opened it for a sniff. "Good hashish," he said.

Carrie spent her wedding night listening to a sexual miscreant by the name of Easy Ethel describe her life of depravity. Harry's cell mate, named Sammy, smelled of sweat, urine, excrement, and certain fungi known to grow around toilet bowls and in Stanley's refrigerator. He spoke of disassembling cars and furnishings and stuffed toys; toward morning he cried a lot and it came out then that he had also dismembered seven people, one of which was for sure his mother and six others who may have been his father. He seemed to find candidates for this last relationship on a regular basis, and Harry was careful not to give him any paternal advice.

"This here's my tenth time in stir," Sammy said. "I used to keep track on my toes, but I only got nine left." He took off his shoes for clarity. "They said I chopped off ol' number ten with a spade. Don't remember doin' it—I forget doin' things sometimes. You got all yer toes?"

"Yes!" Harry drew his feet together quickly.

"Mmm-hmm. Every one. Yup." And he laughed loosely for no reason. "Say, what's your name?"

"Harry."

"Harry? One of my fathers' names was Harry."

"Did I say *my* name was Harry? I meant my brother's name. He was Harry."

"Say," Sammy said, and the word sounded like it came out of a long cave, "maybe you're my uncle."

"Oh . . . I don't think so."

"How come?"

"Well, for one thing, I'm white and you're black."

"Couple of my daddies was white."

"Was one of the white ones named Harry?"

"Was one of 'em named Harry, was one of 'em named Harry—uh-uh. Nope. None of 'em was named Harry. They was George and Charlie."

"There, see? None of your white daddies was named Harry."

"So what?"

Harry looked into Sammy's eyes and saw that genetics was nonnegotiable.

"I got to think this out," Sammy said. "You stay put." He picked Harry up and hung him by his pants from a hook on the wall. Then he curled onto his bunk for a nap.

High up on the wall, Harry felt seraphic. A certain vertigo was present, and he thought he might either throw up or void his intestines. The important thing, he kept thinking, was to miss the sleeping homicidal maniac.

When Sammy finally awoke, he was clearheaded and contrite. "Why are you stuck to the wall?" he asked. "Did I do that? Tell the truth, did I do another bad thing?" He lifted Harry down and fluffed him like a pillow. "Sometimes I do bad things. Then I don't remember."

After the police determined his innocence and released him, Harry asked that the six bottles of ginger ale be delivered to Sammy; Carrie, likewise, left Stu's garter belts for Easy Ethel.

"It was dope, dope," she said when they reached the sidewalk. "Not an aphrodisiac. Dope. I spent my wedding night in jail because of your sicko brothers and their hashish and garter belts—my Gawd, what kind of family have I married into? I can hardly wait to meet Nicki."

"Hey, Harry,!" came down to them then, and from the sixth-floor cells an arm groped into sunlight.

"Say hello to Nicki," Harry said.

{16}

Alice went on the honeymoon; Harry and Carrie stayed home. Home was Alice's house, and despite the scorching August heat it seemed to contain the presentiments and fortifications of another season, as if Winslow's death had left it suspended in winter with the storm windows in place, the outside faucets turned off, the implements of summer rusting and webbed in the basement. Once a week one of the Fletcher children came and mowed the lawn. The water meter reader gave up after three knocks, but the unpaid paperboy called mournfully and pawed at the door like a neglected pet each evening. Inside, the newlyweds ate little, ignored the phone, and screwed each other's brains out.

"Oh, Harry, make me your sex machine!" Carrie pleaded. "Make me...make me...make me...."

Since most of their conversation came during intercourse, they learned to speak in rhythm, in passionate bursts and breathless stanzas.

"Darling...wouldyoulike...peasoup...orcrackersandlettuce...fordinner?"

"Lettuce...sweetheart."

"Lettuce...again?"

"Justlettuce."

"Gottakeepup... yourstrength...darling."

"Rabbits...eatlettuce."

When Alice came back she paid the paperboy and announced that she had bought a ski lodge in New Hampshire.

"It's very small," she said, "and very rustic. There are two tiny hills and a lot of trails. I plan to advertise for beginners and conservative types who like to be close to God."

Harry foresaw the end of his college education before it began and got a job delivering pizzas. Since the pizza parlor was next to a pharmacy, he got another job delivering prescriptions. This arrangement lasted only two days because he got confused and delivered a large anchovies and hot peppers to a woman who was dying of gastroenteritis and hemorrhoids. The drugstore fired him but the pizza parlor was forgiving. In future years he would often eat pizza at moments of adversity, and it would come to him that this simple food was the cultural dish of neurotics. During the mornings and afternoons he worked out with his AAU club. If he could go a decent 1500 in the Regionals he might be able to talk scholarship with Harvard or Cornell. He hadn't swum the 1500 since the summer before and even in half-assed shape was bound to improve. He worked harder than he had ever worked in his life, tapered six days, and when the big race came was only two seconds over his best 400 on the way out. Then at 1100 meters he began to tighten up. He was well ahead of his wildest dream at this point, but his arms were like lead and he dropped off so much in the last 400 that he finished with a mediocre time.

With a towel over his head he moved to the adjacent practice pool, throbbing and near tears.

"I'm proud of you, son," Alice said, kneeling above him. "I know how disappointed you are, but you worked too hard, and you had too little time, and you went out too fast, and none of those things are reasons to feel bad. You know you really don't need that scholarship. The ski lodge will pay for your college education. The lodge will pay for everything."

Carrie was waiting by his tote bag. "Thank God it's finally over," she said.

"What do you mean?"

She shrugged. "Get dressed and I'll meet you in front."

Going up the hill to the parking lot, he asked again, "What did you mean?"

"There's your mother," she said.

"What did you mean, 'Thank God it's finally over'?" he demanded that night in bed.

"Oh, come on, jock, hang it up." She laughed without humor.

"You mean quit?" He was up on one elbow now.

"Are you seriously thinking of swimming in college without a scholarship?"

"Why not?"

"Um. Has it occurred to you that you're married?"

"Lots of jocks are married."

"Oh. Do they stay married?"

"What are you saying?"

"I'm saying that you ought to give a teensie-weensie bit of consideration to the fact that you're a husband about to become a student about to become a father. Time to put away our toys and get serious about living, don't you think?"

The silence began to ring between them. "You want me to get a job, is that it? Well, I intended to get a job."

"And still work out? Maybe you can deliver pizzas between sets. Cheese, pepperoni, and chlorine—slightly soggy crusts. Way to go, Moon."

"What is it, the money? My mother's helping us out."

"Oh, yes, Momsie. Momsie pays the bills, forgives us when we're bad, and picks up the pieces when we've lost another race."

"You ungrateful bitch."

"End honeymoon."

The open wound they had become bled quietly in the dark for several moments.

"Carrie the bitch: get pregnant, get married, get lost," she said then. "Did you think I was going to sit in pool balconies forever? It's very exciting watching you go up and down. Want to know how many tiles there are on the balcony wall at the old alma mater? Oh, God, I hope hell isn't watching a conveyor belt of swimmers flopping over every twenty-five yards."

"Maybe *you* should go to college," he said.

"Maybe *you* should have the baby!"

She was worrying about the baby, he thought. That was it. That was why she was making these demands. "The baby isn't due until March," he said.

She grabbed his hand and put it on her belly. "March is when it happens for you. It's happening for me right now."

If it was there, he couldn't feel it. A baby was still just an idea, a prophecy. He was falling slowly through space again.

"Oh, Harry, I know what swimming means to you. Haven't I always been there? But it was just a...a way of proving your manhood, a rite of passage, and now you are a man. You don't need it anymore."

Rite of passage? To a descendant of Jonathan Moon water was a destination.

"I can't quit," he said.

"I don't see that you have any real choice," she said.

The next day the coach at Ross State Teachers College called and offered him tuition and books.

They got an apartment off campus that was surrounded by water on three sides—two open ditches and a storm culvert. Since the apartment was decorated in early ocean liner style and approachable only by a broken walkway suggestive of continental drift, Harry felt buoyant and at ease while Carrie was all at sea. Alice paid the rent and floated weekly "loans." It was a muggy fall, and great swarms of mosquitoes came up from the ditches night after night. Harry filled the holes in the screens with wallpaper paste as he papered their bedroom and when they woke the next morning it looked like someone with a very bad cold had spat through every window. Carrie made him poke the gobs out with a pin, and that night the mosquitoes were back.

"It's too bad we can't just donate all this blood to the Red Cross," she said, flailing between her shoulder blades.

He brushed her back. She was naked, and he thought he detected the tiny blur of the carnivore's flight against the paleness of her hip. He brushed there, too.

She turned over and ran her hand down to his roots.

"Haven't initiated this bed yet," he said and slid two fingers between her knees. "Going up."

"You certainly are."

He caressed her quietly then, barely within the hair at the base of her belly, and she responded by opening and arching toward him. He kissed her swollen breasts and grasped her buttocks beneath him. Already they seemed to flex together like a hand in a glove. He worried that he might hurt the baby, that his passionate thrusts might puncture her womb like a balloon.

"Tell me...tell me if it's too hard," he panted.

"Oh-h, Harry," she moaned and dug her nails into his shoulders.

Suddenly there was a loud explosion. They both felt it. He yanked out and rolled free. "Carrie!" he cried.

"What the hell was that?" she enunciated clearly.

"It wasn't you?"

"Do I look like I'm packing a heater? Of course it wasn't me. It sounded like the walls were coming down." She had the light on by this time.

"I thought your womb had blown up."

"Dumb, Moon. Must've been outside."

They turned off the light and resumed petting. He traced his nails down her sides, and she started snickering.

"Know what I thought?" she said. "I forgot you weren't wearing a rubber, and I thought it blew up!"

He stopped tracing. "We've never had to use a rubber."

"So what?"

"So, what do you mean you forgot I wasn't wearing one, like . . . like you're used to doing it that way?"

She "tsk-ed" her tongue off her teeth.

"Are you?"

"Am I what?"

"Used to doing it that way?"

"Oh, sure. I'm practically vulcanized."

"God, Carrie. I thought . . . I thought—"

"You thought what, that I was a virgin? Like Heather maybe, huh?" She laughed scornfully. "Good ol' Heather, the virgin queen. You men are all alike. You're so proud of yourselves you can't imagine any other hunters getting off their shots before you have us stuffed and mounted."

"'You men are all alike,'" he repeated slowly. "I think I married a demo."

"Listen, Moon—" she got out before a second explosion stopped them cold.

On went the light, and they scrabbled around the mattress back to back like a couple of children lost in the forest.

"Over there," she said, "it came from over there. It's the wall. It's crumbling. We've been hit by an earthquake and an aftershock. I'm getting out of here." She snatched the sheet and fled.

Harry got dressed. He put on clean underwear and socks, a white shirt and tie, and his best suit. He brushed his shoes, his teeth, and his hair and neatly arranged a handkerchief in his breast pocket. From out on the broken walkway he heard her whisper huskily for him to bring her clothes. Swathed in white and spanking in the breeze, she looked exceedingly chaste, he thought. The sheet whistled as she struck down mosquitoes. He ambled out and said, "Wheat paste."

"Are you out of your fucking mind?" she whined. "I've been standing here semaphoring for half an hour."

"Wheat paste," he said. "I used it on prepasted wallpaper and it sucked all the moisture out. The paper exploded."

The paper continued to explode for a day and a night, but they didn't make love again for six weeks.

This first period of abstinence was conducted along the lines of two types of war: cold and guerrilla. The cold consisted of moves and countermoves, omissions, indictments, and provocations. For example the indictment form might find him doing dry land exercises while she ate ice cream and watched TV. To countermove, she might then add a cleaning solvent to the toilet tank. This kept him from diagnosing his urine. Bright yellow meant he was dumping vitamin C, a green tint was B-complex, orange meant dehydration and fatigue, but when Harry studied the bowl now he had to subtract the blue. Guerrilla warfare, on the other hand, was just sniping. It might be a one-liner, or it might develop insidiously.

"Why did you cut your pork chops into geographical shapes?" she asked one night.

"What geographical shapes?"

"South America, I believe."

"All pork chops look like South America."

"Is it your history course? Are you studying the southern hemisphere? Have you discovered the broad concepts of the Monroe Doctrine? Or is it some hot little tamale from Rio in your English class?"

She found Vietnam in his meat loaf, the Rock of Gibraltar in a chicken breast, and an omelet form of the Canary Islands.

He sniped back at her culinary arts but only in front of company, where he felt safe from swift and violent reprisal. "This is my wife's favorite dish," he might say, raising a well-fried drumstick, "chicken-gone-to-hell. Wait'll you try the char-broiled salad and the killer hors d'oeuvres." He was particularly hard on poultry. "Have some chicken nodule soup," he would offer. "Rooster cancer isn't contagious."

When she found out he hated carrots, she couldn't buy enough of them. Alice gave her the whole story of the battle to save his eyesight after Winslow had galloped him into the arch, along with the recipe for carrot creole that the TV talk show host had published, and Carrie served carrots at every meal. Harry used the raw ones for doorstops.

As a last act of insolence, he took her aluminum baking nails and hammered their mattress to the box spring. "Maybe that'll heat up our bed," he said.

This was an indictment-conciliatory snipe, and Carrie knew when she heard it that he wanted nooky. "Mushrooms remind me of penises," she said one evening as they walked along a damp path behind the library. "Little penises sticking up out of the ground, ready to shoot off their spores. Do you ever feel like shooting off your spores?"

"All the time."

"Well . . . ?"

And they did it right there on the cold, damp ground among the mushrooms.

"Oh, Harry," she cried afterward, "six weeks out of our lives; how could we? What's happening to us? You go to workouts in the morning instead of sharing breakfast with me. Then you go to class, then you go to workouts instead of coming home to talk to me."

"You could come to workouts with me."

"That's not sharing. What kind of a relationship is that? You want me to be a spectator to your life."

A spectator to his life. That was the way they had gotten close. Why hadn't he seen then that it was just her maidenly game?

There were several dozen married couples enrolled at Ross State and living in the apartments around campus, and Harry didn't know any who were getting along. They were like naughty children who had committed sex or precociousness or stupidity and been banished to a land of crumbling walkways and torn screens to serve out their immaturity. Their unmarried counterparts romped on a giant playground called campus, committing indiscretions and lunacy, seemingly sanctioned and forgiven beforehand simply because they were confined and single. Harry thought about these things at workouts. He was easily the most accomplished swimmer in the subdued program at Ross State, and Coach Reinke and the team held him in awe. That Harry knew more about interval training and fluid mechanics, about technique and pace and kinesiology than even the coach was taken for granted, but when they went into the dual meet season and he still hadn't tapered, Reinke asked him what the hell he was doing.

"What the hell are you doing?" he said. "You were swimming distance when I got here this morning, and you loosened up at least two miles this afternoon, and then you swam an hour straight at the end of practice. If you don't cut down soon, your fillings will rust. I don't want a rusted, waterlogged freestyler when we go down to Clairmont this Friday."

"Tell you what," Harry said with polite arrogance. "First time I get beat I'll cut out everything but the posted workout."

He wasn't going to get beat in this league, and he needed those long swims. He was a purist, an agonist, and something—the rhythm, the cardiovascular intensity, the priming of his muscles with heated, potent blood—spoke of universal consciousness and linked him to a flow of time and energy that need not be understood. So he swam on, away from Carrie, away from immaturity, destination unknown. But along the way he took Heather Latko.

Meanwhile Carrie suffered hemorrhoids, varicose veins, backache, puffiness, shortness of breath, mosquito bites, sexual abstinence, and her husband's sniping. But she didn't suffer loneliness. Harry's obsession with swimming was just the last hurrah of an unfulfilled ego, she thought. It was only the fact that he could be so totally distracted from a fresh marriage, impending fatherhood, and the responsibilities that now faced them which worried her. She had never wanted more than Harry. He was dumb but gentle of heart and one of the few eligible males who had never regarded her as a mammillary freak. If this was aiming low, it was because a husband was not the focus of her life but a prerequisite. They would be quite happy together, she felt, once he gave up his hobby and got a decent job and the baby was born. "*I* am out of circulation; *I* am not attending college; *I* am bearing a child for us," she reminded him. "*You* are *swimming*."

She hated to nag, to point out her sacrifices, but she wasn't going to be his second mother. Then in December she found a crisis to solve the crisis.

The day broke cold and gray, a catatonic extension of the foregone night, and she felt pains immediately on rising.

He looked at her uncertainly. "You okay?"

"Sure."

He shrugged. "Well, I'm going to practice."

"Keep in touch"—she smiled—"with reality."

"What does that mean?"

"It means don't let me stop you."

He didn't.

By eight thirty she discovered she was bleeding; the pains were like contractions. She called the doctor at home, and because he was going to the hospital late he actually stopped by. He gave her a cautious pelvic exam, ordered her to stay in bed, administered a shot of estrogen, and left some phenobarbital. Harry was supposed to be back before his ten o'clock class, so the doctor left.

At ten thirty she took the sedative.

When Harry came back at four he saw the breakfast dishes as he had left them, then the towel with the blood on it and a medical syringe on top of the garbage. She was in the bedroom, as gray and catatonic as the day.

Despite fatigue, she caught every nuance of the collapse in his face. "The doctor gave me a shot," she said. "The baby has a fifty-fifty chance."

He sagged beside her. Hung his head. Raked his fingers through his hair.

She drew her hand across her belly. "I need a prescription filled for secobarbital," she said. "And I'd appreciate it very much if you'd leave me alone. The smell of chlorine makes me sick."

Her crisis dragged through Christmas, and Harry never left the house except to shop for groceries. When the doctor who had ordered her to bed ordered her out of it again, she rose up blazing.

"I suppose you're going back to the pool now," she said. "I suppose it doesn't mean a thing to you that you nearly lost the two people who depend on you."

She cried then and apologized, and he was more struck by her apology than her anger. It was New Year's Eve, and he hadn't planned on working out that day, but late in the afternoon there was a knock on the door.

"Hey, Moon, it's me, Nino!" Nino announced when Harry opened it. There was something more than typical redundancy in this. Some note of sadness, of a stark plea for existence, as if the young man standing there—whiter and thinner than Harry had ever seen him—was in danger of extinction.

"Nino!" He laughed. "Hey, Carrie, look, it's Nino!"

"I hitchhiked up," Nino said, jerking his thumb. He tried to smile at Carrie but seemed embarrassed by her pregnancy. "Can't afford no car yet. I'm workin' at Ollie's Sunoco now."

"Ollie's. Son of a gun."

"I ain't workin' out no more." He flung his hand up in a cavalier way and avoided Harry's eyes. "Maybe next year. Maybe I can go to night school and then junior college. Gotta get the ol' grades up."

There wasn't going to be any next year, Harry knew. Even tutored he would have been ineligible after one term. "It's good to see you, Nino," he said.

"Hey, how about you? Tore up all the pool records already?"

"One or two."

"Yeah." Nino laughed and jangled all around. "I knew you would. I been tellin' everyone Harry Moon is famous by now."

Carrie drummed on the refrigerator.

"Nice apartment you got here," Nino said. "Say, ya think I could see the pool?"

They walked to the IM building. A few students were out in long knit scarves and wool coats, walking with their heads down and a sense of preoccupation and purpose that rendered Nino implausible in his grimy work shoes and exaggerated gait. He made a snowball and threw it a mile, and Harry thought how free he was and how ignorant of that freedom.

Harry produced his own key on the steps to the IM building, and they went inside. Cathedral-like space fell away from them in three directions. Harry led him down the middle corridor, the echoes of their steps seeming to extend their presence.

"If I'd known it was like this...if I'd just known," Nino kept saying. He ran his hand along the tiles, the shower fixtures, the scales, whirlpools, and steamroom doors.

"This is my locker," Harry said.

"J-Thirty-four."

"Want to swim?"

A wild, anxious look crossed Nino's face. "I forgot my suit."

Nino would have swum nude in the White House pool in front of Lady Bird Johnson. Besides, there were several suits in the locker. He was afraid to get in the water, Harry realized, afraid to show how out of shape he was.

"I just wanna watch," Nino said. "You go right ahead and work out, ol' buddy. Never mind me. I wanna say I saw Harry Moon work out. So you go right ahead. I'll just sit in the balcony and watch."

Harry felt tremendously sad. He put on his suit, and neither of them spoke again. The pool had a bulkhead and a diving well and spacious stands on either side. Nino climbed slowly to the top and Harry turned on the underwater lights. The pale green suffusion reached only to deck level. If he had looked up, Harry could scarcely have distinguished the phantom at the top of the stands.

Nino watched with a fierce pride. There was Harry turning over like a well-oiled machine, hitting his turns with a vengeance, driving off the walls, splitting the green fire. In the gloom at the top of the stands his own hands looked faded and ghostly, but he could see every atom of Harry Moon. A half hour passed, an hour, two. Then Nino understood. None of the savants on campus would have understood, but Nino did. He rose up slowly and plodded down the steps to the rail.

"Hey Moon," he shouted, "don't stop! I got to go now, but you keep on goin', okay?" Nino knew how important it was to keep going and never stop. If you stopped you were through. "I got to go now...but don't you stop. Don't ever stop...okay? Good-bye, Moon...." He swung over the rail and moved slowly down the deck.

Harry kept going and going, but Nino Torkie looked back once and was gone.

ERRORS
OF
THE
MOON

{17}

When Alice invited her boys up to see the lodge, they came. But they came one at a time over a period of four years, as if each required his own winter. The lodge itself was going great guns. There were five overnight cabins and a large parking lot for day skiers. Alice stayed up at the main building, renting equipment and collecting trail fees. She cleaned and stocked the cabins herself, kept the books, and built a fire if the temperature dipped into the teens. Now and then she took a day off, or went shopping, and on these occasions a retired grocer down the hill held the reins for her. Skiers seemed to be healthy, wholesome people, and there was little that couldn't run itself. This was contrasted by the moral decay of her sons, whose annual arrivals made her wonder if God wasn't balancing her books.

First came Nicki. After his parole officer gave him permission to travel, Nicki got into his Lincoln Continental and drove north. Outside Fitchburg, he was stopped for speeding and given a ticket. The ticket was made out to Millard Fillmore, which is what his ID said. When he crossed the state line into New Hampshire he pulled into a rest stop, changed license plates, and took another wallet out of the trunk. He did this with a conciliatory air, as if in his own fashion he was following the rules of the game, bending in an obverse way to the laws of state and society. The concept was tested just north of Concord. This time he was pulled over for a burned-out brake light, and the ticket was made out to Ulysses S. Grant.

"Unusual name," said the officer. "You're called after some general, aren't you?"

"A Greek admiral," said Nicki.

The rest of the trip was uneventful. "My son, my son!" Alice exclaimed when her presidential conglomerate arrived. "It's about time. Where have you been? Where have any of you been? Do you know, you're the first one to come. The first born and the first to come."

"Gosh," said Nicki.

"Have you seen Harry's baby yet?"

"No."

"Sit down and I'll show you her pictures."

Nicki sat down and stared at his mother while she ooh-ed over Harry's baby girl, born two weeks earlier. When this was done, Alice collected her maternal gushings into the photo envelope and folded her hands.

"Now, what are you up to?" she asked.

"Selling insurance," he said, unwrapping a stick of gum.

"Insurance? What kind of insurance?"

"All kinds."

This was partially true. If you wanted your house to suffer wind damage, for instance, Nicki would come out with a sledge-hammer and rupture your awnings. He had a touch for this and could just as well work on your aluminum siding with a ball peen hammer to simulate hail. Just last week he had burned down a garage without even scorching the attached house.

"Oh, good," Alice said. "You can sell me a policy."

"Actually, I promote insurance. Someone else does the selling."

Her eyes narrowed then, and the brilliant light that had filled her face since his arrival fell to the twilight of the room.

Nicki snapped his fingers. "Almost forgot." He went out to

the car, and when he came back he had a beautiful full-length fur coat. "Here," he said, "try this on."

"Oh, Nicki. It's—" She broke off, caught between ecstasy and suspicion.

"It's *real*," he finished for her.

She slipped it on, her eyes remaining downcast. "But... where did you get it?"

He chewed gum furiously for a moment. "Oh, I've got a friend who raises them in his apartment. He buys insurance from us."

"An apartment? He raises them in his apartment?"

"Just on the side. He's also got a farm. I get them for a song."

Alice dropped her arms to her sides and the sleeves fell over her hands.

Nicki laughed. "Guess it's a little long. Take it off."

She took it off and he flashed out the door. A minute later he was back wearing a coat of his own, carrying another over his arm. "Try this," he said.

"You've got three coats?"

"Well, I had to get the right size."

"Your friend gives them to you for a song, you said. He has a farm, you said."

"Hell, he's got minks running all over the place. A coat or two is nothing to a mink farmer."

"Mink?" Alice seemed to find direction. "But these are silver fox."

Nicki stopped chewing. "Yeah. Silver fox. That's right. He raises silver foxes in the apartment, I think. They're running all over the place there too. You can't raise minks with silver foxes. The minks would eat them."

He was chewing furiously again.

Alice slung the coat over her shoulder and went to the closet. She reached in, extracted a shotgun, and passed quietly outdoors. Seconds later there was a loud concussion. Nicki swallowed his gum. The second report seemed to free him up, and he ran out the door screaming, "What the hell are you doing?"

What she was doing was blasting his "minks." She had hung the coat on a branch, and now it lay in tufts and thatches all over the snow. Turning slowly, she fixed her eyes on the garment he wore and began to reload.

"Maybe you'd like to take that one off before I put it out of its misery," she said.

"Are you crazy?"

The breech slammed shut and the twin barrels came up. "So much for common sense," Alice said. "You never had a lick of it anyway."

"Mom, it's me!" Nicki shouted.

"Stand fast."

"Oh, my God! Mom!" He ran into the woods like a gigantic flying squirrel in the huge flaring coat.

She tramped after him until his flight faded into the deep interiors of the forest she loved; then she returned and walked slowly around the Continental. This, too, was part of his misbegotten gains, she realized, and, leveling the 16-gauge, she first put out the windshield, then peppered the trunk. The trunk shot also atomized the remaining brake light. Late that night as she lay in bed she heard the engine leap to life and the wheels spin down the driveway. "Insurance!" she said. "I'll take a hundred thousand term on you, Nicki."

Next came Stu. This was ten months later. He arrived in a yellow Mercury, wearing new shoes, socks, boots, suit, gloves, hat, and one of Nicki's fur coats. The clothes had a precast quality about them, like a cocoon, and the watch, the ring, and the mirrored sunglasses he wore hung from his flesh like radiant shrapnel. All this hastily acquired opulence rendered him as fresh and bright as a butterfly. The yellow Mercury was, in fact, a Monarch, and Stu was on his maiden flight to celebrate metamorphosis and renounce past failures.

To finance this he had begun to blackmail the three wives who had taken advantage of his neighborhood introductory offer. Since one of them had given him genital herpes, he felt justified. He knew that if it was Mrs. Prittikin, the other two were not guilty, and if it was one of the other two, then he had in all likelihood passed the gift that keeps on giving to the remainder, but in his self-righteousness he felt he need not be selective toward fallen women and so blackmailed all three.

Alice noted the car, the coat, the boots, the hat, the gloves, and the sunglasses and immediately felt sorry for him. She knew from these and other signs that Stu had become more perishable than ever. There was nothing to him now but the gloss he had donned, not even the prosaic honesty of hope he once had. His expectations were snuffed out like a candle, his tears turned to wax dribbles, the oily after-smoke descending over him and imparting a thin sheen, a smoke screen that hid his ashes.

He stood in the driveway, ceremoniously removing his gloves.

"Some lodge," he conceded, nodding in a general way.

"Some son," Alice said. "So many new things—did you rob a bank?"

Stu tossed his head. He wondered why she had to ask that question first. Finally he said in a drawn-out way, "No-o. No, no, no."

"Good. Leave the bank robbing to Nicki. Where *did* you get all these things?"

"I sell insurance." He said this almost before she got the question out. "Hey, where is everybody?"

"A few are in the cabins, most are on the trails. You should see it on weekends. Did you bring your skis?"

The car was obscured by branches and shadows, and she couldn't tell if it had a rack.

"No," he said.

"Well, I've got plenty of equipment. You can take a rental pair."

Stu turned and whistled. The car door opened and a girl came crunching through the snow out of the shadows. She was at least six feet tall, 190, and built like an amazon beneath her red ski sweater and tapered white slacks.

"This is Daisy," Stu said.

"Hi," said Daisy in a well-marinated voice, and Alice smelled cigarettes and rum.

"Daisy and I are engaged," Stu said, but seemed not to share the spirit of this good news with his betrothed.

"How wonderful," said Alice.

The young couple skied all afternoon and when they returned to the lodge Alice showed them pictures of "Harry's baby." Stu kept nodding, but Alice sensed that his attention, like his fussiness with removing gloves, was merely kinetic energy over a vacuum. Stu was miming life; his instincts were toward some dark and impossible existence.

"I suppose all this talk of babies is a bore," she said. "Don't mind me, I'm a deprived grandmother who's sick of snow conditions, the weather, and the wax of the day."

"I like babies," Daisy said.

"Well, isn't that nice. Maybe you'll provide me with a conversation piece or two after you're married."

Stu grinned and tossed his head again. It was as if his neck hurt and he loved pain. "We're not rushing into things," he said. "Daisy comes from a very conservative family."

Daisy cleared her throat. "You wouldn't happen to have a bathroom, would you?"

"No," said Alice, a little annoyed. "We go in the snow. Of course we have a bathroom. We've always had a bathroom. It's down the hall and left through the kitchen."

"We're not too sure about children yet," Stu said when she was gone. "Daisy has sensitive ears."

"Well, buy her some plugs. What would the planet Earth be if everyone had sensitive ears?"

"Quiet?" Stu guessed.

"Very. I'm going to get us some tea."

She rose and went to the kitchen, but before she could fill the kettle she was arrested by the sound of Daisy urinating in the toilet. It was a sound she hadn't heard since Winslow died. Either the girl was a cow or she was standing up. Compelled by a force greater than propriety, Alice grasped the knob and pushed the door open.

"Does Stu know?" she asked.

"We never got that far," Daisy rumbled. "He just likes to sniff my underwear."

"That's all you two do?"

"Is there anything else?"

"Lord help us if there is."

She dreaded Stanley's visit. She knew it would come the following winter. Whatever was happening was following the sequence and spacing of their births. She saw not that the fatalism she had scorned as cowardice in Winslow was real and apparently contractible. She imagined it as a chalky spirit, dislocated by his death and coming to rest in her. She had taken it lightly that awful summer in Vermont with her boys, believing it to be an eccentric season, but Nicki's criminality had become as irreversible as his puberty, and Stu's depravity was also permanent. What hope was there for a boy who had read *Popular Mechanics* for the dirty pictures? There was no accounting for this. It went beyond the reach of God and motherhood, dimly associated with accidents of perception.

So Stanley came at the appointed hour the next year, and lo, he had become a terrorist. Aided by hallucinogenic visions from gods with long chemical names, he had come to grips with politics and formed a worldview that included kidnapping, bank robbery, extortion, assassination, and pipe bombs. These were the holy tools of a new world order, he assured her. Revolution was inevitable, and the end would more than justify the means.

"What end?" she wanted to know.

"Justice for the masses. Death to the fascist pigs." He was the same old unexcitable Stanley; there was something insincere and marionette-like in the rhythm of his gestures.

"At least you don't sell insurance," Alice said. "But you sound like the Committee to Hold Hands at the Equator. Is that what you are?"

"They were ignorant children," he said. "We've got to get out of Vietnam and stop meddling in people's revolutions."

"Your father fought in World War Two," she said.

"I love K rations."

"Are we still talking, son?"

"I don't know."

Outside, large snowflakes were falling, and it seemed as though the world were coming apart in silent, bloodless chunks.

"Do you miss your father? Why didn't you come to his funeral?"

"Funerals are no fun, and there's nothing to eat there."

She waved her hand in front of his eyes.

"I bought Dad an electric grave blanket," he said. "The flowers all light up in their centers when you push a button. Did you see it?"

"No. I don't go back there anymore."

"Batteries probably dead now anyhow."

"I don't understand Nicki," Alice said after a pause. "And I don't understand Stu. But I'd like to understand you, son. What is it you want to give to the world?"

"Peace," he said. "And tolerance." Nodding for a moment, he added, "And love. Why can't we love each other?" Just then a black car swept up the drive, and Stanley dropped to his knees. "Oh, Mom, they're after me. Help me get away."

"Who are they?" Alice asked in dismay. "What have you done?"

He looked soulfully into her eyes, whispering confessionally. "I've tried to bring peace and tolerance and love to the world. But those men out there don't want it. They're fascist CIA pigs, and they're after me for stealing dynamite in New Jersey."

Alice blanched. She didn't remember rising to her feet, but she stood there swaying and pointing to the rear of the lodge. "The skis," she said.

Stanley bolted. "The revolution thanks you!" he called from the hallway.

He had the boots on before the agents finished circling his car, and by the time they entered the lodge he was wrestling a down vest, poles, and skis out the backdoor. Whether or not his mother slowed them down, he never knew, but he got the vest and skis on at the head of the trail before he heard the order to halt. The trail dropped sharply right off the bat, and he double-poled frantically into a dip and a loop. At the top of the first rise a shot rang out. The bullet passed cleanly through the side of his loose-fitting vest, but he fell from sheer fright. He felt he had been hit and that his very essence was flowing out of him. Actually it was goose down that was flowing out of him. Two years earlier his brother Nicki had fled along these same paths as a flying squirrel, and now Stanley soared through the forest like a gigantic molting bird.

The snow seemed to be closing in on him, and he was scarcely surprised when it bit off the end of his ski pole. He had blundered off the trail where denizens of the deep lurked like sharks under the crust. He pulled out the pole, and it was just a gnawed stick. The rest of it was stuck in a coyote trap, but Stanley knew only that Mother Nature was a fascist. With one pole, and trailing feathers like a sliced pillow, capture was inevitable.

"You should've sold insurance like your brothers," Alice told him wearily when they brought him back to the lodge.

A year was barely enough to get ready for Harry's visit. That there would be such a visit over and above her own trips to Ross State and her children's reciprocal journeys home in the off-season, Alice was sure. Harry would come alone and in crisis. It might be a decision to quit school, a pending divorce, terminal illness, or—darkest of possibilities—something wrong with the baby. So consumed was Alice now with the rhythm of fate that she sought only to disrupt its liturgical chant, to break its dreary claim on the calendar of her life.

When Harry inevitably arrived on a ponderous day of a dogmatic week in March, she threw a streamer at him, tooted a party horn, played a tape of "Pomp and Circumstance," and presented him with the keys to a new Chevy Malibu.

"There's a baby seat in the trunk," she said.

Harry's eyes glistened. "You put me through school. Why this?"

"Because you're almost matriculated. It's a graduation present."

"Mom...Mom." He shook his head. "I don't want to seem ungrateful, but you should've given it to one of the others."

"Pooh," she said. "You can't drive a Chevy in cell block twelve. The last time I saw Nicki, you could've parked this car in the trunk of his. Without opening it," she added, remembering her last blast with the shotgun. "And Stanley, he doesn't need a car, he needs a tank. He says he's going to lead an army against the Pentagon when he gets out of Lewisburg. I wrote and asked him whatever happened to the gentle Stanley who said everything was natural, and he wrote back, *Don't piddle with the noncommittal.* What would he do with a car? Load it with TNT and park it on Pennsylvania Avenue, that's what he'd do."

"Stu could use it."

"Look, son, I'm not doing this just for you. Actually I wanted to buy a baby seat for Stephanie, and the car was attached. If Stu ever fathers a child—if Stu ever fathers anything —I will buy him the Cadillac division of General Motors. Now enough of this. I wanted you to have a great time when you finally came to see the lodge."

This was closer to the truth than any of the other reasons she gave for her generosity, but Harry hung his head and seemed too despondent for cheering. It was exactly what she feared.

"I won't have any long faces here," she said. "You'll infect the tourists. New Hampshire law forbids pessimism. Now, I want you to pick out some skis and boots back there and hit the trails. Get some fresh air in your head, and when you come back we'll have a nice visit. You have no idea what a little snow and silence can do for you. God talks to you out there. It's a religious experience. Stanley even tried it when he was here, and I do believe he heard God."

Harry looked a little livelier after this description. "Why don't you come with me?"

She looked at him blankly. "I don't ski," she said.

He was gone two hours and came back refreshed. It was the old paradox of exhaustion and renewal. "I haven't had a workout like that since I quit swimming." He sighed.

"You never should've quit, Harry. It kept you vital and looking ahead. I always felt you quit because of me, so you could get that job at McDonald's and pay for your own groceries."

"I told you the truth, Mom. It was because of Carrie." He drummed his fingers on the Naugahyde couch. "And she was right."

"Nonsense. A young bride feeds on attention and sacrificial offerings. After a while you learn that what's good for one is usually good for both."

"Well, it hasn't worked out that way."

She waited. Harry drummed.

"It's my gambling," he said at last. "I don't lose much. But I lose."

"Oh," Alice said, almost relieved.

"I started out just playing poker at the dorms—nickel-dime stuff. Then it was sports, never more than a buck or two. I can't resist a raffle ticket, pinball, or pool. If someone goes to Las Vegas, I give them five dollars to roll for me. I buy Irish Sweepstakes tickets and lottery tickets from any state in the Union. *Reader's Digest* and the Ramolo Missions send me stuff by special courier, and I've never won a damn thing. Even when I worked at McDonald's, I took my salary out in french fries, malts, and Big Macs just so I could keep collecting bonus game cards, but I couldn't get the *O*. Last year I joined the church so I could play bingo. I've even bet on traffic lights, menus, and the weather. I always say a little prayer to God to let me win, and sometimes I do, but then I just keep on betting till I lose."

"Is there anything you don't bet on?"

"The stock market and UFOs."

Alice regarded him thoughtfully, unable to divine the connection between all this speculation and his fatalism. "And it's ruining your marriage?"

"I don't know. I guess. If you gave me odds, I'd bet we'll split by the end of summer. Carrie doesn't understand."

"Understand what?"

Harry looked at her a little surprised. There were some things that were either self-evident or beyond comprehension; you couldn't communicate them. "How I feel when I've got a bet riding," he said.

Alice wanted to ask how but recognized the strain on her credibility as a listener. She looked to the fireplace and Winslow's picture above it and the timbered pitch of the roof she had bought with his legacy and back to Harry's face. Over all swam an orange glow, as if they shared a common ether. And then she knew. Harry was fighting fatalism. The optimism she had labored to indoctrinate him with as a child was still there, struggling to stay alive. Despite what had happened, he was still the hope of the Moon family. Marriage, college, fatherhood, a job —these were his enemies. They had awakened him in the middle of a dream. He needed that dream. It was an assignation with his own potential, and it lay in some unknown realm at some unknown time. Perhaps it was success as an athlete. Who could say what urgings of his genes needed resolution? Maybe the instincts of a fish had been preserved through evolution to call insistently to Harry Moon. At any rate, he was not ready to subside in the mainstream, to become predictable and banausic. The future stretched before him as regular as a checkered tablecloth, and gambling was a rip right down the middle. That's what he got out of a bet riding.

"I understand, son," she said.

"Then what should I do?"

"Gamble. But don't win. You haven't found the right game yet."

｜18｜

Like smoke from Delphi, Alice's advice lay languidly on the air inviting interpretation and seeming to chart the future for Harry. This lasted until Carrie greeted him at the door, holding Stephanie's tiny worn-out oxfords. "Seven come eleven, baby needs a new pair of shoes," she said. Then the smoke vanished.

She had a way of making everything he did seem immature. She also left the impression somehow that she herself was soaring to ever-increasing heights of maturation and purpose. He was falling behind, he knew, in the race to grow up, in his integrity as a father, in his goodness and worth as a human being. She read voraciously and sat in on classes where attendance was not taken, so that her knowledge seemed broader and deeper than his and probably was.

"You're always throwing her up at me," he said about the baby. "Have I ever neglected her?"

His ugly tone provoked Stephanie's tears and he went off to the bedroom feeling guilty, angry, and defeated. The next morning he took two steps into the dining room and his feet went out from under him. Stephanie came and stood over him. "Daddy fall down," she said. He looked up into her blue eyes, pallid brow, and softly glowing hair and knew that whatever he said next must reflect both reason and the intensity of the moment. Beyond Stephanie he saw Carrie holding a can of Endust and a rag mop. She was smiling as though the knowledge that nothing sticks to Endust had just been given her by seraphic presences with light shining through them.

"Maybe we can buy Stephanie a pair of shoes with suction cups," he said.

"I'm sorry I took that cheap shot about your gambling."

"A bet is like fishing. You toss out a line and you never know what might come back."

"So, fish."

She bought him a Zebco rod and reel from K Mart at Easter, and he went out in May just to humor her. He had always considered the sport slow, sadistic, and unnecessary to the consumption of fish, so he took her favorite barrette off the dresser and used it for a lure rather than buying tackle. There were red daredevils, royal coachmen, gray ghosts, pork frogs, and hula poppers, but Harry had a gold barrette with a bent prong that plowed through the water like a submarine. When it wasn't plowing it sank to the bottom—a dense, inanimate piece of metal. But no matter where or how it went, fish stalked, struck, and leaped at it. The strikes came with such ferocity that he often had to disembowel the fish to get the barrette back. There seemed to be some mysterious demiurge never suspected in the antecedents of fish.

He kept trying new and less likely locations. By this time there were twenty seekers of enlightenment following the young man with the Zebco rod and reel and gold barrette lure. Eagerly they took his abandoned spots in their boots and boats, and one even tested a pool with his sonar fish detector only to shake his head. Harry's fascination with fish yielded to a dim fear of fishermen. What was this covetous and barbaric world of hooking limbless creatures?

In a gesture of reconciliation, he offered the mangled largesse of his labors to all takers. He was glad to get rid of them, these dead and dying fish with their cadaverous mouths and saturnine eyes. Finally, he traded a bass, iridescent with scales and blood, and a marled pike for two yellow carp and a hideously ugly sucker. These he took home to Carrie.

"Ugh," she said, "couldn't you have caught some fillet of sole?"

She put them on the porch and all the cats in the neighborhood came as the fishermen had.

Harry was pleased that he would never have to fish again, but he had hated cats ever since the accident with the taxi and the garbage cans which he had caused by stepping into the street with his 3-D glasses on. Carrie took in one of the strays for a pet. "Puddie," Stephanie called it. Carrie called it "Toots." Harry never called it at all. Naturally it liked him best. It prescribed figure eights around his legs with its tail held high, walked over his books as he tried to study, and slept on his chest. Smoke-gray hairs clung to his sweaters, his slacks developed snags, and nothing he ate was not first sampled by Toots. To top it off the cat suffered from some form of hard pad disease and clumped around the rooms like it had two pairs of jackboots on.

Harry bore it all until the morning he went in the bathroom to brush his teeth and there sat Toots licking his toothbrush. He decided to floss and gargle. Toots sat in the sink and batted the floss around as he sawed between his teeth. "Garrr-rrrgh," Harry went. His head was back, his eyes closed. In this position he completely forgot the cat. Bobbing forward, he spat in the sink and was instantly impaled. He must have screamed, because Carrie and Stephanie arrived immediately and the cat left.

His chest looked like a huge fuzzy strawberry, but all he heard was "Heah, Puddie," "Poor Toots." Over the tables and up the drapes, under the sofa and through their legs the cat shot, finally taking refuge in a paper bag. If Harry had left it at that, he might have come off merely lacerated and ignored. But in pain and anger he kicked the sack clear across the apartment.

There was no joy in Mudville that night. Toots fled to parts unknown. Harry slept on the sofa listening to a pair of sportscasters argue politics while singles, doubles, and stolen bases accumulated in the background. A piece of gauze crisscrossed with white tape covered his chest. He had suffered the fierce scrutiny of a three-year old, and guilt pursued him in his dreams, where he found himself interviewed by ABC News. "Our viewers would like to know if you kick your cat, Mr. Moon. Do you kick your cat? Did you kick poor 'Puddie' and make your daughter cry? Do you also beat your wife, Mr. Moon?" The camera rolled into his face and up his nose. There in the hollows of his sinuses the questioning continued: "Do you ever pick your nose, Mr. Moon? Have you ever had halitosis? How's your love life?" Other reporters were calling, the echoes of his name rebounding through his sinuses. He saw CBS and NBC peeking up his nostrils. "Mr. Moon, Mr. Moon, may we get the inside story, Mr. Moon?" He watched the dark shapes of cameras rolling toward him through his nose. "Hey, Harry—

may we call you Harry? Our viewers would like to know your side of it, Harry. Were you harassed, maligned, pressured, or goaded into kicking 'Puddie'? Are you a victim of society? Do you understand your rights? Was it the President's fault? So, you won't answer, eh? Hey! Hear that, America? Harold Moon denies you your right to know. Your First Amendment freedom is being abridged by Harold Moon. Let's hear it for Moon." In came a mighty, nasal swell: "Guilty! guilty! guilty!" "Now, Mr. Moon, perhaps you'll be more cooperative. Our viewers would simply like to know, do you hate Mommie? Do you ever masturbate? Would you break down and sob for us? May we take pictures of the inside of your bathroom?"

One of the reporters lit Harry's chest on fire, and he awoke with a shriek.

A blinding light stabbed into his face. "I just wanted you to know, if Toots doesn't come back, we're getting another cat," came Carrie's voice. In her left hand she brandished a flashlight and in her right the bandage from his chest hung, covered with hair.

The next day they held a funeral for Toots, and Harry was obliged to bow his head and pray aloud. On the third day Toots rose from the dead. Harry heard her hard pad on the porch: *clump ... clump ... clump.* The cat without grace was back.

"Here, pussy, pussy," he said that evening when the cat sat between Carrie's legs.

Carrie looked up into his eyes. "I'm sorry," she said. "I've been hard on you."

"We've been hard on each other," he said magnanimously. "I'm hard now."

"We've got to talk first, Harry."

"About what?"

"About everything. Why do you gamble?"

"For the same reason I swam."

"Why did you swim?"

He shrugged. "I need to do something great. No one in my family ever did anything great."

"The Moon family needs a savior, so you're going to run off and crucify yourself on craps tables every night?" She let that settle on him. "Don't you want to be close?"

"Of course I want to be close. I've always wanted to be close."

"Name one thing that shows you want to be close."

He thought about it a full minute. "When we first got married, I bought everything in pairs," he said. "That was because I was conscious of you."

"The reason you bought things in pairs was because sub-consciously you wanted to keep us separate—a jar of mustard for Carrie, a jar for you."

"I suppose the reason I bought things in triples after the baby was born was so that Stephanie could have her own jar of mustard."

"Could be. You're not really close to the baby either."

"Not as close as you, that's for sure."

"And what's that supposed to mean?"

"Just that you always complained about being a spectator to my life, and now you're making yourself a spectator to Stephanie's."

"It goes with the hormones, Moon," she said, getting very dusky. "I'll get over it in fifteen or twenty years!"

"*You* name one thing that shows you want to be close to *me*," he said then. "When have you ever cared that I had personal goals since we got married?"

"Magazines," she said promptly.

"What?"

"I used to read all the magazines you read so that we had something to talk about."

"We should've read different magazines, I don't remember us talking much."

They sat staring at far-flung points in the room until the sting subsided.

"All right, Harry," she said then. "I'll tell you what we can share. You give up gambling and I'll run with you. I'll leave Stephanie at the day care center and we'll run." She moved into his lap and ran her hand inside his shirt. "In the meantime, I'm going to take a hot bath."

All she had to say was "*hot* bath" and he stiffened like a pointer. The thought of his wife's sexual parts immersed in water had him half liquefied already, and he beat down his resentment of what she was extracting from him in the way of change. Running was not the answer, running would not replace swimming or gambling, because he would never win at it. But now the Samson in him was lying down, and Delilah was taking a bath.

When they actually did run in the next few weeks, she

· 144 ·

nagged him to slow down and afterward walked around for an hour hunched over as if someone had punched her in the stomach. "I love it," she wheezed, though it was clear that what motivated her was a force as elemental and negative as hate.

Harry hated it too. "I've found someone to run with us," he announced brightly one afternoon.

"What for?" she demanded suspiciously.

"For inspiration, for social intercourse."

"Intercourse, eh? What's her name?"

"Upsilon Lambda Phi."

"A whole frat? Are you out of your mind?"

The frat connection was an expatriate swimmer named Dan Dreiman with whom Harry had once worked out. He was now in premed and too busy to swim. He was blond, possessed a four-point average, and had a terrific smile.

"I'm Dan," he said to Carrie with a luster Harry had never seen before.

"Well, nobody's perfect." She shrugged and rapped the chandelier with her shoe, dislodging dust in Harry's lunch.

"My wife made some soup but it died," Harry said.

Dreiman continued to beam at Carrie, as if he had discovered a dark corner that needed lighting. "How do you like your new Pumas?" he asked.

"I prefer glass slippers."

"Hey, Dan, tell her about that red-headed professor who teaches humanities," said Harry.

"Schwendler?"

"Yeah. Schwendler. Tell her."

"It's not a mixed company story, Harry. I'd just embarrass Carrie."

"For crying out loud, Dan, this is my wife. Oh, all right, I'll tell it. You know that Professor Schwendler in humanities—straight as nails and all airs—well, guess who starred in last week's smoker at Upsilon Lambda? You got it, big as life and dressed like a horse."

"I like your shorts," Dreiman said to Carrie as if Harry had said nothing at all.

They drove to the starting place in front of the IM building. There were nine fairly trim males and a pair of whippetlike coeds on hand. The air smelled of burning green wood and rotting canvas, and as the runners stretched, a flock of ambulatory pigeons kept turning away.

Carrie stood with her arms crossed.

"If you fall behind just stay on the bike paths," Harry said. "We'll come back this way."

"Oh, don't worry about little old me, I'll just follow the gobs of spit."

He had done it. He had escaped, Harry thought. The running would no longer be a private act of fidelity between them, juxtaposed against his passions for swimming and gambling. But when he looked back and saw gallant Dan Dreiman, apparently resolved to keep pace with his wife, he had his first taste of ashes.

‖19‖

The aftermath of Stu's passion had progressed beyond Harry's. Whereas his brother's complications arose from a twisted heart, Stu's came from a twisted mind. Blackmailing his former lovers was a harrowing business.

For one thing, he didn't trust mailboxes. He had once sent away for a book on hypnosis guaranteed to give him power over people, but the publisher had procrastinated. Where was the promised blueprint to absolute control over his environment? The weeks of a sultry summer had slipped away along with untold opportunities to enslave haughty nymphets and obnoxious enemies. How could he become an effective person, respected and obeyed, as the ad promised? If he ever actually got the potent little cabala in hand he would use it first on the Roads to Mastery Publishing Company, he had threatened. But from the misty shores of Hoboken, New Jersey, had come silence. After he wrote his third letter of inquiry he hid by the mailbox to make sure it was picked up. The truck wasn't long in coming. It rumbled and squealed to a halt, disgorging a sinewy man with grimy gloves and a red bandanna. The man squinted against the smoke from his cigarette as he grasped the mailbox and emptied it in the back of the truck. An unseen driver then committed some mechanical act, and up went Stu's letter on a dais strewn with the remnants of his civilization. The sinewy man reattached himself easily, and the feral transmission roared away. It was then that Stu scrutinized the red, white, and blue mailbox and realized it was a patriotic garbage can left over from the Fourth of July.

Since he never trusted mailboxes after that, collecting money from the three wives he blackmailed became complicated. Mrs. Fletcher, for instance, had to leave her payoff in the cup on the fourteenth green of the course she played every Monday. Usually she was so afraid he would pop out of the bushes that she blasted her next tee shot into the river. Mrs. Mallory, on the other hand, shoved her hush money up the downspout of the garage. When it rained, Stu collected sop in the truest sense. Lastly, Mrs. Prittikin had agreed to leave her money in a Cracker Jack box on top of a wire trash basket in the park. It was the same park Harry had proposed to Carrie and later been arrested in, and it seemed now to acquire a penchant for dramas in the lives of the Moons as Stu used it for extortion and the events that happened one white, still day in August.

He should have known when he hefted the box that something was wrong. Mrs. Prittikin always included loose change, as if to imply that she was being squeezed down to the last nickels and dimes of her soul, but this time the box was light. Dressed in matching yellow shorts, socks, and shirt, Stu felt very much a part of the sun and the day and the inevitable facts of survival. "Got to get my jack, Jack—yummy Cracker Jack, Jack," he sang, and it wasn't until he took out the note and read it that he felt another bowel attack coming on. *I'm right behind you,* it read. *Don't yell or run or I'll blow your lousy balls off. Turn right at the bridge and get in the rowboat.*

He glanced backward and saw Mr. Prittikin—Tony Prittikin, the butcher at Grand Union—wearing a dark suit and tie and carrying his right hand in his pocket. Stu's beautiful yellow shirt, shorts, and socks were about to be swallowed by the hulking shadow of a butcher in a dark suit; he discovered in this the helpless terror and injustice of life no matter what the weather.

Birds continued to sing and a pair of wryly smiling ducks rose and waddled off on orange feet, but Stu Moon lurched awkwardly down a dappled path to certain death. He smelled the decay of the river, which was dotted with death in the form of struggling insects. Here was the froth and foam of used elements dissolving, there was the rotting wood conveyance upon which he would float to a suitable point where the current ran strong and submerged trees would grapple for his body.

"Get in," said Prittikin, and Stu realized that the stench of decay was butcher's breath.

When the boat slid away from the bank and they faced each other, he told himself that Prittikin was just a man—although a very angry man. He probably read the Sunday comics, celebrated Christmas, and now and then put a little extra lean beef in the hamburger.

"I suppose you want to talk," he said. Prittikin didn't answer, and Stu thought he was wrong about the Sunday comics. The man had no sense of humor. He rowed with the rhythm of predestination, as if meshing with some larger and inflexible machine powered by retribution. Stu tried for nonchalance, for daring at the moment of danger. "Did you hear the one about the horny sailor who spent the night in an oarhouse?"

Prittikin kept rowing. The boat rose and fell on powerful strokes, cutting the gluey water with urgency and stealth.

Why am I telling him jokes about whores? thought Stu. And how could Mrs. P. marry a man with hairy hands and no neck?

And then he saw the anchor, a V-8 juice can filled with concrete.

"How about if I return the money?" he asked. "I could sell the car, the stereo, all my clothes—" Here he began sobbing. "You'd make a profit, Mr. Prittikin. I'm sorry about your wife. We only did it once." The oarlocks squeaked relentlessly, and he wanted to sing "Row, Row, Row Your Boat" or read the Sunday comics to make the leaden figure laugh. "It's the herpes, isn't it?" he cried. "Oh, God, if you only knew how I've suffered. I didn't give it to her, you know. I mean I was just passing it on. I mean . . . oh, God, how I've paid for it. The blackmail was just to cover my medical bills."

Prittikin slowed and lost cadence when Stu said that about the herpes, and Stu saw he hadn't known.

"Wrap the rope around your foot," Prittikin grated.

"Oh, please." Stu's voice was as thin as a dog whistle. "If you kill me, I won't be able to give you the formula for this marvelous herpes salve Daisy gave me. You take Oil of Olay and Shoe Saver and just a touch of Dr. Scholl's—"

"The rope!"

"Daisy's my wife!" Stu screamed. "I've got six kids and they're all crippled!"

The butcher lunged forward, enveloping him with bad breath and rope. They were between an island and a sewage plant where the water was as black and flat as molasses. Prittikin yanked him to his feet. Stu had a premonition of a short flight and an icy plunge. He would scream and be muted by ebony torrents filling him like a glass. The fish would nibble, the mud would suck, the chemicals of man would slowly gnaw him to the bone.

"One..." said Prittikin, swinging the anchor.

"Remember the ten commandments!"

"Two..."

"Daisy's salve really works—"

"Three!"

Over went the anchor, over went Stu, over went the boat. But the worst part of it wasn't the ebony torrents filling him like a glass. The worst part was Prittikin's breath. Because Stu was standing chest deep and the butcher was wrapped around him.

"I'll save you," Stu said.

Prittikin let go. His suit and tie looked darker but otherwise unruffled as he stood in the river.

Stu danced a lazy cancan in the mud, slowly twirling his other leg to unwind the rope. Then he wrestled the boat over, found the oars, and began bailing with a plastic bottle that had been wedged under the seat.

Prittikin said, "We're going to the island. There's rattlesnakes on the island."

The main thing about the island was that nobody went there. Besides the snakes, it was strewn with garbage and poison ivy. So that was where Stu was led and made to stand on various scree slopes. He stood on scree slopes north, south, east, and west but no snakes came. Then he stood in an inland quarry, and finally Prittikin ordered him to roll in poison ivy. In the end, he was ordered into the boat and rowed back to the park, where he was told they would drive to his apartment.

Like a fly in a bottle, he rode in Prittikin's car, slowly asphyxiating and receiving daylight and compound images from the pitiless world beyond the glass. There were lovers and shimmering bike wheels, beds of flowers, children with rainbow-colored ice-cream cones, and butterflies brighter than his shorts. But the flowers had no fragrance and the children, who were surely laughing, made no sound. They seemed remote, because they looked happy, and sunshine fell on them while he was merely a passing shadow. He saw his dentist, the newsboy, a pair of neighbors, and a cashier from the corner drugstore. The cashier waved. On the stairway to his apartment he saw his landlord, but Prittikin's breath closed around him like a gag.

"Your wife home?" Prittikin demanded at the door.

"I don't know. She comes and goes."

"What about your six kids?"

"They're all at camp."

"Crippled kids' camp?" He put his hand on the doorknob. "If your wife is home, I'm going to rape her. And if she isn't, I'm going to cut you into ribs, chops, flank steaks, and mankindburger."

Rape Daisy? Stu felt rays of hope. "Oh, please don't rape Daisy," he said. "I couldn't live with that."

Prittikin opened the door, and the first thing Stu saw was an empty rum bottle on the table and the bedroom door closed. "She's taking her nap," he said. "Please don't rape her."

Prittikin pushed him into the closet and jammed a chair under the handle.

"I'm going to bring her out here so you can watch through the keyhole."

The next thing Stu heard was the bedroom door opening, then Daisy swearing, then bedsprings. Either Prittikin had lain down or Daisy had stood up. But then Stu heard the body being dragged past the closet and tossed downstairs. "Goddamn sex maniac," Daisy rumbled and freed the closet door.

"Oh, Daisy." Stu buried his head in her diaphragm. "It was awful. That man tried to drown me and kill me with rattlesnakes and he was going to butcher me if he didn't have his way with you."

"There, there," Daisy said, patting the top of his head.

"I was so afraid for you, but I couldn't yell or he would've killed me."

"There, there."

"He's Mr. Prittikin, the butcher. I'm afraid he found out about his wife. I'm afraid the others might find out too!"

"There, there."

"I'm afraid we'll have to do without so many fine things now, Daisy. I'm afraid we'll have to struggle."

Daisy held him at arm's length. "You mean no more seven-inch spiked boots and black lace garter belts?"

"Yes, but we've got more than that going for us, don't we? We'll just have to make do with what we've got."

"What have we got?"

Pain crept into Stu's eyes. He was about to play the role he had forced on Mrs. Prittikin the morning he had walked out. "Tuesdays and Fridays?" he asked hopefully.

"I'm busy Tuesdays and Fridays."

"Thursdays, then."

"Can't make Thursdays."

The pain intensified but, rather than flaring into hate as Mrs. Prittikin's had, it merely brightened like a starving ember consuming its last bit of fuel and went out.

⟩ 20 ⟨

Harry got his first job at Bauvier Junior High School in a town called Haversack. Haversack lay at the crossroads of abandoned commerce which included a defunct mine, a burned lumber mill, and a bankrupt textile industry. From his first step inside Bauvier, Harry sensed its age-encrusted weariness, its down-to-the-bone gloss and hollowness, as if it had been picked clean by generations of ravenous children hungry for life. He had gotten the job because of a death in the English department, and the senescent staff acknowledged him as one greets an undertaker younger than oneself. Behind their dry smiles and wrinkled eyes was a foretaste of the unknowable, but his own sense of doom was at least as profound. This was it. A room. A terminal resting place. Harry Moon, teacher.

There were two days of preparation before the students arrived, and he brought Stephanie with him on the second, hoping to charm the principal, Mrs. Feedly, and ease his own feeling of dislocation. But everyone seemed to see through this, and though Stephanie was disarming—"I'm three and a half, wanna see my wart?"—Harry faced the arrival of the students like a springbok isolated from the herd and going down to a pack of jackals.

He had thought himself unworthy of them, but as they swept through the building strewing candy wrappers, swearing, and shoving, a great cloak of civic order and social morality seemed to descend over him. Instead of rediscovering the chrysalis stage of his own youthful innocence, he was faced with containing an alien and barbaric race.

"Are you gonna make us read?" one of them demanded at the door. "We read last year."

"If you say my name, don't mess it up, okay?" came from a girl on the other side. She had hair cropped to her skull but Harry knew she was a girl because she rubbed all over him in the crush. Her first composition would be about the "Anal Beauty Pageant."

The bell rang as if connected to every frayed nerve on the ancient staff and seemed momentarily to intimidate the students, who more or less sat down. Harry wrote *Mr. Moon* on the board to the sound of saliva and gum, and the darlings stared at it a few seconds as if sounding out the four letters. Finally the girl who had rubbed all over him screamed with laughter and everyone broke up.

"I knew you was gonna make us read," lamented the first boy, who looked as if he picked his nose with a stick.

"I'm Mr. Moon," Harry said, and the laughter erupted all over again.

"Moo-on!" someone strained rectally.

"I teach seventh-grade English," said Harry. More laughter. He dropped his briefcase on the desk and opened it to get the class list. Gales of laughter. "I don't see anything funny in that!"

he barked. There was silence, then a snicker, then gales of laughter. By this time Harry was feeling twelve years old. "Now I'm going to read your names, class, and if I mispronounce one or two, don't feel bad, because my father's name was Ferdinand, my mother's name was Liza, so when I was born they called me Fertilizer!" Dead silence. Harry read. When he got to the girl with the short-cropped hair he said "Satchel Morgan," and she leaped to her feet.

"Sasha! Sasha!" she screamed. "I told you not to mess it up. Why does everyone call me 'Satchel'? It's not fair. Just 'cause I've had ringworm and my hair hasn't grown out, it's not fair!"

Some saving instinct, stronger than his child psychology courses, came to Harry's aid then, and he paced slowly up the aisle. "If you don't shut up, little girl, I'm going to beat you with a wet skunk," he said precisely, and turning on the rest of them he explained that though he loved mankind—indeed, *because* he loved mankind—the punishment for further disruption would be to be led around the room seven times by the eyelids.

After that he was known as a hard teacher, and his car was often modified in the parking lot during lunch. Since Bauvier also had an elementary wing, his reputation for torture spread to the lower grades. This was enhanced when a first-grader ran into him with a wet poster painting one day, and by way of reprisal he convinced the obnoxious tot that he was a dwarf and would never grow. The information got back to the child's parents, and in due course Harry's presence was requested in the office. He tried to convince himself that the meeting with Mrs. Feedly, the principal, had nothing to do with the fact that he was a probationary teacher, but when he walked into her inner sanctum she made him as welcome as an ovarian cyst.

"I hope you're not terrorizing your students, Mr. Moon," she said in part. "One of the things we look for here at Bauvier is compassion. Without compassion, what have we?"

The words "discipline and obedience" hovered on his lips, but he confessed an error in judgment and thereafter avoided the elementary wing. He also avoided Mrs. Feedly and compassion. It wasn't until he met Raymond that he got compassion.

This meeting took place in his second year. By that time Harry realized he was getting more of an education than he was giving. The roots of human weakness and compromise lay before him in simple acts, and he was helpless to alter them. Where would he begin? With tardiness, with skipping breakfast? Was the student who forgot his pencil to be given another and another? Did dying grandmothers expiate all missing homework? Were divorce, alcoholism, and unemployment the universal exemptions for failing children? The frailties were legion and endemic. And who was to blame? Was it parents, teachers, television, the school social worker? Was it society? The administration? Or was it no one?

In danger of drowning in fatalism, he came to school one day and discovered Raymond writing on Mrs. Feedly's car with chalk. He did not know the student's name was Raymond, only that he was a sixth-grader who always seemed to be sitting outside the assistant principal's office.

"Practicing your block letters?" he asked.

"I'm writing 'fuck,'" said Raymond, without looking up.

F-C-U-A, Harry read. No wonder the world was screwed up. "That's not how you spell it," he said.

"How do you spell it?"

"F-U-C-K."

"Thanks."

"Don't mention it."

That was compassion.

The next time Harry talked to him was when the whole school got together on the front lawn after the Clean-up, Fix-up, Paint-up Parade. "Pee-rade" was the way Mrs. Feedly pronounced it; "We are going to have a pee-rade." Mrs. Feedly introduced the pee-rade chairman, who introduced the mayor, who introduced the pee-rade queen: Miss Cleaned, Fixed, and Painted. Harry stood with the other teachers, and Mrs. Feedly turned and looked into his mouth just as he yawned. The mayor was also yawning, or gasping for breath, and there was some question in Harry's mind whether that hoary personage would live long enough to speak. When the chairman was introducing him, she said, "In a minute the mayor will recognize someone very important," and Harry could just see the wheels grinding slowly in the old head as the dimly lit mayor tried to recognize someone. Then he glanced up at the library window and saw a wisp of smoke. He slipped away and climbed to the third floor, but by that time he only smelled the cigarette. Raymond had his feet on the librarian's desk. Harry wanted to collar him and shake him up, but he sensed the futility in this and instead sat down at a nearby table and folded his arms. You weren't supposed to fold your arms, according to his child psychology courses. That was bad body English. It said you were closed-minded. Harry thought it was restful.

"Everyone's supposed to be at the parade," he said.

Raymond shrugged. "I felt like reading."

"What are you reading?"

"Nut one."

"Never heard of it. Any good?"

Raymond shrugged, and Harry's glance fell on a fluorescent tube lying on the desk. NUTONE, it said. Nut one.

"How's your spelling?" he asked.

"Good. F-U-C-K."

Harry shook his head. "How old are you?" Raymond was thirteen even though he was only in the sixth grade.

"They're calling your name," Raymond said.

Harry listened to the drone coming up from the lawn. "Really?"

"Somethin' about the English department."

Harry tried to stare him down, but Raymond kept on grinning. Maybe they really did call my name, he thought and bolted down the three flights and out on the lawn. But the mayor of Haversack was still trying to recognize somebody, and when Harry looked up he saw Raymond grinning out the window at him.

That summer Raymond did three things. He quit drinking, became a Christian, and stole a Saturday night special with which he shot and killed a neighbor's dog. Harry heard about the dog. Mrs. Feedly told all of Raymond's teachers that fall. "He's on probation," she said, "and we don't have to put up with any nonsense. One false move and we refer him for alternate schooling. Frankly, the sooner the better." Whatever happened to compassion? Harry wondered.

Raymond missed the first eight days of school that year, and when he showed up in fourth-hour class on the ninth, Harry kept him after the bell.

"You missed language orientation, room rules, book intro, and student autobiography," he said.

"I'm also missing lunch," Raymond complained.

"Look, son, I want you to know that you've got a chance in here. You don't have to fail. I'm not an uptight grammarian, I'm just an adult in charge of seeing that you learn to read and express yourself as well as you can so that you get a decent job and don't get crapped on all your life. Words are the name of the game, son, and I'm sorry you missed all mine the last eight days because they would have built your confidence and opened your eyes. Now, I'm going to give you a crash course right here to show you how smart you are. See this sentence?" *The koby dotots demeeched nonbortly,* he wrote. "What's the subject of this sentence, Raymond, what one word is this sentence about?"

Raymond shrugged.

"How about *dotots?* Let's say *dotots,* okay?" All the kids had gotten *dotots.* "Now, what kind of *dotots* are they?"

Raymond shrugged.

"*Koby* maybe? Do you think they're *koby dotots,* Raymond?"

"Yeah."

"Right. Right as rain, Raymond. *Koby dotots.* Now, what did the *koby dotots* do?"

"They went to lunch."

"How could they go to lunch? That's not even in the sentence."

"How the hell should I know? Don't *dotots* ever eat?"

"They *demeeched,* Raymond. The *koby dotots demeeched.* Look at the sentence. You see how easy it is? Now, how did they *demeech?*"

"God, I wish I knew."

"There are only two words left, Raymond. *The* and *nonbortly.*"

"*The,*" said Raymond.

"They *demeeched the?* How could they *demeeched the?*"

"*Non . . . bortly.*"

"Right! See how smart you are? How did you know all that? Words aren't holy, Raymond. God didn't create them. They're just grunts and scribbles that get born and die, and in between people use them. You've been using them since you were one year old—without benefit of formal grammar. They're your link with the world, and you're a real expert."

"Yeah?" said Raymond, and he didn't come back for eight more days.

Harry seemed to be teaching a class in the dull and prosaic. Nothing he said was relevant, and the young bodies slouching before him were a separate creation altogether. He felt as though he were Jules back in Chewbagin, where gravity made exorbitant demands, and he actually careened when he lectured. He got so absentminded that he walked into the boys' john with his lunch tray one day. The cafeteria was serving cannelloni—he loved cannelloni—and he was obliged to scrape it into the toilet in front of some seventh-graders as if he had come there expressly for that purpose. "Hello, Mr. Moon," they chorused politely. He understood now the catatonic reserve of the staff, who were stunned and alienated. The fate of the human race was sealed, if Bauvier Junior High was any indication, and he anguished over his part in it. If the Raymonds of the world played hooky, it lessened his own culpability.

There was very little he could grasp conclusively about the decline in human quality, except that all girls wrote "a lot" as one word (*alot*) and all boys wrote it as two (*a lot*). He suspected that mothers secretly inculcated daughters at puberty. "Alot" was a watchword, a feminist symbol. When Harry reflected aloud on this, the class grew serious and worried-looking.

One day Sasha Morgan brought a frog to school for a demonstration speech. Sasha was in Harry's first hour ninth grade now and her hair had grown out, turning her into a great quilled bird. He sat at his desk while she took out her frog and handed him an extension cord. "Plug that in," she said. Lethargically he obeyed. The cord was attached to a transformer and the transformer to the frog by means of copper wires. *Zin-ng* went the frog. It had been taking hopeless hops, due to the fact that its ankles were shackled, but now it went *zin-ng!* Harry turned pale. Sasha smiled. The frog reverberated, layout position.

She picked it up like a tuning fork and rapped it smartly on his desk. "This is how you electrocute a frog," she said.

The class was alert. Girls were gurgling hysterically, boys were panting like apes.

Harry tottered up, up, out of his seat, stammering, sweating. "Ah . . . ah, Satchel—"

Swiftly Sasha produced a scalpel, flipped the frog, and skillfully slashed doors in its white waistcoat. These she threw open, revealing the frog's plumbing and a dull ruby heart the size of a gumdrop, still beating.

Bereft, Harry grabbed the scalpel and plunged it into the frog's chest.

"You killed Kermit...." Sasha said dazedly. "Kermie...you killed Kermie."

A great sigh of dismay rose from the class.

"You killed Kermit!" Sasha shrilled. "I raised him from a pollywog and you killed him. *I* wanted to kill him!"

Harry cleared his throat and endeavored to hide the slaughter. "Sometimes...sometimes in the interest of science we have to—er, ah, mangle an amphibian," he said.

Satch sobbed for the lost opportunity to snuff out a life and let Kermie drip back into his shoebox. On the school records that year Harry anonymously recommended that Sasha Morgan be held back spayed.

As the year went on, it was Raymond who depressed him the most. When failure notices went out the second quarter, Raymond signed his *Bullshit*. Because he was the brother of Stanley, Harry was one of the few teachers who recognized states of chemical induction, and Raymond generally came to class so high he needed an elevator to sit down. If Sasha should be spayed, Raymond should be sent to dog obedience school.

Besides *Bullshit*, Harry got him to write two things that year. The first was his autobiography, but because Harry never read these until he got to know the students better, he looked at it last. The second thing, which he read first, was a composition about what you would do if you were stranded on an island with your worst enemy. It was a three-page assignment and the choices seemed to be to kill, coexist, or make peace. Most of the papers dealt with elaborate and prolonged torture. Raymond's was one sentence long and did none of the three. *When I smelt his Seegrums I kilt myself,* he wrote.

"Who *is* your enemy?" Harry asked.

Raymond's eyes snapped then. "I knew you didn't care," he said inscrutably.

Harry shrugged it off. Another reason he didn't read the autobiographies at the start of the year was because they were a useful escape valve. Whenever he found himself hating a particular student, he pulled out the autobiography. These artless accounts of friends and families, of birth and death, of injuries, vacations, favorite toys, divorce, homes and hopes and hobbies never failed to achieve artistic truth under such circumstances. This was especially true of the unlovable authors, and Harry usually wound up crying for them. It was almost a fixed rule: if the kid could make you hate him, his background made you cry. Harry didn't hate Raymond until midyear.

Raymond had printed:

I was born in Ochtober or September 1961 with a busted showlder. Thats because my Mom was abused. My brother was born dead. My other brother was a junky. He didnt die till he got hit by a motorcycle. Well then I started schol and it was a riot. Miss Kaplans was the funnest. All we did was goof around. My Mom was glad I went cawse I was pretty distructive. I was always breaking things. My dad didnt care. They were always talking about devorce. My dad drinks Seegrums which he steels from the warehowse where he works. When I was six I got a bike and smashed it into the side of a ice creme truck. After that I got rabbitts but my sister burned down the garage with cigaretes. Then my dad got snakes which he kept in wire cages. Once one got out and Mom kilt it with my dads luger. He beat her up for that. I got held back in 1st and 4th grades. They said I had the attenshun span of a 5 year old. In 2nd grade my Mom got pregnent again and thats how we got Sherri. I wanted a boy at first but as she got bigger I liked her beter then a boy. She use to cry for me to tell her storys at nite. When she got sick I was the only one who could make her take medasin. Well then she died and I cried for about a year. Anyway I got shot in the eye with a B-B in 5th grade and they took me to the hospitel. They covered my good eye and shined a light to see if I could see it. I said yes. So then they x-rayed it and got the B-B out. I got one stitch and a peice of plastik on the back. They said I had a ruptshard rentanna. So now they bought back 20%. I really dont no what to writ cawse I never wrot about myself before.

When Harry read this, he understood Raymond's indictment, "I knew you didn't care." Raymond had confided in him, had told him about the "Seegrums," had kept track of what Harry should have known; and Harry hadn't read it, hadn't understood who Raymond's worst enemy was. Or why. He was sitting in the bathroom of the tiny Cape Cod he and Carrie had just made the down payment on, and a wave of pathos swept over him. Harry had learned to hate Raymond, had read his story, and now he was crying.

‖21‖

Stephanie was everything except eternal. At the age of six she still made cute little mistakes, but her self-assurance and independence were devouring her childhood like a newborn turtle eating its yolk. Carrie longed for another baby to nurture.

"I need something awkward and vulnerable," she complained to Harry.

"How about a crippled rabbit?"

"Something I can rock, something transparent and beautiful."

"I shall invent the glass canoe."

"Oh, Harry, don't you want another baby? What's more precious than an authentic human being with all the parts in miniature—your parts—a life you can make and shape? Show me a miracle as old or as grand as that. Nothing else comes close. Look at all the love and feeling Stephanie has given us. Oh, Harry, when she crawls into your lap, doesn't your other knee feel cold?"

"No."

"Maybe it's because you don't hold her in your lap enough."

"Maybe it's because I'm wearing the pants in this family."

She scowled. "Can't have babies while you're wearing pants."

It came down to a mortgage and bills on his side of the argument, trifles as far as she was concerned. They would always eat, dress, live in a house. Harry was putting paper ahead of flesh. How could he let sterile fears run their lives? It seemed to her that in his cold, analytical resistance he no longer loved nor cared for them with the same intensity. He was blind to the important things, caught up in the smallness of details and stress. She had to make him see this somehow. If only he would spend more time with Stephanie, if only he could be there to hear her ask for the "Eleanor's glue" instead of getting it secondhand like a scripted joke, if only he would be like other men.

And then Dan Dreiman called.

She answered the phone, and it was as though his lustrous smile and blond hair entered the room. The hair brought sunshine and seemed to surround her with energy and optimism. The satellite that carried their voices long distance traveled from horizon to horizon and yielded the task to its next in line, but Dan Dreiman did not care about indebtedness to public utilities. He was in his last year of med school, married, the father of two-year-old twins and one four-year-old girl. Peggy was expecting again. He was excited about it.

"How do you do it?" Carrie gushed.

"The same way everybody does it," he said directly, and somehow this sounded very funny to her.

Carrie laughed. "No, I mean the finances. How do you make it?"

"Loans."

Carrie laughed.

"We owe everybody."

Carrie laughed.

"Everyone invests in a doctor."

Carrie laughed and laughed. Dan Dreiman was too busy pumping out energy and optimism to worry about bills. Harry would've blown his brains out.

Dan wanted to know all about her. Was she still reading Updike? Did she ever run anymore? Had she changed her hair? Why wasn't she pregnant? All women should be pregnant (Carrie laughed and laughed). How was Stephanie? Did she like school? Another satellite rolled overhead. He was coming through Haversack next month, he said. Could he stop and see them? Only if he stayed a week, she said; Harry would be delighted. Well, maybe overnight, he agreed, and they settled on a weekend.

When Harry came home he stood in the doorway sensing change. The living room looked barren and unsettled in some way, there was a pile of clothes on the dining room table, and nothing emanated from the kitchen. She's leaving me, he thought starkly. Then he heard her clumping up the basement steps—it was either Carrie or Toots, the cat with hard pad. He heard humming then and deduced that the cat probably could not do this. "I didn't know you had no musical talent whatever," he said when she entered the room.

She kept on humming.

He pocketed his hands. "When's dinner?"

"When I make it."

Long silence. "Oh."

She had stopped humming as she meted out material across a curtain rod. "Why do you always do that?" she said.

"Do what?"

She crossed her eyes and bobbed her head with the oafish words: "'When's dinner?'"

"You look beautiful when you're snotty," he said.

"Not funny."

"I'm never funny to you anymore."

"Oh, Harry." She played out the material violently, lost track, and started again. "Do we always have to be funny? Can't we just be civil? I'm sick of laughing. Can't you just come in and ask me something? Ask me how I feel, or . . . or what I did."

"What did you do?"

She clicked her tongue against her teeth.

He wanted to mimic her but couldn't cross his eyes. "Well, since you never ask about *my* day, or how *I* feel, let me tell you: The average person can stand fifty-five social contacts a day. I am not an average person, and I hit fifty-five before first bell. By the time I was packed into the room with thirty-two ninth-graders the temperature was already ninety-five and I felt like Rice Krispies and milk were oozing out of my pores. Sasha Morgan, who leases her brain but forgets to pay the bill, changed her nylons in class. Second hour started in on the 'Moon' jokes and song titles, and by lunchtime the whole school was bowing to me and calling me 'Reverend Moon.' Third hour Gayle Arroyan, who has big shoulder blades, wore her bra backwards and *everybody* noticed. Fourth hour Raymond told a beautiful story about fat Mrs. Clyde bending over to dry between her toes in the athletic office just as Shellie Lyons came in, ramming the doorknob up her rectum. Raymond did not use the word rectum, and he said the doorknob got stuck. By the end of the day the temperature in the room was a hundred and forty and all the books began to smell like vomit. It's the glue, but half the class got sick anyway."

"Welcome home," said Carrie.

"What's that supposed to mean?"

"It means you ought to be glad to be here."

"I am glad to be here." She was sucking her cheek, and he perceived that she had left him already. "What are you doing to the curtains?"

"Making new ones."

"What happened to the old ones?"

"I'm having them cleaned and burned."

"God, Carrie." She wasn't looking at him. She never looked at him. He always had the feeling he was running after her when he talked. "Look," he said, "we've got to cut down—"

Just then the alarm on the stove went off like a chain saw chewing through a tin roof. Harry hated that sound. It made him stiffen like Sasha Morgan's high-voltage frog. "What's that?"

"It's time for Stephanie to come in and watch *Mr. Rogers,*" Carrie said.

"A TV alarm? My kid's got a TV alarm?"

"Steph-anie!" she hollered out the window.

"Today's children are faced with many choices: channels two, five, six, and eight," Harry sneered.

"Dan's coming," Carrie said abruptly.

"Dan?"

"Dreiman. He wants to see the house."

"You mean that's why everything is torn up in here?"

"Nothing is torn up, Harry. I've been planning these curtains a long time. They're simple and cheap. Like you. I'll start dinner in a little while."

"What time is he coming?"

"Next month."

Stephanie rushed in then, breathless and aglow. She was just the right height to disembowel him with her bony shoulder, but Harry stepped in front of her and swung her into his arms.

"Daddy," she said impatiently, "I'm going to miss *Mr. Rogers.*"

"Oh. Well. Can't miss *Mr. Rogers.*"

"Oh, Daddy."

He set her down and she flew to the set.

"Why don't you go see about the lawn," Carrie said.

"See what about the lawn?"

"Just stare at the dirt. It'll come to you. Keep repeating: I want to protect my investment."

He didn't know what he wanted to protect, but he went out and stood on the lawn. He knew he was crude and rude and unromantic, but it wasn't the way he wanted to be. He wanted to come home and get out of his head and into his heart. But to do so seemed to sanction and venerate the indifference she showed him. He saw himself as a field slave, shuffling in with his floppy, faded hat in his hands and, grinning ear to ear, saying with alacrity, "Yessum, Miss Carrie!" "You may attend me as soon as I am done with my daughter, the cat, the telephone, and the television," said the house mistress. "Yessum, Miss Carrie!" He would not pay homage to this.

What had happened to the girl who sat tirelessly in pool balconies sympathetic to his dreams and appreciative of his efforts? The answer, he feared, was simple and irrevocable. She was not tireless after all. He had not even really loved her then. But she had seemed to love him, and he had become first dependent, then grateful, and finally addicted to her. Was this how true love began? Then, as she had supplanted his goals and follies one by one—his swimming, his gambling, his grasping for freedom and self-esteem—he had slid down her list of priorities. What was it his mother had said? Young brides feed on attention and sacrificial offerings. Well, he had run out of sacrifices. The tokens she demanded now seemed to be abject husbandry, dutiful fatherhood, grateful lover. "Yessum, Miss Carrie!"

He looked at the lawn.

It was piebald, but what vegetation there was seemed given over by thirds to loose-necked dandelions, miserable tufts of broad-bladed grass, and some scrunched-up blue blossoms he couldn't identify. His neighbor putted flawlessly in the adjacent yard and callously asked if he had used a can of Grass-B-Gon. Harry replied that if the man's basset continued to defecate on his lawn he would use Dog-Gone administered through twin barrels. He had mowed the dirt so often it had ruts in it. Now he decided to proceed scientifically. The last box of grass seed he had purchased contained coupons for free soil and plant analysis. Yielding to a sense of purpose and hope, he carefully packaged the samples from his yard as directed and mailed them off to the company. They wrote back two weeks later:

> Dear Mr. Moon,
> The soil sample you sent us is a high quality, granulated asphalt, and we here at GreenGro feel that if it wasn't for the radioactivity you might be able to hot-roll an A-1 parking lot.

The plant sample was moss and they wanted to know if his backyard was a rock. He promptly fired back a soil sample from that, too. Their final opinion was that his house had been built on a meteorite of some kind and that he should contact his local observatory. The letter closed:

> We regret having developed no products at this time suitable for promoting grass on extraterrestrial objects.

Harry decided to pave the lawn. He had no idea how to go about this, but he purchased ten fifty-pound bags of Redi-Mix with the intent of lightly glazing his environs. When Carrie saw what was about to transpire she prostrated herself in front of the wheelbarrow. Since his understanding of what he was doing was not concrete, Harry agreed to take the nine unopened bags back. But he still had a wheelbarrow full of wet cement, so he quickly gathered all the canine bowel movements he could find in his yard, dipped them, and stuck them in ordinal rows on his neighbor's porch.

D-Day was closing in. Dan Dreiman Day. Carrie washed, dusted, waxed, and polished the house, top to bottom. She defrosted the refrigerator, scrubbed the bathroom tile with a toothbrush, and cleaned around the toilet to the last pubic hair. A quarter of their food budget went for cleansers that month. She cut her hair, made herself a top and a pair of slacks, and went back to jogging. The window shades acquired borders, new curtains went up, and some withering house plants—neglected for months—suddenly flourished under intense care. When Harry commented that he had never seen the refrigerator so well organized, she snapped, "I always keep a clean refrigerator!" She was not to be crossed in those days, and he spent most of his time outdoors watching the weeds grow, watching a huge robin who kept trying to eat the hose, watching to see if his neighbor was going to remove the concrete poop. Then Dan Dreiman arrived, and Carrie seemed to soften and expand as brightly and quietly as sunshine.

At first she only smiled, exchanging socially relevant pecks on the cheek and yielding pert answers. Harry did most of the talking. But when he asked about Dan's family, the answers evoked her laughter, and Harry felt the shifting of attention.

"The twins are superexcellent," said Dreiman, pumping out energy and optimism. "And Jenny lost a tooth already."

Carrie laughed.

"She bit into her spoon."

Carrie laughed.

"She was eating oatmeal, and there was the tooth stuck in the oatmeal."

Carrie laughed and laughed.

Harry sensed a simpatico he couldn't share. He knew this was a cute story, but his wife's reaction seemed disproportionate, and he realized it wasn't just cuteness that engaged them. It was joy and warmth and some deeper human trust that induced the sharing of feelings.

He told a joke of his own. "The inventors of gene-splicing were Joe Doblotski and Agnes Flots, who, while wearing their Lee Riders on August fourth, 1974, managed to get extremely close up in his room in the South Bronx," he said.

Carrie ran her hand down the curtains.

"That's dumb," Dan said, and Carrie laughed.

Sadly, Harry realized that he had been an inadequate husband. His wife's needs would have been better served by a Dan Dreiman. He bore this revelation to the dinner table in a kind of transcendental peace, as if he had been martyred and freed by the same stroke. The candles flickered in the conversation and seemed by their shadow-casting to orchestrate a world of secondary meanings.

"What are you taking?" Harry asked.

"Female anatomy," replied Dan.

"Ever have second thoughts?"

"Not really. The end justifies the means. So what are you up to?"

"I teach pause patterns in Elizabethan and Jacobean drama to the brain-damaged."

And so on.

The candles searched Dreiman's face but found only the energy and optimism. His lustrous smile and blond hair seemed compatible with this search, converting it to a display of radiant honesty. This aspect of his character was totally disarming, even commanding. Surrounded by Moons, he played a solar role.

"I like your house," he said. "That last place you had was a cave."

Carrie laughed.

"Even the glasses look superexcellent."

Carrie laughed.

"These glasses?" said Harry. "They're just specimen jars we got from the Red Cross."

Carrie didn't laugh.

"We use jelly jars," Dan said.

Carrie laughed.

She laughed all night. She laughed spontaneously. She laughed convulsively. She laughed with the helpless joy of a child overwhelmed by a superior presence. Harry smiled sadly.

As the weekend flowed by, the warmth and trust between Carrie and Dan broadened into something tangible. There were probing pats and nudges, stroking, brushing, touching innocently and obviously in front of Harry. In an effort to dilute its significance, Harry and Stephanie were included. By Sunday evening Harry's arm was limp from friendly punches, and Stephanie threw up after being repeatedly tossed in the air. When it came time to say good-bye, Dreiman draped himself devotedly over his friend, and Harry realized what was coming.

"You're the salt of the earth," Dreiman said. Then he turned to Carrie. "And you're the pepper."

He took her roughly in his arms, patted her, and lightly kissed her on the cheek. This happened so naturally that he went on talking, as if he had only tested the sanctioning of the situation and the real good-bye was yet to come.

The charge in the air was palpable. Harry felt like an ion detector. He had seen the posturing, the alacrity, the mutual awareness of each other's presence in every word, glance, and gesture all weekend, but now he sensed the magnetism. They were like a pair of gentle wrestlers getting ready to grapple, aware of their positions, self-conscious of the distance between them, gauging what they could get away with, waiting, calculating. Dreiman kept saying cute things, but Carrie was no longer laughing. She stood poised and acquiescent, and when he made his move she fell spontaneously and without hesitation onto his lips, eyes closed—to shut in her fantasy, to shut out Harry's cold look.

"Sure was superexcellent, wasn't it?" Harry said as Dreiman's car faded down the street.

That night she insisted on sex and kept her eyes closed the whole time. Harry felt as though he were having a dinner of leftovers; her kisses were "seconds," offered in quantity and each one the same as the next. After that, things returned to normal. The refrigerator amassed its old clutter, the bathroom tile moldered, and Carrie's jogging dwindled to nothing. Last to go were the house plants, which one by one dropped their blossoms, rusted, and sank silently into the soil from which they came.

⁅ 22 ⁆

Just as his father had, Harry came to regard the entry and exit of dogs in his life as a staunch omen. They had followed him from the gates of the cemetery at Winslow's funeral and reappeared most often at times of peace and tranquillity. But now they were gone again; there seemed to be no reason for it. Even the next-door basset disappeared, as if out of mortification for its immortalized feces. Was this the death knell of his marriage?

The basset was replaced by a Doberman, and when Harry saw his neighbor sneak over and extract one of his discarded yellow tennis shoes from the trash, he grew suspicious. Thereafter he could hear the Doberman masticating his footwear in its doghouse on the front porch.

A few days later he was walking down the street and there

was the yellow shoe on the lawn, laid open like a grapefruit. Thinking to retrieve it, he took two steps in that direction, but the wind was blowing toward the doghouse and out sprang Cerberus, lathering for the kill. Harry faltered, though the Doberman was chained. He advanced one more step toward the shoe, and the doghouse began to move. It grated over the rows of concrete poop still stuck to the porch and came bounding down the steps toward him. Forgetting the shoe, he sidled and then fled toward his own property, but the Doberman dragged its doghouse in hot pursuit.

"Carrie!" he shouted.

She came and looked through the screen.

"Open the door!"

"Are you crazy, Stephanie's in here," she said.

"Open the goddamn door!" he screamed.

"Oh, Harry, don't be such a baby. He can't catch you."

The oval scraped in the lawn by the doghouse looked like Aqueduct now.

"Run down to the post office," she suggested, and then she saw that the cat was trapped in a low tree in the middle of the oval. "Oh, Tootsie!" she wailed.

Grabbing a can of carpet cleaner she raced out to attack the Doberman. Foam spurted out and the killer dog stopped dead, whined, then actually cringed before the asthmatic, snaking can. "Leave Tootsie alone, you bad dog!" she admonished after she had chased him back to his yard. Then she drew a ring around the doghouse with carpet cleaner to forbid further travel.

The Doberman remained in seclusion, but still Harry's strays were missing. They stayed missing until the last day of June. That was when he got the call from the hospital: "Mr. Harold Moon, son of Alice Moon . . . ?"

By the time he got there she was annexed to two machines and a plastic bag. The machines had something to do with her heart and kidneys, the plastic bag fed fluids. She seemed already half transferred to the elements through this symbiosis, and he went around to the unencumbered arm before dropping to his knees. "Please, Mom," he pleaded, "they're not naming kids Alice anymore. Where will all the Alices of the world come from, if the old ones die?"

She opened her eyes. "Harry, listen. Children free women from their husbands. Having babies makes them holy and fulfilled and self-righteous. If they don't have enough children they become bitter and insecure. That's your choice . . . Harry. A wife who's self-righteous or insecure."

And then she died.

They knotted together in grief, all except Nicki and Stanley.

Nicki intended to come. His lawyer was supposed to get his bond reduced after he was arrested for chinchilla smuggling and arson. Harry saw them going down the corridor of the Justice Building on TV. It was one of those shame-on-you stories where the reporter and camera run alongside trying to get an interview while the felon hides his face. Nicki made no effort to hide, but just before the elevator doors rolled shut he gestured toward his companion and said into the microphone, "I'm sorry, gentlemen, but my client here has nothing to say." When the elevator doors opened on the courtroom corridor five floors above the departing newsmen, the lawyer stormed out, gave Nicki the finger, and took the stairwell back down. The bond hearing was postponed.

Stanley was still in Lewisburg—though parole was imminent.

Stu, Carrie, Stephanie, and Chewbagin were at the funeral, a few neighbors, some of Winslow's relatives, and the miscellaneous. Harry was saddened to see that Jules was not there. Someone said he had been too ill to travel, and it seemed to Harry then that two guiding forces had gone out of his life at once, leaving him alone with people he did not really know or love. He stood apart at the parlor window, listening to the dreary eloquence of a summer rain that shattered on the black asphalt parking lot and beaded on the freshly waxed hearse, his hands locked behind him as if he were a closed loop turned inside out. He felt sad and contrite, but the gentleness of contrition and the admonishment of the rain were pleasant somehow and evoked images of authority and love. The smell of the rain off dandelions and asphalt revived the smell and taste of the Black Jack gum his father used to bring home and left his heart aching.

He did not think of his mother.

The reading of the will was delayed a month for Stanley's release from Lewisburg. Nicki had made bond also by then, so all four brothers sat in the lawyer's office. Harry had a bias about the looks of dishonest people which fit the lawyer. It had something to do with their complexion—particularly when they were young—and the stringiness of their hair. The lawyer was young and sallow and mottled and had stringy hair. His suit and tie looked, to Harry, like a cheap disguise.

"With your permission, I'll read the document," he said.

Nicki and Stanley sat very still, Stu smiled, Harry crossed his legs and fought back tears.

The lawyer read. "'Being of sound mind and body I, Alice Viola Moon, dispose of all my worldly assets upon my death as follows: to my son Nicki, his father's slipper with which he was once beaten, but not long enough; to my son Stanley, the contents of my medicine cabinet and all over-the-counter or prescription drugs on the premises of either of my two residences; to my son Stu, any and all girdles, bras, pantyhose, panties, trusses, or other garments commonly known as unmentionables which I am not wearing at the time of my interment; to my son Harry, with rights of survivorship for his wife Carrie and their natural issue at the time of my death, equally, all else, real or intangible, including bank assets and real estate properties. May each of my heirs find in these bequeathments the return of their love and devotion paid in full.'"

Nicki and Stanley sprang to their feet, Stu cried, Harry sat very still.

"I knew she wasn't herself these last few months," gibbered Nicki. "I knew it. She was getting very chummy with her furniture. Six weeks ago she complained to me that her piano had varicose veins."

"The will was executed seven years ago," the lawyer said.

"Even then," said Nicki. "She was always in a hissy-fit. She shot at me once, did you know that? I gave her a mink coat, and she chased me through the woods with an elephant gun."

"I think it's a joke," said Stanley. "She tried to burn down a mountain in Vermont one time, remember that, Nicki? Great sense of humor."

Stu shook his head and talked to his hands. "I never liked her girdles. They made me sweat."

Harry stood up then, taller and angrier than he had ever been in his life. He was witnessing something as tasteless and transparent as a Lucite toilet. "Nicki gets the house, Stanley the lodge, Stu half the accounts," he dictated in a guttural voice, "then the three of you can go to hell. That way you'll never run into Mother again."

When he left the lawyer's office, the strays were waiting for him.

{ 23 }

The first thing Stu did with his share of Alice's money was to pull his watch, ring, and mirrored sunglasses out of hock. Clasped again in the metallic goodness of life, he went after the matching yellow clothes and then, for accent, a white T-Bird. The last thing he went to buy back was Daisy.

But Daisy was servicing a man named Eliot Budnipper under roughly the same terms she/he and Stu had enjoyed, and it took him nearly a year to find her. Budnipper owned a hair salon called Ringlets and Tresses in Maine, where Daisy was a specialist in spit curls. When Stu wafted in like an Indian summer come to rescue her from winter she pretended not to notice him.

"Daisy!" he exclaimed, as if they had just happened to bump into each other in Budnipper's hair emporium.

"Not here," she grunted and wrote her phone number on a customer's hair in Dippity-do.

Stu circled the customer and left.

When the number turned out to belong to a steel mill, Stu hired a girl to deliver a note that read, *If you don't care if I kill myself, write "good-bye," on the bottom of this note.* Daisy wrote back *I care alot* and included another phone number. (She wrote *alot* as one word, like a girl, but Harry Moon wasn't around to add this corollary to his theory.) Stu called the number that evening and this time got a rape counseling center.

"I'm going to kill myself," he said.

"Sorry, this isn't the suicide hot line," the counselor informed him. "Unless you've been raped, I'm afraid we can't help you."

"You don't understand, my girlfriend Daisy gave me this number."

"Has your girlfriend been raped?"

"Not that I know of. Once a butcher tried, but she threw him down a flight of stairs."

"You don't understand, sir. If you just want to commit suicide, there's nothing we can do for you. We only counsel rape victims."

"*You* don't understand. I just wanted to talk to Daisy. She—"

"Daisy? We have a counselor here named Daisy. Would you like to speak to her?"

"Is she six one, one hundred and ninety pounds?"

"I'm sorry, sir, we don't give out our counselors' statistics."

Several moments floated by in which Stu felt himself falling into the earpiece, and then Daisy's marinated voice caught him.

"Stu?" she said. "Is that you?"

"Daisy! Thank God."

"I'm sorry, Stu. I realized after you left the beauty shop I'd given you the number of the foundry where I used to roll steel. It's hard to write with Dippity-do. How have you been?"

"Miserable."

"Life goes on," she said.

"Yes, it's been going on all around me. Oh, Daisy, I need you. You're my essence, my being, without you life is just so much Raisin Bran without the raisins."

"There, there."

"Come back to me, Daisy."

"I never liked bran, Stu. We have so little time on this earth, and yet we must drink, we must eat, we must savor our victuals."

"We can do that together."

"I told you I can't stand that lousy bran."

"It doesn't have to be bran anymore, Daisy."

"What?"

"I can afford milk and honey again."

"Milk and honey?"

"And seven-inch spiked boots and black lace garter belts."

"Black lace?"

"Yes, yes. Give me your address."

"I'm living with Eliot. That's why I couldn't give you my home phone."

"Eliot Budnipper?"

"He's very jealous. I have to buy my lingerie from female clerks. All my conversations with men are limited to twenty-five words or less."

"You're living with Eliot Budnipper?"

"Yes."

"The same way you lived with me?"

"More or less."

It couldn't be much less. "Well," he said. "Well, give me your address."

"Ah, Stu, I wish it were that simple."

He didn't want to pursue that, but he sensed suddenly that he was bidding for her against Eliot Budnipper. "I've got a new car," he said. "A white T-Bird. I figured I could get you a nice yellow dress to match my suit and we could ride in that nice white T-Bird, Daisy. What d'you say?"

"No can do, Stu."

"Oh. Then it's him."

She laughed heartily.

"Hardly. It's just that Eliot is good at business arrangements, and it could get messy."

He was bidding against some *thing*, Stu realized; not affection for a rival, not opulent circumstances, some *thing*. "Listen, Daisy, listen to me. It's not right to let anything stand between us now. Everything can be just as good as before. I'm practically a millionaire. I can buy Budnipper with my cookie jar. I bought stock, I bought land, the IRS discovered an error and refunded me a small fortune with interest. Everything I touch turns to gold, Daisy. Trust me. Tell Budnipper to go join a salmon run; tell him you're leaving."

"Oh, Stu," she said.

He gave her his phone number, and two days later they met in a coffee shop across town. She was wearing white silk and red pumps with black net stockings. Stu handed her a dozen daisies. The details of the day, the coffee shop, and their attire were vivid and indelible, and the fate of the world seemed to hang on the moment.

"Everything is fine," she said. "I told Eliot, and he said,

'Fine, fine, just tell your boyfriend to give me five thousand dollars for the prints and everything will be fine.' "

"What prints?"

"That's what I couldn't tell you on the phone. I'm afraid I used rather bad judgment in letting Eliot take some compromising pictures of me. But he said his virility was all bound up in a thirty-five-millimeter camera and he got off by clicking the shutter at sex objects. I'm not very photogenic."

"Budnipper's got dirty pictures of you?" Stu said. She looked hurt and airy, but Stu was devastated. There was nothing in their previous relationship that would've been worth five grand on film. "Budnipper's got dirty pictures of you and he wants five thousand dollars for them?"

"Yes." She looked at her nails. "I told you he's a good businessman. If I get rough with him, he'll hold copies back, but for five thousand Eliot's trustworthy."

"What can he do with these . . . prints?"

"He can send them to my mother." Her voice wavered, but then she smiled so broadly that her lipstick went from scarlet to pink. "Oh, Stu, what difference does five thousand dollars make when we've got so much? Open your cookie jar and throw him the crumbs."

"It's the principle of the thing. He's screwing us."

"Who cares who Eliot screws?"

Stu's lips fluttered. "I do."

"I see. What happened to the big spender? Why are we meeting in this cheap café?"

"Cheap café? You call this authentic replica of a Shakespearean coffeehouse cheap? I'm surprised you let the ambience throw you. Shows what a cheap creep like Budnipper can do to your standards."

"So you're not going to pay the five thousand?"

"And give in to blackmail?"

She stood up like a flag unfurling. "Someone's standards have changed, haven't they?"

Stu had a little more than sixty-two hundred dollars left from his mother's estate, but he knew even before Daisy left the restaurant what he had to do. The sun could become a white dwarf before he'd find another human as cooperative and understanding as Daisy. Then he thought about poverty. Twelve hundred wouldn't last long. He bore this dilemma all day and into restless dreams that resolved themselves at dawn with the image of Daisy wearing a little girl's frock and glass slippers outside a Fotomat singing "Some day my prints will come." This imperative of the heart settled it, and when Budnipper arrived at Ringlets and Tresses from his health club at noon, Stu was waiting for him.

"So," he said when they were alone in the office.

In the corner was a long mahogany coffin with a brass hasp. Stu stood knee deep in carpet and tried to think of emasculating things to say.

"Well, there's no accounting for taste," Budnipper said. "Have you got the five thousand?"

"Have you got the prints?"

"Come now, fellow blackmailers ought to be able to trust each other."

Stu winced. So Daisy had told about that too.

"Let's see the prints," he said.

Budnipper opened a drawer that had the acoustics of a tomb. "Do you prefer Daisy as a woman or a man?"

"You bastard," Stu said.

Budnipper threw the pictures across the desk. "Suit yourself."

Stu glanced at the first one and nearly passed out. "Oh, my Gaw-wd...." The hand holding the picture felt like a ten-ton crane falling on his libido. "Ahh-h...oh, Daisy!" Stu wept.

Budnipper moved to the corner, dropping his fingers on the mahogany coffin as artfully as a pianist striking an introductory chord. Loosing the brass hasp and lifting the lid, he came up with the glistening midsection of a thick snake.

"Meet Chester," he said. "Chester the congester."

Stu fumbled with his wallet, whisking a cashier's check free.

"Don't you want the negatives?"

"The negatives...where are the negatives?"

"Chester's got them." The reptile's flat head leaked over one end of the coffin.

"You're a jolly one, aren't you?" Stu wiped his eyes. "What do you specialize in, terror and humiliation?"

Budnipper studied the check, then reached into Chester's boudoir and came out with a packet. "Pythons are harmless," he said, tossing the negatives onto the desk.

Outside in the empty emporium Daisy stood alone. "Hello,

big spender," she said when Stu emerged. "Are we inseparable again?"

Stu's left ventricle seemed to be doing all the work. "Inseparable," he said. "Unless you decide you want to go back to him."

She nodded as if understanding his hurt. Then she spun the chair and opened the cabinet under the sink. She took out a bottle of Liquid Plumr and a tube of Nair. She added small portions of each to a large jar of Dippity-do and mixed them with the handle of a hairbrush. Then she put the solvents back, recapped the Dippity-do, and stood up.

"There's nothing madder than a bald-headed woman," she said. "And there will be several screaming for Eliot's blood by this time tomorrow. Then I can't go back. Satisfied?"

{ 24 }

So Stu bought back Daisy with his share of the inheritance. Neither Stanley nor Nicki were to have such fluid destinies in the last days before they left the country. They were men of property, now, and thus obliged to tend real estate.

Stanley in particular found this difficult. He had mourned the good old days of napalm and Agent Orange when there was plenty of work for protesters and revolutionaries. After Lewisburg the world had looked like the end of a party to him, strewn with full ashtrays and empty cups. Betrayal throbbed in the air like a hangover. Old comrades were slinking about in gray suits and white shirts, tethered to the corporate enemy by their neckties. But then his mother's will was read and his brother came across with the ski lodge. Stanley went to New Hampshire to be reincarcerated.

A glance at the ledgers showed him that his mother had violated a cardinal principle of American enterprise: She had paid taxes. She had also run her business with too much hospitality, he thought. The cabins all had TVs, and there were magazine subscriptions, dryers, auxiliary quartz heaters and complimentary ice, coffee, popcorn, and hot cocoa, according to the faded sign in the lodge. Stanley canceled the subscriptions and sold the TVs to pay the utilities and head the mortgage. Then he jacked up prices, made some new signs, and waited for snow.

But the leaves were still on the trees, their hot colors blanketing the forest like a lava flow, when the first couple arrived. He was a sailor, she a waitress, and they had just gotten married. Now they were honeymooning in her father's Olds Cutlass. They had no skis, no money, and no future. They wanted to park the Cutlass in the lot by the lodge and sleep in the back-seat. How much would Stanley charge them to use the "plumbing"? they asked. Despite years of secular innocence and rebellion against the venal establishment, Stanley had a sense of avarice and opportunism. "Fifty cents a visit," he said and the rosy ardor in their faces whitened. The waitress perhaps saw in him the spleen of a customer who complained about the silverware, the wait, and the temperature of his roast beef and vindicated them all by denying her a tip; the sailor may have seen the bleeding manner of a Captain Bligh. They hauled forth a pair of battered suitcases, plunked two quarters on the check-in desk, and retired to the facilities. The sailor immediately reappeared, strode self-righteously out the front door, and returned with two pillows and two blankets. Stanley heard the bathroom door lock. From all this two-by-two deployment he gleaned that he had more or less rented them an ark for fifty cents.

"You've made two trips!" he hollered through the door. The water came on then, and he jiggled the knob. "What do you need pillows and blankets for? You're not doing laundry in there, are you?" He dropped to his knees and peeked through the keyhole. "Oh, yes . . ." he gurgled carnally. "Oh, yes."

The sound track began then, groans of passion climbing the tile walls, piercing the steam like the flashes of flesh gleaming on the floor. The sailor worked in labial ecstasy on the waitress; Stanley worked on the keyhole. The sailor stroked his bride's wide-flung thighs; Stanley clawed the coffered door. The sailor steamed north for a navel engagement; Stanley rammed his nose against the doorknob. Pain cleansed his brain, bleaching his desire like a white sheet drawn over a corpse. This hermaphroditic door was as close as he would ever get to a lover, he thought, and felt a wave of gratitude that the heedless couple had shared their sexual graphics and erotic cries with him. When they emerged sometime later in a cloud of steam, he handed their fifty cents back and invited them to sleep on the couch in front of the fire. They bluntly accepted, and throughout the night he lay wide-eyed on his bed in the dark, listening to the upholstered joy enunciated by the springs.

The second car pulled in the evening of the first snow: a burly driver in a fatigue hat, a scrawny woman with a pinched face, two children whose animation in the midsection of the station wagon made them look like four, and a gigantic graying Afro riding in back. The rear bumper stickers read I'M A VIET-NAM VETERAN in orange and yellow letters and FOOTPRINT OF THE AMERICAN CHICKEN along with a peace sign. As they got out, Stanley saw that the graying Afro was the rump of a brindled sheepdog.

The burly driver came into the lodge and looked at Stanley as if he were Viet Cong. "Where's Alice?" he asked suspiciously.

"My mother's dead," said Stanley.

"Oh. Your mother."

The woman, the children, and the sheepdog all came in then. The children, a boy and a girl, were eight or nine years old. The dog acted like another sibling, accustomed to sitting at the table and sleeping in a bed.

"Alice won't be here this year," the man announced to his family. "This is her son."

The children made disappointed sounds, the dog growled.

"I'm Stanley," said Stanley.

"I'm Joe," the man said. "This is Shirley. These are our kids, Jason and Julie."

"That's Rover," said Jason stridently.

Rover. Stanley felt he had come face to face with Middle America.

"We stay here every year after the first good snowfall," Joe informed him. "Alice took care of us. Cabin, skis, boots—everything One-A. We don't know anything about waxes. Alice took care of that."

"Well, just before she died she told me everything she knew," said Stanley.

"Hey! What happened to the free popcorn sign?" Julie shrilled.

"How about cabin number three?" asked Stanley.

"We always stay in number one," said Joe. "One-A, remember?"

"One-A."

"Hey! What happened to your free hot cocoa sign?" Jason demanded.

"It's not free anymore. My distributor quit giving it to me out of the goodness of his heart."

"Your rates are up," Joe noted, looking at the card. "Seems like a lot of things have changed. I hope the cabins and the skiing are the same."

"Identical," said Stanley. "Same trails, same snow—we kept it in the refrigerator all summer."

Shirley touched her silvered sunglasses and turned away, subtle body English that told Stanley he was a creep. They were increasingly unhappy when he asked them to pay in advance and to understand that coffee and ice were no longer complimentary, but they paid up and went to the cabin. A minute later Julie returned bearing a message from her father. "Someone stole the TV from cabin one," she said. On the way back she passed Jason, who was instructed to inform Stanley that the phone had likewise been ripped off. After that an austere silence came out of the cabin until both children returned with two halves of a communiqué.

"My father says for you to set us up with skis and boots right now," said Julie.

"My father says that after you take care of us come to the cabin and fix the toilet," said Jason.

"What's wrong with the toilet?"

"It's blowing bubbles and making waves."

"Mommie says there's something down there," added Julie.

Stanley suddenly realized that they were weighing his authority against their father's, or perhaps the power of dollars to buy obedience, and he frowned into their searching, scarlet faces, saying, "Skis and boots require a deposit."

The little girl held out a ten-dollar bill in each hand. "This one's for me, and this one's for Jason."

Stanley knew as much about skis as he knew about plumbing.

"Aren't you gonna put the wax on?" Julie demanded. "Alice always put the wax on."

"Of course I'm gonna put wax on!"

"Then how come you had us put our skis on first?"

"I always do it that way. Lay down on the floor."

He rummaged around until he found a box of tubes marked WAX—KLISTERS. The tubes were different colors and carried some kind of printed legend. He had no idea what the temperature was, or whether they were having "corn" snow, or any of the other things mentioned on the tubes in four languages, but there was no point in being fussy. A glob of blue, a dash of red, a squirt of purple—he laid the beads from tip to tail—and suddenly he was like a committee of spiders spinning too many webs in the same spot. The stuff followed him, floating in the air, building filament bridges that multiplied like hydras from surface to surface.

"You look like a silkworm," Julie said.

"Stand up!" he ordered. "Snow ho! Get lost!"

They struggled to their feet, but of course that was the end of it. Jason managed to get half a cracked ski up, leaving the other half welded to the floor. Julie looked as if she had jumped out of an airplane into the La Brea tar pits.

"Holy moly, you don't know what you're doing!" she shrilled. "I'm going to tell my dad! Holy moly!"

Stanley foresaw financial ruin. The floor of the lodge looked like a gross of Snickers on a hot griddle, and these little brats were going to run ramble-scramble through the world and broadcast his incompetence.

"You kids are too weak to ski," he said.

"I'm gonna tell my dad! Holy moly!"

Jason, still standing on one foot, began to cry.

"All right," said Stanley, "I guess I put a little too much wax on. Here, I'll give you half your deposit back."

"Dad-dy!" screamed the little girl.

"Okay, here's your whole deposit. Anyone can make a mistake. Put your foot down, Jason, and I'll unlace your boots."

Jason put his foot down. On Stanley's shoe.

Stanley's face looked like a used blotter, but he brought himself under control. "Look, kids, I'm going to level with you. You're my first customers, and I'm a little nervous. I don't know thing one about skis. I mean—you saw, right? Do I know anything about skis? You said I look like a silkworm, right? Not even a good silkworm really—I mean, how do those little green caterpillars handle this stuff with no hands or fingers yet? So, I'm asking you, give me a break. Don't tell your folks. They might leave and spread the word before I have a chance to redeem myself. Don't tell your folks, and the popcorn is free!"

Jason sniffed and shifted his weight on top of Stanley's foot.

"What about hot cocoa?"

"Don't tell a soul ever, and the hot cocoa is free too. In advance. I trust you." He dropped to his knees and tore the broken ski off his shoe. The shoe looked as if it had been polished with a belt sander, but he smiled hideously. "You can stay down here while I fix the toilet, okay?"

"Where's the comics?" demanded Julie. "Alice always had *Wonder Woman* and *Donald Duck* for us. I'm not staying without *Wonder Woman!*"

"Well, I've got all kinds of wonder women," Stanley said. "Here." And he brought out a stack of *Hustler*s.

"Holy moly," said Julie.

He really didn't relish seeing G.I. Joe again. The bumper stickers on the wagon had preordained their relationship— Vietnam vet, American chicken—but he thought he could go look in the toilet, then offer them cabins two through five to keep peace. They could even take the number with them. Cabin number two, alias number one. He knew they wouldn't, though. He had sensed a driving force in Joe that went beyond the nostalgia of this annual visit or perfectionism or even their instinctive dislike of each other. As soon as he entered the little cabin with its hermetic tightness he felt it again, sharper this time, as if Joe had been backed into a foxhole, bayonet fixed. Rover was cowering under the sink like a pile of dishrags.

"Well, well, had a little trouble with the toilet?"

"This place stinks," said Joe.

"These things happen. I'll have it fixed in a jiffy."

"What's wrong with your shoe? Looks like you shined it with a belt sander."

Stanley whisked the curtain aside and peered in the bowl.

"Uh-huh, uh-huh, just what I thought. Wave prefarction of the lower bowl. You probably ought to move to another cabin."

"Fix it," said Joe steelily.

"Oh. Okay. Yes, I think I can bang on the pipes a little... loosen the rumber maybe."

"That's the water inlet. There are no pipes. You need a plunger."

"Well, I'll just rap the bowl a few times." And Stanley grasped a wooden dowling that was leaning on a stud and began banging.

The next thing he knew his head was underwater and he had good news and bad. The good news was that there was no wave prefarction of the lower bowl; the bad was that Joe had him by the neck and shoulder and the words "Stinking Cong!" were ringing through the toilet.

Stanley braced his elbows on the rim with the strength of ten and made a contest out of it. He looked like an overenthusiastic grasshopper bobbing for apples. On the upthrusts just above the waterline he clamored for mercy, but his voice running around the contours of the bowl had the mellow inertness of a Rudy Vallee. Shirley's voice was going, too, like castration cold turkey. Stanley never put it together. Even after he was released and sat with one arm companionably around the bowl he couldn't put it together—the man with his hands stuck to his temples, the woman shrieking and doing push-ups on the man's chest, Rover clawing at the door, suitcases devouring clothes, a montage of color and shapes and inscrutable relationships. He didn't put it together until after they were gone and he had returned to the sanity of the lodge, with its pictures of shameless women and depraved acts strewn all over the hearth, and its empty boots and plastic skis pasted to the floor.

The next morning three more guests arrived. The first was a gaunt youth with wire-rim glasses and teeth as orange as a beaver's who backpacked in under a tent and a sleeping bag. He wanted out of the storm, he said, and Stanley put him in cabin five. The next two chugged up in a small flatbed truck which Stanley thought he had once seen in a Buster Keaton movie. There was a man and a woman and collectively with the truck they must have had three centuries behind them.

"Where's Ray?" the old man brought out slowly when Stanley went to meet them. He held his teeth in his hand, and his voice sounded like it came from under a blanket. "Where's Ray? Dead? We ain't been here in fifty years. I s'pose Ray's dead."

"Ray's prob'ly dead, Floyd," said the woman. "We ain't been here in fifty years." Except for her teeth, she looked exactly like Floyd, as if the shared tribulations of a lifetime had worn them even.

"I'm Stanley, the new owner. Ray told me all about you. You're Floyd, right?"

"Right. Hear that, Inee? Ray told this boy all about us."

"And you must be Inee," declared Stanley.

"Why, that's amazing. How did you know that?"

"Ray told me."

"Ray told you? But how did he know we were coming? This here's our fiftieth anniversary. We came here on our honey-moon in . . . ah . . ."

"Nineteen twenty-five," said Floyd.

"Nineteen twenty-five," Inee repeated. "This here's our fif-tieth anniversary."

"Oh, so you're back for a second honeymoon."

"Our second honeymoon," they agreed in unison.

"Well, if there's anything I can do to make it more pleasant, just let me know."

"You can keep the fire burning," said Floyd. "Inee and I never got out of bed the first time, and Ray kept the fire going. We want everything the same."

"Everything the same," said Inee, nodding.

Floyd turned to her and held out his hand. "Better give me your teeth, dumplin', that part's gonna be better than nineteen twenty-five."

She extracted her dentures, and he put both sets in the toolbox on the truck. Then he toted two satchels out of the cab.

"Let me help you with those," Stanley said.

"Just keep the fire goin', sonny. Everything like nineteen twenty-five, ya know." And hefting the satchels carlishly, Floyd led his paramour straight to cabin three.

Stanley walked around the truck as if he had discovered a time machine. It had come from another dimension, bearing two anachronisms who had divested themselves of age as simply and symbolically as removing their teeth. The trees, the sky, and the cabins suddenly seemed ancient and interesting to him, and he regretted not venerating them sooner. He had come here like the snow, blanketing everything with his flakiness and rendering it expressionless. How was it, with all his meditation, his ardor for things natural, his chemical journeys into essential truth, that he had missed the body, spirit, and sense of history of this place? It stood like an outpost on the border of space, a gateway to nature and a setting for some as yet unnamed gem. He saw now that he had been led here to identify its ultimate purpose. But what was it?

He went up to cabin three, where Floyd and Inee were already in bed enjoying love without teeth. There was a faded rose curtain drawn partway across the room, but it was full of holes and rents and Stanley could piece together a composite lump of ghostly flesh beyond. The flesh seemed to be stirring. He laid a few sticks on the grate, crumpled a newspaper underneath, and lit it.

"Just like nineteen twenty-five." Floyd's voice came gummily through the curtain.

"Nineteen twenty-five," echoed Inee lugubriously.

Stanley went back to the lodge. They hadn't wasted any time. And in a cold cabin, too. It had probably been cold in 1925, he thought, but he regretted selling the quartz heaters out of the cabins. The fire would not last long—neither would Floyd and Inee, though—and a half hour later he went back with a load of wood. As soon as he entered he saw that the mound of flesh was still quivering. This was truly amazing, he thought. Or was it the way of all geriatric lust? Maybe they were just trying to keep their balance. He stoked the fire, added some heavier logs, and went away. An hour later, again laden with wood and concern for the temperature of the cabin, he returned. This time he heard Inee say, "Oh, Floyd!" while he was adding to the fire. Her voice sounded as if it were dredged out of a drawer, but he understood that this was passion.

They were still mounted and quivering on the third and fourth visits, and he began to suspect that it was a monumental sham, that this canescent concupiscence was somehow a joke they had come here to play on him. He went back to the truck and sat in the cab. The windshield was yellowed and, despite the frost, which was closing over it like a cataract, he could see that it was layered with some kind of scale that made it look like lemon sherbet. He could smell oil—clean oil—and old leather and tobacco from the Red Man pack on the seat.

In the boot were heavy, blackened tools, an umbrella, the remnants of a straw hat, and a cloth purse. The hasp on the purse was shiny with wear; Stanley opened it. Inside was a cracked mirror in a tortoise frame and two pieces of cardboard bound together along one spine. He opened the cardboard, and there was a society page article decaying into an archipelago of newsprint. The gist of it was that Floyd and Inez Cavendish had been united in holy matrimony at First Presbyterian in Delaware, Massachusetts, on December 5, 1925. Somehow in the process of aging, or perhaps in a radiant burst from the photographer's flashpan, the faces of the bride and groom had bleached out, and now the picture stared out featureless, receptive to new identities. Ironically the only exceptions to this were their teeth, smiling forth and promising permanence. Stanley got out and opened the toolbox. They weren't the same teeth, but he thought they were still smiling.

He waited two hours this time, and when he went back they were still mounted but not moving, and the fire had gone out. The cabin was ice cold. A little apprehensively he rebuilt the fire, glancing all the while at the stillness on the bed. Finally, he rose up and faced them.

"Just like nineteen twenty-five," he said. And then he said, "Oh, God."

He couldn't bring himself to part the curtain. There was no need. They weren't moving. They weren't even breathing. They seemed closer to each other than before, as if in the final collapse their flesh had merged. It was, in a terrible sense, beautiful. Two eternal lovers ineffably bound in the bower of their initial consummation, nesting in a kind of poetic halo imparted by the rosy, ragged curtain as thin as glass.

But Stanley was terrified. He lurched back to the lodge and huddled on the couch in front of his own blackened grate. He had let the fire go out. They hadn't been able to generate enough heat to stay alive. The specter of Lewisburg hovered over him, and he began to cry. He was an ex-con; the jury would blame him somehow. He had sold the quartz heaters and two people were dead. He had failed to tend the fire. Those two wonderful ancients had shown him the meaning of this place, and he had let them die. Oh, how sad, he thought. To discover your soul and lose it on the same day—how sad.

He sat there a long time, knowing he had to call the police but reluctant to start the procedure that would desecrate a memory and decimate a life. The police or their agents would break Floyd and Inee apart and place them in separate body bags and conduct autopsies. They would vacuum them with trocars, spill them in the sink of a pathology lab, and bury the pieces in plastic sacks. Then they would bury Stanley. He would plead euthanasia or accident but they would bury him. Why should he rush into that? Why not just sit here until the pure snow buried them? Why not wait for divine lightning or hellfire to do the job? Hellfire. That was it. Cremation.

Unfurling from the couch, he ran all the way to the cabin. The fire was nearly out again, but he culled the embers onto the hearth. Behind the veil, the ancients were waiting for eternal life, he felt, grateful for his understanding. He rolled the embers under the hem of the curtain and watched the flames rise. And then he went outside.

But he was scarcely through the door before he heard the shouts, and Floyd and Inee burst out into the snow naked and livid as newborns.

"That how you tend a fire, boy?" screamed Floyd. "That how you treat guests?"

"You're alive!" Stanley cried.

"Of course I'm alive. But if I'd stayed in there I'd be roasted. Think I come out just to show you my testicles was descended?"

"He's just like Ray," said Inee, "that stupid son of a bitch."

"Just like Ray," agreed Floyd. "Stupid son of a bitch,"

"Ray burned us down the first time, too," said Inee. "That was cabin six."

"Stupid son of a bitch," said Floyd. "Burned us down right over there."

"Just like nineteen twenty-five," said Inee.

"Just like nineteen twenty-five," said Floyd.

They went up to the lodge by themselves, donned boots and blankets, and got into the truck. "Just like nineteen twenty-five," Stanley heard Inee's voice above the motor as they chugged away.

He stood in the snow, watching the cabin burn, remembering that his mother had once burned down a mountain and thinking that arson and stupidity ran in the family.

The morning after the fire he looked out and there was the gaunt youth with the wire-rim glasses and beaver teeth who had backpacked in and been put in cabin five. He still wore his backpack and his boots but other than that he was stark naked. Since it was only forty-two degrees out, Stanley was intrigued.

He put on his fleece-lined jacket, his stocking cap, and his gloves and boots and went out to talk to him.

"I couldn't help but notice that you're naked," he said.

"Naked is natural," the youth answered.

It was exactly what Stanley would have replied five years earlier.

"I'm into nature," Stanley said, "but I draw the line at freezing my balls off."

"It helps the seeds to germinate," said the youth. "I put them in the ground naked, and it helps them to know that their father suffered with them. Suffering is natural to the birth process."

Stanley noticed then that he had a little spade. He scraped away the snow, chipped open the earth, and dropped in a seed from his backpack.

"You're their father?"

"Yes."

Stanley took off his hat, gloves, and jacket. He unbuttoned his shirt and unzipped his fly.

"Thanks," said the youth. "You're very understanding. I go all over the country planting these seeds, and no one ever understood before."

"I used to be a terrorist," Stanley said, as if that explained it. "My name is Stanley."

"I'm Johnny Cannabis-seed. When these plants come up, smoke one and remember me. It's a form of communion."

"You must be very lonely."

"Yes...lonely. I used to have a dog named Vesuvius. But she broke wind all the time, and one night she fell asleep by the fire after eating a can of kidney beans and ignited."

"That's sad," said Stanley. He watched Johnny Cannabis-seed father a few more plants and then he said, "Would you mind if I zip up my fly? I think I'm getting frostbite."

"Certainly."

"I'll take off my shirt if you like." This was a significant gesture. Stanley hadn't taken his shirt off in front of anyone since he heard a girl on the beach say about him, Oh, God, if only I had tits like that!

"That's okay," said Johnny. "I forgot, you haven't had any squirrel mushrooms to keep you warm."

"Squirrel mushrooms?" Stanley looked into Johnny Cannabis-seed's eyes and perceived the friendly patronage of a guru. "I'll take a dozen. How much?"

The gaunt youth waved him to follow and led him through the snow to a knoll some distance into the woods. Here the earth was piebald with icy crusts and mud and knobbed with tall mushrooms. A pair of squirrels were nibbling away on the umbrellas, and one of these fell flat on its back, barrel-rolled, then swayed to its haunches.

Johnny walked within a yard of it to pick a mushroom; Stanley watched in astonishment. He had never seen squirrels high before. The mushrooms must have contained a hallucinogen like psilocybin. He realized now that he had discovered a spiritual leader, someone who knew and loved the secrets of this setting, someone whose coming had been presaged by Floyd and Inee. Whatever was to become of him, whatever he was to do in the wilderness of New Hampshire, this was the docent of his destiny.

They ate mushrooms all morning, and by noon they were both running naked in the snow, planting marijuana seeds. A busload of skiers from a high school in Franconia pulled in and pulled out again without opening the doors, and the teenagers pressed themselves wide-eyed to the windows like bottled olives. "I was once one of them," Johnny reflected, "a fly in a jar, en route to the dung heaps of civilization. Daddy had high hopes for me and bribed my way into the best medical school in Maryland. As my handwriting deteriorated, his expectations for my career leaped from male nurse to Surgeon General. But the only thing I was good at was collecting exams, research papers, and assignments from the school incinerator. By the time the scandal broke I was getting straight A's and doing two hundred dollars a day. They caught me because half the senior class was also getting straight A's. My files were larger than the Dean's, and because of Daddy's influence they made me Director of School Archives instead of expelling me. Well, everything was cool until I killed my best friend in a hockey game. He was groping over the ice for his contact lens and I caught him in the temple with a slap shot. We were playing a scrub game on a frozen pond, and the next spring I saw a bat crawl down to the edge of that same pond and get a drink of water at sunset. I knew right away it was him—my best friend. I mean you don't see bats out walking at sunset every day. Well, I followed him home and he went to an old hollow apple tree. Somebody had planted marijuana all around the trunk. I tried to pick him up and he bit me. Well, you really can't blame someone you've killed with a hockey puck for biting you, so after I finished with the rabies shots I went back to the apple tree and cured some of the grass. As soon as I smoked it, it came to me. The apple tree, rebirth, grass—I was meant to go around like Johnny Appleseed, replenishing nature."

Stanley hung on every word. "Yes, yes," he said, "I understand."

They went back to the lodge and french fried some of the mushrooms. Then they sat by the fire all day munching and smoking grass. The radio was on and seemed full of elusive meaning. "We'll hear Dan Rather on Miss Universe right after this message," said the announcer, and Stanley sat rapt, waiting for the passionate groans and gasps of Dan Rather on Miss Universe. Literal truth teased him like some not quite definable silhouette on a bedroom shade.

They ate mushrooms and listened to the radio all winter, and the cumulative effect of the drug was short-term memory loss, so that Stanley would often sit with one shoe on and not a clue as to whether he was taking them off or tying them up. They also suffered from "spore breath," in which anything organic they blew on grew mold within six minutes. This was too remote a phenomenon for either of them to notice, however. They blew on their coffee, their soup, on finger burns and flies, and the result was iridescent minestrone, green flesh, and insects that glowed in the dark. Johnny had intended to stay only a week or so, but by the end of that time he had only a vague memory of purpose and less will. The winter of oblivion passed painlessly, and Stanley emerged in spring unaware that hundreds of skiers had taken advantage of his lethargy, that his lodge was now famous for its free hospitality, and that Triple A had written it up, citing as its only drawback the hazard of squirrels that lay on their backs on the trails utterly indifferent to slaughter. Then in late May the mushrooms stopped growing, and guru and acolyte alike gradually unwebbed. When Johnny Cannabis-seed's mind had cleared sufficiently he said to Stanley, "When you think you've reached the ends of the earth, remember the world is round. I have examined a mountain grain by grain and in the end it wasn't there. The future is in the past."

"My past was in Lewisburg," Stanley said.

"I mean for you to go back to your roots. You should purge your mind. Mental blocks and intestinal blocks are often made of the same material."

"I used to be a terrorist."

"But you weren't born a terrorist. What were your roots before that? What are the roots of your roots? You must go back to your roots' roots if you want to be rerouted."

So Stanley left the smoke-blue trees of New Hampshire and went to England.

⑆ 25 ⑆

While Stanley was ruining the lodge and Stu was buying back Daisy's services, Nicki took his mother's house and turned it into cold storage for hot merchandise. The days when he had crammed contraband into dresser drawers upstairs were gone forever, and for the better part of a year Nicki stacked TVs neatly in one room and stereo receivers diligently in another. Stolen paintings checkered the dining room walls in a discernible attempt at classification, and upstairs there was a bathtub full of jewelry and gold accessories. That these vague constructs met some legitimate criterion of order eased his conscience, as if he sensed his mother's troubled heart gliding from room to room.

But Nicki roamed the night world of crime with equanimity, directing panel trucks and appraising the possessions of others on the wrong side of locked doors. He specialized in skylights and carried with him a set of tools that could excise glass like cutting pizza. In this manner he transgressed into the home of a well-known artist who was at that same hour appearing on the "Tonight Show" in California, according to *TV Guide*. This particular artist had long since established his forte with droll caricatures of famous personages, whom he somehow turned into ashen-faced animals of the forest. The skill must have become effortless and tedious to him because his studio was cluttered with the distractions of a causeless life: television, refrigerator, wet bar, and a subscription to the *Daily Racing Form*.

Nicki turned on the TV, and there was the famous artist sitting two guests away from Johnny Carson. One of the guests was hanging out of her dress at both ends. She was the obligatory birdbrain who discoursed loudly on her quirks as she tugged this way and that. "I like ketchup on my oatmeal," she said. "I keep the ketchup in the cookie jar. I keep the cookie jar in the linen closet so my cat can't get it." She crossed and uncrossed her legs and hitched a falling shoulder strap.

"That's really strange," Johnny Carson said. "People keep things in the darnedest places." She uncrossed her legs, tugging and hitching, and Carson panned innocence at the audience as if he had just seen the darnedest hiding place.

Ed McMahon led the laughter, and then the famous artist said, "I keep two Salvador Dali prints in the refrigerator of my studio."

Nicki jumped up and flew to that appliance.

"Salvador Dali right there in the fruit drawer with the bananas and pears," quipped Carson.

"No, in the freezer actually," said the artist. Nicki opened the door of the freezer, which was separate and disconnected. "Under the ice cube trays," said the artist. But his voice didn't come out of the television this time, and he had a nickel-plated revolver in his hand as he stood in the doorway.

The "Tonight Show" was a rerun, and the famous artist had been asleep in his bedroom downstairs when the set came on. He didn't know about the rerun, and he ordered Nicki face down on the floor while he watched the end. Then he called the police.

The judge Nicki came before at ten o'clock the next morning was known for his peculiar sentences. Nicki had come before him three times as a juvenile and on each occasion had received fantastic probations. The last time was for purse snatching, and he had been ordered to join the Boy Scouts and help one hundred little old ladies across a busy intersection.

Each of the little old ladies was supposed to sign a voucher, but most wouldn't, and if it hadn't been for a feebleminded aberrant who claimed to have two breasts—one above the other—and who signed eighty-seven of his vouchers, he might be a Boy Scout still. She had made him take her hand and help her across eighty-seven times as it was.

But this time his old nemesis was not going to give him probation. This time the judge bound him over for trial and set bond at fifty thousand dollars.

‖ 26 ‖

The fall after his mother's funeral, Harry returned to Bauvier and there was Professor Schwendler, the red-haired humanities teacher from Ross State who had appeared as a horse in Upsilon Lambda's stag smoker. She had changed her name to Agnes Eldrige and dyed her hair blond in order to get the job that had opened up with yet another death in the English department, but there was no mistaking the voluptuous proportions or the vulnerable pathos in her expression. "I knew someone would recognize me sooner or later," she said to him when they met in the empty faculty lounge. "I'm at your mercy."

He stared at her uncomprehendingly.

"Loose lips sink ships," she said.

They were sitting at opposite ends of a long table that seemed to be getting longer.

"If you're talking about that smoker, forget it," he said.

She laughed curtly and tossed her head. "Oh, God, the smoker." She had a cigarette going on the lip of an ashtray, but she fumbled in her purse for another. "I had to take that damn horse's head off."

"I'm the soul of discretion," he said.

She flicked her Bic furiously and torched the cigarette in the middle, inhaling as though she had just discovered air. "I don't know if I can take this. No matter where I go, someone will know me. Maybe I should just kill myself."

"Nobody in this town watches smokers. The Bijou is running *Birth of a Nation*."

"Oh, it's not just the smoker." She laughed harshly. "I'm as shameless as a cat. I have these sexual compulsions under inappropriate circumstances. My shrink says it's perversity; I'm trying to work out some self-hate."

"Is that why you left Ross State?"

"I didn't leave. They fired me for assigning my freshman humanities class a composition."

"Wow. They fired you for that?"

"I asked them to write a sex scene with their mother in it."

"Oh," said Harry. He thought a minute, then added, "That's not so bad."

"No? What would you think of a woman who was handed the microphone at a testimonial dinner for the Dean of Admissions and elected to suck it?"

"You did that?"

"It came out of the speakers like someone hopping through quicksand with galoshes on. They had to pull the plug to get me to stop."

"That's unbelievable."

"I told you I was as shameless as a cat."

Harry tried to hide his awe. "Everyone's got problems," he said.

"Yeah? What problems do you have?"

In the face of so much naked truth, he was inclined to candidness. Maybe it would even prevent Agnes Eldrige's suicide, he thought; how awful to have the soul of a professor from his alma mater on his conscience. He told her all about his marriage falling apart, how he felt he had become a mere figurehead in a family that revolved around childbirth and the trail to puberty, how he had seen that Carrie was much more compatible with Dan Dreiman than with him, and that they hadn't had intercourse or any meaningful dialogue since spring. The mention of Dan's name was enough to start his wife's crossed legs rocking, pumping heat to her sexual fantasies, he told Agnes, which was true, except that it was the pumping of Dreiman's energy and optimism that Carrie was in rhythm with.

"She calls his wife long distance every week," he said. "She says they're best friends. She can't remember thing one about what I like to eat, but she's an almanac of dates and trivia about the Dreimans."

"You call that a problem?"

Harry looked slightly abashed.

"Listen, fella, how long has it been since you told your wife you liked her cooking? When was the last time you asked her what was on *her* mind? Sure she goes for this Dreiman guy. He's outromancing you. He's winging in with all the joys and none of the problems of life. Your wife likes that. He's her fantasy. Don't you have fantasies? Did you think she was going to hang up her dreams just for you? She's not in bed with him, is she?"

He couldn't bring himself to tell her about the kiss. That was too painful. Harry had a vivid memory. "I don't think so," he said.

"Then it's just an innocent fantasy. Don't press it. You'll drive them together. Take my advice and appreciate what you've got. And if it bothers you to see your wife's head turned by a fantasy, bring her presents, take her out, talk to her. She'll reward you with love, loyalty, and hours of pure joy."

"Sounds like directions for owning a collie."

"More like a cat," she reflected. "Pet 'em, feed 'em, but don't mess with their independence." She seemed to like using cats in feminine contexts.

The door opened then and Mrs. Feedly, the principal, came in carrying a lunch tray. "Did I hear someone say they owned a cat? I love cats. Cats are divine. I love all animals, really. I think it's because they're like children, don't you?"

Her tireless falsetto imparted a false brightness to the world, and there was no need to answer her. Harry watched her bend to her soup, thinking she looked rather like Tweedledee and Tweedledum of his own painful adolescence. Agnes stared at her with widely innocent eyes and sucked one of her cigarettes with exaggerated slowness.

"I've got a dachshund actually," Mrs. Feedly said, dabbing her lips. "Her name is Kootchie. Felix named her. I've never told anyone this, but her real name is *Hootchie*-Kootchie. You know, like the naughty dancers?" She covered her mouth with her napkin, wincing merrily. "The reason he named her Hootchie-Kootchie was because she does this funny little dance and falls down on her . . . tail. Felix says it's because her head is so far from her tail she doesn't know what she's doing."

"I have the same problem," said Agnes.

Harry couldn't watch.

He stopped for yellow roses on the way home, and when he got to the door he hollered, "It's Mr. Wonderful!" Toots ambled in and tried to use his leg for a scratching post. Then he remembered. This was the day Carrie took Stephanie to Brownies.

He dropped the roses in a glass of water and went into the living room. Toots crawled into his lap and began to purr. She had gas, but the heat of her body and the fact that she was a cat seemed linked with Agnes's advice, and Harry put up with her. They were still sitting there when the rest of the family came home at five fifteen.

"It's Mr. Wonderful," he said when Carrie sat down to read the mail.

Her sitting down in his presence was itself unusual and propitious, he thought, but she looked at him as if she had just discovered mold in an egg salad sandwich.

He smiled but his lips felt leaden. "I really like your cooking," he said.

Again she looked up, this time her brows knitting angrily. "I had to take Stephanie, Harry! Your dinner will be ready soon."

He saw that his goodwill was being misinterpreted. It was too little, too late; their problems were of a more terminal nature than he had portrayed to Agnes. "I didn't mean anything by it," he said.

"Fine."

"By the way—"

Just then Stephanie appeared in the archway. "Oh, don't wear those shoes, honey," Carrie said. "They're too tight on you. You'll have to wear your sandals until your father gets around to taking us shopping."

"By the way—" Harry resumed when Stephanie had gone to change shoes, but the cat suddenly yowled and sprang from his lap.

"Harry, you hurt her!"

"I didn't hurt her! How did I hurt her?"

"I don't know; she whined."

He covered half his face with his hand. "By the way, what's for dinner?"

"I don't know yet," she said frostily and went to answer the phone.

Stephanie called to him that the hall light was burned out. Why did they have to turn on lights in the daytime? Why did they have to look at him as if he was cheap and unreasonable when he told them that? Why couldn't they have a decent conversation?

He heard Carrie hang up the phone and open the freezer door. Water ran in a pan. Something plopped. The can opener whirred. Two burners came in contact with utensil bottoms. Then she was back, sitting down, looking at a magazine.

"Where'd the yellow roses come from?" she asked.

"Dan Dreiman sent them," he said hopelessly.

She crossed her legs and began pumping. The magazine pages flew. Her eyes darted restlessly.

"I don't see a card. How do you know he sent them?"

"He didn't. I just wanted to see you rub your thighs together."

She froze then. Magazine, legs, eyes. "You're a fart, you know that?" she said, real pain in her voice.

"I want to talk, Carrie. I want to get a baby-sitter, take you out somewhere, and talk."

"No," she said, anger still gathering.

He called the sitter anyway.

He washed the dishes, straightened the house, and ran Stephanie's bath. Afterward he tucked her in bed.

"How come the soap still has sharp edges?" he chided.

"I washed real good," she said, "but, Daddy...soap isn't good for you."

"Isn't it?"

"No. It makes your skin slippery and it tastes awful when you get it in your mouth and it stings in your eyes."

"You're silly," he said, and she sighed contentedly.

"Daddy?"

"What?"

"Don't forget, you owe me a quarter."

"What for?"

"For Herbies."

Herbies were Volkswagens. Each time they saw one they

called out the color, and the first one to see the designated color of the day won. Yesterday it was yellow. "Red Herbie...blue Herbie!" he had called, deliberately overlooking the yellow ones until she saw hers first.

"You've got sharp eyes," he said, kissing her cheek.

"Daddy?"

"No story," he said. "It's late, and your mother and I are going out."

"I wasn't gonna ask that. Daddy?"

"What?"

"Do you love Mommy?"

"Of course I do."

"Does Mommy love you?"

"Yes."

"Do you and Mommy love me?"

"More than...spider soup."

"Then why are you gonna go away and leave me here?"

"Sometimes grown-ups have to be alone," he said.

"Alone together?"

"Sometimes. Sometimes alone all alone."

"Are you and Mommy gonna be alone together or alone all alone?"

He took her arms from around his neck then, and quietly kissed her, and quietly left.

When the baby-sitter came, Carrie reluctantly followed him to the car. They hadn't spoken since the flare-up in the living room, but she had showered and changed into a light blue skirt and blouse. There were only two theaters and three restaurants with any class in Haversack, and he drove past them all. There was one cemetery.

"What are we doing here?" she asked incredulously as he drove between the granite entrance columns.

He stopped the car, doused the lights, came around, and opened the door. She allowed herself to be led among the markers and mounds while the silence pressed in. It was a huge silence on a very calm night, surrounded as they were by so many still presences. When the magnitude of this settled on them, he gestured to the stones and said, "Do you suppose they ever argued?" He took a few steps, shoved his hands in his pockets, and swung back. "I wonder what they argued about. Doesn't seem to matter now, does it? We all wind up here. Maybe you and I will lie forever right over there."

"What's your point, O histrionic one?"

"The point is that there's no point in continuing this cold war between us. It's cold enough here. Life is short, Carrie. We're wasting it."

"I agree."

"What should we do about it?"

"Have babies."

He hung his head. "Is that what matters?"

"If it didn't, there wouldn't be anyone left to stand over these stupid graves."

"All right, Carrie, you traded your bed for a crib and wound up sleeping on the couch. As far as you're concerned, we've been personally mandated to carry on the human race all by ourselves. That's all that matters."

"When you come right down to it . . . yes."

"What about us?"

She leaned over a headstone and cupped her mouth. "You hear that, down there? What did you go and die for? Now all you have is descendants."

"And there's nothing else between cradle and grave?"

"Of course there's something else. There's enjoying life. There's raising your children."

"There's also living," he said. "I don't want to be a spectator."

"Oh, God, here we go again. My husband didn't get to climb his mountains yet. His family had such big hopes for him, but he did a dirty thing at Lake Seymour, and Wifey took away his swim-swim and his gambling—that's gamboling—and made him grow up too fast."

"And you never appreciated the sacrifices."

"Sacrifices! What about *my* sacrifices? Who went to college?"

"You got what you wanted."

She gaped at him through the darkness. "Which was?"

"Me. A baby. A home with a windup husband who goes to work every day, comes home to play with his daughter, and sits at the head of the table on Sundays. I'm a wooden masthead, a bowsprit—"

"Well, make up your mind, Cap'n Moon. The Crap Island boat is sinking while you run around the deck."

"The one thing you can't have is for me to like it," he continued. "You want me to be grateful and worship you for this lovely role you've created for me. But I don't. I can't. You've ignored me to death. When we started out, you were always in my corner. You wanted me to succeed—"

"Mick-ey . . . Mouse . . . Club," she intoned.

"Then you sprang the real you, and we started to rust away. You know, I might've given up—I might've resigned myself—if you'd been just a little smarter. If you'd come to *me* once in a while, if you'd stood still when I came to you, if you hadn't let any and everything that had to do with Stephanie and your world come first, I would've jumped through hoops for you. It worked before we were married, Carrie. All you had to do was make me feel important, and I'd be as dumb as ever. But it's hard to fake that in a marriage." He paused, tasting blood. "So you got yourself another stud."

"Oh, yes, I love Dan Dreiman. We go to bed together all the time."

"You don't have to. You don't want sex; you want sexuality. That's how a woman cheats."

She laughed harshly. It reminded him of Agnes's raw laugh when she had abandoned her pretenses that morning in the faculty lounge.

"So now you're an expert on women," she jeered.

"A man cheats with sex; a woman cheats with love," he said. "It's easy to cheat with love. You can do it with glances, with body English. You can even do it with good-bye kisses and never admit that's what you're doing. You get what you want, and as long as he doesn't get what he wants, there's no mess."

"Don't tell me what I want! I know what I want. I know what I *feel!*" The last word came out so hard that he realized she was starting to cry. "Yes, I want children." She took up in charged bursts. "Is that so terrible? I gave up a lot, you know. I gave up a whole lot. I went from my father's house to yours, and I never had a chance to taste freedom. I could have been a brain at college and made a career. . . ." She gave herself a couple breaths to check the tears. "I know, freedom is a myth. Well, that's easy to say when you've had it."

"It's bondage that's the myth," he said.

"Well, I'm imprisoned by a myth, then. Have I ever complained about that? All I ever wanted was for you to love me and Stephanie. And I never loved Dan Dreiman!"

"I've tried to love you, but you never appreciated my love. I don't blame you for Dan Dreiman. If it hadn't been him, it would've been someone else. I thought at first that it was just the baby, that it was mostly her demands that made you forget all about me. And that's still true. Another baby and I'll be extinct. I don't have to die to have nothing left but descendants; I'm a zombie husband now. But you certainly had enough time for Dan Dreiman. So I guess it's a matter of the right man, too. I don't fulfill your needs."

"I don't fulfill yours."

"Agreed. It's basic. You're in the habit of ignoring me; I'm in the habit of resenting you."

"So what do we do?"

"I don't know."

They stood there among the dead feeling dead, and then she said, "I think you should go away for a while. You've got a lot of feelings to work out about me."

He did.

The following Friday he called in to work sick, packed a suitcase, and went into Stephanie's room. "Daddy's going away alone all alone," he said.

❘ 27 ❘

From the first hour of his journey, Harry seemed to be in mortal danger. This did not really become apparent to him until he was airborne in a small, ugly, propeller-driven plane en route to Norfolk. He had noticed, of course, that the ancient craft swayed down the runway and that the passengers applauded when it eventually lifted off. "What's going on?" he asked the stewardess. She was not like most stewardesses, he saw then. For one thing she chewed gum like it was flubber, and for another she was fat. She was so fat that when she waddled down the aisle he could see her cheeks outflanking her long hair and the plane reverberated. In answer to his question about the applause she said, "Oh, they're regulars, they are."

"Welcome to the suicide flight," said the smartly dressed man to Harry's left, who naturally overheard his question. "Bet you never heard of Discount Airlines, but you jumped at their rates, right?"

"Right," Harry said apprehensively.

"Thought so. That's how I started."

"Started what?"

The stranger laughed. "The reason their rates are so low is because they discount old planes. This baby's maiden flight was Kitty Hawk."

Harry felt a wave of nausea and closed his eyes.

"But she hasn't crashed yet," the stranger revealed.

Harry opened his eyes and surveyed the "regulars."

"Now you're wondering if they can all be that cheap, right?" said the stranger. "Well, some are, some aren't. Some are thrill-seekers, some are ignorant, some are suicidal. But none are like me."

Harry looked directly at him.

"John Hancock," the man said and stuck out his hand.

For one horrifying moment Harry imagined that he was here to ply a ghoulish trade in the jaws of death. "You don't . . . sell insurance for John Hancock?" he got out.

"No, of course not." The man laughed. "My name just happens to be John Hancock."

"I see."

"Actually I sell insurance for Quickie Life of New Jersey."

Harry closed his eyes again.

"For ten dollars and forty cents I can insure you for the rest of the flight, if you hurry," said John Hancock. "We already got off the ground, so the price is down. Now, you're probably asking yourself what good is a policy if this baby starts to shudder in the air and goes down in a fiery holocaust, right? I mean, what chance does a flimsy piece of paper have when flesh and bone fuse at thirty-two hundred degrees Fahrenheit, right? Well, I've got this little lead box here under my seat—solid as anything they put the flight recorder in—and that's where I put your policy."

Harry felt the plane shudder, and his eyes flashed open. It was the stewardess coming back up the aisle.

"If you like, you can keep the little lead box under your seat," John Hancock was saying. "Seats aren't going to be here anyway, if we go down. They'll be on the ceiling. Floor bolts are just about rusted through." He waggled his seat to emphasize the point.

"No...no, thank you," Harry said. He clawed at his throat. "No thanks to everything."

"Say, you're not gonna swoon, are you? I didn't mean to make you swoon. If you're gonna swoon, I'll call the steward-ess."

"No, I'm not gonna swoon." Harry tossed his arm limply over his head.

"I hope I didn't offend you. You look funny. Did I offend you?"

"It's all right."

"I may be the only insurance man working this flight, but there's others making money off it, you know. See that guy over there, briefcase and Pierre Cardin suit? Know what's in his briefcase?"

Harry lolled in his seat, his eyes bugging out. Oh, please, God, don't let it be a bomb!

"Stock portfolios," said John Hancock. "He's the leading scientist at a laser fusion lab. Every other Thursday he takes this flight, and while he's in the air the stock in his corporation goes down. All the insiders sell out. He's got a standing order to buy then. When he lands safely, the stock jumps back up and he sells. I'm getting ready to lay a bundle on him. Fly and buy; he's got the right idea. Sure you don't want any insurance? We've still gotta land, you know."

"I'm sure."

"Say, you're sweating, mister. Don't swoon on me, now. Can I tell you a joke? How about a joke to cheer you up? What d'you get when you cross Iraq and Mexico?"

"Airsick."

"Wrong. Oil of Olay. Get it?"

Just then a male voice crackled over the loudspeaker. "Charlie, Baker, Able, Fox. This is your pilot," it said. "We don't know exactly where we are, but weather reports indicate severe turbulence somewhere in our vicinity. A two-inch hailstorm has been reported on the ground. If you hear knocking on the outside of the craft, or the windows start cracking, don't be alarmed. We'll probably make it anyway. And don't answer the knocking. That is all. Roger and out." There was snickering from the cockpit just before the speaker went off.

Harry pictured a tiny storm, two inches square, crawling along the ground below them.

"Don't answer the knocking? What the hell's he talking about?" Hancock said. "Excuse me, I've got to sell some insurance."

When the plane landed uneventfully everyone applauded again, including the stewardess.

Harry was so wrung out by all of this that when he got to Norfolk he dropped into the cool darkness of a theater to figure out his next move. The movie was *Peter Pan,* and as his eyes grew accustomed to the light he saw that the theater was filled mostly with women and very young children. Some of the women were pregnant; he could tell by looking laterally along the rows. They all seemed to have such large lips and eyes—the exaggerated beauty that belonged to a child but in an adult looked grotesque, he thought. Carrie would have loved this. He had forgotten the plot, but suddenly the picture began to hang together for him, and he realized he was watching the story of his life. Here was an ancient boy who refused to grow up. Here was a budding girl whose chief obsession was motherhood. "Come back with me, Peter, and we'll raise the lost boys together," Wendy pleaded. He couldn't remember how it ended, but he wanted Tinker Bell to win. It was Tink who shared Peter's life and wanted him to go on as he was. Once, Carrie had been Tink. Now she was Tank.

He was sitting on the edge of his seat, waiting to see how the movie would come out, when the man came in. He was just an average man in a light dress shirt and glasses, but he had a briefcase, and he sat down across the aisle from Harry. What kind of man goes to *Peter Pan* with a briefcase? Harry wondered. He had his own suitcase on the seat next to him, but he wondered about the man with a briefcase. Captain Hook was trying to gaff Peter, and Harry noticed that the man across the aisle kept one hand hidden. He remembered the scientist aboard the plane with his "stock portfolio" in a briefcase hedging doom. John Hancock carried a lead box. Why was his life suddenly filled with pregnant women and sinister parcels? He gazed acutely at the thing in the aisle and thought he heard ticking. It grew louder as he stared. It *was* ticking! But now he saw the crocodile, which had swallowed a clock along with Hook's hand, slog across the screen, and he couldn't be sure. How long had the croc been there? How much time was left in the briefcase? In the croc? There was a pregnant mother and a little girl sitting right in front of the man. Why on earth would a man who hid his hand come to see *Peter Pan* with a briefcase? Certain that an explosion was imminent, Harry leaped to his feet.

"This man has a bomb in his briefcase!" he shouted. "This man has a bomb in his briefcase, everybody!"

The man with the glasses looked flabbergasted. A woman screamed. Above the loudspeakers the crocodile ticked bombastically.

"I'm just a traveling salesman," said the man with the glasses.

"There's a bomb in the theater; we're going to be blasted to kingdom come!" came from the first row. More screams. Pregnant women were jumping out of their seats everywhere.

"I'm just a traveling salesman. I sell diapers!" hollered the man with the glasses.

He struggled to open his briefcase, but Harry tried to stop him. The house lights came up and the aisles thundered with pregnant women.

"Diapers!" shouted the salesman, and the case flew open, spewing samples all over the seats.

A few enterprising mothers-to-be collected them on the way out. And then the picture went off the screen with a sound like a needle skating off a record. Harry would never know what happened to Peter Pan, just as he had never known Disneyland. He didn't wait around for a refund.

As soon as he left the theater he took a cab to Virginia Beach and rented a room at a place called Long John Silver's by the Sea. He wanted to swim in the ocean. "Are there any sharks out there?" he inquired of the bewhiskered manager.

"Well, it is the Atlantic; I expect there's some." He answered so thoughtfully that Harry couldn't be sure of the sarcasm.

"I mean right offshore? I came here to swim, and I don't like sharks."

"They're not a real popular item with anyone," said the manager, "but no shark ever bothered a guest."

Harry had read in the paper of a man losing a leg as he stood knee-deep off New Jersey, but he didn't say anything. He went to his room, unpacked his suitcase, and turned on the TV. A chorus of pregnant women were singing "The more love you give, the more you end up with" and looping their arms out in front of them. He turned it off and got into his suit.

On the beach, he picked up his first stray—an old graying Labrador with three legs. The ocean was hard as slate and marbled with foam, and the dog watched him enter with a kind of knowledgeable forlornness. Harry sensed at once the magnitude of the element. It exhilarated him to think he stood at the beginning of something so vast, and he felt an impulse to strike out across it. The foretaste of destination was as mythical and seductive as the freedom Carrie sought, he thought. And as necessary. What a pleasant eternity that would be, thrusting waves aside with a tireless freestyle while lesser, limbless things undulated beneath him. Limbless. He looked ashore and saw that his Labrador friend had been joined by another three-legged dog. This one was big and dim-eyed and hoary also. A thrill of horror went through him. All of a sudden the waves sounded anxious to get in. *Rush . . . rush . . . rush . . .*

He felt the same intense peril he had felt in the plane going up and in the theater filled with rushing patrons. Something was stalking him. Was it death? Were these the cues of an angry deity? Had he fallen from grace by leaving Haversack? The plane had not crashed, the briefcase had not exploded, but were there really no sharks? He stumbled ashore and scampered up the beach. As soon as he was dry and dressed, he checked out of Long John Silver's by the Sea. "How come all the dogs around here only have three legs?" he tossed with his key to the manager. "How come there aren't any little ones?" Long John Silver only had one leg, he remembered on the way back to the airport.

That the brushes with death were a relinquishing of divine protection, an acknowledgment by God of his lessened worth in absentia from his family, seemed confirmed by his safe and uneventful trip home. He arrived in Haversack early Saturday morning and checked into a motel. Somehow it became a defeat to return so quickly, and after several hours' sleep he took a train to Chewbagin. There he spent Saturday night and all day

Sunday. The only place he went was the graveyard Jules had shown him as a boy, where, to his sorrow, he came upon a new stone chiseled with the name JULES OBADIAH STENNER.

"I wish you were here. I wish you were here, Jules," he said and wept.

The date on the stone was August; he had missed him by only a few weeks. This man in whose senile lapses he had seen only philosophical pauses was lost to him now, like his mother, like his wife. Despite his love, everyone seemed to be escaping him. He could no longer make meaningful contact with the supporting cast of his life.

"Jules?" he called. "Remember how you used to tell jokes over these graves? Well, I've got a joke for you. What do you get... what do you get when you cross Iraq and Mexico?" He listened to the wind blowing down the mountain then and knew there was no one here. Maybe they had been here for Jules, who could walk in either dimension, but they weren't here for Harry Moon, who stood in between.

He left at dusk and boarded the train. The mantra of the wheels and the inevitability of his destination produced a sense of failure he tried to resist. He was going back with no answers, his feelings for his wife as unresolved as his role in the destiny of Moons. She said she loved him. Did she believe that? Which of them was she lying to? Or was his definition of love an impossible code of fidelity she couldn't be expected to honor?

The train ghosted into Haversack about 5 A.M., and since it was now Monday and the station was close to the school, he decided to sit in the playground until seven, when the custodian was supposed to arrive to open the door. That would give Carrie the illusion that he had been gone an extra day. He wanted to jangle alarms in their marriage, he realized. They seemed to be down to ultimatums and demonstrations. The ultimatums were hers, but the demos were his.

When he got to the playground he went automatically to the swings. He hadn't swung in years, and now he rocked and climbed to reckless heights. One of the eye bolts emitted high poignant notes with each pass, not unlike the cry of a cardinal in search of company, and he noticed as the dawn came over the trees that he wasn't alone. Someone lay next to the fence. There was something familiar in the high sloping head, thatched with ragged hair. Harry scuffed his feet, dropping to earth.

"Raymond?"

"What?"

"What are you doing here?" He got off the swing and walked toward him.

"It's a free country."

"You should be home in bed," Harry said. "I can't believe you're out this early."

"I ain't out early. I'm out late."

"You haven't been home all night? Don't you know your parents probably have the police out looking for you?"

Raymond laid his head back down, and Harry saw that he was bedded in newspaper.

"Did your parents have a fight? Are you a runaway? Get up."

Harry got his suitcase. It was still too early to stow it in the school, so he thumped back down the street with it, Raymond on his other side. He was mad enough to confront Raymond's father—if the boy couldn't have a hero, let him at least have an overlord who ran a bed check once a night, Harry thought.

The house was notorious in the neighborhood and not unknown to the police. Harry had been there once before to identify Raymond to a truant officer. It looked stark and broken-down in the dissipating gloom. Why weren't the lights on? Why weren't there two adults frantic out of their minds running around? He zigzagged up the disintegrating porch and blasted the door.

He blasted it three more times, then looked at Raymond.

"I'm out permanent," Raymond said. He hadn't bothered to come up on the porch.

"Your folks left," Harry said, stunned. "You moved?"

"Not me."

Harry came straight down the steps, snapping off the rotting edge at the bottom. "They left you," he said tentatively.

Raymond shrugged. "I don't care."

"When?"

Shrug. "Eight days ago."

Eight days. Raymond never kept track of anything, but he had counted eight days. Hope by the number.

"Where did they go?"

Shrug. "Don't know. Don't care."

"Didn't they tell you, didn't you see them packing?"

Shrug. Raymond was looking down the street tapping his foot. Even in profile he looked humiliated and crushed. Finally the silence was too much. "That's what I get for goin' to school," he said. 'They did everything while I was in school. Even kept my sister home. I come here afterward...." He stopped. "Don't matter to me none."

It mattered a lot.

Harry's heart fell like the swing falling from its arc. A boy had come home from school and there was nobody there. His parents had run away. Raymond threw him a rapid glance, and Harry saw the whites of his eyes. He remembered the day his brothers had led him away from home and abandoned him and how his father had found him in front of a bakery. "You must be hungry," he said. "I'm going to call in sick today. Let's go home."

Carrie would scream, he knew. Carrie would scream very loudly. So be it. He only hoped she wouldn't do it within earshot of Raymond. The baby she wanted was on the way, saving them the time and trouble of intercourse, pregnancy, and labor. Also infancy, childhood, and most of adolescence. It sat well with his mother's deathbed advice, too. Having babies makes women holy, fulfilled, and self-righteous, she had said. If they don't get their quota they become bitter and insecure. That's your choice, Harry. Well, he was opting for self-righteousness. But this was one baby that wouldn't supplant him.

{ 28 }

When Carrie heard about Raymond coming to live with them she screamed. She took Harry out to the garbage can in the alley and screamed at him. "Helpless and vulnerable?" she screamed. "You call that kid in there with a beard a baby? I said I needed someone helpless and vulnerable!"

"You said *awkward* and vulnerable, actually. Raymond is both. But if you don't want to open up your heart to a child who came home and found his parents ran out on him, I'll just tell him to forget it."

"Oh, sure. Lay some sin on me. Sometimes I don't understand you, Harry."

"I know."

So she went back in to open up her heart, but Raymond read its tentative warmth as easily as a billboard and also the fear of guilt behind it. He played on the fear of guilt. He tested it with loud music, unresponsiveness, the breaking of dishes, and mistreatment of the cat. An example of all four was when he dropped a cup of coffee on Toots. Toots did the java jive, and Carrie got hysterical. She tried to crawl behind the refrigerator to retrieve the anguished cat, chastening Raymond at the same time. Raymond had the transistor blaring, and it sounded very much like the cat. "Turn that crap off!" she shrilled. The music went off, but when she emerged scratched and bleeding from the space between the wall and the refrigerator she saw that he had the earphone on. "You did that on purpose," she accused. "You broke the cup, scalded the cat, deliberately turned that music up, and now you're ignoring me."

"The President's been shot," he said.

"What?"

"They just broke in with a bulletin. The President's been shot."

"Oh, my God."

"He's been shot . . . three times."

The cat was howling, but all Carrie could say was "Oh, my God."

"Two shots hit him," Raymond said.

"Oh, my God, where?"

"In Chicago."

"I mean *where*."

"One in the head . . . one in the neck."

Tootsie wailed.

"Oh, my God."

"He's still alive."

"Turn it up," Carrie commanded.

"They're trying to stop the bleeding. Oh, no . . . !"

"What? What?"

"Oh, no!" Raymond pounded his fist on the wall and ran out the door.

Carrie scrambled to the TV set in the living room. The UHF channel was showing "Mr. Fix-it Snakes Our Plumbing" at that hour, and even President Ford's demise had not superseded the critically plugged toilet. She flipped to Channel 2, where a bulldozer was halfway across Oliver Hardy. Life goes on, she thought fleetingly, but the President had not been shot on channels 5, 6, or 8 either, and suddenly she knew who should be assassinated that day.

Then the back door opened and she grabbed the rocker to sit in judgment on Raymond. But it was Harry. He came through the kitchen.

"The refrigerator howled at me," he said.

"This isn't going to work, Harry."

"What isn't?"

"You know what."

He went around behind her and dropped into a chair facing the window. "We never solve problems together," he said. "We seem to communicate by indictment."

"Why do we have to solve Raymond's problems?"

"I brought him home to solve your problem. You wanted a baby."

"That's not why you brought him home."

"Okay, I've got a big heart too."

"You've never been able to distinguish what you want your actions to mean from what they actually do mean, Harry."

They continued to sit, staring in opposite directions for a minute or two, until he got up and came around in front of her. "Look," he said. "What is it going to take to make this work?"

"A frontal lobotomy for Raymond."

"What's Chief Boilingblood done now?"

"Oh, come on, Harry, we're not equipped to handle hardened cases here at Happy Valley. I want to be able to lift up the phone and not interrupt an obscene call, I want to leave money on my dressing table, I want to take a bath without having to plug up the keyhole along with the tub."

"So we need a separate phone, an allowance for Raymond, and a bathroom without a keyhole."

"Great, Harry. Make a list. Write it all up. Insure domestic tranquillity and provide for the common defense."

"Give it time, Carrie. Give it time."

He was insane if he thought she was ever going to love baby Raymond. "Time" was not the watchword here—unless it was followed by the word "bomb." He could not deny her a real baby forever, she thought, not if there was an ounce of justice in their marriage. She had joined the legions of repressed women who had been cheated out of their independence, their potential, their very maturity by possessive and critical husbands. It wasn't fair. How much more could she give? In a just marriage she would have been encouraged, exalted, indulged. So why was her worth tarnishing? He had invaded her very fantasies and accused her of infidelity because those fantasies were more tangible than his. She liked another human being who happened to be male, and Harry acted like they were already in bed. He couldn't understand simple warmth. To him tenderness between the sexes was only a prelude to intercourse. He might give lip service to love for its own sake, but that wasn't his big worry. His big worry was sex. All romance was sexual seduction. That's why she had cut him off at the bedroom. It was the one and only statement she could make.

When Raymond came in for dinner she pretended to be preoccupied. She felt his marmot eyes searching her face for anger and hate as she set the table, and she knew he would test her again soon.

It came when she undressed for her bath. She had just bent over to try the water steaming out of the tub when she felt that the keyhole behind her had suddenly become a bay window again. Sidling out of range, she grabbed up a spray can of Lysol and crept in from the left flank. Then she let him have it. There was a sharp gasp and much stumbling. That's mud in your eye for Toots, Raymond!

But Raymond came to breakfast exceedingly bright-eyed. Harry came in winking. His left eye looked like a misplaced nipple.

MOON
RISING

{ 29 }

Just before the Halloween
after his mother died Harry went down to the basement for a
can of bamboo shoots and stayed the weekend. Peace and neu-
trality invested the cool dampness of the cellar, and the serenity
that comes with decay beckoned him. He felt compatible with
the elements that wafted out of the drains. Here were the discarded containers of the life upstairs, here lay the casualties of
usage—clothes to be washed, toys to be mended, ancient objects
too worn to be rehabilitated but too nostalgic to die, dying
slowly then and placed here to be shrouded with dust or rust
and forgotten. Harry was one of these. Vestigial. Peripheral.
The only difference was that he had made his way to the basement by himself.

Upstairs the organic unit of mother and daughter talked
on in a private language made up of familiar words but incom-
prehensible themes. The phone rang, dishes broke, alarms went
off, but they seemed to do so in some kind of sequence that left

the continuity of conversation intact. Harry was no longer there to collide with these disruptions, to be interrupted or overriden or ignored. He was here. The floorboards rumbled and snapped overhead like thunderclouds, and the nails of the flooring stuck through between the beams like the beginnings of a sharp and desolate rain, but the spiderwebs in the basement softened and lightened the corners, as if to give the thunderclouds a silver lining.

He stayed in the basement Saturday night and all day Sunday, eating dried prunes and apples and drinking at the laundry tubs. They had a toilet downstairs, which was a handy thing after two days of dried prunes. Carrie sent Raymond down on Saturday afternoon, but Harry only asked him about school, as if they hadn't been there together every day.

Sunday night he started upstairs, remembered he'd forgotten what he had come down for, and went back to the cellar for a can of bamboo shoots. They were all out, and he surfaced into his estranged household empty-handed.

After that he spent most of his free time in the basement. He talked to meter readers, a pair of Jehovah's Witnesses, and salesmen of all types in its rational coolness. The Jehovah's Witnesses seemed drawn to his dejected spirituality housed belowground, and they trooped down the stairs without touching walls or banister to quote him whole scriptures by turns. He became the neighborhood sideshow. Only Raymond recognized something lonely and defiant in Harry's retreat. Sometimes he would come to the foot of the stairs and smoke a cigarette. Harry wouldn't say anything about the cigarette, and Raymond would nod and smile as he was leaving. It was the closest they ever got.

Just before Christmas, Harry was sawing out the pieces to a wooden cart for Stephanie when a newsboy and a route manager came to the door. It was the old Help-your-carrier-win-a-trip-to-Washington-D.C., and Carrie sent them downstairs. Harry gave them an audience but continued sawing.

"Hi, I'm Phil Parker, your local representative from the *Herald*," said the route manager. "And this, of course, is your neighborhood newsboy, Johnny West. Say hello to Mr. Moon, Johnny."

"'Lo, Mr. Moon."

The hacksaw kept nipping through plywood like a yelping

dog, but Harry recognized Johnny as the purveyor of fireworks who had sold Raymond M-80s in October.

"Young Johnny here is saving up for college, Mr. Moon," said Phil Parker. "It's good to see such enterprise on behalf of our youth, don't you think? Now it just so happens that to help him do this the *Herald* is running a program for Johnny here and others like him. We feel so strongly about sending him to college that we're offering him the additional incentive of a free trip to Washington, D.C., if he can enlist more new subscribers than the other newsboys. We notice that you haven't subscribed yet, Mr. Moon, and we thought you'd want the opportunity of helping out your neighbor Johnny here."

"Johnny here?" Harry stopped sawing.

"Washington, D.C., is the capital of our great nation," Phil Parker explained.

"I've heard of it."

"Johnny here has a chance to go there if you help him out. You don't want to take that opportunity away from Johnny here, do you, Mr. Moon?"

Johnny here was picking his nose and flicking his fingers over the laundry.

"Won't I be taking it away from one of the other newsboys if I help Johnny here?" asked Harry.

"But Johnny is *your* neighbor and newsboy, Mr. Moon. He grew up right here on *your* block. His mother and father know you and see you on the street every day."

The boy had been sent here last summer from Newark to live with his aunt and uncle, Harry knew. For that he felt sorry, but he detested promotions that went beyond incentive into shame, guilt, and coercion.

"Tell you what," he said. "This is such a wholesome thing your paper is doing, I really hate to take away *your* opportunity to subsidize Johnny by fattening your accounts. And I happen to have a ticket here." He waved a refund coupon from a pack of Eveready batteries. "This is your chance to win three free high-jump lessons for a paraplegic of your choice. Moreover, if you buy one a week for a dollar, I'll keep ninety cents and give my little girl a dime to go to the zoo. You don't want to keep my little girl from going to the zoo, do you?"

The route manager looked weary as he guided Johnny West up the basement stairs.

It was snowing out, and the soft motes piled up outside the

basement windows. Harry skated a rag over the puddles left by his visitors and looked at the coupon in his hand. It was about the size of a lottery ticket. He hadn't bought a lottery ticket in a long time. The pain of hope had long since eased in his life, and he smiled to think that he had once winged selfish prayers toward God for material gain. Was his father's fatalism the elemental force that had sent him to the basement to be purified? He had no vain ambitions now; he desired neither reconciliation with the world nor rapport with his wife. The basement had simplified him and cauterized his wounds. The snow was cooling and whitening his heart. It was time to go up. He was invulnerable now because he was worthless, and just to prove it he went out and bought a lottery ticket.

"Hello?"

"Hello."

He called her from the drugstore. Before verification. Before he showed anyone else the ticket.

"What would you say if I said I'd won a color TV?"

"Red, green, or yellow?"

"What would you say if I won a car?"

"I'd say you popped your clutch."

"Yeah?" Energy in his voice. Like Dreiman's. Like hope.

"Harry, did you win a car?"

"No."

"What are you up to?"

"What would you say if I won a house?"

"Did you?"

"What would you say if I won nine and a half million dollars?"

She didn't say anything.

{ 30 }

Harry bought a Kawasaki 1250 and a new suit. Carrie bought a microwave oven. They signed Stephanie up for piano lessons and paid cash for a spinet. Stray dogs snubbed Harry, sensing in him the nouveau riche. Except for that, nothing really changed, he thought. Certainly not the honor of the Moons. There were charities and eccentrics who had read about them in the paper and who wrote or called to plead their causes, there were tax obligations to be met or evaded, so they changed the phone number and put their trust in the convolutions of counsel, and soon their marriage resumed its antagonisms.

But the students and faculty at Bauvier saw a changed man. Harry no longer feared dismissal. It was as though he had acquired the deed to his own prison. The length of his sentence was now finite, and he could choose the release date himself. At the end of the first marking period he awarded varsity letter *E*'s to his failing students. He also issued lifetime unexcused tardy slips to his habitually late pupils, laminated and trimmed in gold. The day after he got the Kawasaki he roared in, assigned one student to rat on anyone touching the chrome and another to carry his helmet, and strode down the middle of the hall like the Führer followed by the junior Wehrmacht. To Sasha Morgan, eating a banana on the south stairs, he said, "I see you've found the appropriate diet for your species." These and other excesses eventually came to the attention of Mrs. Feedly, who called him to the office. "Mr. Moon," she said crisply, "did you or did you not say to your classes that the cafeteria serves yesterday's garbage with food coloring? Do you or do you not drop the *H* when you pronounce the name 'Jack Hass' in your third-hour class? And do you intend to continue thundering to school on that machine you chain to the fence?" Tipping with both hands, she poured her glasses on, scrutinizing him quietly. "Is it the wealth, Mr. Moon? Is that why you've grown so irresponsible?"

This insight appealed to the remnants of his sense of duty, and he returned to class committed to clean up his act. Money had not made him happy. Could it be that what he needed was not freedom but rather a stronger commitment? For several days he wore the proper clothes, drove a proper car, and appeared at the proper places at the proper times. For this he expected to be warm and full and loved. But the students sensed his vulnerability and baited him with silliness and obnoxiousness.

"Your nose is funny," said an emboldened Sasha Morgan on Friday in the middle of a discussion of verbs. "One nose hole is bigger than the other." Then she screamed, or laughed—indistinguishable acts in her repertoire of expressions. The rest of the class sounded like a mass case of piles nearing resolution.

Harry smiled gently, but he was thinking that if these children were the future of the world, then to hell with civilization. "No, Sasha," he said, "actually I've only got one nostril and a small mouth. You, on the other hand, have a large mouth, an enormous mouth. When you open it, I can see the back of the inside of your skull. Though your brain is not loaded, you keep shooting off that mouth. I could shoot back, child, but I don't hunt small game."

The class labored in a deeply intellectual silence.

"Oh, yeah?" retorted Sasha presently. "At least I'm not ugly."

"I'm not really ugly, child," said Harry. "God let me choose my face, and since I was already humble, I chose this one. And remember, I got mine first. Yours was left over."

After that he thought a lot about napalm and recognized that his time in the company of children was drawing to a close. He began to understand W. C. Fields. He went home that night and found his plastic garbage cans blasted all over the snow by M-80s. The cans had cost him twelve dollars apiece at Sears and were warranted for five years. But what was twenty-four dollars compared to the kind of freedom Jules had enjoyed? No, they couldn't hurt him, these adolescent guerrillas. He was no longer their hostage. Carrie heard him laughing as he shoveled garbage and snow.

For all that, he remained unhappy. When had he been happy? he wondered. As a child? He looked through an old album that had belonged to his mother, and it seemed to him that the boy in the pictures was deliberately hiding his feelings, as if he recognized in the process of photography some obtrusive and disinherited spy from the future. If only his mother and father were alive, he thought. Who else could he ask, who else had been there from the beginning? He made a Saturday appointment to see Dr. Ufunker.

Carrie needed the car to take Stephanie for her piano lesson that day, so Harry took a bus.

When he came into town he saw the cemetery where his parents were buried, radiant with snow, and their house on Diebold Street, painted a ghastly green now. He walked from the terminal to Ufunker's office, arriving twenty minutes late. The receptionist frowned at him, but he had never waited less than an hour to get in anyway and there were still three patients ahead of him. He sat down in the desolate waiting room and stared at his shoelaces.

Neither the gold-toothed Daddy Warbucks who swore in ice-cream flavors nor the old boxer from New Amsterdam were there, but one of the patients kept swinging forward in his seat for a look at him. This one was a withered old man with white eyelashes and eyebrows that hung down like bangs, who presently leaned onto the withered old lady next to him. "Ask him, Martha," he husked.

"Now, Willard," she reassured him.

"Ask him."

Their whispers were loud and sibilant off the barren walls. Harry smiled politely.

"Willard wants me to ask you if you're from 'eaven or t'at ot'er place," the withered old lady said.

"I beg your pardon?"

"'Eaven or t'at ot'er place. Willard wants to know if you're an angel. 'E t'inks 'e's dead and 'e wants to know w'ere 'e is. If you're an angel, mister, it would 'elp a lot."

Willard's worried face peeked past her elbow like a gnarled bole on a white oak tree.

"Well, I'm an angel then," said Harry.

Willard's O-like mouth reposed and his brows unknit.

"T'anks a lot, mister," the woman said. Leaning toward Harry, she confided in a stage whisper, "'E's got necromimesis —t'inks 'e's dead. Doctor's going to take X rays." She swayed back but immediately leaned sideways again. "Me, I've got kraurosis of t'e brain. My brain tissue's s'rinking. It usually 'its t'e vagina, but wit' me it 'it my brain." She swayed back and forth again. "Don't seem to make no difference, t'ough, except I can't remember one of t'e letters of t'e alp'abet."

"Which one?" asked Harry out of politeness.

"I can't remember."

"Say Jack Hass," said Harry.

"Jack 'ass."

"It's the letter *H*."

"T'ank you."

"Don't mention it."

"I already did. O'-o'. W'at's t'at letter again? It's as t'ough it got squeezed out. I t'ink my brain just s'runk again."

"*H*."

"Yea'. T'at one."

Willard's face knotted like a hairy fist. "Which place is he from, Martha?"

"'E's from 'eaven, Willard. Not t'at ot'er place."

"Why don't you just say hell?" It was the third patient across the room.

"'ell," said Martha.

But by then they had all recoiled from a foul emanation.

The third patient was an ashen-faced man with eyes like rat droppings, and he yanked out a paper sack and held it over his mouth. His words resonated the paper so that he sounded like a large bass kazoo. "I'm sorry," he said. "It's my breath. I forgot to use my muffler. If I breathe through my nose, it's not bad. At three feet you might think I'd been eating radishes dipped in Mange Cure. But as soon as I open my mouth it's like Shoe Saver and brake fluid in a septic tank. It's very embarrassing. No one comes to my birthdays for fear I'll blow out the candles. Once a hummingbird dropped dead at my feet."

"'Ave you tried baking soda?" asked Martha with concern. "Baking soda and a sprig of mint is w'at I use on our dog."

·   222   ·

"I've tried everything. Cigarette filters, activated charcoal. Once I ate a pair of Odor-Eaters, size twelve. Nothing helped."

"Where's he from, Martha?" Willard wanted to know.

"Detroit," said the man.

Willard swiveled his hoary old head toward Martha. "Is that in heaven or hell?"

"It's in between," she said.

"Oh. Purgatory."

When Harry's turn came, he felt like an anticlimax. Before him had gone a man who was dead, a shrinking brain, and a case of death-dealing halitosis.

"Harold Moon," Ufunker read from the card without familiarity. He had aged like a piece of cheese, shrinking and yellowing, and Harry noticed he was wearing a pair of perforated kid gloves with GRAND PRIX printed on them. "What's the problem, Mr. Moon?"

"I guess I'm just depressed. I seem to be losing my importance. It's as though everyone has forgotten me. May I sit down?"

Ufunker recognized him for the first time then. "Well, well, how are your mother and father, Harry?"

"You signed their death certificates."

Ufunker blinked, Harry sat down.

"If my mother were still alive, I probably wouldn't be here," he said. "I would've gone to her for advice and direction. But she's gone and I'm lost. I suppose I ought to see a marriage counselor or a psychiatrist, but I just didn't feel like going to a stranger. You've known me longer than anyone else, that's why I came to you."

"I see." Ufunker flexed his gloves. "Well, I could take X rays, I suppose. You may have brain damage, you know. Sometimes depression is pathologically induced—"

"I know what caused it," Harry said. "I want to know what to do about it. I want to know what kind of person you think I am and where I stopped being happy and what I should be happy with."

Ufunker began thumping his foot. "Well, you were only a five at birth, you know."

"Was I happy then?"

Thump-thump. "You cried." *Thump-thump.*

"Don't all babies cry?"

"Unless they're stillborn." Ufunker pulled off his gloves. "It's because they've been taken out of the womb. The womb is a wonderful place. We all secretly yearn to go back there, you know. I've often thought we ought to sleep in some kind of womb at night. The waterbed comes close, of course, but you need to be immersed. If we all had a womb to go back to at night there would be less suicide, less crime, and fewer defective carburetors built in Detroit."

He went on talking about wombs and when he finally ran down, Harry asked, "Is it possible to be unhappy in the womb? Do you think some babies set impossible standards because of prenatal perfection?"

"Anything is possible."

"Then maybe that happened to me."

Thump-thump, thump-thump went Ufunker's foot. It sounded just like a beating heart. "You cried at birth, so you must have been happy in the womb," he said.

Harry thought that was a good point.

He went back to Haversack, and on Monday morning he arrived an hour earlier at Bauvier and got the pool key from the engineer. He hung his clothes in the coaches' office and put on his swimming suit.

The pool was a mere twenty yards long, four lanes, and the sign on the wall read BATHER LIMIT 65. He went to the edge, came down slowly, and uncoiled like a watch spring bent on releasing all its pent-up time at once. Out, out, out, he soared, defying the claims of earth, air and water. Then he shattered the polished surface. This was his womb.

He swam without counting, dreaming of the ocean and the feeling he had had at Virginia Beach. The womb was big, global in fact, and he needed a destination, a far shore to get to. The swim he had begun this morning must end at a worthwhile place or it would never end at all. There were many paths in the sea but none of them seemed right. There was the Long-distance Senior Nationals—four miles. Too short. There was Lake Michigan. There was Catalina. There were half a dozen seaboard swims. And then the reedy flesh that had beckoned him over the years from a hundred different depths in lakes and pools and puddles spoke to him from the green shadows wavering beneath him, and he heard his ancestor calling him home. "The English Channel," Jonathan Moon said.

❴ 31 ❵

By the time Harry got out of the water on the morning of his first workout he knew exactly what he was going to do for the next eight months. He would kiss off his job at Bauvier as soon as he got another pool to train in, and he would swim, swim, swim. At the end of the summer he would go and face the Channel.

"I'm going to swim the English Channel," he said to Mrs. Feedly as soon as she was in her office. "I'm quitting in order to train. I suppose you want two weeks' notice. It's in the contract —two weeks."

"Contract be damned," she said. "I'll take your classes myself. Did you leave any lesson plans?"

Her eyes looked like two ditches that had suddenly filled with light, and Harry saw in them the depth of his maladjustment and isolation.

"I was going to read them *The Cat in the Hat Comes Back* and do walk-the-dog with a yo-yo," he said. "They're into animals right now."

"I'm not surprised."

"I'd like to go on using the pool in the mornings."

"Recreation swimming for the general public is on Thursday evenings."

"You mean if I quit teaching, I can't swim?"

The light in the ditches flickered on the word *if.* "I'll make an exception," she said. "Just be off school property a half hour before the bell."

It would have been better if she was shocked, flustered, and conciliatory, he thought, but there was no use being petty about it. He was as relentless as a compass needle now. He stopped at the library, got everything he could find on Channel swims, and went home. Carrie was going to burst an aorta when she understood what he was up to. He gave her the easy news first.

"I quit," he said.

"Makes sense. You can afford your own gold watch now." She fingered through the library materials. "What are you going to do, swim the English Channel?"

He watched her fade into the kitchen. She had said it flippantly, but she understood. Understood and didn't care. Then he went upstairs and wrote a letter addressed to the cemetery:

Dear Mom,

Today I quit work and began training for the English Channel. I know you always wanted me to be a teacher, but it just didn't work out. I really tried. I gave it a few years, but all I saw was the decay of Western civilization. You wanted me to be noble, and if I'd stayed in junior high any longer I might have wound up on the window ledge of the third floor with the pigeons or held a room full of seventh-graders hostage with a pipe bomb. I don't like pigeons and Stanley knows where to lay his hands on munitions, so it's a good thing I quit when I did.

I went to see Dr. Ufunker and he asked about you. He told me to go back to the womb. I don't know what I'll do after the Channel, but that doesn't seem important now. Maybe the sharks will get me and I'll see you soon. I have the feeling it's in God's hands. Stephanie and Carrie are fine.

Love, Harry.

When he went downstairs Carrie was waiting for him in the rocking chair. He hated these audiences in which he came before her, so much like command performances. He had pursued her from room to room and chair to chair in quest of conversation, and it seemed she had the tactics of a sphinx when it came to choosing a place for marital strife.

"What are you going to do about us?" she began.

"What are you talking about?"

"Presumably when one swims the English Channel one goes to England. What about us?"

"It's something I've got to do alone. I didn't think there would be a problem."

"There is. It's called Raymond."

"Maybe we could send him to camp," he suggested.

"Harry," she said with a sigh, "Raymond was another one of your obsessions. I don't know how many women would have accepted a junior felon thrust into their lives—it's probably listed in *Ripley's Believe It or Not*—but I was stupid to be one of them. I have a daughter to raise, and she doesn't need a lying, stealing, sadistic, swearing, smoking, cough medicine junkie for a brother. Think a minute, Harry. You brought him here. If you go to England, take Raymond with you. But don't bring him back."

"What are you saying? What am I supposed to do, drown him? Oh. You're telling *me* not to come back."

"I didn't say that."

"Well, what the hell did you say?"

"I said Raymond's time is up."

"Maybe my time is up."

"Maybe."

She wasn't rocking, wasn't looking at him, and she looked incalculably older. It was that which he regretted most, the deflowering of her face. How had she come by such a glint of steel? How many angry, silent hours had it taken for the granite to form? He saw that she had taken a long journey into her mind and arrived at disdain and regret and guiltless infidelity. He was no more to her now than whiskers, spent mouthwash, and trimmed hair in the sink. And what was she to him? Clean socks in a drawer? Infidelity and oatmeal?

"When are you going to England?" she asked quietly.

He shrugged. "August."

"August! That's eight months—eight more months of Raymond. No, Harry."

The way she said it he knew she would give in. He had eight months. "I'll see that he's gone by then," he said.

He awoke the next morning with a dull, unrequitable ache. It was, he knew, the sexual analogue of his desire to swim the Channel. Even in high school his workouts had been paced by visions of Heather Latko. Now his swims were longer and more monotonous than ever, his chimera more sustained and intense.

To begin with, he tried straight swims—eight, nine, ten miles, and one ghastly sixteen-mile affair that destroyed his eyes and bored him out of his mind. The 20-yard pool was a dishpan, and he grew nauseated from flipping over every few strokes. To combat this he did a lot of kicking on a board. Most Channelists had used only a two-beat kick, he read, but leg cramps were still a problem, so he worked on his legs a lot and this also eliminated the flips. He had to get used to goggles—which he had always disdained—and he took cold showers to approximate the 60-degree chill of the Channel. Until he could get to open water in the spring, he decided to swim intervals and IM. The intervals consisted mostly of 400s in sets and the IMs were long medleys of all four strokes, but they broke up some of the tedium.

Harry weighed 186 pounds and was not particularly stocky. He decided to put on another 15 pounds, if possible, despite the caloric demands of training. Since Carrie refused to turn her kitchen into a pastry shop, or even to be tempted by the gluttony he proposed, he spent a lot of time slurping malts and eating sundaes in one parlor or another. He also snacked on marshmallows, whose calories, Carrie did not seem to realize, were 96 percent sugar. By late April she had put on eight pounds and he had lost two.

There was a spring-fed quarry outside Haversack, and it was into this that Harry transferred much of his training. The water was 56 degrees, and he had to camp on the cliffs swathed in blankets for better than ten hours a day in order to get in four hours' work. He spent most of his downtime reading, planning, and eating. He could handle sixty strokes per minute on the crossing, he thought, and when he hit the tides go to maybe sixty-eight. The course had to be from Dover to Calais, hopefully straight but probably as zigzag as a lightning bolt. He would have to hire a boat and handlers once he got to Dover. Presumably they would know enough about the tides and the weather to help him choose the best moment. The tides and the weather would still be a matter of luck then, but the cold would be a matter of preparation. He had to put on weight. He could coat himself with lanolin and Vaseline, but he still needed the weight.

He began to notice the profusion of diets in the marketplace. There was the drinking man's diet, the ice-cream lover's diet, the cake eater's diet, the sweet tooth diet, the chocolate diet, and the cheater's diet; there were *Calories for the Thin, Shed 'n Bread, Lose 'n Booze,* and the ambitious, all-purpose tome for the sexual gourmet called *Pound-Off.* Each of them seemed predicated on some unrelinquishable human frailty which could be recklessly indulged so long as one followed the remaining regimen. Harry decided to try the frailties and chuck the regimens. All of them. At the same time. He brought home a dozen books and carefully excluded everything they said to eat from his diet except for the human frailty. By the end of June he had gained seven pounds.

The water temperature in the quarry was now up to 62 and Harry was putting in five hours a day, mostly freestyle and kicking. But he needed an open course, he felt, and once a week he motorcycled down to Lake Seymour for long swims of ten to fifteen miles. There, adjacent to the beach where he had lost Heather and discovered Carrie, he sensed the paradox of trying to possess or achieve something so perfect that all the failures and losses it replaced became insignificant. If he failed in this, there wouldn't be a goal big enough to redeem his life, he thought. And as he swam, the water around his ears giggled at mortal logic and mocked some silver detail in Heather Latko's voice.

All through his workouts that year he had been taking honey and orange juice to keep from burning protein, but the honey left him queasy and the orange juice sometimes came up in cold water. He knew he would need something stable but effective over the Channel crossing, since he might be in the water anywhere from ten to twenty hours. The special demands of that kind of stress called for expert metabolic advice from someone truly creative in pharmacology. So he wrote Stanley in England and in due course got back a reply saying that the summer tax bill was coming due for the ski lodge, and if Harry would pay the four hundred dollars Stanley would arrange for delivery of two gallons of imperishable elixir guaranteed to float him across the Channel like a cloud. Harry paid the four hundred and sent a second letter with the caution that he didn't want to join the fog over the Channel. Then came a glassine bag full of red powder, postmarked Pittsburgh. Attached were these instructions:

Sprinkle powder in underwear before passing through Customs. When safe, take off underwear. Boil same in 2 parts club soda, 1 part vinegar. Throw underwear away—do not incinerate! Strain liquid through nylon sock. Place result in large wok and stir-fry six pounds of mung beans. Throw mung beans away (handle with rubber gloves). Pour liquid from wok through 40% orlon sweat sock. Bottle and store away from sunlight.

Harry took a quarter of the powder and made a half gallon. The mung beans turned into black discs and the orlon sweat sock dissolved, but the end result was a colorless liquid that looked like water and smelled like boat fuel. He tried some on the cat, and she couldn't get enough of it. It softened her hard pad and put her in heat. Since she had already been spayed, he thought this was remarkable and poured some in Carrie's coffee. The effect this time was less certain, but Carrie took a shower at ten o'clock and another at two, and the hot water heater never came on. So Tootsie strutted around with her tail in the air, Carrie showered, and Harry took a thermos of the stuff to Lake Seymour.

He swam hard for an hour and waded ashore for a drink. If it tasted like anything, it tasted like weak tea with a cloying aftereffect. He swam for another hour and took another drink. He did this for four consecutive hours and emerged feeling fine and without nausea. Except for his travel itinerary, he felt he was ready for the Channel.

Now came the hard part.

The Raymond part.

Raymond was not a child with problems—problems implied solutions—he was an end product. Whatever was genes and whatever was environment, these were done with. Harry had carried him for a while, cried over him, knocked on his door, but Raymond wasn't home. The most he had given Raymond was a little revenge, a chance for the boy to resist and reject him just as he himself had been rejected. And Raymond did this with the finesse of a de Sade. What was left was a holding pattern until he joined the army or got a nothing job or took to the streets. The streets, most likely. Carrie was right, they couldn't subject Stephanie and themselves to the waiting and the futility. Eight months ago Harry had known this.

But then he got a call a week before summer recess at Bauvier. "I just wanted you to know, Raymond's parents are back in the same house. They haven't enrolled the little girl, but the counselor talked to the father. The father says they left Raymond to teach him a lesson. He says the boy can come back if he wants to. Please don't think I'm offering you advice, Mr. Moon. I just wanted you to know." It was Mrs. Feedly.

The cardinal rule was that a child is better off with his natural parents under almost any circumstances. Almost. But only Harry had read Raymond's two compositions. Only Harry knew how intense Raymond's hatred for his father was, how deep the hurt and indignation at rejection. Would Raymond even *go* back?

He never mentioned the call from Mrs. Feedly to Raymond or Carrie, and he put off what he had to do until his travel arrangements were made, until he had swum his last workout at the quarry, until the eve of his departure. Then he took Raymond for a ride on the motorcycle.

The night slipped by them in a cool rush laden with insects and, because he had given his helmet to the boy, Harry took the sting of some of these against his face. It seemed to him then that he was a cruel Goliath striking down tiny creatures with his momentum. They soared for miles around the agrarian extremities of Haversack, but at last they circled inward to the diseased artery Raymond knew so well. When they reached the last block, Harry killed the engine and drifted to a stop.

The front windows were lit and Raymond saw his sister playing at the table. He got off the cycle, took a few steps up the broken walk. At first Harry thought he was compelled by the sight of his sister, but as the minutes lengthened it became apparent he was waiting. Harry dropped the stand and got off.

"It's your home," he decreed behind Raymond.

Raymond slowly shook his head, the helmet aglint with reproving moon.

"They're your folks."

Raymond shook his head faster.

"I want you to remember us," Harry said in a choked voice. "I love you, Raymond. You can come see me anytime." The words were mud in his mouth. "Anytime, Raymond. I want you to remember us. That's why I'm giving you the Kawasaki."

Raymond turned with malevolent delight. The consummate bribe. One motorcycle for one waiver of love. It vindicated all his cynicism, all his anger.

"Sure," he said evenly.

Harry tried to say something else, but the mud stuck and he turned for home carrying a cinder for a heart. The next morning he said good-bye to Stephanie and Carrie, sent Raymond's things by cab to his parents' house, and left for England.

⦃ 32 ⦄

No sooner had Harry left for England than Carrie received two desperate phone calls. The first was from Nicki just after his hearing in which the judge had set bond. There was only place Nicki could get fifty thousand dollars.

"Is Harry there?" he asked over the phone.

"Harry's gone to England," Carrie said.

"Oh, God. Oh God, oh God. Look, Carrie, I'm in the slammer and I need bond."

"What are you in for this time?"

"For being in the wrong place at the wrong time. I swear, I was watching Johnny Carson, and I went to the refrigerator, and the next thing I know I'm under arrest."

"I know a woman who got pregnant seven times watching Johnny Carson," Carrie said. "Her husband only functioned at midnight."

"Fifty grand, Carrie. I need fifty grand."

"You want us to give you fifty thousand?"

"It's only bond," he said. "You'll get it back."

"That's not the point."

He began to sound hysterical. "Have you ever been in jail?" he shrilled. "Have you ever been in a dirty little cage with a toilet bowl and no seat, surrounded by animals who would kill you for cigarettes and line up to commit perversions on your tender body? You're my one lousy phone call! Harry would do it in a minute, you know that, Carrie! Harry would fly down here to save his brother from death and dishonor!"

She had spent her wedding night in a cell with Easy Ethel and had seen Nicki for the first time waving out of an upper-story lockup, but she declined to remind him of this. "Okay, Nicki," she said. "Dishonor is your stock and trade, but we'll post bond. And if you screw this up, I'll drop a hot steam iron on your privates."

So Nicki got out, and he might have actually showed up for the trial, but he took a young lady to whom he had bragged of his daring and skill on a tour of roofs, and on one of these he accidentally dropped her through the skylight. They were disco dancing to a transistor radio over the heavy lattice frame, and he missed a catch. For several minutes he peered down into the darkness, but a terminal stillness prevailed beneath the disco version of "I Fall to Pieces," and Nicki left the roof, the state, and the country all in a matter of hours. He went to England.

The second call was from Stu. Daisy had gone through his remaining twelve hundred dollars before Budnipper even found out she had sabotaged the Dippity-do with Liquid Plumr and Nair. She thought there was no end to this wealth, of course, and Stu was forced to put his watch and ring in hock again and finally to use the white T-Bird as collateral for a five-thousand-dollar loan. By this time the bald-headed women who had used the Dippity-do were lining up in droves outside Ring-lets and Tresses and babushkas were selling like hotcakes. But faced with the specter of once more confessing bankruptcy to Daisy, Stu could not enjoy Budnipper's dilemma. In desperation he did what Nicki had done. He phoned his rich brother.

"Harry went to England a million years ago," Carrie told him. "He called in from another planet sometime this morning, but the reception was not good and he chose not to speak to the subspecies called 'wife.'"

"England? Where in England?"

"Wherever the English Channel is. On the coast, I believe."

"How do I get hold of him?"

"Good question. You might try a barrage balloon, or a note in a bottle. Sometimes he talks to fish."

"Carrie, I'm up against a wall. I need money."

"Is there a bank on the other side of the wall? Look for a door, Stu. Nicki got our last fifty thousand earmarked for stupidity."

Stu swallowed hard. "When is he coming back?"

"Another good question. Oh. You mean Harry. Harry is essential to Moonlight Bay. He may never come back. Why don't you go find him? Are you still living with that person of the third sex? Take it with you. England has lots of fog. You may never be noticed."

Then she hung up.

Stu felt as if he'd just rolled through a lion's cage at feeding time. But going to England was not a bad idea. It made sense to get Daisy as far away from Budnipper as possible before they went broke. Why make it easy for her to go back to that crud? If she didn't have any money, she couldn't fly home, and it would be hard to explain Liquid Plumr and Nair in the Dippity-do by satellite. Finally, he would be able to find his brother on the shores of the English Channel, he felt, and that might be his long-term salvation.

On the way to the courthouse for passport applications, they passed Budnipper's. It was starting to rain and the remnants of waves and curls on the women lined up outside the shop were dissolving like mud headdresses in a downpour.

"I'll never turn another spit curl in this town," observed Daisy. "But maybe in England I'll rule the waves."

{ 33 }

The last time Harry had flown was the suicide flight on Discount Airlines. This time he went first class, and the difference was uplifting. There was no swaying down the runway, no faltering flight, and the plane did not reverberate when the stewardess waddled down the aisle. The stewardess did not waddle, in fact, or chew gum; she was a slim Bahamian with skin like caramel-colored marble. Instead of a pilot calculating the odds of a safe landing over the cabin speakers, Roger Miller was singing "England Swings." Harry had never understood Miller's effervescent nonsense syllables sprinkled here and there, but the melodious tour de force of the song made him feel a sudden love for the passengers around him and a sadness that he had left for a foreign shore without remembering to take a picture of his wife and daughter. He smiled at the woman to his right and began to improvise his own nonsensical version of buzzes and boops.

"Would you mind not singing that? It's my favorite song," she said.

Harry smiled abashedly and lapsed into silence. When the song was over, he turned to the woman on the other side, stating brightly, "I'm going to England."

"We're all going to England," she said. He lapsed into another silence, and she added wearily, "Your first trip, huh?"

"Yes. My first trip. How about you?"

She laughed a little harshly. "I spend more time in the air than the moon." Harry wanted to tell her that his name was

· 235 ·

Moon, but now that she had begun, she opened up about her life. "I'm looking for my third and fourth husbands. Can you believe that? How old do you think I am? Forty? Fifty? Well, you're wrong, I'm thirty-five. Thirty-five and I'm looking for my third and fourth husbands. It's depressing. I got married when I was sixteen to a forty-three-year-old brain. I thought he was the Wizard of Oz. His swear words all had seven letters. If he didn't like what came out of the pulpit on Sunday, he stood up and argued. If he did like it, he applauded. He died of smoke inhalation when I was twenty-nine. Three packs of Camels a day for forty years. Some brain.

"My next husband was a press secretary for a famous sex symbol. He covered her for three years—after she took off her clothes for him. When I found out, he left me. Number three is a game nut. He loves crosswords, jigsaw puzzles, quizzes, and contests. The last time I saw him he was going on a scavenger hunt. That was two years ago. I get a card every week from a different place. The last card said he needed a blade of grass from Wimbledon and a book from the University of Oxford library. Three months ago I almost caught up with him in West Germany. He needed a strand of barbed wire from the Berlin Wall."

"You're very faithful," Harry said.

"No, I'm persistent. I told you I was looking for husband number four, too."

"Where did *he* go?"

"He didn't go anywhere. I haven't met him yet. But I'll be damned if I'm going to dump this jackass I'm hitched to now until I get a replacement. They don't come with warranties, you know. Say, are you married?"

Harry spent most of the seven-hour flight in the bathroom to avoid deepening his candidacy for number four, and when they landed at Heathrow he rushed off the plane.

He had sprinkled the powder for Stanley's elixir in his underwear as per instructions and went quickly through Customs, but when he slipped off his pants in the airport rest room his pubic hair came with them. This reminded him of Nino shaving down at the State Championships, and he bought a postcard on which he dedicated the Channel crossing to his old friend and mailed it on the spot in what the counter girl called a "pillar box." Then he took the Underground to London, emerging into a city whose fabled skyline of ancient, engraved structures seemed hostage to young, faceless ones. There was bloodless St. Paul's and the Tower of London, but they looked arthritic and frozen somehow in the keeping of homogenized corporate attendants. Old England on pension to new.

Harry cashed travelers' checks in a bank and registered at a hotel called something-something Ltd. He ate roast beef and Yorkshire pudding in the hotel dining room, and then a piece of apple pie down the street, including a huge chunk of translucent cheese, because the proprietor of the shop said, "An apple pie wi'out tha cheese is loik a kiss wi'out a squeeze." It was the only thing anyone said to him that transcended commerce. After that he retired to his room, where he all but melted his electric razor by plugging it into a 250-volt socket. In the morning he took a "coach" to Dover.

Through the window he got his first view of the austere Channel and its horizon. The overcast sky looked like cheap flannel tucked into a slate-green sash. And there were the white cliffs like scored glaciers ebbing from the cold grays and blues of Dover. He inhaled all this as he stepped from the coach and thought he would never be closer to the elements than in that one sentient breath. By noon he had a lodging—a pension, they called it—and was plunging into the icy grip of Dover Harbor for his first workout. Here he felt the full power of the sea, coming, as it was, not from some quarry's gouged-out sides or the basin of a lake but from great depths and endless expanses. East he would go, east to France. Over the route of conquerors and kings and armies in force or disarray, from one country to another, across an aorta of the ocean, he, Harry Moon, naked and unassisted, would pass. When he sat on the shore watching the tide make its reptant way up the beach, he said to the Channel, "Stretch yourself, make yourself as wide as possible, I will persevere."

The next day he asked the woman who ran the pension where he could hire a trawler for a Channel swim and she said, "You'll be wanting to see Freddy Flywater and Sam Santa, I expect." He followed her directions to a row of tightly squeezed rooms stacked three stories high against the cliffs and capped by a mansard roof. The bell card to one of these read "Flywater and Santa Ltd." His ring extracted a short, thin man, about thirty-five, with a face as narrow and squeezed as the rooms and a mouth like the flap of an envelope, from which a cigarette dangled. He had hard, tiny eyes beneath the brim of a soiled billycock hat and a red silk scarf around his neck.

"I want a tender for a Channel crossing," Harry said simply.

The man looked back over his shoulder, shouting, "Hey, Freddy, we got another one!" There was the sound of a toilet flushing and Sam Santa grinned. "Freddy's spending a penny in the loo. What's your name, mate?"

"Harry Moon."

"Well, I'm Sam Santa and this here's Freddy Flywater."

The second man came forth fastening his pants and stuck out his hand. "So, you wanta swim, eh?" this one said. "Well, you've come to the right place. We're professional handlers. Handle I'd say . . . I'd say about—how many attempts would you say we handle a month, Sam?"

"I dunno."

"Ten or twenty, wouldn't ya say?"

"That's right. Ten or twenty."

"There. Ya see. Ten or twenty. Oh, we're experienced at attempts, we are."

Freddy Flywater was probably in his late fifties, a barrel-chested man with no discernible neck and with white hair sprouting from his gray shirt like fleece. He had a round, burnt face, pug nose, and bad teeth that made his mouth look like a damp knothole. His boyish blue eyes and blue sailor's cap were the only things that seemed to have made friends in that face.

"I just want a dependable boat and someone who knows the weather and the tides," said Harry.

They took him down to what they called the quay, where an aging hulk bumped against the dock. Harry looked it over from stem to stern without understanding a thing about its seaworthiness, except perhaps the name: *Driftwood*. He supposed it didn't matter much what went with him as long as they could navigate to Calais. They haggled about price, the cost of petrol, and then, when Harry said he wanted them on standby for the best possible conditions, a retainer. They kept calling his swim "an attempt." Finally he agreed to their retainer and they agreed to quit saying "attempt."

He went back to the pension to distill Stanley's elixir from his powdered underwear. The lady of the house was obliging about the use of her kitchen. "Ain't you young to be cookin' and such," she said. "Most men your age would be between the age

of skirts and the age of tools. You're a strange one, you are."
She saw everyone as one "age" or another. Her grandson was at
"the age of crumbs," she herself was at "the age of bingo." But
when he dropped his underwear into the boiling club soda and
vinegar, she quit talking about ages and crossed herself. Harry
wound up with a gallon and a half, which he stored in two
plastic jugs.

For the next six days he listened to the interminable English weather reports, conferred with Freddy Flywater, worked
out, and waited. On the evening of the sixth day the reports
looked good, favorable neap tides were due, and the wind,
which had blown to Force 7 the day before, all but vanished.
Came the dawn, Harry Moon stepped off Shakespeare Beach
and into the English Channel.

He wore a white rubber cap, goggles, and several pounds
of Vaseline and lanolin. The fog was violet, the water was violet,
the white cliffs of Dover were violet, but Harry Moon was as
white as the ghost of his ancestor as he slipped along doing
sixty-one strokes per minute. Calais was twenty-five miles away
to the southeast, but he would swim close to thirty to beat the
tides. The trawler gurgled to windward some twenty feet away.
Freddy Flywater filled the wheelhouse and Sam Santa leaned
against the gunwale, staring. He stared and stared. With his
hard, tiny eyes he stared. Harry couldn't make out the eyes too
well, but every few strokes the water would sheet just right over
his goggles and he would see Sam Santa's long squeezed head,
billycock hat, and upper lip like the flap of an envelope. Staring. Staring with his nose, his ears, his long nimble fingers
which hung over the side as if he were dying. He looked like an
empathic funeral director. Harry tried not to notice. But when
he breathed to the other side, he lost track of the boat. He
began breathing every other stroke. At the end of an hour
Santa waved his billycock and whistled shrilly. Harry stopped.

"Time for your bottle, mate!" Santa yelled.

Harry was to stop ever hour for a feeding. They had a baby
bottle which was filled from the jugs of Stanley's elixir. Harry
was to unscrew the nipple and quaff the ration. With a gallon
and a half there was no danger of running short. Santa tossed
the baby bottle and it immediately sank to the bottom of the
Channel.

Harry looked at him in dismay.

Santa grinned sheepishly. "Good thing you didn't drink that stuff! Weighs a ton!"

"You filled it to the brim!" Harry shouted back. "You were supposed to leave some air in it!"

"Right. Sorry, mate. Here I'll lower the jug on a rope."

Harry continued to tread water. The fog was burning off; Dover Castle was still visible behind him. Ahead, the sky gradually thickened into opacity with no sign of the French coast. This was good. If you could see all the way, it meant the wind was too brisk, he had been told.

"All set!" Santa called, and the jug winged out.

This time it did not sink. Harry sank. Treading furiously, he managed to get a swallow or two and recapped it.

"Empty some of this next time!" he ordered. "And would you mind not staring at me while I swim?"

Santa turned to Freddy Flywater. "Think the blighter's gone daft with salt water, Fred? Says he don't want me starin' at him."

Flywater shrugged. "So, don't stare. He's payin', ain't he?"

"He ain't takin' his feedin' well, either," said Santa.

"Then he'll have enough left to turn around and come back, won't he?"

Harry saw Santa in the wheelhouse after that, his billycock just a silhouette alongside Freddy Flywater's cap. The next few hours were almost serene. He swam as if, along with the beating of his heart and the rhythm of his breathing, it was a necessary and effortless bodily function. The feedings went smoothly, and he was relieved to see that his handlers had the good sense to empty some of the elixir before tossing him the cumbersome jug. What was actually happening did not occur to him for some nine hours. Dover Castle was long gone by then and the coast of France tantalizingly close. They were making for the bay at Wissant when they stopped for a feeding. Neither Santa nor Flywater came out of the wheelhouse, and Harry heard them laughing like a couple of adolescent girls. Finally one of them tossed the plastic jug. This seemed to be excruciatingly funny to them. It hit the water and skated up a trough. Harry saw that it was empty. "Wrong one!" he shouted. Convulsive giggling erupted from the wheelhouse. The other jug came sailing out, hitting and bobbing like a cork. "This one's empty, too!" Harry hollered. Great peals of laughter and foot-stomping thundered through the hull. It hit him them. They weren't dumping the stuff, they were drinking it, easily a gallon between them. Stanley's elixir, and they weren't burning it off like he was in the 60-degree agony of the Channel. They were now stoned and in God knows what condition to navigate!

He wanted to climb on board and attack them with the plastic jugs, but he realized that his only hope of victory lay in their muddled senses. The tide was running like a conveyor belt, and the wind was twisting around. He swam to the other side of the *Driftwood* and hollered for them to start up. All he got was giggling and the conking out of the engine. For the next twenty minutes they fiddled and laughed and triggered abortive spurts on the starter. When they finally got it going, they churned circles around him, spilling diesel fuel. He seemed to be swimming in an oil slick. He had picked up his tempo to about sixty-eight strokes per minute, but he was no longer sure which way the tide ran, and by the time he realized they were heading out to sea, it was useless to challenge either the wind or the tides. "Hey! Hey!" he shouted. There was a final round of insane giggling before they sped off.

He was picked up eight hours later by a Polish freighter in the North Sea. None of the Poles spoke English, which was just as well, because he was delirious by that time and chattering that his daughter was in love with a VD automobile named Herpes that starred in Walt Disney movies. By coincidence the freighter was bound for Dover, so he was waiting when Flywater and Santa returned very sober two days later. They had run down a sea lion and limped into Dunkerque the day before.

"Ten or twenty a month, eh?" Harry said. "You handle ten or twenty Channel swimmers a month, you said. How come I didn't see any of those poor bastards floating out in the North Sea?"

Freddy Flywater scratched the white fleece on his chest, and Sam Santa rubbed the brim line of his billycock as if excavating a memory.

"Because none of 'em ever got as close to Calais as you did, mate," said Freddy Flywater.

"That's right," echoed Sam Santa. "The rest of 'em drifted into the Atlantic, we think. Caught an early tide, they did. You was quite lucky, Mr. Moon. Quite lucky to get that far, I'd say."

TOTAL
ECLIPSE

} 34 {

The Moon was down, overcome by its own lunar tides. Harry was so depressed that he didn't call home for three days. His sense of destiny now seemed like a cruel hoax. He was sorry the Polish freighter had saved him, and he thought about returning to the sea like a tardy but obedient lemming hurling himself off the white cliffs of Dover, but the pension lady's grandson—the one who was at "the age of crumbs"—kept watching him in awe, and out of consideration for the child's innocence Harry did not kill himself.

The boy was about seven, and he had been standing with a hairbrush in one hand and an ice cream in the other when Harry returned from his "attempt." It was the only thing Harry remembered as he dragged in—the boy licking the hairbrush instead of the cone. "Play elsewhere," he told him. "How do you play Elsewhere?" the boy wanted to know. "Is it very much like mumblety-peg? I know how to play mumblety-peg."

Harry was so sore in the shoulders he could hardly dress.

The first night back he slept in his clothes rather than struggle out of them, and when he dropped his pants to wash in the morning he ended up scrubbing his shirttail. As he came shuffling out of the bathroom the boy grinned knowingly. "It's not what you think," Harry said, but the boy's elfin worldliness reminded him of Stephanie, and he thought that he should call home.

He collected a sackful of coins and went to the nearest "kiosk." It was 1:30 P.M. in Dover, 8:30 A.M. back home. He got the overseas code and shoveled money into the box. He dialed slowly. It rang once and he knew from the long pause between the picking up of the receiver and the voice that it was Stephanie.

"Helloo-o," she cooed.

"Hi, hon."

She got very breathy, and he could picture her grinning from ear to ear, wiggling all around. "You sound funny," she said.

"I'm calling from another planet again."

"Which one?"

"It's called Britain."

"Guess what."

"What?"

"I forgot my line in the play." She was in a recreation department play that summer.

"That's all right."

"I knew it, but everyone kept saying it to me and it sounded different. Then I forgot."

"You'll have lots more plays."

"Are there any plays on your planet?"

"I think so. Tragedies."

"What's a traj-edy?"

"Something sad."

"Have you ever been in one?"

"One. A few days ago. How's Mommy?"

"Fine. She's upstairs with Uncle Dan. Wanta talk to her?"

Uncle *Dan?* He wanted her to have said Uncle *Stan.* But Stan was in England, and Harry felt the cold of the English Channel stealing back into his flesh.

"Uncle Dan brought me a Bicentennial doll," she said.

Harry felt his insides crashing off the cliffs of Dover. Uncle

Dan. Eight thirty in the morning. Upstairs. Suddenly he hated himself, hated the phone, hated even the precious voice that had told him these things.

"I'll get Mommy."

"No. That's all right, hon. I really called just to talk to you."

"She'll wanta talk to you," Stephanie insisted.

"Well, I'd rather have you surprise her. You can tell her you got a call from another planet, and she'll think you're very grown up. I've got to go now, baby."

"Daddy?"

"What?"

"Did you do that swimming thing yet?"

"Not yet."

"Oh."

"Good-bye, sweetheart."

"'Bye."

The click of the phone was like a steel door walling away his heart. He went back to the pension without a thought or a feeling. Later he went up to the cliffs where he could survey the Channel and think about it. Why shouldn't it happen? Two people who were an accomplished fact rushing together in his absence. He hadn't had relations with Carrie in over a year; the silence between then had grown until it roared with invective. What had kept them together this long? Fate hadn't brought him here for fulfillment; it had brought him here for dismemberment.

He felt as if everything was being scripted by a god who wrote soap operas. He had challenged Carrie, challenged the Channel, but the timing of revelations such as the one he had just discovered by phone seemed fraught with malevolent will. It was his father's fatalism, and he was into its Armageddon.

He went back to the pension braced for crisis and shock. If the Queen of England were waiting for him, he would not have been surprised. But it wasn't the Queen of England, it was the Queen of Hearts, and he was stupefied.

"Heather..." he said.

"Hi, Harry."

She was only slightly less radiant. The puffiness of her lips reappeared now in a fuller neck and cheeks, but this only made the substance of his dreams bigger than life.

"I read about you in the paper," she said, "and since I was in London..."

The warm glow of a transcending fruition began to spread through him. She had married her Rhodes scholar two years after the prom, and now her husband jetted from capital to capital in pursuit of more corporate lucre than they could ever possibly need while she dallied a country or two—an affair or two—behind. This candid remark seemed aimed at Harry's loins but it took a chip out of his heart. Devouring her celestial beauty, he still could not conceive that she was neither chaste nor created on high just for him. "I don't believe this," he kept saying as they moved toward friendship, frankness, and finally fornication. The illusion lasted into the bedroom where he undressed her—"I don't believe this"—and gazed upon her flawless body—"I don't believe this"—and to the brink of entry, where he realized she was merely human after all. Momentum alone was not enough to finish the act. Whereas once his sex drive flared and consumed itself like a match, it now slowly heated up and dribbled like a candle. He was unable even to penetrate. "I don't believe this," she said. It reminded him of the arrogant way she had once declared, "I'm going to be infested," the day of the Brownie investiture when they were children. The smile she left him with had the cloying aftertaste of Stanley's elixir, and he realized how thoroughly his gods had deceived him.

He sat on the pebbled beach all night, staring at the sea. A lunar path swam straight across the Channel to his feet, and he thought here was the essential symbolism of his life: moon and water. Why was it so important? Why had he left a wife and daughter and bought off a longing boy with a motorcycle? Where did he belong? He rose, and the moon's wake shattered beneath his feet. When he had gone waist deep, he turned southeast, swearing he would not leave England except to swim to France.

It was the final comic blustering of a frail human will. At noon he called Carrie to tell her, and she said, "Raymond ran his motorcycle over a cliff and drowned in the quarry yesterday."

Harry took the next bus to Heathrow, and the next plane home.

｛ 35 ｝

Harry remembered neither taking off nor landing. The plane out of Heathrow was a piece of metal that sat dead in the sky while the earth spun. When New York passed below, it fell and lay dead on the runway. Harry wondered what kind of coffin Raymond lay in.

He took a train to Haversack, a long empty night train that wailed mournfully and wriggled through the darkness like a worm through a grave. These dreary images were inescapable, he felt, because he would have to explore and explain Raymond's death to the tribunal of his soul forever. He had read Raymond's obituary a year and a half ago when he assigned the composition: What would you do if you were stranded on an island with your worst enemy? Raymond's worst enemy was his father. Harry had known that. He had known it the night he took Raymond back home to his father on the motorcycle. Still he had taken him, left him on the doorstep, and even presented him with the gleaming instrument of his suicide. Harry's conscience dictated a revised question: What would you do if I took you back and left you with your father? *When I smelt his Seegrums I kilt myself*, Raymond had written and now had effected so indelibly. Meanwhile Harry had stranded himself on an island called Britain, where he had been his own worst enemy.

He went to the quarry the day after he got home and saw the skid mark and dove off the cliff into the spot where Raymond must have plunged, and he stayed underwater a long time, thinking, feeling, crying tears that never formed. This was

Raymond's funeral. Two days after that he went to the church for the public ceremony. There were dozens of students there who had hated Raymond and a score of adults who had never had a kind word for him. Most of the adults were Raymond's teachers, but all of them were strangers.

Harry resisted the sham and pomposity of it, and it seemed to him that Raymond stood next to him, sharing his scorn. Why did you use the motorcycle, Raymond? Was it to hurt me? Was it to make me your murderer? Raymond just sneered, and Harry understood that he had murdered him with insufficient love, not a motorcycle. If Reverend Jules were alive and decrying the waste of burying the dead with their possessions, what could he have stripped Raymond of?

At the grave site, Harry noticed how unhealthy everyone looked. The cemetery was flowering, the trees were vibrant, but the faces looked ashen as they followed the casket to the hole in the ground. Harry had a habit of categorizing people by stroke. The bulky minister was a butterflyer leading ostentatiously. The children breast-stroked in his wake, their heads bobbing in unison for a look at what lay head. Bony Mrs. Feedly cast about on her back, looking for a clear lane. Harry's eyes went to the small lake in the middle of the cemetery where a single black swan glided. This was Raymond, black and silent and alone. Then he remembered. Raymond was a nonswimmer. Raymond had drowned.

The minister's words tangled in a sinewy breeze, but Harry heard the symbolic handful of dirt rain onto the casket. Carrie cried then, and he took her hand and led her away, but before they got to the car a man ran up behind them and started yelling. It was Raymond's father. "Hey, Mr. Rich Man," he said, "I'm gonna sue you for everything you got!" He was wearing a suit and tie, but he looked somehow hastily dressed, as if he had rushed here from a world of languor and nudity. "You hear me, Mr. Rich Man? Everything you got!"

Harry held the door for Carrie, trudged wearily around to the other side and drove slowly from the cemetery.

They went home and embraced Stephanie out of fear of the consequences of life. "Did they bury Raymond?" she wanted to know. "Is Raymond in the ground? Why couldn't I go to the funeral?" She spoke so rationally about it that they saw there really wasn't any reason. And yet it seemed as though the Angel of Death had passed over their house and spared this child by the thickness of a bedroom wall. How precious she was. How temporary. Even out of reach of death she was leaving them day by day. Harry saw this for the first time now and did the futile things that tardy fathers do. He took her to the zoo in Philadelphia, the Museum of Science in Boston, a circus and three shows in one week. He bought her a dollhouse, a rock tumbler, a second bicycle, and six stuffed animals which completely filled her bed. When she appeared suddenly in the backyard below his upstairs bedroom window, he shot three rolls of movie film through the glass. By the end of August he had the film back from the drugstore, and he realized with a pang that all he would keep of his daughter were her artifacts and ten minutes of a long-ago child swinging in the backyard. Growing up was another kind of death, in some ways worse and more painful than sudden termination.

He had not spoken with Carrie except in cursory bits since his return from England. But the week before Labor Day they took Stephanie to a cabin on a lake in the Adirondacks for three days, and there, sharing a swing seat on a wooded bluff overlooking the beach, they watched her play in the sunset as they unloaded on each other.

"Nicki called," she began.

"When?"

"Last month."

"Last month! What did he want?"

"Fifty thousand dollars."

"Fifty thousand!" The swing seat steadily accelerated. "What for?"

"Bail."

"Good ol' Nicki."

"I gave it to him."

"You *what?*" He half turned and the swing developed arrhythmia.

"You wanted me to leave your own brother in jail with perverts and killers?"

Harry straightened around and the swing slid back into pace.

"He skipped out," Carrie said then.

"He skipped out!" Harry bounced around this time and they seemed to be circling each other on the aberrant swing. "You gave him fifty thousand and he skipped out?"

"That's right."

The sunset sheeted the beach orange, and the woods seemed to throb with reflected light. They fell into a furious rhythm.

"Stu called too," Carrie said.

"When?"

"While you were on vacation."

He laughed forcibly.

"He wanted money, of course," she said. "I told him you were in England. I think he went to find you."

"While I was on vacation," he repeated acidly. "You mean while *you* were on vacation in bed."

"What's that supposed to mean?"

"'Mommy's upstairs with Uncle Dan,' that's what it means. Couldn't you at least have gotten a sitter for Stephanie and gone to a motel?"

"I suppose so. Peggy was here with him, and she had to watch all their kids anyway. You know you really are an asshole sometimes. They were on their way to Bar Harbor and detoured a hundred and fifty miles to see you, so I invited them to spend the night. It was really embarrassing when Stephanie announced your call at breakfast. How was your holiday? Lots of little wenches for you to breast-stroke with?"

At least *his* infidelity was over, soured and sunk in a far-away sea, he thought. Carrie's fantasy was love, a tender assortment of attitudes he and she had never been able to achieve. And Dan Dreiman was still the Anti-Love of their marriage.

"That must have made it even more exciting, having Peggy here," he said. "That way you prolong the longing and never have to face the disillusionment of culmination."

"You're sick."

"Does it disgust you to see your flirtations for what they are?"

She threw her head back with a hollow laugh that gave the swing a new eccentricity. "You know what your problem is, Harry? You know what's behind this grand delusion of yours? It's fear for your perfection. Here you went and married ol' Carrie, and now you're scared of rejection."

"I admit being a casualty of rejection," he said. "In the order of existence I rank somewhere behind the doorbell, the phone, and the cat."

"I shouldn't answer the doorbell?"

"Oh, by all means answer it. But if it's Peggy Dreiman don't pretend she's your best friend just to obscure your enthusiasm for her husband."

"I think your perfectionism has something to do with your brothers," she said "They're all such failures. You still feel a need to compensate—"

"All women want to preserve their virginal prerogatives," he went on. "It's understandable that you want to be rediscovered, to be desired. That's what *your* self-worth is all about. After all, you spent your adolescence testing it out. It gets to be a habit that no one mate can satisfy."

"First, there's Nicki, public enemy number one. I guess you figure he makes you look bad, huh? Then, of course, we have Stanley, who knows not how to wash. Someday he will be swallowed by a clump of dust. Two jailbirds in one family; you're probably afraid it's hereditary."

"The real thing about rejection in this family is that you want your power to reject back," he resumed. "You want men to dangle at your whim, hoping, longing for you. I never did that, so you rejected me."

"Having Stu for a brother would emasculate anybody—if he is in fact a brother and not a sister. Whichever, he's the epitome of nonachievement. Is that why you have to make it, Superjock?'

By now they were rocketing off into eternity on an anger-powered swing. Stephanie looked up and waved gleefully at this exuberance. Behind her, storm clouds shared the coming of night and a cold wind touched the bluff.

"So, I'm a dreamer in search of perfection, and you're an indifferent wife who would've been happier with somene else," Harry said.

She didn't argue.

"I never thought your standing by my side was just part of the mating ritual," he said. "I thought you'd be with me forever."

"I never thought your manhood would need proving after we got married. I thought you'd want a family."

"I'm going back to England." He looked at her as if this required an answer. "I'm going to swim the Channel."

She dragged her feet and the swing jolted to a stop. Then she went down to the beach to help Stephanie with her sand castles.

⦚ 36 ⦚

After Harry left for England the second time, Carrie took Stephanie to Boston. They marched through museums and arboretums, through the Common and Public Gardens, soared past Bunker Hill Monument, the State Houses, and Beacon Hill, and finally, along the harbor heading north, slowed until they came to rest at a coastal beach near a cluster of whitewashed and spired towns. They were having fun.

"Are you having fun?" Carrie kept asking.

Stephanie thought so, but she studied her mother more than the scenery.

Time seemed to stop on the little beach, and it occurred to Carrie that people aged five or six seconds at a time in the aftermath of pain or shock, until the accumulation of these put them beyond feeling and they ceased to experience passion or power or awe. She did not want to be beyond feeling. Oh, God, how could she grow old with just one child! Why couldn't Harry understand that children were their power over death, their expression of life? He was so afraid of losing something that he was losing everything. And all he could do was complain that their conversation was forever being edited for "kiddies." She wondered if succeeding in his swim would finally put his ego to rest. Maybe then he wouldn't be so selfish about sharing his life with children. But she saw a dead fish at the high-tide mark and thought that this was Harry after his victory, used up by the sea, bloated, empty-eyed, and posturing on the shores of his conquest, his mouth open for yet another telling of the tale.

A teenage couple who had been splashing each other in the shallows came ashore and lay in the sand. The boy was lean and tan in a pair of faded cutoffs, the girl budding and willowy. She lay half on top of him, his thigh rising between her parted legs. Carrie could see the warmth and vibrancy of their skin from twenty yards away. She lay back and thought of her own lover. He was not Harry and he was not Dan Dreiman, he was someone she had never spoken to. If he spoke, he would say something stupid, so she never let him speak. He just stood there, blocking the sun, his face a bronze mystery in the surrounding glare. Then he dropped to his knees and slowly plied his lips and hands over her body.

She awoke perspiring and rose to her elbows in search of Stephanie. The wet sand bridges of a series of canals were collapsing, and Stephanie was feverishly restoring them. Carrie looked for the teenagers, but they were gone. The dead fish at the high-tide mark that reminded her of Harry was gaping at her, she thought. Yes, Harry, I've been unfaithful to you once again. There is no fidelity in womankind, only virginity.

"Hey!" she shouted to Stephanie. "How's your sunburn?"

Stephanie dropped to her haunches, and the sand bridges sheered off layer by layer until the canals were just little lagoons. She sucked her cheek, then pointed across the ocean. "Is Daddy over there again?"

"Yes. Somewhere."

Stephanie pushed down the remaining bridge with her hand. "Are children more important than daddies?"

"In a way. Why?"

"Are mommies more important than wives?"

Carrie sat up, dismayed.

"Why didn't you go with Daddy?" Stephanie asked then.

The waves seemed to pause.

"*You* are going to school next week—" Carrie got out.

"I could've stayed with Gramma and Grampa."

"Stephanie, what's got into you? I *want* to be with you. I'm your mother."

"I don't want to grow up," she said. "I don't want to be a grown-up and not be important anymore."

Carrie stood over her, feeling shocked and vestigial. Suddenly the tot crouching woodenly at her feet seemed immensely cruel and ungrateful. She was being betrayed. The object of all her love and sacrifice was turning on her.

She went and stood in the surf. The sand melted out from under her feet with each surge, draining her anger into the sea, and she thought that this was where the words had come from. The sea had put the words and the wisdom in Stephanie's mouth. The sea was a resonator for Harry. Standing on the threshold of a great global ocean, she felt it metering out its message, and each wave aged her with the five or six seconds that follow pain and shock.

HARVEST
MOON

{ 37 }

Harry sat next to a witch on the plane to England. She told him this as soon as he sat down. "I'm a professional witch," she said. "As a gesture of friendship, I'm prepared to grant you one wish."

Harry fastened his seat belt. "Don't do anything to the pilot, okay?"

"That's your wish?"

"Yes."

"What a waste."

"It's my wish."

"Okay. But I wasn't going to do anything to the pilot anyway. I'm a white witch."

He looked her over then. She wore pumps, a paisley dress, and a mood ring. Her hands were fat, or swollen, and covered with freckles. She looked as if her makeup had been applied by an undertaker.

"I'll guarantee a smooth lift-off, too," she said. "I don't like long runs and sudden lift-offs."

Harry wondered why she didn't take a broom. Then the pilot delivered his welcome speech, the stewardess came by, and the plane eased down the runway and into the air like a fish floating to the surface of a pond.

"Thanks," Harry said.

"You're welcome. Say, you're all right. Usually I get some jackass who asks me why I didn't take a broom. Would you like your skull read?"

"I beg your pardon."

"The bumps on your head. You want me to read them?"

"No." He waved fussily.

She saw that he had been preoccupied. "Well, then, how about your palm?"

He clenched his fingers.

"No? What about your horoscope? Your fortune? They serve tea in the middle of the Atlantic. I'm very good with tea leaves."

"I don't drink tea."

"I knew that," she said triumphantly. "As soon as I said that, I knew you didn't drink tea. I'm psychic, too."

He grabbed up a section of a newspaper someone had left next to his seat and pretended to read.

"You've got the want ads," said the witch.

"I'm looking for something."

"We're all looking for something. You won't answer too many New York ads in London, though."

"There's a column on marriage counseling too," he said. He folded the section noisily to that spot and made an effort to read. The first letter was from a woman who complained that her husband refused to put the cap back on the toothpaste and it was driving her crazy.

> Little dribbles of toothpaste get all over the sink and the medicine cabinet. If he leaves the tube open on top of the toilet tank, it gets there, too. And the tube always bubbles at me when I squeeze it.

The marriage expert wrote back that the woman's husband was deeply psychotic and must be given an ultimatum to accept intensive care or else she should leave him flat.

"I do seances too," said the witch. "You've lost someone, haven't you?"

Harry shaded his eyes with the paper. "I've lost everyone."

"Oh, but they're not lost. They're just waiting. Outside the pale. So close. I can help you reach them. Here. Take my hands and close your eyes."

Harry grasped her hands.

"Don't peek!" she commanded. "Yes...yes, I see them. They're waiting for you. One, two, three...four of them. You're going to take a long journey."

Harry opened his eyes. "Of course I'm going to take a long journey. I'm on a long journey now."

She opened her eyes too. "Now you've done it. You chased them away. I was about to say you were going to take a long journey and find them."

"There aren't four people in the world I want to find."

"Maybe not now," she answered, "but there are four, all right."

She was so far off base, he couldn't believe it. Here he was breaking up with his wife, haunted by a young boy's death, his brothers trying to bleed him dry and his parents dead, out to redeem his failure at the sole goal he had set himself, and this freckled sideshow had missed it all. He offered to sell her the original Mona Lisa, three for a dollar, and they got in a big row.

"You're lucky I'm a white witch," she said. "If I wasn't a white witch, I'd glue your testicles to your underwear!"

The stewardess finally separated them.

By the time he read the travel poster in a London bus station, he had forgotten her. The poster read:

THE BICENTENNIAL
OF THE MOON FESTIVAL
In the Hills of Gloucestershire

For 200 years the people of the tiny village of Bourk-on-the-Wold have celebrated the death of Erasmus Moon. The term "lunacy" was given special meaning by his four sons— one a thief, one a social degenerate, one simpleminded, and one a drunkard—who kept the Cotswold district in chaos for years until they fled to the Colonies in 1767, never to be heard from again. Erasmus Moon is said to have been responsible for a typhoid epidemic in 1769, the accidental poisoning of Bourk-on-the-Wold's water table in 1771, and the unintentional destruction by fire of the town-cathedral in 1773, causing many to revert to paganism. When Erasmus fell ill with ague in 1776, the doctor took his time in coming and the priest did not come at all. The whole town turned out for his funeral and got shamelessly drunk. This gala occasion, then, is the basis for the pagan festival that has endured for nearly 200 years. There are those who say that the patriarch did not merely die in 1776 but that his spirit went to the Colonies, where it joined his four sons in helping England lose the war. Come join us in the Moon Festival, Bourk-on-the-Wold, mid-August to mid-September.

Harry did not believe he was related to Erasmus, and he did not believe the brothers four were waiting for him, but he exchanged his coach ticket to Dover for one to Gloucestershire. To the heartland he sped, those pale green hills that rise like vertebrae on the limestone spine of England. The cottages were quarried from the earth, honey-colored riddles of stone queued up in leas and dales. These were often hedged or hemmed with red and yellow flowers, conveying innocence in the parental gray shadows of a mill or a cathedral. This fostering impression of cathedrals was enhanced here and there by a scowling verger or the martellato voice of an organ booming across the land. Then came Bourk-on-the-Wold.

There was no organ, no verger, and no cathedral here. There were cottages and inns, small shops, and a manor house. And ruins. The ruins were accentuated with crepe and pagan figures carved in oak. A huge blackened pit straddled by three spits marked the nave. This was clearly the cathedral Erasmus had burned down. Off to one side, a Christian churchyard seemed to huddle in terror and dismay, its tablets leaning inward and blanched white. Still farther apart was a pile of stones. As Harry watched, a family trooped to the site bearing stones and a camera. The father took a picture while the others hurled their stones onto the pile. When Harry got off the bus, he went back to the site and read the oak marker:

This is the grave of Erasmus Moon. Legend has it that only stones from the burned cathedral, used in pagan ceremonies, can hold him in his grave. These are available at the Village Gifte Shoppe at 50p.

The Village Gifte Shoppe was a pub that sold bitters, stout, shandy, and a cider that cleared plumbing. The stones were a sideline. Harry bought a pint and wandered on to the Moon family homestead. This was a cottage like all the others except that it was a half kilometer from the village and had pens and an ancient sheep-dip trough. When he saw the trough the old feeling of haunting presences returned. It was the one Erasmus had thrown Jonathan in when the boy came home drunk, and here for the first time Harry sensed that he had caught up with the sentinel who beckoned him from cold, dark lakes and reedy ponds. "You're home, Harry," said a voice it took him a moment to recognize.

He turned, and there was Stanley.

"I looked it all up," Stanley said. "I checked it all out, and I came here looking for my roots. Four brothers left here in 1767, and one of them is our direct ancestor. Take your pick. Jonathan spent more time in the bottom of this trough than he did in bed. Samuel was degenerate, Benjamin was a thief, and Alexander was spaced out. It's like we're descended from all four of them in some way."

"Jonathan," Harry said with certainty. "I came from Jonathan." And he poured the remnant of his pint of bitters into the trough.

They spent the afternoon in the village eating something called "Scotch eggs" and drinking shandy. Toward evening the sky inked up and lightning winked over the hills, but a crowd was gathering and everyone was talking about the Ceremony of the Stones, which was to take place at midnight. At seven a fire was kindled in the ruins and a number of stones from the cathedral walls were placed in the pit. A man in eighteenth-century costume paced the village square, recounting Erasmus's sins, chief of which was the begetting of four sons to carry on his errors. "Tonight a licensed exorcist will oversee the placing of the stones on the grave site to reaffirm the bonds that keep Erasmus in hell," he said. "Come one, come all, to the cathedral at midnight. A freewill offering will be taken to help defer the fee of our exorcist, who has come from the ends of the earth to be here."

"Malevolent sons of bitches," Stanley observed.

"Everyone needs a scapegoat," said Harry.

At eleven thirty the village began to empty out. At ten minutes to midnight, Stanley said, "Let's go toast Erasmus." So they climbed the hill in the dark and sat on the stones over Erasmus's grave drinking shandy.

"Here's to all the Moons now and forever, all the moons in the universe!" shouted Stanley. "Here's to Erasmus and his four sons!"

They touched cups and drank.

"Here's to the new Moons," said Harry. "Us and our brothers."

Stanley stood and dropped his pants, offering his backside to the chanting mob at the cathedral. "Here's a moon for all your madness."

"Here's to Carrie and Stephanie," said Harry. "Here's to Nino ... and Raymond."

Stanley pulled up his pants. "Here's to Johnny Cannabis-seed."

"Here's to Jules," said Harry. "Here's to Professor Schwendler, alias Agnes."

"Agnes?"

"If I have to toast Johnny-what's-it-seed, you have to toast Agnes. The world kicked her out for disturbing the peace—for distributing a piece."

"Okay. Agnes."

They drained the shandy and tossed their cups on the grave as the procession started out of the ruins, illuminated by a wagon load of flaking crimson stones. "The stones that fell keep Erasmus in hell!" they chanted.

It seemed cruel and unreal, this commercialized hate.

"The stones that fell keep Erasmus in hell!"

When the procession got close enough to see them, the hooded figure in the lead stopped. Then the column stopped. Stanley took a step forward.

"The Moons are back!" he cried.

There was some tittering from the crowd, who thought it was a setup. But the hooded figure did a genuine double take.

When Harry saw her fat, freckled hands in the glow of the stones he knew. He never saw her face, just the fat, freckled hands and the mood ring, but he knew it was the witch from the plane.

"I know this one," she said, pointing at him. "He's a crazy. You didn't tell me there was a crazy here. I quit!" With that she tore off her hood as she stalked away. The last thing he heard as he and Stanley kicked over the wagon was her shrill reminder: "I told you there were four people waiting for you!"

She meant the original brothers Moon, of course.

They hitched a ride to London in a lorry and by noon the next day were back in the pension at Dover with the woman who was at "the age of bingo." She took one look at Stanley and said, "No pets," but she was obliging enough when he used her kitchen to brew Harry a new elixir.

Harry bypassed Sam Santa and Freddy Flywater to obtain a smaller boat of even less integrity. This one was owned by a demonstrative young couple who called themselves Honey and Horny and had christened the boat likewise. Horny said he knew the Channel to Calais, and Harry took him at his word. For the next two weeks the sea was rough and out of sorts with the sky, which cuffed waves and was spat at in return. Harry worked out little but walked the beaches morning and night, his hands in his pockets, his pantlegs fluttering, and his eyes searching the horizon. The wind slapped his face with rags of water and blustered in his ears, portraying itself lord and master. But an even more elemental force was draining the heart out of him. The plummetlessness of the sea, the opacity of the horizon, and the rigidity of the cliffs—these things seemed to confine him to the unsupporting sand and its sterile sameness. He lacked identity; he was a mere grain on the face of the universe, he thought. But the sand was just a plenum, imperturbable and yielding, and gradually he saw that the elemental force he felt was loneliness. Across the ocean Carrie stood in the same sand, as stark and stiff as he, stung by Stephanie's indictment and only beginning to feel the same loneliness. It was a stupid ocean that separated them—but an ocean.

On the tenth day at Dover, Stu suddenly appeared. He was out of money and out of Daisy. She had been discovered by a designer who created fashions for giant hermaphrodites. Stu fell on Harry's shoulder and cried for all the miserable things he had done to him. He was sorry for pissing in the ginger ale and giving it to him for a wedding present, sorry for hammering his Sunday school pin into a pellet when they were boys, sorry for cutting his bicycle spokes. Harry forgave him and said he could help Stanley on the boat. This fraternalism was repeated four days later when Nicki showed up. Like Stu, Nicki had eventually zeroed in on Dover as the departure point for

would-be Channelists. Harry was well known for his prior encounter with a Polish freighter, and everyone in Dover knew he
had returned. Nicki said he could never go back to the States
and begged forgiveness for the fifty thousand dollars, along
with permission to join the crew. Harry was overcome by this
unexpected support, and on the fifteenth day, over a viridian-
colored sea, the *Honey & Horny* embarked on a culminating
journey with the brothers Moon.

As soon as Harry entered the Channel the loneliness returned, sharpening the chill. He should have been psyched up
at this point, euphoric with energy and confidence, but he felt
abandoned. Where was the beckoning presence? Where was
Jonathan? Heretofore he had swum to an ancient pulse, but
now he was alone in the sea.

Less than four hours out, the waves began running high
and the *Honey & Horny* rose and fell, so that one moment he was
looking down on her deck and the next he could only see her
hull. Horny was at the wheel, but Harry's brothers sprawled on
the deck grasping cleats and lines, as white as gulls. When he
called to them for an estimate of the distance, Nicki peered over
the gunwale like a "Kilroy was here" caricature, Stu waved
weakly, and Stanley just shrugged.

He rose opposite them, his cap and goggles and the ghostly
spread of lanolin rendering him impassionate. "Too rough!" he
shouted and fell with the wave.

That was when Stu crawled to the rail. "Harry," he dredged
out, "you're all the hope this family ever had . . . If you quit now
. . . I'll kick your ass . . . all the way back to England!"

Harry seemed to tread a little higher in the water then.
Here was Stu, quite possibly the most devitalized creature on or
under the Channel, including the clams, threatening to kick his
ass back to England. The effect was galvanic. He set off at an
incredible seventy strokes per, and within fifteen minutes the
sea had calmed. But the torrents of the day yielded to seaweed,
then jellyfish, then fog, and finally delirium. They rose one
after the other, like little dooms. At fourteen hours he was nauseated from swallowing salt water, his hands clutched rigidly at
the sea, and the boat horn had constantly to call him back. It
was getting dark. But he kept thinking about what Stu had said,
and he knew he was all of them now. The brothers Moon. Old
and new. A dynasty of ignominy. They needed a hero.

Throughout the night he swam, fixed on death or conquest. But the fog layered in and by 4 A.M. the tide caught him, swift as a river, and bore him south. He didn't know the boat had lost him until he heard the horn, sounding now like lugubrious sobs from eternity, and by then it was too late. There was no longer anything to go by except the tide and the waves.

When the dawn finally took and the fog began to pull apart like cotton candy, he saw he was totally alone. Long corridors of empty sea opened and closed between white bluffs. Stroking on nerves, he picked up the pace and an hour after daylight broke through the tide. Quite suddenly there was something tangible on the horizon. A thin line ran through the ephemeral wastes that lay ahead, he thought. It had to be Calais or the bay at Wissant or at least France! He put his head down.

When he lifted it again he was in the fog once more and there were voices dead ahead. They were female voices, shouting in French. Some women had glimpsed him, he thought. He must be very near an arm of the bay or a peninsula. He swam, lifting his head every few strokes, expecting to see them on the shore or perhaps a pier. But then he realized that there were no waves crashing, just the voices, and they were arguing.

They loomed out of the fog like pilings, three fat ladies floating in the English Channel. He could tell they were fat by their cheeks and by the way they confronted each other, amply spaced like angry icebergs. In their steadiness he wondered if they weren't standing on the bottom.

"How far to the beach?" he croaked.

They stopped arguing, their puffy eyes narrowing like startled clams. The one in the yellow bathing cap directed something lengthy and shrill at him.

"I don't speak French," he said.

"She wants to know if you are from the clinic," said a second woman, who had rubber flowers on her cap.

"Clinic?"

The second woman translated this for the first and got a reply. "She says if you are not from the clinic then get the hell out of here."

"How far to the beach?" he repeated, teeth chattering.

"Two, maybe three miles."

He squinted at them stuporously; they floated without effort and seemed impervious to the cold, but they did not look capable of an out-and-back swim of six miles. "Do you have a boat?"

"Yes."

He glanced around. "Where?"

She pointed straight down.

The woman in the yellow cap delivered another tirade.

"She says if you have come from the clinic to apologize, it is too late. We have sunk our boat and we are going to commit suicide as soon as we decide who should drown first."

It crossed Harry's mind that he was hallucinating. Hallucinations were listed as hazards of a crossing, while obese suicidal trios who rowed out of France and scuttled their craft were not.

"What clinic?" he asked tightly.

"Dr. Dubois's Ferme de la Femme Grasse, of course." Fat Lady Farm. Harry gathered as much when she said that they had been kicked out for smuggling bonbons. "We have been humiliated, no one wants us, and so we have come to this," she finished tearfully.

The tears needed no translation, and the other two started to sob along with her. The third one had a mouth like a carp, which made poignant gulping motions as she cried.

Harry was dismayed. The English Channel was growing saltier by the minute. "Stop, stop!" he cried hoarsely. "You can't commit suicide. The world is full of rejection. It doesn't mean you aren't loved."

The woman with the rubber flowers demanded to know who loved them.

"I do," Harry said.

This was translated and replied to. "Prove it," said the woman with the rubber flowers.

Harry could not prove it. He was in the middle of proving something to himself. He could not hug them, he could not save them, he could not hold their hands. If he so much as touched another human being his Channel swim would not be recognized.

"I've come from Dr. Dubois," he said. "I wasn't supposed to tell you that, but he's very sorry. He's sorry for humiliating you, sorry for accusing you of smuggling bonbons, sorry for not caring enough—"

A zesty translation and exchange bubbled forth. "We accept his apology," said the woman with the rubber flowers. "And we want to know how Dr. Dubois is going to save us."

Harry gazed stupidly through his goggles. "Dr. Dubois is very sorry about that too—" he began, but the carp mouth was already gulping and Harry sat miserably in the water while three French women bawled because he would not cancel out the redeeming venture of his life.

Hell. Hell. He had saved a lion once, hadn't he?

"Can you swim at all?" he asked huskily.

They couldn't swim at all. They tried, but they were like immense beach balls, buoyant but effectively limbless.

"I'll tow you," Harry said.

And so they formed a human chain, something like a pontoon boat powered by a single rubber band. And it would have been a happy ending for the French ladies, except that he couldn't make it. He knew even before they had covered a quarter mile he couldn't make it. He wasn't going to save them. He wasn't going to save the brothers Moon. He wasn't going to accomplish anything. But he swam on. He swam without hope or expectation, dragging his arms back through the water as much as pulling his body forward. And that was when he saw the rock.

It was a smooth stone barely above the surface of what must now be low tide. You might see it if you knew it was there, but he nearly collided with it. He looked for more, a reef, a shoal. These things never cropped up alone. But there was just the one stone going straight down into the water, and he knew that this was it. If the women could cling to it until he got back with help, if he *could* get back before the tide rose, then . . .

"I'm going for Dr. Dubois," he said, and his three charges kept repeating it like an incantation as he swam away.

The fog was lifting at last and the beach was plainly visible, perhaps two miles away. He would make it. He would make it, and the chattiness in his head suggested to him that he could still have a recognized crossing, that what he had left behind him was sheer delirium he ought to forget. But when he stumbled ashore within earshot of a pair of fishermen, he did not hesitate an instant. And as for the actual rescue, the only hindrance was the French trio's tearful hysteria over Dr. Dubois's absence.

The lady with the carplike mouth turned out to be a former screen idol whose fleshy kisses had melted French audiences for a decade and a half. This was revealed by the press corps, which descended on Wissant to romanticize Harry's adventure. If he hadn't already been a hero, they would have invented him on the spot. But the French trio was exalted by the role of damsels in distress and couldn't say enough about his gallantry. Within twelve hours the story had been flashed around the world and Harry Moon could have walked back to England on the upturned faces of interviewers strewn across the Channel.

If the French had let him go. But they didn't. Heroes are a French obsession, and they hadn't finished the embellishments yet. When Nicki, Stu, and Stanley finally showed up, they contributed biographical material that would have made a legend blush. They had run out of gas and drifted into the North Sea as Sam Santa and Freddy Flywater had, but by pouring Stanley's elixir into the engine of the *Honey & Horny* they had made the Firth of Forth by sunset. "So ends two hundred years of dishonor," Stu had saluted him. Harry doubted that. The marker at Bourk-on-the-Wold's ruined cathedral was solid oak. It would take a deed worthy of marble to outlast it. What he had done would last no longer than newsprint, he thought. And he was probably right. The *Guinness Book of World Records* would eventually list his feat as the longest rescue approach ever by a life-guard.

At the end of six days the film crews and special-assignment people were packing up, and the lambent flame of fame began to gutter out. Harry Moon was about to descend to earth, taking his place among the momentary who live on in trivia and bits of infrequent nostalgia. The standards for nostalgia are far less rigid than those of history.

But history was not done with Harry. ·

One of the last media hypes surrounding the rescue was a BBC reenactment that had him towing his buoyant trio to the illusive stone. They had to wait for low tide, of course, and even then it took Harry several hours to find it. Which wasn't bad, considering how long it had been lost. A professor from Oxford saw the broadcast and became intrigued. The next day he had a trawler with divers and special equipment go over the area, and that evening he mentioned with typical British reserve to a departing reporter, "You may wish to dally a day or so longer. I believe Mr. Moon has discovered Atlantis."

FULL
MOON

So much for the past.

The final element of this account hovers at the border of tomorrow. Just before the brothers return to England, Carrie appears on a touring bike in a Nava helmet and Cabretta gloves. Sticking out of her saddlebag is a copy of *Time* with Harry's picture on the cover.

"*C'est la vie,* sport," she says to him. "Bet you think I came because you're famous and because the French broads are messin' with my hunk, right? Well, you're wrong."

"I'm glad you came, and I don't care why," he says sincerely.

"I came because I wanted to. I stashed the kid with my parents and got to Dover an hour after you hit the outgoing tide. It took me a week to get up the nerve to cross, after I heard you were everybody's man of the hour. You don't look like the man who discovered Atlantis."

"It wasn't my most important discovery this trip."

· 273 ·

"Yeah?" She squints at him as if to read the unspoken part. Then she says, "Well, maybe you want to bike with me, then. I can see you're not going to ask about how I couldn't get a bus down from Calais and had to rent this thing and what a kick it turned out to be and—I think I'll tour Europe and Asia. Wanta come?"

He grins. "After I take care of some unfinished business in my ancestral hometown."

"Like what?"

"Like making up for the sins of the father. Like buying up a certain burned-out cathedral and turning it into a theme park for troubled children."

"Raymond would have loved it."

"Yeah." He is glad she understands the Raymond part. "But I always wanted my own Disneyland anyway," he says. "I'll start with a wave pool and a water slide called Bourk-on-the-Wild."

"You're crazy, Moon."

"Crazy. That reminds me, I'm going to build a rehabilitation institute near the theme park for Nicki, Stu, and Stanley, too. We'll call it Atlantis. It'll say so in marble."

"God knows, they need help."

"Help? They're gong to run it. It's the world that needs help, and I can't think of a better place to start than Bourk-on-the-Wold. You should see what they do for kicks after sundown. I figure Nicki can handle gambling therapy, Stu oughta be a whiz at sexual dysfunction and marriage counseling, and if Stanley hasn't got an herbal cure for every drug addiction, the world is not round. Then there are these three French ladies who might do the suicide hot line...."

And so on.

Whether or not any or all of this ever comes to pass, the return to Bourk-on-the-Wold is not forever. The brothers Moon of 1767 are not the brothers Moon of the present, and their destinies may only mesh here and there like the gears of an unpredictable clock. What is certain is that the clock will keep imperfect time.

There is nothing in all of this to suggest fundamental change. One imagines a future premised on the genetic ironies of the past. Stanley perhaps will live the longest—like Alexander—and after years of senility and stupefaction, owing to the largesse of Johnny Cannabis-seed, be found frozen on his skis in the woods, forever in flight from the CIA of his past. The cabins surrounding him may be in flames, but even that heat will not thaw him out of eternity. When they finally find a cure for herpes, Stu may interpret this as the power of prayer and join a religious order. Is it too outrageous then to assume he will contract some other sexual malady—as Samuel did from his deaconess—and die, say, of a withering virus and a spiritual depravity? Nicki, alas, is destined for justice at midnight. One sees him stuck in the broken back window of a bookstall in Abbey Lane. A burglar alarm precisely above his head tattles acidly for nine hours before someone finally comes. By this time he is quite deaf, but the ringing of phones, or the bells in his cell block, somehow produce silent vibrations in his head as merrily lethal as those which killed Benjamin, the chicken thief of the belfry, over two centuries earlier. Harry will be the only one to escape his atavism. His lone brush with drowning had come on his first Channel attempt when he was swept into the North Sea. The dark side of the Moon turned away from him at that moment, and Jonathan never beckoned again. We see Harry, then, on his deathbed far in the future, surrounded by generations of new Moons and newer Moons. Suddenly his heavy-lidded eyes ignite and he sits bolt upright. "Carrots!" he cries. "Bring me carrots!" But before the banished vegetable of his childhood can be summoned, he expires. Outside, a lone stray barks at the moon.